Half a Dozen Paces Through the Thicket, She Heard a Twig Snap Underfoot. . . .

Turning, she came face to face with the captain. He was hatless, as ever, and one lock of hair hung across the cruel scar that marred his brow.

She met his gaze, uncaring that her wet flimsy shift revealed the most intimate contours of her body to those searching blue eyes. She was aware that her heart was beating a wild tattoo and that her lightly draped bosom was rising and falling to her quickened breath, and that, surely, he must divine the reason for it.

He took the few paces that separated them, looked down into her eyes. The whole of her world, the sun-blessed island where they stood, the lark that sang overhead, the wind in the top branches, the grass beneath her bare feet, all nature and all life, were gathered into one, and became part of the hands that he extended toward her bare shoulders to draw her to him. . . .

Emmie's Love

JANETTE SEYMOUR

PUBLISHED BY POCKET BOOKS NEW YORK

Another *Original* publication of POCKET BOOKS

POCKET BOOKS, a Simon & Schuster division of
GULF & WESTERN CORPORATION
1230 Avenue of the Americas, New York, N.Y. 10020

ISBN: 0-671-83129-1

First Pocket Books printing January, 1981

10 9 8 7 6 5 4 3 2 1

POCKET and colophon are trademarks of Simon & Schuster.

Interior design by Catherine Carucci

Printed in the U.S.A.

Contents

Part One

The Idyll

Chapter One

"Perry, I tell you that we should have gone by way of the Strand. At least the Strand is lit up in parts."

Peregrine Manners laughed into Emmie's ear. She was aware that he had unfastened the clasp of her cloak, and that he might at any moment insinuate a hand against her bare shoulder. But there was time enough to deal with that emergency when it was upon her; meanwhile, it seemed important to make her point, in order that he should heed her and order the driver to turn the hackney carriage about before they got too far into the dark maze of streets behind Drury Lane.

"You fuss too much," said Manners. "We're no longer in the days of the Mohocks. The streets are well patrolled. Besides, it's quicker this way. And you *did* tell me that those two old biddies insisted on your being home straight after the theater."

"The Strand would have been nearly as quick," said Emmie. "All these turns and twists! How can this be a shortcut?"

"Frightened of footpads?" mocked Manners. And,

because he delighted to shock her of late: "Scared of being raped?"

"Don't be tiresome, Perry," said she, detaching his hand from her shoulder. "Talk to me about something sensible, do."

"What do you want me to talk about?" He sounded sulky, like a little boy who had set his heart upon the big red apple in the middle of the dish and has seen it taken by another. Of all the young men of her acquaintance, family and friends, Perry Manners had been the last to grow up, and the one who most frequently regressed to boyhood. She wondered how soon, before they reached her aunts' house in Leicester Square, he would make the attempt upon her breasts. It would be a pity to part under a cloud of resentment, because he really could be a most agreeable companion when he behaved.

"Talk to me about your commission," she said. "It is all signed, sealed and delivered?"

"Absolutely," he said. "I have a lieutenancy in the Buffs, and it cost my father two thousand guineas, to raise which he had to sell the estate in County Cork. I expect to be out in the Peninsula by Christmas. Hope the Duke doesn't polish off the Frenchies before I get there."

Emmie had the droll thought of England's hero, the Duke of Wellington, deliberately withholding his hand against the French in Spain till he was joined by Perry Manners. And she smiled into the darkness.

"Maybe you'll be sent to the Americas instead," she said. "Now that the war over there isn't going too well."

Manners clucked his tongue impatiently. "You don't understand, do you? Ladies can't be expected to understand these things, I suppose. Why, the Navy will settle with those Yankee bounders by the end of the year and have 'em suing for peace. They don't have a chance."

It was on the tip of Emmie's tongue to mention that

the small matter of the American Revolution had not been resolved so neatly or favorably, but she forbore from doing so.

"When shall we see you in your uniform?" she asked.

"I'm to go for the first fitting on Monday," he said.

"You will look so handsome that we'll all be swooning," she said.

"Will you now?" he said throatily, and Emmie knew that her comment had been misinterpreted, for his hand slid to her neck again. "Will you now, little Emmie?"

She sat bolt upright. "Did you enjoy the theater?" she asked brightly.

He lowered his hand, shuffled in his seat. "It was well enough," he said stiffly. "I'm not much for high-flown theatricals."

She smiled. The entertainment they had just witnessed at the Theater Royal, Drury Lane—a charity performance in aid of Relief for the Soldiers in the Peninsula—had been a ragbag of patriotic flimflam comprising scenes from Shakespeare's *Henry V,* verses written by the Poet Laureate in honor of the victories at Fuentes de Onoro and Albuera, interspersed with *tableaux vivants* of Britannia surrounded by the tutelary goddesses of the English rivers, and displays of real fountains and fireworks; and about as far from being "high-flown" as the thespian art is capable. Perry had sat up and taken notice of Britannia and her attendant goddesses, but had dropped asleep through Shakespeare.

"A pity Prinny didn't come," said Emmie.

"Too drunk, even, to be carried out to his coach, I shouldn't wonder," said her companion, and muttered a scurrility under his breath. His Royal Highness the Prince Regent was passing through one of his frequent bouts of unpopularity with the citizens of the capital, who had opportunity of witnessing the royal excesses at close quarters.

The hackney carriage's iron-shod tires thrummed around a cobbled corner, causing Emmie to sway toward her companion. He took the opportunity to slip a hand around her waist and hold her there.

"Surely, we must soon be at Leicester Square," said Emmie, making the calculation that she must give him no more than a few moments before she rid herself of the hand, or it would be established there by right of conquest.

"There's no hurry," said Manners. "You will be home soon enough. Too soon. Oh, Emmie. Beautiful, beautiful Emmie . . ."

"Perry—please . . ." His free hand was kneading her shoulder, from which he had slipped the protective cloak. Beneath it, she wore a high-waisted frock of sprigged muslin in the newest—and distinctly scandalous—mode. Her bosom, forced high by the top of her stays, while certainly masked from his eyes by the concealing darkness within the carriage, was nevertheless virtually unprotected from an importuning hand. And his mouth was against her neck. What was more, his breath smelled of spirits, and she knew then that he had taken brandy in the theater buffet during the interval—in addition to the bottle of claret and more brandy that she had watched him drink during dinner in the ladies' supper room at his Pall Mall Club. Not only overamorous, but also far from sober!

The process of disentangling herself, once begun, swiftly progressed from a simple readjustment of hands to the beginnings of a struggle. Her only consolation was that he did not get unpleasant, but, then, Perry was not the sort to get unpleasant under any circumstances. Petulant, yes; unpleasant, no. His mouth—moist, warm, murmuring endearments—remained at her neck and shoulder. One hand obstinately remained around her waist. She had two free hands to fend against his other. And surely the lamps and house lights of Leicester Square could not be so far distant.

"Hoy! Whoa, there, cabby!" A cry came from out of the darkness of the narrow, high-walled street ahead.

The hackney carriage slowed to a halt.

"Sorry, genn'lemen." The voice of their driver.

"Sorry? Sorry be damned, you dog. You will take us to Piccadilly, all four."

"I have a fare already, genn'lemen. I beg you to stand aside so I may pass on."

"The damned hell you will, you saucy fellow. A fare you say? Then you shall turn him out into the street, so that his betters may have the benefit."

Emmie, who had been listening to the exchange outside the carriage with growing alarm, leaned forward to peer through the side window. She could see nothing. Save for the dim light of the carriage lamp slightly above her head, close by the driver's seat, the street was in total darkness. And the lamp revealed nothing.

Nothing, except . . .

"By gad!" cried one of the men outside. "There's a filly in there. There in the lamplight, see? She's ducked back out of sight now."

"A good looker, is she?"

"Worth a tumble!"

"Let's have a look at her!"

Manners, who had removed his arm from about Emmie's waist and had abandoned his efforts to insinuate his other hand inside her bodice, took firm hold of her hand and murmured in her ear.

"Don't be alarmed, m' dear. A party of drunken fellows on their way home from a rout, I shouldn't wonder. Leave 'em to me. Nothing to worry about. Drunk or no, they sound to be gentlemen."

At that moment, the carriage door was wrenched open.

"A light here—bring a light! Let's see what good fortune has delivered into our hands."

The shape of the open doorway was filled by the silhouette of a man in a high-collared, caped coat and

a tall hat. Emmie strained her eyes to distinguish his
face, but it was in the most profound shadow. Next
moment, she was blinded by a shaft of light that
streamed out from the open trapdoor of a carriage
lamp held in the hand of another of the intruders.

"By God! What a morsel we have here, gentlemen.
Do you regard those raven tresses? And those eyes?"

"Do you see the bubbies on her? Egad, I'll make
my close acquaintance of them before the night's
much older."

"Now see here, gentlemen!" admonished Peregrine
Manners, assuming the deepest voice within his range.
"Enough's enough, and you have had your bit of
sport. The young lady is quite willing to overlook your
bawdy talk. Off with you now, while there's no ill
feeling."

"And who," came a drawling voice from out of the
darkness, "is this spavined youth with the mother's
milk still a-dribble on his chin?"

"Genn'lemen, genn'lemen, I beg you to desist.
Stand aside and let us go on our way." The voice of
the driver.

They did not even deign to reply to him. From out
of the lantern's beam came a gloved hand that fastened
itself about Emmie's wrist. She screamed when she
was dragged bodily from her seat and out into the
night, to stumble and fall on her knees at her captor's
booted feet. Crouching there, on hands and knees
upon the cobblestones, she saw Peregrine Manners
leap out of the carriage. In his hand he carried his
silver-knobbed cane. Clearly in the lamplight, a tongue
of steel snaked out from its hiding place in the cane.

"By gad, the young whippersnapper's got a toy
swordstick!" cried one of the night intruders—he who
carried the carriage lamp.

"Keep your light upon him, Jack," said another.
"I'll teach the whelp to draw upon his betters." A tall
figure in a high-collared coat loomed forward into the
stream of light that also illuminated Manners, who

stood, white-faced and defiant, with the slender blade of his swordstick outthrust.

"Keep back!" said Manners. "I warn you that I mean business."

"Perry!" cried Emmie. "Be careful—*please!*"

A hand clamped down upon her upper arm and held her tightly.

"None of the caterwauling, my little filly," said her captor. "Still your pretty tongue while we settle for young cockalorum, then you shall have our undivided attention, I promise you."

She watched in horror as the two figures in the lamplight faced up to each other: Manners, shortish of stature, pathetically young-looking; his opponent tall and broad of shoulder under the heavy, caped coat. The latter carried a walking cane that he held before him defensively. It was to be wood against steel.

"Drop that blade, whippersnapper, and you may well survive this night with nothing worse than a whipping!"

"Try and take it off me!" responded Peregrine Manners.

With an angry snort, the big man lunged with his cane. Manners parried, made a riposte. His opponent staggered back, clutching his forearm, and the cane fell from his fingers and clattered to the cobbles. Emmie saw a thin stream of carmine issuing from his sleeve.

"By the devil, the bastard's pinked me!" roared the wounded man. "Right through the confounded wrist!"

The grip on Emmie's arm tightened convulsively.

"Enough of this tomfoolery!" exclaimed her captor. "Get in there and strike him down! Are we going to be beaten by a stripling with a toy skewer? Get at him, I say!"

She saw Manners's peril, then, saw a dark form creeping around the rear of the carriage to come up behind him.

"*Perry!*" she screamed.

It was too late. An arm was wrapped about Manners's throat from behind, dragging his head back, chokingly. A kick was aimed at his loins. He with the dripping sleeve raised his stick to strike. The confused press of struggling figures moved out of the shaft of light, the coach lamp having been laid on the ground. There came the heavy thud of the descending stick. And again.

"He's down! What shall we do with him?" The question came out of the darkness. Instinctively, Emmie knew that it had been directed toward the man whose hand was upon her, holding her down upon her knees. She craned her neck and looked up. He was a looming shadow, tall, lean, powerful. The wide brim of his tall hat entirely hid his face.

"What shall we do with him?" The question was repeated.

Deep, harsh, merciless, the answer was shouted over her head: *"Stone his damsons!"*

She screamed and struggled to free herself and rise to her feet, but it was no use, for his grasp was like a band of steel. Then, impatient of her efforts, he slid one arm about her and, lifting her with no more effort than if she had been a rag doll, he bore her across the cobblestones to where a line of iron railings bordered a dark yard. He lifted up the struggling, frightened girl and impaled the waist of her gown upon the spear point of one of the railings. She felt, and heard, the sprigged muslin rip as the point entered, tore and finally snagged against the back lacing of her stays. When he took his hands away, she was suspended there, her slippered feet just clear of the ground, her fingers scrabbling upon the cold iron uprights. Helpless.

"Stay there, little filly," came the mocking voice from the shadowed mouth. "Your turn comes later." And turning on his heel, he went back across the street.

Breathless and panting, she hung there, the whole weight of her body taken upon the lacing of her stays, which tightened intolerably, nipping her waist and chest. Breathing became an agony. By a tremendous effort, she contrived to reach one hand up behind her back and finger the taut loops of lacing that encircled the top of the spike. There was nothing she could do to free herself. Impossible to claw through the strings with her fingernails.

Those men—those predatory beasts of the night—when they had done whatever they were doing with poor Perry Manners, would come to her, hanging as she was, helpless. . . .

A choked cry came out of the darkness. It was echoed by another. A clatter of hobnailed boots announced a running form that crossed the street in her direction.

"Oh, my gawd! It ain't right—it ain't natural!" the hackney carriage driver cried. He ran with staggering steps, like a man drunk with horror, his hands pressed to his brow.

Another scream from across the road. It died in a whimper.

"What are they doing?" wailed Emmie. "Oh, can't you do something to help him—please?"

The man peered up at her, cursed a slow oath under his breath.

"Gawd 'elp you, Miss," he said.

So saying, he reeled away into the shadows, fearful of helping her and sobbing brokenly. She was alone.

Alone—but not for long.

Presently, when they had had their fiendish sport with poor young Peregrine Manners, they swaggered across the street toward her: four well-made figures in high collars, with linen stocks that hid their mouths and chins, and pulled-down hats that shadowed their questing eyes. The one in front, who bore the carriage lamp, directed its beam toward the limp figure in the

sprigged muslin, who hung like a sacrificial lamb, helpless against their hands, their eyes, their lustful
thoughts.

Their acknowledged leader, he who had hung her
there, who had given the unspeakable sentence upon
Peregrine Manners, was the first to reach her.

"Well then, gentlemen," he drawled, "let us see
what she's made of, eh?"

And, taking off his gloves (they were lilac-colored,
and of the finest velvet—she could see them clearly in
the lamplight) and slipping them into the capacious
pocket of his caped coat, he advanced his hand—his
strong, well-formed hand with scrupulously well-tended
fingernails—toward her bodice. There was an audible
intake of breath from his companions.

"Egad!" exclaimed one of them. "This is going to
be a night to remember and no mistake. What a prize
we have here."

The questing hand was in no hurry; it lingered about
the edge of her bodice; a well-tended fingertip briefly
and caressingly touched a small mole that announced
the perfection of the upper slope of her right breast;
it described the contour of her neckline, trailing along
her shrinking flesh from shoulder to shoulder. She
willed herself to close her eyes, to cry out for help, to
scream, but, like a rabbit fascinated by an adder, she
could do no more than stare in fascination upon
the probing fingertip that so suavely outraged her
body.

"Oh, come on, old feller!" sniggered one of the
blank faces behind the lamplight. "Enough of the
shilly-shally. If we're all to have this filly, and again
and again, 'tis a long night ahead of us. Strip the little
bitch and let's get started."

"Crude and overeager, as ever, my dear Jack,"
murmured her tormentor. "Just like a bull at stud. I
tell you, this tender morsel will greatly be improved
by a modicum of dalliance. Bring the light nearer. You
see the slight flush on those cheeks, those smooth, and

oh, so damask cheeks? I tell you, that is not entirely occasioned by terror. No, indeed. Nor should the quickness of her breathing be laid entirely at the blame of her overtightened stays. I tell you, Jack, that I have already lit a small fire in the heart and loins of this delicious morsel, which when fanned to greater intensity—as is my intention—will be much to the advantage of you all, when your turn comes to worship at the portals of Hymen."

This oration, which had been accompanied by a slight questing of the well-tended fingertips within the limits of the terrified girl's bodice, won a guffaw of approval from the speaker's three companions.

"Gad, you're a silver-tongued devil and no mistake, Snakey," said one.

"Snakey, you may take all the time you please, for all I care," said another.

"She's quite young," said the third companion. "And a virgin, d'you think?"

The leader—the one they addressed as Snakey—cupped Emmie's chin in his hand and lifted her face up into the best of the lamplight. The intensity of the beam caused her to close her eyes, or she might have seen his face quite clearly.

"Nineteen or twenty, no more," pronounced Snakey. "As to whether she's lost her cherry, well, we shall soon discover that for ourselves. Or, perchance the filly will tell us of her own accord." He gave Emmie's ear a gentle tug. "Well, my fancy, has some bright sprig run off with your maidenhead already, or are you whole?"

"Please . . ." whispered the tortured girl.

"Answer me sprightly, filly," said he whom they called Snakey. And there was now a hard edge to his voice, as from a man who was not used to waiting for an answer. "Answer up: are you maid or no?"

"I—I am a virgin," breathed she, in so small a voice that it could scarcely be heard.

"Yoicks!" cried one of her tormentors.

"Tally-ho!" whooped another. "The game's afoot, Snakey! Who's to be first at the fence?"

"Silence, all!" cried Snakey. "You'll all have a turn at the jump, but, by God, I'll be first over!"

With that, he seized the center of Emmie's bodice, where the sprigged muslin was tied in a tiny lovers' knot, and, in one downward thrust of his hand, ripped the gauzy material from neck to waist. Another, and firmer, grip on the waistband, and the garment parted at the hem and fell at the suspended feet of the hanging girl.

"By my oath!" murmured one of the men in awe. "Lady Luck has brought us good fortune this night, and no mistake."

"Regard those bubbies," said another. "What fool was it who said that when you've seen one pair you've seen all? I tell you there's no two pairs alike. And this filly has the finest I ever beheld."

They stood back a pace, while he who held the lantern directed it to the best advantage upon their victim. Emmie, bereft of her gown, and clad in nothing but her stays, a pair of pale pink stockings, tied with ribbons at the thigh, and her slippers, made what shift she could of covering herself with her hands; but even that pitiful inadequacy was denied her when, with a laugh, Snakey seized one of her wrists and held it firm. Shamed and helpless, Emmie bowed her head and closed her eyes against her bitter tears.

Then they were crowding about her, kneading at the milk-white orbs that overspilled the tight corseting, probing her hips, her bared thighs. Brandy-laden lips sought hers moistly. The most extravagantly lewd declarations were breathed into her horrified ears. When their attentions became more precise, she threw back her head and screamed to the sky, which won her a curse and a savage slap across her bare breasts. And then the brute called Snakey, throwing aside the skirts of his coat, commenced to unbutton the lappet of his breeches. . . .

Salvation came out of the night, down the winding, cobbled street. It came in the form of a swift phaeton drawn by a pair of high-stepping horses.

"What goes on there?" A voice out of the darkness.

"By gad, they're footpads!" Another voice.

Emmie opened her eyes to see her tormentors in confusion, looking to each other and toward the new-comers in the phaeton, which had drawn up by the curb a short distance away. And, finally, they looked to their leader.

"What do we do, Snakey—stay and fight?"

"It's four to two, Snakey."

"Yes, but look at the size of that feller in the shocking bad hat, Snakey!"

Snakey looked, and gave the curt order. "Cut and run!"

They ran, all four. The men in the phaeton leaped down in time to scuffle with the last of the runaways, and a couple of punches were thrown. But darkness added to the confusion, and Snakey and his cronies, moving at the rush, were able to break through and make good their escape in the warren of narrow lanes and alleyways that stretched between Long Acre and Leicester Square.

Silence. Emmie opened her eyes to see her rescuers returning from the fruitless pursuit. She could make little of them in the darkness, save that one was tall and well-made, and the other—the wearer of an extravagantly wide hat—a veritable giant who over-topped his companion by a head and a half.

Emmie shrank back against the cold bars upon which she was suspended, and again covered her intimate parts with trembling hands, fearful that she had exchanged a quartet of scoundrels for a pair in the like mold. But the first words of the lesser of the two new-comers set her mind at rest. They were delivered in a firm and pleasing voice in tones of compassion.

"Zounds, Jago, see what the swine have done to this lady!"

"Lawks-a-mussy, sir. Have they killed her?"

"Ma'am, are you all right?" Even as he spoke, he was peeling off his coat and holding it out toward her, covering her bareness from their gaze. Still holding the coat around her, he took her about the waist, lifted her up and unhooked her from the cruel spike. Trembling, mouthing incoherent thanks, she let herself be gathered up in her rescuer's arms and carried to the phaeton, where she was laid down upon a plumply cushioned seat.

By the light of the phaeton's lamps, she now saw that one of her rescuers was a grave-faced young man with ginger side whiskers and the ruddy complexion of one who spends a great deal of time in outdoor pursuits. His companion had the look of a pugilist, being of middle years, with a broken nose and a thickening about the eyes and ears that betokens one who follows the bare-fisted trade.

"Permit me to introduce myself, ma'am," said the young man. "Jock Ballantree, at your service. And this is Jago Jackson. First—and do not answer if it distresses you too much—have those swine hurt you so much that you should see a physician? Second, if you are well enough, shall we not take you straight home? Third, that being so, where do you reside, ma'am? Take your time in answering, I beseech you."

Emmie, despite her turmoil of mind, could not resist a smile at the droll manner of Ballantree's address.

"I have not been hurt, sir," she replied, "And for that I have you gentlemen to thank—which I do, from the bottom of my heart. And . . ." She broke off, an expression of sudden horror passing across her features.

"By heaven, ma'am!" exclaimed Ballantree. "What ails you?"

"Perry!" said she, brokenly. "Oh, Perry, how could I have forgotten, even for an instant?" She made to get up, casting about in the surrounding gloom with staring eyes.

"Who be Perry, ma'am?" asked the giant Jackson.

She told them, then. And when they had heard, they went to search, admonishing her to stay where she was. She crouched in the phaeton, huddled under Ballantree's heavy coat, listening to the clatter of their booted feet on the cobbled darkness, listening to the murmur of their voices as they moved slowly to and fro, searching, searching.

"I see him, sir!" cried Jago.

"Yes!"

Running footfalls.

"How is he?"

"Turn him over, careful now."

"What have they . . . ? *O merciful Christ!*"

Emmie could bear to hear no more. Clasping her hands over her ears, she threw back her head and screamed to the night, the eternal cry of Woman in her agony.

It was big Jago who escorted her to her aunts' house behind Leicester Square, gravely handed her into the care of her aunts' butler, who came in answer to the summons upon the elegant front door, putting on his wig as he came. The aunts were abed—and had so been since eight of the clock, as was their custom, come hell come high water—and were by that time fast asleep in their great double bed, side by side, hair in plaits, bonnets tied under their chins, mouths agape, snoring a duet in counterpoint. But before retiring they had instructed the butler, Standish, to summon the Watch should Miss Emmie not return home by ten, which should give Mr. Manners ample time to bring her from Drury Lane. If Miss Emmie was not back by ten, then Standish must summon the Watch, but not the sleeping aunts, not under any circumstances.

In the event, Standish had himself nodded off over the kitchen fire, and it was past eleven when the knock on the front door sent him scurrying. He gaped to see

Miss Emmie most curiously disheveled and wearing—
of all things—a gentleman's bottle-green hunting coat,
and accompanied by a devilishly rough-looking giant
with a broken nose and cauliflower ears, and bearing
upon his head a most outlandish hat. Neither Miss
Emmie nor her escort troubled themselves with en-
lightening him as to the reason for her condition or the
company she was keeping, but contented themselves
by bidding each other a good night and shaking hands.
Blinking in amazement, the butler watched Miss Emmie brush past him with a perfunctory "Goodnight,
Standish," run lightly up the stairs two at a time, enter
her room at the top landing and slam the door behind
her.

Once in her room, Emmie gave way to the agony
in her mind by throwing herself upon the patchwork
quilt of her cozy little four-poster bed and bursting
into heartbroken sobs. She cried for her shame, for
terror, for relief and release—but, most of all, for poor
little Peregrine Manners, who would never wear the
uniform of scarlet with the buff-colored facings, never
march to victory behind the Duke, never paw pretty
girls in hackney carriages again.

While Jago had escorted Emmie home on foot (a
mere five minutes' walk—the whole nightmare episode
had taken place but a turn in the twisty road from the
lights and bustle of Leicester Square), it was Jock Ballantree who had driven the cruelly maimed Peregrine
Manners to a physician, in the hope of at least saving
the young man's life.

Emmie was still weeping, still wakeful, when the
summer sun thinly lit the prim bedchamber that was
always hers when she visited her aunts in London.
Then, at the dawn's hour she drifted away into sleep,
and (such is the resilience of the young) was able to
triumph over the new wounds that lay upon her mind,
and dream of unimaginable delights. In particular, of
a certain Toby Stocker, with whom she was deeply

and sincerely in love. Toby, a mere footman by calling, nevertheless possessed the finest figure in Oxfordshire, with a pair of shoulders on him that would
not have disgraced a wrestler, and a pair of legs on
him, and a suave promontory at his loins that tight
buckskin breeches showed to full advantage.

In waking life, Emmie had done no more than exchange hot glances with the eminently desirable footman; in her dreams that dawn, while the sun rose over
the trees of Leicester Square and the morning chorus
of starlings filled the still air, she and the eminently
desirable Toby were alone in a moonlit garden, together in a rose-covered bower. She, nude, was accepting his most intimate caresses. He, clad in his
customary buckskin breeches and livery coat of saffron yellow with black braiding, could not, in her eyes,
have been more alluring if he had been naked also.
Matching her lover's ardor, the untried girl caressed
his cheek, his firm shoulders, insinuated her small
hand into the bosom of his shirt and stroked the thick
pelt of fine hair, and his firm nipples, then boldly descended to the pride of his loins . . .

She woke near noon. A fine rain skittered at her
window, and all London lay under tumbled storm
clouds. Springing from her bed, Emmie stripped and
washed herself in the basin. Her aunts' exiguous circumstances permitting the luxury of only one cham-
bermaid, she shifted for herself by emptying the slops
out of the window into the alleyway below. And, while
she was doing so, she saw a yellow phaeton draw up
by the front door of the house, and from it alight a
well-made figure in blue broadcloth and a tall hat, from
under which descended a riot of ginger thatch. He did
not notice the girl up at the window, but, tethering the
horses to the ring of the mounting block, gave a firm
double beat upon the door knocker, by which time
Emmie was struggling into her stays.

She had progressed as far as running a comb through

her raven-black hair when a knock on her door, followed by a discreet cough, announced the summons of Standish the butler.

"Hem! You are awake, Miss?"

"Yes."

"The Misses Amberley present their compliments and a good morning to you, Miss, and request the pleasure of your company in the white drawing room. There is a visitor, Miss. One Sir Jock Ballantree, Bart."

"Thank you, Standish. Tell my aunts that I will be down presently."

"Yes, Miss. Thank you, Miss."

She deftly wound her hair into a chignon. News of poor Peregrine, she hoped fervently. And so her rescuer was a baronet, which was interesting. She recalled his curiously droll manner of speech, and was glad to have the opportunity of seeing him again. A nice person: the sort who would be useful to have around in a shipwreck, perhaps.

Her only decent, clean gown was a striped silk, which she wore with a sash of dullish pink and slippers to match. Emmie looked at herself this way and that in the pier glass and quite liked what she saw. News of poor Perry. She must hurry.

The door of the white drawing room was open when she descended to the hallway. Her aunts were sitting in their twin armchairs on either side of the Adam chimneypiece, and their visitor perched on a stool between them, his hat lying upside down by his feet. He rose at Emmie's entrance and bowed with an almost Roman gravity, taking her proffered hand and depositing upon it a kiss that was like the touch of a butterfly. His honest, bucolic countenance was full of concern, and his cornflower-blue eyes clouded with anxiety as he met her gaze.

"I trust you are well, or better, ma'am," he murmured huskily.

"Better by far than when you saw me last, Sir

Jock," she replied. "But, please tell me, how is . . . ?"

She was interrupted by her aunts. The Misses Amberley, both maiden ladies, of adjacent years, exactly similar in appearance and temperament, customarily spoke in alternate phrases, like a pair of poll parrots sharing the same cage.

Aunt Sarah said, "Emmie dear, you will wish not to permit Mr. Manners to escort you to the theater again . . ."

"For it appears," continued Aunt Clarice, "that Mr. Manners is not a gentleman in whom the custodians of a girl of tender years can repose any confidence . . ."

"In short," concluded Aunt Sarah, "we have it from Sir Jock, here, that Mr. Manners was so far gone in his cups last night that he not only delivered you home an hour late, but was struck with the vapors and obliged to repair to a physician."

Emmie murmured to Sir Jock, *sotto voce,* "Don't worry, as you will have ascertained, they are almost totally deaf, and their vanity prevents them from using ear trumpets. Speak freely to me. How is he? How is Peregrine Manners?"

"Very poorly, when I called to inquire this morning," said Ballantree. "But he will live."

"That's a mercy, at any rate," said Emmie. "And what of—what of those animals who assaulted us?"

"I laid evidence before the magistrates at Bow Street, ma'am," said Ballantree, "but I fear that lack of evidence of identity will preclude any hope of arrest."

"Their leader was called Snakey," said Emmie. "And there was another who was addressed as Jack. I told you that, did I not?"

"That you did, ma'am," confirmed Ballantree. "And I mentioned as much in my deposition to the magistrates. Snakey and Jack. I stated also that, in your opinion, all four were well-bred and well-dressed gentlemen."

"Gentlemen!" exclaimed Emmie, and shuddered at the thought of herself suspended from the dark railings, her body exposed to their questing hands and eyes. . . .

"What are you talking about, Emmie dear?" piped Aunt Sarah.

"Apart from Mr. Manners's revolting state of intoxication, how did you enjoy the theater, dear?" asked Aunt Clarice.

"It was very diverting!" shouted Emmie.

"I hope I may call upon you again, Miss Dashwood," murmured Ballantree.

"I regret, Sir Jock, that I am returning to Oxfordshire tomorrow morning," said Emmie.

"That is to Flaxham Palace, is it not?" he inquired.

"That is so, sir," said Emmie.

"If ever I am in Oxfordshire, and in the vicinity of Flaxham, I beg leave to call upon you there," said Ballantree.

"That will be very agreeable, sir. But I have to warn you that my grandfather is rather . . . odd, and does not take too kindly to visitors," she said.

Ballantree smiled his grave smile, his cornflower-blue eyes crinkling most attractively at the corners. Emmie remembered that those eyes, also, had feasted—however briefly—upon her nakedness.

"That is common knowledge in society, Miss Dashwood," he said. "Nevertheless, I will brave the marquess's displeasure and call upon you if I may."

"Was His Highness at the theater, Emmie dear?" asked Aunt Sarah.

"And accompanied by that dreadful, dreadful Mrs. Fitzherbert?" echoed Aunt Clarice.

"Only the Duke of York occupied the royal box!" shouted Emmie.

"Eddie York, I remember him well when we were gels," said Aunt Sarah.

"Danced appallingly," said her sister. "Very bad breath."

"I must take my leave," said Ballantree.

Emmie gave him her hand. "I can never thank you enough for saving me last night," she said. "And, again, for keeping the news of it from my aunts."

He bowed over her hand. In doing so, she was aware that his gaze flickered briefly over her corsage. And she knew, as if she had entered behind those cornflower-blue eyes and seen into his mind, that he was recalling the secret roundness which lay concealed beneath the striped silk.

Emmie Dashwood was an orphan. Her mother, the youngest daughter of the Third Marquess of Beechborough, had died soon after her husband and father of her only child, the Reverend Arthur Dashwood, M.A. (Oxon.). Ostracized by her own father for presuming to exercise her choice by marrying the man of her heart, a poor clergyman with only his stipend to support them, poor Lady Jane Dashwood had, in the end, been reduced to doing her own washing and cooking, not to mention suckling her own babe instead of putting her to wet-nurse. Grief, coupled with inadequate diet and the rigors of motherhood, was too much for the gently reared aristocrat. She was carried off in the harsh winter of 1793 by a galloping consumption, and the infant Emmie was brought to Flaxham Palace, Oxfordshire, seat of the Beechborough marquessate, there to join the tatterdemalion horde of orphan cousins and maiden aunts, discarded mistresses, unemployed imbecile relations and sick, idle, impoverished and dying relations who inhabited the gaunt, unheated wings of England's most unlovely stately home. It was a fetid place where priceless tapestries were eaten to rags by moths and rats, and every room had a piss-corner.

Tom Cradock, founder of the Beechborough line, had been Paymaster-General to the great John Churchill, and had raised the monies, by fair means and foul, that allowed the English army to wrest vic-

tory in the Low Countries. The war over, the fate that
disposes its favors so disproportionately brought
Churchill the Dukedom of Marlborough and his paymaster the lesser degree of Marquess. For Marlborough, a grateful nation built the splendid palace of
Blenheim on a fair sward of high ground above Wood-
stock. To the paymaster was given a scarcely less ornate abode, Flaxham Palace, which lay in a miasma-
haunted piece of swampland in a turgid backwater of
the Thames. Within fifty years of its building, Flaxham
was crumbling with dry rot, the Death Watch beetle,
woodworm and more rats than any floating hulk in
Wapping or Rotherhythe. Heirs innumerable sickened and died in infancy. Young wives took pale and
succumbed to wasting diseases. Only the successive
marquesses, to the number of three, thrived in Flaxham's unhealthy atmosphere; and the then current
marquess, father of poor Lady Jane and grandsire of
Emmie Dashwood, had survived four wives, innumerable mistresses and the attentions of a different
serving wench brought to his bed each night, to
achieve the ripe old age of eighty-seven, with all his
teeth, most of his hair and all his appetites intact.

It was in trepidation of being reunited with her
grandfather and his immediate circle that Emmie was
driven through the high, ornamental gateway of Flaxham two days after her hideous experience in London.
The gatekeeper and his wife and children came out
and doffed caps or curtsied as the crested coach swept
past on its way down the long drive that led to the
unsavory hollow in which stood the great, gaunt seat
of the Beechboroughs.

Grandfather Beechborough was a lecher, and no
ties of blood or honor kept his gnarled hands from
straying. It was rumored that he had sired children
from his own sisters, and had had carnal knowledge
of his own mother. He had certainly, and on several
occasions since her ripening, allowed his hand to alight

caressingly upon Emmie's shapely rump with more
than grandfatherly affection.

If the marquess was a libertine, his nephew and heir,
the Honorable Eustace Cradock, was a fiend incarnate. Blackballed from the best clubs in London, bereft of his commission in the Coldstream Guards,
banned from the Royal Enclosure at Ascot, he had
lately achieved the supreme accolade of vice: to be
declared persona non grata at St. James's Palace. That
the Prince Regent, voluptuary extraordinary of England, found the Hon. Eustace's proclivities too gamy
for his royal taste was an inverted distinction indeed.

The marquess and his cousin played interminable
bezique in the palace orangery, surrounded by their
cronies and sundry wenches of their choice. It was
through the glass walls of the orangery, in company
with various of her contemporary cousins, that Emmie
had been introduced to the facts of life; for Beechborough and his circle paid no regard to niceties when
the urge to copulate came upon them, but merely took
the wench who had attracted their fancy and mounted
her before the assembled company. And the assembled company scarcely troubled to look up from their
bezique. Only the round, regarding eyes of the children, peering in through the glass walls, heeded the
salutations to Hymen that were regularly performed
upon the orangery sofas, the marble-topped tables,
even the tiled floors.

Notwithstanding the deleterious upbringing, Emmie
at the age of twenty was as unspoiled in mind as she
was pure in body. Though not unaroused by the contemplation of the sensual, she elevated sensuality to
the plane of the spiritual. A child of a bawdy age,
living in surroundings of extreme libertinism, she
nourished in her heart an unsullied image of what
should be the nature of physical knowledge between
a man and a woman. In short, she was an incurable
romantic. And every fiber of her romantic heart was

currently directed toward the adoration of Toby
Stocker, the footman.

Stocker was her own age, and incredibly handsome
in the blond, hawk-faced Viking mold of an Eastern
Counties male. Well over six feet, and lithely built, he
was the epitome of all the heroes in the novelettes that
filled Emmie's idle hours. Others among her contem-
poraries, her cousins, and even haughty Petronella
Pallance, who was cousin only in name, fell under the
spell of the handsome young footman of Flaxham Palace. But only Emmie knew him at all in the intimate
sense. . . .

The incident had taken place in the spring of the
previous year, when the rising sap had found an echo
in the urgent desires of the young romantic that was
Emmie Dashwood. One morning early, driven by a
nameless compulsion, she rose and, dressing herself
in only a chemise and slippers, went out into the park
that fronted the rambling pile of the great mansion.
Away across the water gardens she espied, in the rising mist, the ghostly forms of antlered deer, heads
erect and staring in her direction, ready for instant
flight. At her passing, a cloud of wood pigeons rose
from a lofty elm tree and whirled away toward the
sun. She came at length to the river bank, where,
among the concealing rushes, she slipped out of her
chemise and entered the cool benison of the slow-
moving water.

She lay floating for a while, moving gently among
the rushes, safe from all eyes, enjoying the ecstatic
sense of freedom that her nudity kindled within her
spirit, intoxicated by the sights and sounds of the new
spring, by the kiss of the moving water, by the knowledge of her own youthful loveliness. All at once, she
heard the sound of footfalls moving through long
grass. In a trice, Emmie ducked low in the water,
covering her breasts with her folded arms, cupping
them in her hands, her skin prickling with a sudden
terror. Crouched close by a thick screen of rushes,

she peered out to see who had disturbed her idyll and was shocked to behold a tall figure in the saffron and black livery of the Beechboroughs. It was Toby Stocker, whom she barely knew by name, but whom she had noticed serving at table. She had remarked privately upon his splendid appearance.

What was he about, she asked herself. What was *he* doing down by the river so early in the morning? She prayed that he would move on quickly, that he would not chance upon her chemise and slippers that lay behind yonder bush—happily out of his sight.

She continued to watch unseen, crouched low behind the screen of reeds, a dozen paces from where the tall young footman stood. And it was when he turned and looked the other way that she saw he was carrying a towel and what looked like a cake of yellow soap.

Merciful heaven—he was going to wash himself!

Or—*bathe himself* . . .

Dry-throated on the instant, her breath quickening, her heart commencing to thump so that he should have heard it, she watched the tall footman shrug out of his frogged, yellow tail coat and lay it carefully over the limb of a spreading willow tree. His neckband followed, carefully wound into a ball and placed on top of the coat.

Emmie swallowed hard. Trembling-lipped, she let her mind furiously race over the limited options open to her. She could declare herself, or she could remain silent. To call out to him, to sternly announce herself as Miss Dashwood, followed by a demand that he instantly withdraw, would bring upon herself only a temporary embarrassment. The footman would instantly and without question depart. Male servants—even male servants employed in a den of licentiousness such as Flaxham under the Third Marquess—would not dare to thrust their unwanted attentions upon their noble employers' female kin, however naked and helpless.

So why, Emmie asked herself, did she remain silent?

Her eyes never left his fingers (very long, lean fingers) as they unbuttoned his shirt at breast and cuffs. She gave a sharp intake of breath when he peeled off the shirt and disclosed his upper torso, richly muscled at shoulders, breasts and upper arms, and pelted with a fine coating of blond hairs that rose from navel to neck. So close was she that she could see his nipples pucker and stiffen—like her own—in the morning breeze.

He posed there for a few moments, rubbing his hands up and down his forearms, flexing and unflexing his smooth muscles, brushing back a lock of flaxen hair that fell across his brow. Naked, huddled, afire with emotions that she had never dreamed of experiencing, Emmie Dashwood watched. And adored.

When his hands fell to the lappet of his buckskin breeches, she all but cried out with a rush of intense feeling that caused her heart to miss a beat and her whole body to describe itself in her mind: limbs and torso, every last inch of her skin, every stiffened hair. If she had been offered the kingdoms of the earth and all the treasures of Araby, if she had been granted a century of youth and beauty unspoiled, or the gift of eternal life, she could not have dragged her adoring gaze from the blond Adonis on the river bank as he drew the buckskin breeches over his lean flanks, and, stooping, down the length of his muscled thighs and calves.

Straightening up, he stood revealed to his hidden adorer in the nude splendor of his young manhood: tall in the sunlight, Grecian in repose. Heart-rendingly vulnerable. Ductile.

She watched through her tears, as, stooping, he took up the cake of common soap and, dipping it into the shallows, commenced to rub it over himself: chest and shoulders, arms and hands, face, neck, then his lean stomach and flanks, his loins and buttocks, his back as well as he was able. When he was lathered and rubbed, he waded, thigh-deep into the river, so close to her that she caught the soapy smell of him, and dashed water over himself; this being done, he then immersed himself completely, not ten feet from the nude girl who watched him from behind the screen of rushes, and whose sole desire was to slide under the water and join him, breast to breast and flank to flank, in an eternal kiss of ecstasy. . . .

"We are here, Miss. Miss Emmie, ma'am, we have arrived."

The coachman's prompting aroused Emmie from her erotic reverie. She felt her cheeks color mightily before the fellow's gaze, for it seemed impossible that some sign of her inner thoughts should not have shown on her countenance. She swallowed hard.

"Thank you, Tinkler."

"My pleasure, ma'am." The coachman handed her down, and expressed the private thought that here was a filly who had grown into as fine a young mare as was ever brought to stud, and that he, Ned Tinkler, would give much to attend to the breaking of her.

No one greeted her arrival. She marched up the steps and under the great portico to the massive front doors. Flaxham, built in flagrant imitation of Blenheim, consisted of a massive central block and two long, adjoining wings. Unhappily, the first marquess had been badly served by his architect—a less than brilliant pupil of the great Vanbrugh who had built Blenheim. For anyone with an eye for proportion and style, there was something ever so slightly wrong with the general appearance of Flaxham: either the central block was too powerful for the wings, or the wings out of kilter with the central block. It was not only in refinements such as these that the building failed. Due to a structural defect of the roof and gutterings, the

walls and pediment on the front facade were streaked
with green mold, and the stonework was visibly rotting.

One of the heavy bronze doors was ajar. It creaked
open to her touch, and Emmie entered her ancestral
hallway. She immediately caught sight of a flash of
saffron and black livery rounding a distant corner, and
called out. To her disappointment it was not Toby
Stocker, but one of the older footmen, who upon her
inquiry informed her that the family was at luncheon
in the small hall. Emmie, who had not eaten since
leaving the posting inn at Thame that morning, and
who possessed a notably fine appetite, determined to
avail herself of the opportunity, and made straight for
the small hall, which lay at the far end of the southern
wing.

The sounds of the family in full cry after victuals
greeted her long before reaching the door of the small
hall. She caught the bass laugh of her grandfather, the
eldritch cackle of one of her great-aunts, the tipsy gig-
gle of—no doubt—one of Uncle Eustace's latest dox-
ies and several babies howling.

She entered the small hall—a misnomer of a title if
there ever was one, for the chamber was as long as
the nave of a middling-sized church, and on foggy
nights the high-pitched, hammer-beamed roof was
sometimes invisible in wraiths of mist. A long refectory table ran down the center, and another formed a
T at the far end. It was at the top table that the marquess, his sisters, his nephew Eustace, and various
favored women sat. The rest of the family was disposed down both sides of the long table. They numbered about fifty in all.

"Why it's Emmie. Come here, lass, and let me have
a look at you," Archibald Cradock, third Marquess
of Beechborough, called out in his fine bass voice and
gestured to his grandchild to approach him, which she
did with considerable trepidation. Clad, as ever, in
grubby court dress of the previous century, with soiled

lace at cuffs and throat, in a white wig that seethed with lice, Beechborough was not the sort of grandsire that inspired much pride and affection in young women of sensibility. Nor, when she stooped to kiss his cheek and caught the foulness of his breath, was she greatly pleased by the touch of his hand as it insinuated itself from her waist to her buttocks.

"Well, m' dear, and how have you enjoyed yourself in London, hey? How long is it you've been away?"

"Three months, grandfather."

"Three months, hey? Go to plenty of plays and balls, did you?"

"Yes, grandfather."

"Met plenty o' fine gallants, I shouldn't wonder. Any of 'em try to throw a leg across you, did they?"

"No,

"Then the youth o' this country ain't what they were in my young day!" declared the outrageous old man. "For I'd have tumbled you as soon as look at you, young Emmie, and that's the truth of it!" So overjoyed was he by this sally that he threw back his head and collapsed in a paroxysm of mirth that ended in a bout of coughing, from which he emerged purple-faced and calling for brandy.

Emmie took her place at an empty seat near the top table, next to a distant cousin-by-marriage whose name she could never remember. The cousin-by-marriage—quite a young girl, and widowed by the war—was picking at a bunch of grapes and giving suck to one of the half-dozen or so infants who were around the table.

The culinary arrangements at Flaxham Palace were—because of the sheer size of the building, involving a tremendous journey between kitchens and eating places, and also on account of the vast numbers of persons to be fed—of a very rough-and-ready nature. Food—excellent, rich, expensive food—was deposited on the tables in enormous quantities and in no sort of order. Such dishes as were emptied were taken away at the end of a meal; the rest remained, for day after day, till someone noticed the stench. In front of Emmie was a most appetizing-looking game pie, which she nevertheless approached with great caution, first assuring herself that it was not crawling with maggots. It was not; it was excellent. A footman filled her glass with a measure of fine claret, and she set to.

Having rubbed the sharp edge off her hunger, Emmie relaxed and took stock of her surroundings to see how the rest of the family were faring: if there were any newcomers, or if any of the older generations had died during her absence. There had certainly been a couple of births, as far as she could determine.

Everyone seemed to be talking at once, the parakeet chattering providing a continuous background sound. Over the rim of her wine glass, she covertly ran her eye along the top table. Uncle Eustace had a new doxy with him: a highly-colored lady in her mid-thirties, with piled-up hair in the Grecian manner, and one of the scandalous dresses in the new mode that had been imported from Imperial Paris, where it was said to have been originated by Bonaparte's sister, the so-called Princess Pauline. The gown was simply a night shift, high in the waist, low in the corsage, and worn with nothing under. Women of the more shameless sort—and Uncle Eustace's doxy, if Emmie's eyes did not deceive her, was palpably demonstrating herself to be one of *that* sort—even went to the length of damping the sheer muslin before putting it on. Uncle Eustace's doxy might just as well have been naked, as was evidenced by the way her paramour feasted his lustful eyes upon her proffered charms.

Grandfather Beechborough, who had been occupying himself with the victuals when Emmie had entered, had, perhaps as a result of the reunion with his nubile granddaughter, turned his mind to appetites of another sort. He had seized upon a passing serving wench and, having pulled her down upon his knee, was exploring her with his hands and lips. No one took this conduct in any way amiss, not even the old man's sisters, who, dressed like their brother in the style of the 1780s, in figured satins, silks and court wigs, were noisily thrusting food and drink into their black-fanged mouths and chattering like excited monkeys.

It was at this juncture that—someone having called for a cut of the whole peacock that had stood in the center of the table before Emmie, and whose plume of tail feathers had blocked her view of those sitting immediately opposite—Emmie was able, upon its removal, to see that her vis-à-vis was none other than Cousin Petronella Pallance, no cousin.

Petronella mouthed something at her, something she could not hear above the noise of chatter.

"What?"

"You have got fatter!" mouthed Petronella. "You are all cheeks and bubs."

"And you are scraggier than ever!" responded Emmie cheerfully. "A beanpole with bee stings!"

Petronella put out her tongue and squinted evilly. They had been enemies since childhood, had fought in the nursery and in the schoolroom; Petronella had once stabbed her with a penknife in the arm, and Emmie had once nearly drowned Petronella in the ornamental lake. An orphan like herself, the other was her own age and as fair as she was dark, with a sylphlike figure that Emmie—whose figure tended to the Junoesque—held in a private envy that not all the tortures of the Inquisition would have forced her to admit. Petronella, of course, was also in love with Toby Stocker. She also knew—for Emmie had taken great delight in telling her, and in some wealth of detail—that Emmie had gazed upon Toby nude. Petronella had turned white with emotion and had affected not to have believed a word of it.

"It is Sunday, I remind you all!" boomed Grandfather Beechborough in a stentorian bass that silenced all converse. "And I shall require your attendance in the chapel for Evensong. Parson Hackett is conducting the service, and I have bid him give a long discourse on hellfire and such. So mark that you're all present, or you'll court my disfavor. And that includes yourself, Eustace, you dog.'' His last sally was delivered to his heir.

"I shall be present, Uncle," responded the next marquess, his thin lips twisted in a leer. "For I am ever one to take a lively interest in the latest news from hellfire."

"So you should, so you should, Eustace," declared the marquess. "For hellfire's where you're going, make no mistake on that score. And, do you not check your appetites, you'll be there sooner than you think. The fourth marquessate will be the shortest ever, and I'll no sooner have found myself a place by the fire alongside Old Nick, but I'll look around to see your ugly countenance a-grinning down at me."

The Hon. Eustace laughed good-humoredly at that, and when he had finished, he said, "There is no doubt that Parson Hackett is very good on hellfire."

"I never heard better," agreed his uncle. "I greatly approve of Hackett, who is not only sound on his theology, but rides to hounds like the devil incarnate, and can drink his two bottles with the best. A vastly different sort of divine from that father o' young Emmie's." He looked down the table to where Emmie sat. " 'Twas not your father's poverty and low breeding that caused me to cut your mother off without a penny, m' dear, but his mealy-mouthed, canting ways. Forever quoting the Bible against me was the precious Reverend Dashwood, and I would not abide it." And Beechborough, removing his hand from the serving wench's bodice, picked up his brandy glass and drained it in a gulp.

This was a signal for a general breaking-up of the luncheon party, as the family drained glasses, rose and made their way to their quarters, some very unsteadily. In rising, Emmie caught the eye of her Uncle Eus-

tace, who beckoned to her to approach him. This she
did, and fearfully. The arch rake of the Cradocks was
not uncomely to look upon. Apart from a thinness of
the lips and the fact that his eyes were set a mite too
close together, he possessed a complexion and a figure
that would not have disgraced a man who lived a
wholesome life—as the Hon. Eustace most certainly
did not. What Emmie found repugnant was not her
uncle's appearance, but his manner. A few moments'
conversation with him, and she always felt the need
to wash herself all over and clean her teeth.

The purpose of summoning his niece was soon clear
from the Hon. Eustace's opening remark, as, gesturing toward the wanton creature lolling by his side, he
said, "My dear Emmie, I would like to present you
to Mrs. Galloway. Ma'am, this is my favorite niece."

"Howdy-do," said Mrs. Galloway. "Pleased to
meet you, I'm sure."

"Mrs. Galloway is an—an actress," supplied her
swain. "On the stage," he added irrelevantly.

"Poses plastiques," explained Mrs. Galloway. "It's
ever so artistic. Mr. Cradock is forever persuading me
to give a performance before the assembled family."

"I'm sure that would be very nice," said Emmie
faintly.

"Her 'Diana at her Bath' is a revelation," said the
Hon. Eustace unctuously, molding Mrs. Galloway's
well-upholstered shoulder with his fingertips.
"Likewise her 'Psyche at the Well' and her 'Birth of
Venus,' or 'Venus Rising from the Waves.' You must
see them, Emmie dear. I am sure you would find them
instructive and inspiring."

His close-set eyes swam up his niece's body from
hip to bosom, and he licked his already too-moist
lips.

"We have missed you greatly these last months,
Emmie dear. So much has happened at Flaxham since
you have been away. Activities in which you should
have taken part . . ." His voice trailed away to si-

lence, and his pale-eyed stare looked out upon un-imaginable scenes of his own devising.

Emmie took the opportunity of her uncle's relapse into daydreams to murmur some excuse about the need to unpack her things, and took her leave from the Hon. Eustace and his lightly draped paramour. She met up with Petronella on her way out of the hall.

"You lucky creature," said Petronella. "I wish those old biddies would invite me for a stay in London. Pity they caught me creeping in through a window at an early hour, for I don't expect they'll have me again. Did you have a good time?"

"I was nearly raped," said Emmie.

The other's baby-blue eyes opened with wonder. "Emmie, you never were!" she exclaimed. "My, you lucky creature. But why were you only *nearly* raped?"

"It was the most awful experience of my life," said Emmie, and went on to tell her companion about the hideous episode after the theater.

"And they were *gentlemen*, you say?" quizzed Petronella. "And were they *young* gentlemen?"

"Men in their prime," said Emmie. "I never saw their faces, but their leader, he whom they called 'Snakey,' I would say he could have been almost any age."

"And—they did *that* to poor little Perry Manners?" breathed Petronella.

"Yes," said Emmie. "And, do you know, I think I shall live to forget what they did to me, the humili-ation, the terror, the shame, when I look back on it. But what they did to Perry, the cold and callous way in which that man ordered it to be done, I shall re-member all my life. And if I ever . . ." She broke off, shocked by the intensity of her emotions.

"If you ever, what, Emmie?" asked Petronella.

"If I ever meet that man again," said Emmie slowly, "if I ever meet him, and know for certain sure that I am face to face with the man they called Snakey, I shall—*I shall kill him with my own hands!*"

" 'Pon my word, Emmie," breathed her cousin, no cousin, "I believe you would. I really do believe you would!"

The two young women walked together to the suite of rooms in the north wing where, along with a dozen other unattached female members of the family, they resided in richly upholstered squalor and overcrowding. One subject that was uppermost in Emmie's mind—Toby Stocker—was not touched upon by either of them. In fact, despite her attempts to glean the latest news of doings at Flaxham, she found Petronella strangely reticent. The other would begin to recount an occurrence with considerable animation, and then trail off as if it had suddenly occurred to her that Emmie might not approve of what she was about to hear. This prompted a spark of memory in Emmie's mind.

"Uncle Eustace said a rather strange thing to me just now," she said. "Something about certain activities that have been taking place at Flaxham. Activities, he said, in which I should have taken part. Do you have any idea what he could have been talking about, Petronella?"

"Nu-no!" replied the other hastily, and with such a sudden coloring-up and confusion that Emmie was quite certain that she was lying.

Something's been going on, decided Emmie, *and Petronella knows what it is, or has been part of it. I wonder what?*

They came to their quarters: two adjacent rooms in a long corridor of connected chambers that stretched the length of the upper floor of the north wing, which they shared with Cousin Mary Cradock and one of the young widows of the family named Deidre Collingwood. Both rooms were hung with priceless tapestries and paintings, but the wet rot had turned the tapestries to rags and totally discolored the pictures. Four huge four-poster beds almost entirely covered the floor space of the first room. The second—which

the four women used as a dressing room-cum-sitting
room—was furnished in a more Spartan manner,
though the chairs, albeit broken and their upholstery
torn, were Chippendale and Sheraton, and the dressing table Louis Seize. Emmie and Mary were tolerably
tidy and kept their quite considerable wardrobes in
neat piles on tabletops. Not so Petronella and the
young widow, who only needed to inhabit a room for
a day in order to reduce it to bedlam. So there they
lived, those four, in the most complete squalor. Not
since the court of Louis Quatorze at Versailles could
so many high-born personages have been crammed
together in such grisly circumstances as were shared
by the inhabitants of Flaxham Palace. And the sani-
tary arrangements were crude to the extreme.

Dutifully, at seven o'clock, supper having finished,
Emmie took her place in the balcony of the chapel and
watched the remainder of the family file to their pews
below. First came the young ones, infants and all,
even those at the breast. Next, the aunts and uncles
of middling age. After them came the great-aunts,
Beechborough's sisters, one of them leaning heavily
on the shoulder of a black-a-moor boy who had been
sent to her from the West Indies as a present. Then
came the Hon. Eustace, his shifty eyes swiveling
along the rows, and lighting upon first this woman and
then that. His doxy accompanied him, and had had
the common decency to cover her bare shoulders and
bosom with a shawl.

Lastly came the marquess, accompanied by the
Reverend Mr. Hackett, the hunting parson of the parish of St. Agnes-with-Beechborough, from which dis-
trict the Cradocks had taken their territorial title. The
old man assumed his seat in the oaken throne beneath
the pulpit, from which he was able to hear every word
that was declaimed.

In a voice that had gained much power from bellowing on the hunting field, and that had a fruity edge that

came from drinking two bottles of claret with every meal of his life, Parson Hackett announced the first hymn. The great pipe organ sketched the uplifting notes of the first line, and the congregation rose. It was then she saw, with a surge of joy in her heart, that the beloved Toby Stocker was seated in the body of the chapel immediately below her.

She was looking down upon the top of his flaxen head and the breadth of his splendid shoulders. His long, lean fingers were curled around the edges of his hymnal, his head slightly bowed. Quite clearly, she could see the breathtaking way in which the small hairs at the nape of his neck curled lovingly about his ears and over the high collars of his livery coat.

He was close to her. He only had to reach up, and she to reach down over the balcony, and their fingers would be near to touching. Close—as close as they had been on that unforgettable dawn when she had seen him nude. Many times, waking and dreaming, she had lived through that idyll again—but with differences. In her imagination, she had done the unimaginable: instead of crouching in watchful and adoring silence, she had swept through the water toward him, to his waiting arms. But it was all in her mind; it had never happened, and more fool she.

And now she could hear him singing: a pleasant and tuneful baritone that rose above the other servants who lined the pew below. She thrilled to see him raise one hand and smooth back a stray lock of hair—as he had done on that unforgettable, previous occasion, a few breath-robbing moments before that hand had fallen to the lappet of his breeches. . . .

A final flourish of "Amen," and the congregation were silent, then shuffled back into their seats. Emmie remained standing for as long as she dared, since Toby disappeared from her sight behind the balustrade of the balcony when she was seated. And, as she stood there—wonders!—he turned and looked up, catching her eye. She smiled timorously, conscious that her lower lip trembled as she did so. And Toby smiled in return.

She sat down, her knees a-tremble, her breathing quickened. Toby had smiled at her, and had revealed himself in so doing.

There was no doubt about it, no doubt at all: he loved her as she loved him. It had been all there in his smile: the tender and yearning smile of the adoring swain. Such smiles had the lovers of the ages exchanged. Venus and Adonis, Romeo and Juliet, Tristan and Isolde . . .

That settled, the practical side of her mind addressed itself to the problems that lay before them, she and her Toby. The disparity in their social positions would be the greatest hurdle, of course. Grandfather Beechborough, upon hearing the slightest hint of their relationship, would immediately discharge Toby without a reference; indeed, the young footman would likely be horsewhipped to boot. Without a reference, he would take his place among the homeless and unemployed derelicts with which the town and countryside abounded in England of 1813. His only salvation would be to join the army.

No—they needed to be most careful. Toby would first have to secure another position; that done, he must then approach the marquess's bailiff, offer his notice and politely request a reference. And then, let a little time go by—a year or less, for how could she endure to wait so long before she was his?—and then she would join him. They would be married, she and her handsome footman, and make a love nest in a rose-covered cottage on someone's estate.

She shook herself free of such heady delights. Back to practicalities. In her reticule, she carried a small diary with a silver pencil attached. Taking it out and laying it upon her open prayer book, Emmie carefully recorded the plan for their future: THE MARRIAGE OF TOBY STOCKER AND EMMIE DASHWOOD

She scribbled away through prayers, had a blessed opportunity to feast her eyes once more upon her beloved during the psalm, and again during the canticles. He threw a glance upward toward her, and she held it for longer than was wise, and he also. He did not look up again.

Presently, the Rev. Mr. Hackett climbed up into the high pulpit, hitched up his hood, looked down his long, bulbous-ended nose at the assembled Beechborough clan and their retainers and bellowed: *"My text this evening is taken from the twenty-third chapter of the Gospel according to Saint Matthew. 'Ye serpents, ye generation of vipers, how can ye escape the damnation of hell?' "*

Below, in his great oaken throne, the Marquess of Beechborough settled himself with enjoyment for an hour and a half of eternal damnation. Up in the gallery, Emmie, having finished the notes of her wonderful plan for herself and her intended, slipped the diary back into her reticule, or, more accurately, *thought* she had slipped it back into her reticule.

In fact, the telltale diary dropped, unheard above the stentorian voice of Parson Hackett, to the floor close by her skirts.

The diary—she had mislaid the diary!

The awful realization struck her soon after she had gone to bed, had drawn the curtains of her four-poster in order to shut out most of the sound of cousin Deidre's snoring and had searched in her reticule for one last look at the details of her precious future before she went to sleep. By the shaft of moonlight that came through the crack in the curtains, she emptied out the contents of the reticule upon the bedspread, and a prickling of horror spread over her skin. It was gone! She must have dropped it in the chapel!

It would be found. Whoever found it (a servant— one of the family?) would look inside for evidence of the owner's identity, would see the superscription of her romantic yearnings, written in brave capitals as it was. How could they miss it?

She must recover the diary. Now. Immediately. The resolve made, she acted upon it. Emmie slid out of bed in the moonlight, shrugged into her peignoir and slid her feet into her slippers. She listened. No sound but Deidre's snoring. The others slept quietly. She tiptoed out of the room and down the corridor to the staircase.

The chapel lay at the end of the south wing, beyond the small hall, and was a separate building in the baroque style, with a clock tower. As she let herself out of the downstairs door and ran across the great courtyard, the clock struck the quarter hour to midnight. An owl hooted in the copse down by the river. Panting with her exertions, Emmie reached the side door of the chapel and bore down upon the heavy latch. Blessedly, the door was unlocked and it yielded to her touch. She entered and closed it behind her, paused for a short while and listened with a beating heart. There was no sound but the familiar *tap-tap-tap* of a death watch beetle announcing his presence to a female of the species. A shaft of moonlight beamed through the mullioned windows and lit upon the marble and porphyry monument to John Churchill's Paymaster-General that rose, ceiling-high, on the west wall of the chapel, next to the soaring pipes of the great organ. The door leading to the steps up to the balcony stood open. She tiptoed toward it, through patches of moonlight and shadow that lay upon the marble-tiled floor.

Something (a mouse, a rat?) scuttled in the wainscotting as she mounted the steps, and the steps themselves creaked most alarmingly in the silence of the chapel. Reaching the head of the stair, Emmie found to her dismay that the disposition of her surroundings—the balustrade of the balcony, the fact that there were no windows up there—shielded the entire upper floor from the moonlight that filtered in through the windows below. She had no means of illumination with her, and had only an approximate recollection of the actual seat in the front row of the balcony upon which she had sat during evensong. She had to grovel on her knees and scrabble with her fingertips for the feel of the diary.

It took longer than she would have believed: agonizing minutes, during which she realized that it was entirely probable that she had dropped the diary elsewhere but in the chapel. In the event, her fingers finally closed about its shape. It lay some distance from where she had sat. Presumably either she, or one of her neighbors, had kicked against it upon departure.

Breathing a silent prayer of release, she slipped the telltale diary into the pocket of her peignoir and retraced her steps to the stairs.

As she did so, the side door of the chapel—the one through which she had entered—creaked slowly open. She heard, above the sudden, wild beating of her heart, a concerted muttering, as when a group of people gather together in place of quiet to have a discussion. The almost inaudible discourse ceased as abruptly as it had begun, and there came the sound of footfalls passing down the center aisle of the chapel, and the sound was the quiet padding of *bare feet!*

Frightened, yet curious, Emmie peered cautiously over the edge of the balcony, in time to see two dark-robed figures flitting down the aisle toward the altar. One of them carried a lighted taper, a winking star on the end of a long pole. Arriving at the altar, the taper-bearer reached up and lit the four tall candles that stood there. By their light, the horrified Emmie was able to see that the two robed figures were women. Their hair, long and unbound, streamed down their backs. Furthermore, the ankle-length black garments that they wore were of a diaphanous and insubstantial nature and revealed the suavely feminine shapes beneath. Both were barefoot. And both wore concealing black masks!

The lighting of the candles was a signal for more shuffling and padding of bare feet. Down the aisle streamed more black-robed personages, both male and female, and all masked. They took their places in the pews before the altar, where they stood as if awaiting a commencement of some kind of ceremony.

The opening and closing of the side door of the chapel announced another arrival. Craning her neck to gain the greatest advantage, the unseen watcher on the balcony caught the first view of the newcomers: a man and a woman walking side by side up the center aisle. Hand in hand, the couple proceeded to the marquess's oaken throne, where the man, after a deep obeisance to his partner, lowered himself into the noble seat. His consort, following his example, crouched on the marble flagstones in a servile posture by his bare feet.

With a sharp intake of breath, Emmie realized that he in the oaken throne was none other than the heir of the Beechboroughs. There was no mistaking the Hon. Eustace's posture, the arrogant set of his head, the sardonic lips beneath the mask, even the feline glitter of the eyes that blazed through the narrow slits. And the creature at his feet was undoubtedly his doxy, Mrs. Galloway. That voluptuary's black robe, unfastened to the waist, shamelessly disclosed her naked bosom.

At a signal from the figure in the chair, the entire assembly sank to its knees, and the fourth marquess apparent, raising one hand in a mockery of a priest delivering a blessing, then proceeded to declaim a string of words which made no sense to the ears of the listener in the gallery, till, with a gasp of revulsion, it came to her that he was reciting the Lord's Prayer—*backwards*. And then she knew that she was the unwilling and unwitting witness to the rite of—the Black Mass.

Satanism, real or simulated, had been a favorite pastime among the hell-raising rakes of the previous century. In most cases, it had been merely an excuse for rich libertines to indulge in excesses of the flesh. In others—the minority of cases—the Black Mass had been real in every sense, with demoniacal possession, insanity and self-destruction the fates of many of its practitioners.

Was this real—or playacting?

Emmie watched and waited, wishing all the time that she was far from the scene. The Hon. Eustace's sonorous, nasal voice droned on its blasphemies, to which the assembly added occasional responses, such pronouncements as "Praise the time of Dog," which is God spelled backward, symbolizing Satan, and "We hear thee, O High Priest of Darkness," referring to the man in the oaken throne.

The so-called High Priest ended his string of blasphemies by making the sign of the cross in reverse, upon which the congregation rose to its feet. Silence followed, in which Emmie was hideously conscious of a breathless expectancy that had taken possession of the gathering, an emotion so intense that it informed even the inanimate furnishings of the marbled chapel, so that a reclining statue that lay upon the carved and gilded monument seemed also to be waiting for the next proceeding in the unholy ritual.

"Bring forth the maiden sacrifice!" The High Priest's voice echoed loudly in the vaulted chamber.

A shuffling of bare feet, and next down the aisle came three figures, robed like all the rest. They comprised two men and a woman. The latter, who walked between the other two, had her hands bound behind her back, and was held by her companions, as if she were a captive. But it was obvious from her voluptuous walk, by the proud carriage of her head, that she

was a far from unwilling prisoner, and the bonds which
held her wrists were merely symbolic, being of the
lightest golden thread.

On drawing close to the oaken throne, the supposed
captive was halted and turned to come face to face
with the High Priest. In doing so, she presented her
profile to the hidden watcher. If Emmie had had any
doubt about the owner of the unbound blond tresses,
the sight of that masked profile confirmed that the
"maiden sacrifice" was her cousin Petronella Pallance.

The High Priest pointed. "Disrobe the sacrifice!"
he intoned.

This was a signal for Petronella's two companions
to take hold of her black vestment, one on each side,
and rip the flimsy material from neck to hem, revealing
her in total nudity before the unwinking stare of the
entire congregation. Petronella did not flinch before
their gaze, but tossed her proud tresses and threw
back her head as if willing them all, men and women
alike, to feast their eyes upon her slender nakedness.

"Bear the sacrifice to the altar!" commanded the
High Priest.

The two acolytes, both powerfully built men whose
strongly marked physiques were clearly revealed beneath their robes, picked up the naked girl, each with
a hand to an ankle and the other to a shoulder. Holding
herself stiffly prone, Petronella allowed herself to be
borne aloft above their heads, like a corpse upon a
bier; in this attitude she was slowly carried down the
aisle to the candlelit altar, where she was laid as a
bride upon the bridal bed.

Emmie shuddered, fearful for what might follow,
willing herself the strength of purpose to call out and
denounce the blasphemers, or, at worst, to flee from
that place, but she could not summon the courage to
do either.

Several minutes crept past in total silence while the
white form upon the altar made no motion, but lay like

a waxen image, blond hair streaming over the edge of the carved table of marble and reaching almost to the floor, eyes closed, and only the gentle rise and fall of her perfect bosom telling that she was a living and breathing thing.

And then the High Priest cried out in a loud voice: "Come forth, Infernal Master! Accept the sacrifice that thy children have provided!"

At this, the door by the side of the altar—the door leading into the sacristy—burst open by an invisible hand, revealing a fearful figure on the threshold: a figure clad in scarlet robes, with the head and horns of a goat. It stood there for a horrifying instant, arms folded, gazing from side to side at the breathless congregation. Then, with firm tread, it crossed to the altar where the still form lay.

For a while, the infernal being gazed upon the offering. Presently, turning, it faced the congregation and raised its arms. This was a signal for all to kneel. Kneeling, still, they watched—and Emmie Dashwood watched—as the masked creature unfastened the buttonings of the scarlet gown, drew it from his shoulders, and let it fall in a pool of crumpled redness at his bare feet.

"Oh, merciful heaven!" breathed Emmie Dashwood, aloud. "It's Toby Stocker!"

The hideous goat mask was no longer a concealment from her eyes. Alone of all the breathless watchers, she knew and loved the smooth body of young Toby Stocker.

Half-blinded by sudden tears, but incapable of wrenching away her gaze, she saw him spring lithely onto the altar and crouch above the prostrate Petronella, who, opening her eyes upon the cue, reached up her slender arms and, winding them around the neck of the grotesquely masked figure, brought the hideous, animal lips down to meet hers in an unholy kiss.

This acted as a sign to the congregation, causing a stir of excited murmurs and moans of strange ecstasy.

Some with eager abandonment, some shyly and with reserve, commenced to peel off their black robes, revealing that—like the principals in that sensual rite—they had all been entirely nude underneath. The blossoming of flesh was followed by wild scenes of debauchery, as, seizing each other, singly and in groups, the assembly proceeded to reproduce the embraces of the two upon the altar. Lustful kisses were followed by licentious questings of hand and lip; the most outrageous liberties were freely offered and readily accepted, without let or hindrance, here, there and everywhere.

No longer confined to the pews, the frenzied assembly overspilled to the aisles, to the steps of the pulpit, to the pulpit itself—where the Rev. Mr. Hackett had so recently warned of the surety of everlasting damnation upon the wicked—to the marble tombs of the Beechborough clan that lined the walls, to the foot of the profaned altar where Petronella and the masked footman writhed and reeled in tortured ecstasy. And it was to the latter pair—the principal actors in that charade of licentiousness—that all Emmie Dashwood's attentions were directed; she could not have dragged away her gaze if her life had been forfeit.

The Hon. Eustace Cradock, High Priest and master of debauchery, had not finished the night's improvisations. Casting aside two nymphs who sprawled across his knees, he rose to his feet and uttered a word of command, upon which two nude males strutted down the aisle with a dark burden held high between them. A loud and urgent bleating revealed the thing in their hands to be a black lamb, a newborn of the famous Beechborough herd that was renowned throughout the land. They bore it toward the altar where the couple lay entwined and still. The High Priest came after them, accompanied by his paramour; she was bearing a curved knife upon a black velvet cushion.

With a new, more urgent horror, Emmie discerned what they must be about. A cry rose to her lips and trembled to be heard. Heedless of being seen, she rose up, hands clutching the balcony edge, fingers tensed hard against the cold marble. She shook her head in disbelief, willing the unspeakable not to take place.

The nude men lifted the bleating lamb high above the entwined couple, so that its small head hung down and its neck was presented. With a curtsy to her swain, Mrs. Galloway presented the cushion and its gleaming burden, which the High Priest took up in both hands. He then raised the curved knife on high and declaimed in ringing tones, "O Prince of Darkness, behold how the blood of the lamb descends upon the sacrificer and the sacrificed!"

The scream that rent the silence was instantly followed by a long drawn-out cry: "*No-o-o-o!*"

All eyes turned in horror to see Emmie, like an apparition up at the balcony's edge. White-garbed she was, and her face was cast in deep shadow; but all could see that dark and tangled hair tumbled in abandonment about her shoulders. To many minds sprang the thought that they were gazing upon a risen corpse in the cerements of the grave, its hair wild with the damp earth and its face far gone in putrefaction. Panic seized those of the most heated imaginations, and having taken swift root, spread within instants. It was Mrs. Galloway who led the rush for the door, screaming as she ran, naked and uncaring, into the night. In one bound, Toby Stocker was down from the altar, wrenching off his unspeakable mask, his partner abandoned and forgotten. Petronella speedily followed.

Before Emmie had half-realized the true import of the congregation's pell-mell abandonment of their unholy rites, they were gone. No sound but the fretful banging of a door in the night breeze. And the plaintive bleating of the black lamb as it trotted forlornly down the aisle, where the black robes of the devotees lay in scattered confusion.

Shivering, Emmie descended the stair and went out into the moonlit courtyard and crossed to the far wing. Through uncounted windows of the sleeping pile, pale faces were pressed to regard her passing. Of this she was well aware. She knew that the Hon. Eustace and his followers now knew the identity of the hidden watcher who had uncovered their secret and so rudely broken up their rites. Just as she now knew what her Uncle Eustace had meant by the "activities" that had taken place at Flaxham while she had been away, activities in which she should have taken part. . . .

Not being able to bring herself to sleep in the same room as Petronella, Emmie curled up in a sofa in one of the drawing rooms and dozed fitfully till dawn, when she made her way to the great stone kitchens, where the cooks and scullions were already preparing the gargantuan meals that would be needed to satisfy the family for the coming day. Some looked askance to see one of the young women of the house still in her night shift and peignoir, but all curtsied or touched their forelocks, and Emmie was swiftly provided with a cup of coffee and a hot roll of bread with butter. With these she returned to her sofa, and to her disturbing thoughts.

She was finished with Toby—that much for a start. The thought of setting eyes upon him again, let alone enjoying even the simplest of endearments among those she had imagined, filled her with nausea. The first and purest love of her life had died with another woman's satiety.

The telltale diary—she felt in the pocket of her peignoir and it was still there—must have the pertinent pages ripped out and burned, and that she would accomplish instantly. A fire burned in the wide grate of the drawing room. She watched her dreams blacken and curl and be consumed, and in that moment, dryeyed, she passed from girlhood into womanhood.

She returned to her thoughts. Now that she was

privy to the secret lives of Uncle Eustace and his acolytes, she would be treated by them with the gravest dislike and suspicion—she, the outsider. How many did they number, and who were they? Clearly, both the family and the staff of the Palace were included among the unholy congregation. Footmen other than Toby Stocker had swelled the number of ready studs during that night of orgy, for there were no young and well set-up men of the Cradock brood living in Flaxham, since most were either married with establishments of their own, or were serving in the army or navy. During the long vigil from the balcony, she had had plenty of opportunity to speculate upon the identity of the masked revelers, and was almost certain that one of the nymphs who had pleasured Uncle Eustace was her other roommate Mary Cradock, while Mary's *consoeur* in licentiousness had been one of the parlormaids who was frequently summoned to the bed of Grandfather Beechborough. Of one thing she was quite sure: the marquess himself had not been present.

And what next? There was no question of her leaving Flaxham, for she had not a penny with which to bless herself and was entirely dependent—as all the other inhabitants of the Palace were dependent—upon the marquess's grace and favor. She could run away—certainly. But where would she go? Not to Aunts Sarah and Clarice, for sure; the old spinsters, like everyone else, owed the house they lived in, and every crust they devoured, to their cousin the marquess. Let them but give shelter for one night to a runaway member of the family and they would be in trouble.

Bitterly, she told herself that marriage provided her only means of escape. That—or whoredom. She had seen plenty of the latter profession passing through Flaxham Palace as guests of her grandfather and her uncles. The blowsy "actress" Mrs. Galloway was a fair example of that breed.

Yes, it would have to be marriage. But to whom?

Jock Ballantree was a pleasing enough man, but not
of the sort to excite her feelings. Not like—no, not to
speak that name again, not even to think it . . . !

Jock Ballantree might suit her very well. There
would be no love involved, of course, but a tremendous amount of mutual regard. Jock admired her, she
knew it well. Moreover, having had the opportunity
to see her nude, he knew—and was presumably satisfied—with her physical attributes, and would not be
buying a pig in a poke. Yes, thought Emmie, gently
luxuriating against the cushions of the sofa, if Jock
Ballantree came to pay court to her—as he had implied—she would receive him favorably. He was ti-
tled, presumably rich, and undoubtedly possessed
considerable estates. It would be an entirely agreeable
arrangement for all concerned. She would achieve her
freedom from Flaxham and the Cradocks, with a
charming and attentive husband; Jock would gain a
wife and hostess, someone to share his bed and mother
his children. There were worse marriages by far. She
had seen plenty of them.

Marriage, then, would be her passport to freedom—
and not to the false freedom that so many marriages
brought to women, the sort that was more nearly like
slavery. What would take her away from the upholstered squalor of Flaxham Palace would be a marriage
between equals, a marriage a la mode.

Chapter Two

That was on Sunday. On Tuesday of the following week, at the cold hour before dawn when mind and body are at the lowest ebb and the spirit is most easily prized from its fleshly tabernacle, Archibald Cradock, third Marquess of Beechborough, died.

All the following day the bells of the chapel and those of the church of St. Agnes-with-Beechborough tolled the sum of Archibald Cradock's years, over and over again.

The weather being inclemently hot, his obsequies were not long delayed; the interment was conducted by Parson Hackett within the chapel, and the third marquess laid to rest in a marble sarcophagus close by the first and second of the noble line. The service was viewed by the new marquess from that same oaken throne where he had conducted proceedings of a vastly different order a few nights previously. Emmie watched from her usual position up in the balcony, and wondered that Uncle Eustace was not struck dead by the hand of God; similarly Mrs. Galloway, who

53

was in full mourning with an all-concealing veil—a far
cry from the naked trollop who had touted her favors
at every pew in the chapel.

Emmie wept a little for her grandfather, who, despite his bawdy hand, had never shown her anything
but a rough kindness, and who, despite his harshness
to her mother and father, had not hesitated to take her
in when she was a destitute infant. She also wept a
little from fear: the fear of what new order was to be
established under the new incumbent. The unspeakable rites she had witnessed in the chapel—they, presumably, would no longer be secret, but would be an
open sewer for all to regard.

The marble sarcophagus having been sealed, and
the last rites ended, the family filed out into the hot
sunlight. Near the chapel door, Emmie came face to
face with Petronella, to whom she had not addressed
a word since the events of the previous Sunday night.
Petronella had the grace to color up and lower her
blue eyes in confusion, and so did Mary Cradock, who
came after her. In the days between, Emmie had identified many of the masked participants in the Black
Mass by their awkward reaction to her gaze—relations
and servants both. One person she had not encountered—and she had gone out of her way to avoid the
meeting—was Toby Stocker.

Speculation about the new order under the fourth
marquess hung in limbo for nearly a week, during
which time Eustace Beechborough was not to be seen
at meals or at gatherings of a family nature, not even
with his old cronies at their bezique and womanizing
in the orangery. Like a knight keeping his vigil, the
new marquess stayed in his quarters, with only Mrs.
Galloway for a companion, taking all his meals in his
private sitting room and scarcely going forth, save to
walk the grounds in the evening with his hound.

A week following his elevation, Beechborough received a visitor who caused much speculation in the
family. The newcomer arrived in a hired coach, to-

gether with his baggage. He was a finely made, tallish man in his mid-thirties, and wearing the scarlet regimentals of a major of line infantry. All that day, he remained closeted with the marquess, and accompanied him on his evening walk with the hound, a performance viewed with tremendous speculation from most of the windows in the Palace, from whence it was noted that the major was doing most of the talking and Beechborough most of the listening.

Speculation and rumor blew up into a storm the following day, when, after summoning three of his cronies to join him in his sitting room, the marquess then sent a footman to seek out Emmie Dashwood, to present his compliments and to ask if Miss Emmie would please be so kind as to attend My Lord Marquess at her early convenience.

The apartments of the Marquess of Beechborough occupied the whole of the upper floor at the front of the great mansion, overlooking the courtyard, ornamental water gardens and the miasma-laden meadows leading down to the river. The apartments were reached by way of the grand staircase leading up from the entrance hall; and it was with a rapidly beating heart that Emmie trod that upward path as soon as she had smoothed down her hair, put on a little rice powder and the slightest suggestion of scent, and assured herself that the heels of her stockings were not out, nor was she showing too much bosom.

A knock upon the outer door of the marquess's sitting room brought a muffled command from within that she should enter. In doing so, Emmie found herself in the immediate and concerted scrutiny of five pairs of eyes: those of her uncle the marquess, his three cronies, Uncle James, Uncle Herbert and Uncle Josiah Cradock, and the steady gaze of the mysterious major of infantry. They all rose at her entry.

"My dear Emmie," said Eustace Beechborough smoothly, gesturing toward a seat that was set before

the long table at which he and his companions were
sitting. "Pray make yourself comfortable. You know
me, you know these other excellent relations of yours.
It only remains for me to present Major Tredegar of
the Twentieth Foot, who is aide-de-camp to General
Sir Claude Devizes, military governor of Quebec
Province. Major, this is my niece, Miss Emmie Dashwood."

"Your servant, ma'am." The officer bent formally
over her proffered hand.

"Sir," murmured Emmie, wondering what on earth
had induced her uncles to sit in conclave while she
was summoned to be introduced to the aide-de-camp
of some remote military officer.

She composed herself in the seat, laying her hands
upon her lap and looking from one to the other of her
audience with as much calmness as she could muster.
Uncle Eustace, she was amused to note, had taken on
an air of gravity and a way of looking down his nose
that accorded with the dignity of his lofty rank. At
present his gaze was directed toward the cleft of her
bosom, and it took an effort of will to prevent herself
from shielding it with her hand. The crony uncles,
similarly, were regarding her with the unselfconscious
lustfulness that comes with a lifetime's abandonment
of all checks upon the desires. It occurred to her that
they must be missing their daily pleasures in the orangery, which seemed an awful pity.

"Gentlemen, to business," said Beechborough.

"Quite so, My Lord Marquess," said Major
Tredegar. "As My Lord Marquess pleases."

"We will dispense with the strict formalities of title
during this conversation, Major," said Beechborough
loftily. "And you will simply address me and my cousins as 'sir.' "

"Yes, my—yes, sir," stammered the officer, col-
oring, and Emmie felt quite sorry for him.

"My dear Emmie," said her Uncle Eustace, dragging his reluctant gaze from her bosom to her chin,

"the major, here, is an emissary—would you describe yourself as an emissary, Major?"

"Indeed, sir. An emissary. Yes," responded the soldier.

"An emissary from the far-off Canadian province of Quebec, my dear Emmie," said Beechborough. "Now, my dear Emmie, you must know that the major's chief, General Sir Claude Devizes, is an officer of most tremendous distinction, both as to career and family. I am right in saying, am I not, Major, that Sir Claude is one of the Bristol Devizes, the shipping family?"

"That he is, sir," responded the Major. "Sir Claude, furthermore, is now—upon the demise of his cousin—the sole shareholder of the Devizes fleet, and a gentleman of very considerable wealth."

"Wealth is not a consideration that would influence the opinion of a member of the Cradock family one way or the other," said the marquess with a touch of severity. "But it is of passing interest."

"Hear, hear," murmured Uncle James. And the other uncles concurred with this opinion by rapping the table top.

Puzzled, Emmie looked from one to the other of them. The crony uncles, tiring even of speculating upon the contents of her bodice, were heavz-eyed with boredom at the proceedings and almost nodding off to sleep. Only Uncle Eustace and the strange major of infantry remained animated, and pursuing their curious—and most certainly rehearsed—charade.

"So we have General Sir Claude Devizes," said Uncle Eustace, "and he is a millionaire fleet owner of Bristol, aside from being military governor of Quebec Province. And this, mark you, my dear Emmie, at a time when the damned Yankees, having had the temerity and impudence to have declared war on the old country, must manifestly present Sir Claude with opportunities for glory in crushing those confounded colonials."

"Quite so, sir," interposed the major. "Very true."

"What has all this to do with me, Uncle?" asked Emmie calmly.

The crony uncles' eyes snapped open at this, and returned with renewed interest to the line of her bodice. The major's gaze was firmly fixed upon a point two inches above her eyebrows. Eustace Beechborough was smiling thinly.

He said, "Now, I am glad—very glad—that you asked that, my dear Emmie. And I will make frank reply, without further prevarication. The matter of Sir Claude's position and achievements concerns you very nearly. For, to put the point briefly, this excellent gentleman has asked for your hand. In marriage."

Emmie did not reply for a while, and was only prompted to do so when she realized that she was staring at her uncle with her mouth wide open.

"M-marry me?" she exclaimed at length. "But the gentleman does not even *know* me!"

"Ah, but he knows *of* you, Emmie," responded Beechborough smartly, like a man who has anticipated the question. "The late marquess, my distinguished kinsman, received sundry correspondence from Sir Claude, touching upon the latter's wish to marry. Having heard of your attainments, your beauty, probity, modesty, and so forth, Sir Claude stated in the correspondence, several times, nay repeatedly, that he would wish to marry none other than Miss Emmie Dashwood, spinster of the Parish of St. Agnes-with-Beechborough. Ain't that right, Major?"

"Correct in every respect, sir," replied Tredegar briskly. "And I had it, myself, from his own lips. 'None other than Miss Emmie will do, Tredegar,' were the last words he spoke to me as I went aboard the ship at Quebec."

"Well, I am taken completely aback, sir," said Emmie frankly. "I really am."

"And so you should be, my dear," said Beechborough with a look of concern. "It's right and proper

and entirely fitting that a young gel should be overcome with emotion at such a time. Very proper. Very
commendable. Shall I have them bring you a glass of
brandy?''

''No thank you, Uncle.'' Emmie shook her head.
Marriage—and at a time when she had been toying
with that very notion! An opportunity to free herself
from Flaxham and the Cradocks—and delivered right
out of the blue. Of course, it was not Jock Ballantree
who was making the offer, but it could well be a man
just as sound. . . .

''Well, Emmie?'' said her uncle. ''And what do you
think of the idea, eh?''

''What—what sort of gentleman *is* Sir Claude?''
alasked Emmie shyly. ''In appearance, I mean.''

''The picture, Major,'' said Beechborough. ''Bring
forth the picture, do.''

''I have it here, sir,'' said Major Tredegar, and,
stooping, he brought up a leather briefcase, from
which he drew a rectangle of wood, which upon the
opening out of a pair of cunningly fashioned doors
revealed itself to be a traveling case for a picture.

It was of an officer posed before a background of
hot blue skies and white buildings under a searing eastern sun. His face was pleasing, bronzed by exposure
to the elements, the eyes a merry blue, mouth firm, a
proud beak of a nose. His figure, under the scarlet
tunic, was well set-up, and his legs excellent in tight
overalls. The hand that rested on the pommel of his
saber was well-formed and strong. His hair was jet
black, and lightly dusted with gray at the temples. It
was the latter point that caused Emmie to exclaim:
''Oh, but isn't he rather old?''

''Old?'' The marquess gazed at the major in con-
sternation, and the three other uncles were roused
from their torpor, to stare at each other and repeat:
''Old—*old?*''

''Well, Major,'' said Beechborough, ''you are best
fitted to answer that question.''

"Sir Claude is not in—how to put it—the first flush of his youth, ma'am," said Tredegar. "But I assure you that he is very vigorous. He still rides out daily—though on a quiet nag, of course. And, though he is somewhat smitten with the gout, does occasionally dance. Age, ma'am, is not so much a matter of years as of attitude. Don't you think?"

Emmie's eyes flashed back to the picture of the handsome, slightly graying man in the prime of his years. "Quiet nag," "smitten with the gout," "does occasionally dance"—were these words to be applied to *that* man?

She looked closer at the picture. Sir Claude, surely, was a full general. But should not a general have a great deal of gold lace upon his coat? At a quick comparison—her eyes flickered to Tredegar's coat and returned—the man in the picture was scarcely carrying more gold lace than the major.

"When was this portrait painted?" she asked slowly.

Silence . . .

"Perhaps you can answer that, Tredegar," grated the marquess.

"Ah, some little while ago, it was," replied the other. "Let me see—it would have been painted in India, when Sir Claude was lieutenant-colonel of the Forty-fifth."

"But *when* was that?" persisted Emmie shrilly.

"Ah, that would have been during the Third Mysore War," said Tredegar. "Which would put it somewhere between 'ninety or 'ninety-two."

"Seventeen ninety!" exclaimed Emmie. "But—that was over twenty years ago!" She pointed at the picture. "That man represented there is in his late thirties, early forties. And now, he must be . . ."

"Sixty!" snapped Eustace Beechborough. "There is no need in further beating about the bush. Sir Claude Devizes is sixty."

She looked from one to the other of them. Not one of them had the grace to meet her eye, nor even let their gaze linger at her bodice. So that was it. That was the offer. Marriage to a man of sixty. A man who still did a little riding out and danced occasionally. A man who is still very vigorous. Vigorous, she supposed, in the way that these old goats of uncles were vigorous!

She got to her feet.

"Uncle . . ." she began.

"Sit down, damn you!" grated Beechborough.

Emmie obeyed.

"Uncle, I beseech you . . ."

"You will address me correctly, woman!"

"Sir . . ."

"By my title!"

Emmie drew a long, shuddering breath. "My Lord Marquess," she said, "while I am mindful of the honor which this gentleman seeks to bestow upon me"—she nodded toward the picture—"I cannot bring myself to marry a man who is forty years my senior. And that's the truth of it."

Narrow-eyed, the marquess regarded the young woman opposite him. "No, you are mistaken, ma'am," he said. "That is not the truth of it. Here is the truth of it: you will marry Devizes, and you will be pleased and grateful to do so."

"No! No!" cried Emmie, pressing her hands to her temples and shaking her head, till her chignon fell and her hair cascaded about her comely shoulders. Uncle Josiah licked his lips at the sight.

"You will marry, ma'am, or you will starve!" said Beechborough. "You will do worse than Deidre Collingwood, who I am shortly dispatching to live with her late husband's poverty-stricken brood in Ireland. You will do worse than your aunts Ada and Cynthia, who from next week are shifting their quarters to a parish almshouse. There are to be some changes made here, ma'am. The days of idleness and indolence are over, and a new broom is sweeping away the useless and unprofitable personages who clutter the corridors

of my house. You will agree to marry Sir Claude Devizes, and you will pledge your word here and now—
or you will depart from my house, bag and baggage,
this very day. And the devil take you!''

Looking into his furious, close-set eyes, Emmie
made a guess at the truth of the matter. The new marquess had not spent his lonely hours in idleness during
the past days, but had been sorting the sheep from the
goats. In his eyes, the goats would be those members
of the family who partook in the vile ceremony of
which she had been witness, the companions of fresh
debauches of his own devising as yet untried. They—
the favored ones—would remain. The others—the
sheep such as poor Deidre, who never ceased to
mourn her lost husband, and who would surely never
be persuaded to debauchery, the likes of poor old
aunts Ada and Cynthia, she herself—were to be dismissed as useless mouths.

Marriage as an escape—that was how she had
thought of it. She looked again at the face in the picture: the pleasant, humorous expression, the good-humored eyes. Twenty years too late—but still the same
man, for such a man would not greatly change in character. Not so much a husband, perhaps, but more of
a father. The father she had never known.

''If I accept, sir,'' she murmured. ''What then?''

''What then?'' The marquess beamed at her, and
the other uncles beamed at each other. Even the major's unaccommodating features softened with relief.
''Why, my dear Emmie, the contract will be drawn up
immediately. The banns will be read, and you will
marry in the chapel within the month. By proxy. Major Tredegar, here, will act as proxy for his chief. It
is irregular, but has all been approved, since Sir
Claude is on active service, and it is part of the
agreed—ha—terms of the marriage contract that the
ceremony takes place before you depart for Quebec.''

''Can the ceremony not wait till I reach Quebec,

Uncle?" asked Emmie. "Till I have seen the man who—"

"No!" The marquess brought the palm of his hand down upon the table top, but not overly hard. "No, Emmie," he repeated, with an air of heavy patience. "There are ways in which these things are done and there are ways in which they are not done. You, as a young woman who has led a sheltered life, do not understand these things, so you must be ruled by your elders of the superior sex. You will be married in the chapel, with Major Tredegar acting as proxy. And that's an end on't."

"I will regard it as a most signal honor, ma'am," said Tredegar, and in such a silky tone that she was constrained to look sharply at him. For the first time since the interview had started, he had detached his gaze from a spot two inches above her eyebrows and was slyly questing the cleft of her bodice.

The banns were read on four successive Sundays, and they never sounded right to her. "Emmie Laetitia Dashwood, a spinster of this Parish . . . any cause or just impediment." Should she not rise up and scream to Parson Hackett that there was cause and just impediment a-plenty, that she was being dragooned into marrying a man of thrice her age whom she had never seen—as an alternative to starvation and the gutter. But she remembered the humorous—and surely kind—eyes of the man in the picture, and held her peace.

On the Saturday following the banns, she was woken early by the new maid they had given her. The girl's name was Suzie, and she was coal black, being from Jamaica. Not a slave, for slavery had never been tolerated in England—though there had been, and still were, some highly dubious borderline cases. Such a case was Suzie, who was certainly not paid a penny for her services, but worked for a roof over her head and four square meals a day. Furthermor, Suzie had

shared the bed of the former marquess, as had every
personable female servant in the place—although Suzie was barely sixteen.

It was Suzie who bathed her new mistress in the
great wooden tub of Flaxham's only bathhouse, afterward wrapping her in scented towels and escorting her
to the room that had been set aside for the bride.
There, Emmie was dressed in a gown of wild white
silk sprigged all over with white daisies, hand-worked.
On her smooth, raven's wing hair was placed a chaplet
of orange blossom (what sights those innocent blos-
soms had witnessed in the palace orangery!), and she
was handed a posy of the same.

In the cool of the great chapel, beneath the tall tomb
of John Churchill's paymaster, nearby that of the late
incumbent barely cold within his marble sarcophagus,
Emmie was married to the military nabob beyond the
sea. She was entered into matrimony by proxy, with
her hand laid upon that of Major Jack Tredegar of
the 20th Foot. She wept during the proceedings, and
wept still throughout the banquet that was presented
in the great—as distinct from the small—hall, a vast
chamber that projected from the rear of the central
block and was able to accommodate all the extant
Cradocks and their relations by marriage, together
with children both legitimate and bastard, the estate
bailiffs and yeoman farmers of the Beechborough
holdings and their families, along with distinguished
guests from the shires, members of Parliament, both
Lords and Commons. A thousand people were fed
that day with cold roast baron of beef, boars' heads,
an army of poultry, syllabub, pies and pasties galore
and seas of wine and beer.

Red-eyed, Emmie sat through it all, pushing a piece
of cold pie around her plate and willing it to go away.
After the banquet she had a short rest in her room.
Then Suzie helped her change into her going-away
habit: a traveling costume of bottle green trimmed with

black frogging, military fashion, a suitable choice for a soldier's wife. She descended to her waiting coach, with Suzie bringing up the rear with an armful of hat boxes. Most of the family and guests, together with the staff of the palace, were gathered to watch her departure and to wish her God's speed. The marquess her uncle proffered an icy cheek for her to kiss, and Mrs. Galloway dropped a curtsy.

Major Tredegar stood by the coach door, stiff in his regimentals, hat tucked under his arm. He gave her a hand to assist her up the step, and she murmured her thanks.

"My pleasure, Lady Devizes," he replied.

Hearing her new title for the first time gave her a small jolt of surprise that lasted till Tredegar had got into the coach and taken his seat opposite her. Suzie the maid climbed up beside the coachman, and they set off, past a sea of faces and fluttering handkerchiefs.

Her last impression of Flaxham, and of the life she had left behind, was a brief glimpse of one face among the crowd, that of Toby Stocker, gazing up at her wistfully.

They staged that night at the post inn at Chippenham, which was halfway to Bristol. Rooms had been ordered in advance, and she was shown to her room by her host and his entire family, who were profuse in their hopes that her ladyship found it comfortable, and did her ladyship require supper? She declined supper, and told Suzie that she would not require anything more, but would shortly retire. They all left her. She was alone for the first time in all that crowded day.

She took off her short military jacket, and, unpinning her hair, let it fall about her shoulders. She met her gaze in the looking glass of the dressing table, and saw herself for the first time as a married woman: Lady Devizes.

The question of whether she had done the right thing or the wrong thing was scarcely to the point. She had taken the only possible option. The question now was: how would she fare in this marriage?

If her bridegroom did not belie the looks that he had twenty years ago, he would treat her well and kindly. He was rich, and presumably also generous.

What else?

She brought her mind to it with reluctance. It was Major Tredegar who had made the point that Sir Claude was—vigorous. She must presume, therefore, that there was no question of her being a wife in name only. Her bridegroom, when they met, would make demands that were consistent with his appetites. And she had gained a nodding acquaintance of the appetites of a man in his sixties by looking into the orangery. It was entirely possible that her bridegroom would be able to take her virginity with perfect ease. She ran her hand gently over the soft skin of her shoulders and bosom, down to the edge of her bodice. And shuddered at the touch.

The room was small and stuffy. Crossing to the window, she opened it and looked out across the inn yard. A pair of dark figures were briefly silhouetted against the lighted door of a taproom; moments later they swayed together, arms round each other's shoulders, across the dark yard, singing as they went.

It was approaching ten o'clock. She assumed that Tredegar was supping, and was glad that she had not joined him. She did not actively dislike the major, but he possessed an uncertainty of manner—like one who is not quite sure of his strengths and weaknesses—that made her uneasy. During the coach drive from Flaxham, he had conversed pleasantly enough, answering her questions about life in Quebec Province, what the colonials were like, how many servants there were in the military governor's house, and what sort of house it was. On the topic of her new husband he was reticent, and she did not feel like probing him too far, but changed the subject to that of the year-old war with America. On this subject, Tredegar shed his uncertainty and spoke with the received attitudes of his class and caste. Yes, the Yankees would speedily be drubbed by the navy, and any incursion into Canada by their troops would bring them total disaster. The Yankees would sue for peace by Christmas, and, if the British government had the sense they were born with, would be forced to pay heavy reparations for the conduct of their privateers.

Decidedly, she was glad she had forgone his company at supper, and hoped that the transport in which they were sailing to Quebec (despite the might of the Royal Navy, it had been deemed to be more prudent for her to travel in a Dutch merchantman, rather than one sailing under the British flag, for fear of the Yankee privateers) would be large enough, and contain sufficient passengers, for her to avoid him and find more congenial company.

Dismissing Major Tredegar from her mind, Emmie began slowly to prepare for bed, brushing her raven hair with a hundred strokes—as she did every night of her life—till it shone with blue lights. And all the time her mind wandered to the half-forbidden subject of the demands that her bridegroom might wish to make upon her. A score of times she enacted the scene within her mind, and always with variations: how he would approach her, what she would say and do, his manner sometimes gentle, sometimes brusque and demanding.

In this manner, some little time went past, and the inn grew quiet. The last of the carousers from the taproom went out into the night. She heard the sounds of bolts being drawn and locks being turned.

And, all at once, there was a sharp *tap-tap* upon her door.

"Who's that?" she called.

"It's Tredegar, ma'am. Might I have a brief word with you?"

"Major, it's rather late. Won't the matter wait till morning?" she asked. She frowned at her reflection in the looking glass. Really, the man was quite insufferable.

"It will not wait, ma'am. A matter, you might say, of life and death."

"Very well." She got up, threw a shawl about her shoulders and stood in the center of the room to receive him. In that way, formally, without inviting him to be seated, the matter could speedily be disposed of. "Come in. The door is unlocked."

He entered. Her first intimation that he had been drinking came from the fact that the high collar of his tunic was unbuttoned, and the black stock that banded his neck was awry. But he stood steadily enough, his hands behind his back, regarding her evenly.

"Lady Devizes," he said.

"Sir?"

"It is my wish, at this late hour, to take wine with you, ma'am, in honor of your nuptials," he said. He produced from behind his back a long bottle and two stemmed glasses that he laid upon the table close by and filled with a frothing brew. He handed one to Emmie. So amazed was she by his effrontery that she took it.

"To your health, ma'am," he said, pledging her with his glass.

"I thank you, Major," said Emmie, taking a small sip of the wine and laying the glass firmly upon the table. "And now, I must ask you to leave. It has been a tiring day, and . . ."

"A momentous day, ma'am," he interposed. "A unique day in the life of a young woman, when she is brought to the altar. And a tragedy—in your own case—when she is also not brought to her bed, on her wedding night."

Emmie drew a deep breath. "Major Tredegar, will you leave this room immediately?" she said evenly.

He smiled crookedly. Yes, he was decidedly the

worse for drink. And the need was to get rid of him—and quickly—without further embarrassment.

"I had in mind," he said, "to extend my duties as proxy, by not only wedding you, but also bedding you."

"Get out!" she breathed. "Get out, before I summon my maid."

He sniggered. "That little black whore? You'll call in vain for her, my lady. The last I saw of her, she was being pawed by the tapman. Come, finish up your glass and let me pour you another. We have much to discuss before we snuff candles and roll between the sheets."

Emmie said, "If you do not leave immediately, I shall call for help. I shall rouse the entire house and have you turned out of my room by force."

He laughed, took a long pull of his wine and poured himself another bumper glass that he half-swallowed before he answered her.

"No, you will not, my lady," he said. "I do not think that Lady Devizes will shout it from the rooftops that she, niece of a marquess and married only this morning, received her husband's dashing young aide-de-camp in her bedroom at this hour of the night." He took another long swallow of his wine, and watched her over the rim of the glass, his eyes calculatingly evil. "And she half-naked!" he added.

Involuntarily, Emmie looked down at herself, and in so doing, was lost.

"I am *not* half-naked!" she snapped.

For all the wine he had imbibed, Tredegar moved both fast and with dexterity. With his left hand he caught hold of one end of her shawl and, pulling it from her shoulders, hurled it across the room. Emmie, thrown off balance by his sudden assault, and totally unprepared for it, could only stare when his right hand closed on the center of her bodice and ripped it from her breasts. Not content with that, he seized her about the shoulders and completely tore away her upper gar-

ment, rendering her nude to the waist, save for a light
pair of stays banding her slender middle.

Releasing her, he backed away, and laughed when
she covered her bare breasts with both her hands.

"You are half-naked *now*, my lady," he leered.
"And I fancy that you have left it too late to scream
for help. One cry from those pretty lips, and your
reputation—and your husband's honor—fly out the
window."

"You have no honor!" retorted Emmie. "For you
are an animal. Worse than an animal!"

"And you," said Tredegar, "have uncommonly fine
bubbies, do you know that? Come, take your hands
away and let me feast my eyes on them once more.
No? Well, that can wait. Yes, as fine a pair as I have
ever seen. They will please Sir Claude, the old goat.
Do you know what he said to me? I'll tell you, my
lady. He said to me: 'Tredegar, you dog'—that's how
he addresses me, the swine—'Tredegar, you dog, I
don't give a damn which of Beechborough's wenches
you bring back with you, but mark that she is young,
and mark that she has the best pair of bubbies in the
litter.' That's what he said."

Stung to anger, she retorted, "You are lying!"

"That I am not!" he said. "Why, when I put Sir
Claude's conditions to the marquess, he declared that
we must summon the assistance of his three cousins,
to sit in judgment upon you, for, as he said, they were
the prime experts in that line, having handled all the
finest bubs in Oxfordshire. The marquess swore that
you were the pick of the litter in that respect, and the
three old satyrs bore him out. And that is why you are
now Lady Devizes. That, and the small consideration
of ten thousand guineas that Sir Claude paid for you
under the terms of the marriage contract."

She stared at him, watching his eyes, the workings
of his weak mouth, trying to gauge the truth or falsehood that lay behind his wild words.

"Are you telling me that I was—*bought?*" she said.

"That you were," said he. "No dowry went with you, my lady. Why, by all accounts, the Beechborough coffers are nearly empty, which was why the former marquess wrote Sir Claude and offered the pick of his young granddaughters and grandnieces for a consideration. The consideration—and to a man of Sir Claude's wealth, it was picayune—was ten thousand guineas. Paid into the Beechborough coffers in advance, in return for which Sir Claude insisted on an immediate marriage by proxy, lest the expensive young lady changed her mind during the long voyage to Canada."

It was true. There was no cause for him to lie to her, and the manner of his telling, the shameful details of the arrangement, carried the stamp of verisimilitude. She had been bought, like a slave woman, like a horse at the fair. Chosen for her youth and for the shape and firmness of her breasts.

"Will you leave me now?" she whispered. "Please!"

He shook his head. There was growing confidence in his self-mistrusting eyes, and an unfamiliar assurance in the set of his weak chin.

"I'll have you this night, my lady," he said. "I'll play proxy to the end."

He took a pace toward her. She backed away, rounding the table and placing it between them, still cupping her breasts in her hands.

"Keep away from me," she breathed.

He continued to advance, circling the table after her.

"Try me," he said. "You'll have need of the services of a good stud. The man you married is past all that. Fit only for playing the baby to a woman's bubs."

"Keep back!"

"You should have been told, my lady. 'Twas cruel to have hidden it from you. But nothing's lost. Jack Tredegar can be your proxy stud, tonight and any night. Come!"

"If you come a step nearer, I shall rouse the inn!"

He shook his head. He was assured, now. Completely assured and confident in himself and in his ability to bring his intention to a satisfactory conclusion.

"If you had any intent of rousing the inn, you would have done it before now, ma'am," he said. "No, I think your modesty is admirable, but you must not pander to your fine upbringing. Indulge your base desires, as your little black slavey-wench is doubtless slaking hers in the hayloft with the potman. Come!"

"No!"

"You are in need of a good stud. I am a good stud. See for yourself!"

His hands were fumbling at the lappet of his breeches as he was lurched toward her. A resolve fell into place in her mind. It had really been there all the time, but the shocking revelations that he had thrown at her, the very violence of his attempt upon her, had numbed her resolve. The sight of him coming at her, one hand at his loins, the other reaching to snatch her wrist, fired her to action. She snatched up the empty wine bottle from the table and ran to the partly open window. Heedless that her breasts were now open to his gaze, she tossed the bottle out into the darkness. Instants later, it smashed to smithereens on the cobbles below, with a sound enough to raise the dead and to presage the blasting of Gabriel's horn. Immediately, windows were thrown open all round the inn yard. Voices rang out. Windows blossomed light.

She turned to face Tredegar, too contemptuous and uncaring, now, even to conceal her breasts from him. He was not looking at them, but at her eyes.

"Are you out of your mind?" he wailed. "Do you know what you have done? You have ruined my military career and good name! You have quenched my honor!"

"Get down on your knees!" commanded Emmie, pointing. "Bow your head and don't you dare to look at me anymore!"

"Now, see here!" There was still a spark of the new-found resolve in tim, but it was totally extinguished by the sound of running footfalls in the corridor outside, and by a tap on the door.

"Be that you, m' lady? Be you all right in there?" The voice of the innkeeper.

Tredegar's eyes fled to Emmie. His mouth hung slackly open. "Please, my lady," he pleaded. "Please!"

Another knock on the door, louder this time, more urgent.

"M' lady—be you in there?"

Emmie stared implacably at the man before her, willing him with her eyes, demanding his total collapse. It came. With a whimper, the major sank to his knees before her, his hands pressed to his temples, eyes wild with fear.

"I beg you, ma'am," he whispered. "I was drunk—insane! I beg you, for the sake of my wife and children, do not destroy me."

Another hammering on the door, and with it came fragments of a tense converse that suggested that it be broken down.

"Is that you, landlord?" called Emmie in a loud, clear voice.

"That it be, m' lady!" came the answer. "What ails you in there?"

"I did a most ridiculous thing, landlord," said Emmie. "I stood an empty bottle on the windowsill and then brushed against it. I do so hope that the noise of it crashing down into the yard did not waken the whole establishment."

"Oh, it weren't nothing, m' lady," came the relieved reply. "Only it did give me and the missus quite a turn."

"That's all right, then," said Emmie. "I am so sorry. Do please give my apologies to those whom I may have disturbed. Good night to you."

"Good night, m' lady."

The footsteps retreated down the corridor. Tredegar exhaled a shuddering breath, and made to rise.

"Lady Devizes," he said. "I would like to say . . ."

"No!" snapped Emmie. "Do not get up! Not yet. And keep your silence. The events of this evening will never be spoken of to any living soul, either by me or by you. This is not for my sake, nor for the sake of your wife and your children, and certainly not for yours. It is for the honor of the man to whom I am married."

"Oh, I am so grateful," moaned the kneeling man.

"Will you be silent!" said Emmie. "It is my misfortune that you are to escort me to Quebec. You will perform this duty, during which time, apart from the normal civilities before others, you will never address me again. And when you reach Quebec, you will write a letter to my husband requesting an immediate transfer from your present appointment as his aide-decamp. Is that understood?"

"Yes, my lady," he whispered. "Oh, how can I express my . . . ?"

"Get up," said Emmie. "And get out."

She turned her back on him, gathered up her shawl and spread it over her bare shoulders and bosom.

He paused at the door. "It was the drink," he said hoarsely. "It was ever my downfall. And I thought that you—I mean . . ."

"You thought I was whorish," said Emmie. "But you were sadly mistaken. Now get out of here."

When he had left her, she stooped and picked up the torn rags of her upper garment, and in so doing she found that her hands were trembling uncontrollably, and her legs also. Suddenly stricken by an overpowering sense of release, she fell face-downward upon the bed and gave way to a paroxysm of choking tears.

*   *   *

The coach arrived in the teeming seaport of Bristol in the late afternoon of the next day. It had rained throughout the morning, and Tredegar, who by un-spoken agreement had traveled outside with the coachman, had received a thorough soaking. The girl Suzie had traveled inside with her mistress and, doubt-less because of her nocturnal excesses with the pot-man at the inn, had slept the whole way through.

In Dock Street, at the shipping offices of her hus-band's firm, Messrs. Devizes & Young, she was re-ceived with extreme unctuousness and directed to the Norwegian merchantman *Peder Wessel*. She repaired aboard immediately, since it was Captain Harald Michelsen's intent to sail with the evening tide.

The *Peder Wessel*'s first-class passenger accom-modation was in the stern quarter and quite commo-dious. Emmie's cabin was immediately below the poop deck, and possessed a long line of windows that looked out across the dock basin to the city that rose, height beyond height, roofs and reeking chimneypots tiered skyward in the dying day. A young steward advised her in tolerably good English that supper was to be served for first-class passengers in the great cabin before sailing, so she changed out of her trav-eling costume into a simple muslin frock and made her way there.

The stern-quarter passengers numbered eight, and were all Britons. The attraction of voyaging in a ship belonging to a nominally neutral country, at a time when the adventurous American privateer frigates were wreaking considerable havoc among British ship-ping in the Atlantic, had put a premium upon such accommodation, and Captain Michelsen's owners had greatly enhanced their charges. So it was that Emmie's fellow passengers were all of considerable estate. No less than two merchant bankers and their wives pre-sided at top and bottom of the long table set down the middle of the great cabin. On hearing Emmie's title, the most superior-mannered of the bankers obse-

quiously invited her to take the place on his right—
after unseating his own spouse. She was then introduced to the others: an Anglo-Irish gentleman of property, two maiden ladies from Kent and an exceedingly
suave archdeacon of Wells cathedral. All were passengers to Quebec.

The meal, following grace by the archdeacon, was
in the Scandinavian mode, mostly salted and smoked
fish, pickled vegetables, pastries garnished with fruit
and fresh cream. The beer and cider, like the fruit and
cream, were English.

The conversation during supper, because the fellow
passengers were sizing each other up, or possibly because of the daunting presence of the high clergyman,
was stilted to the extreme, and mostly concerned the
war. That is to say the war with Napoleonic France
and the Duke of Wellington's stirring victories in the
Peninsula. There was not a mention of the conflict
with America, for it was an affair upon which, among
polite society, one simply did not dwell a great deal,
it being considered that the Yankees had been guilty
of an act in extremely poor taste by waging war upon
Napoleon's only successful belligerent. Emmie listened with half an ear, but contributed nothing to the
talk around her, save to reply to the maiden ladies'
wistful inquiries about her recently married state and
the reason for her voyage; questions that she answered
sparingly, uncomfortably conscious of Tredegar sitting at the far end of the table, his eyes averted from
her, but listening to—and no doubt dissecting—every
word she uttered.

Escaping from table with the ladies, and leaving the
men to their port wine and pipes, she went out onto
the poop deck for a last sight of England.

Emmie stayed on deck till nightfall, watching the
lights of Newport and Cardiff slide past on the Welsh
shore, till the last of the bell buoys' mournful clanking
died astern and the *Peder Wessel* met the Atlantic
swell.

That night they ran into a storm. Emmie's first intimation of trouble came when her maid Suzie came tearfully to her cabin to tell her that she was feeling sick and scared. Emmie comforted the black girl throughout the long night, while the *Peder Wessel* battled her way through mountainous seas. Scarcely an hour passed without the shrilling of bosuns' pipes and the patter of bare feet on the deck overhead, betokening that the seamen were being sent aloft in the maelstrom of flying water to shorten sail yet again.

At dawn the wind slackened and with it the tortured motion of the ship. Leaving Suzie to sleep, Emmie went up on deck, and was in time to see the veritable last of England fading in the mist: the crag of Land's End and its attendant islets. Captain Michelsen was on deck; he was a tall, taciturn man with a face that seemed to have been hewn out of the rocks of his native shore, and a mane of leonine hair descending from under his cocked hat. He bowed stiffly toward Emmie. Then turned his back upon her.

The days that followed were fine and sunny, and the *Peder Wessel* made good westering before a steady wind of a strength that permitted Michelsen to spread his studding sails. Emmie spent most of her days on the poop deck, under an awning that had been set up to protect the ladies from the ill effects of the sun. Suzie sat with her always. The black girl won many hot glances from the crew of blond Norwegians, who appeared to find her quite irresistible. Suzie, now that her sickness was forgotten, blossomed mightily before their admiration, preened herself like a bird of paradise in the brightly colored shawls and headscarves that she favored, tugged down her bodice to display as much as possible of her swelling young charms and generally behaved in such a provocative manner that Emmie was obliged to remonstrate with her. The black girl took the correction in good part, and continued to preen herself before the sailors.

Of Major Tredegar Emmie saw scarcely anything.

He had even taken to having his meals in his own cabin, and, on discovering that Emmie used the poop deck, took his exercise in the waist of the vessel.

Seven days after putting out from Bristol, in the late afternoon, a cry went up from the masthead lookout that brought Captain Michelsen hastening on deck with his telescope. He roared something up to the man in the crow's nest and was answered. He then put his telescope to his eye and stared away to windward. Emmie was near enough to hear him utter an exclamation, and something that sounded uncommonly like a Norwegian curse. He snapped his telescope shut.

"Pray what is the matter, sir?" asked the archdeacon, who was taking the air on the poop deck.

"It is an American frigate," growled Captain Michelsen. "And making course to intercept *Peder Wessel!*"

Half an hour later they saw her clearly from the poop deck: a lean, slender shape coming straight out of the eye of the wind, leeward gun ports barely out of the water, sails taut as drums, ensign snapping from her mizzen peak. She was shaping a course that would bring her straight at the *Peder Wessel*.

Captain Michelsen, who had been deep in what appeared to be a savage gloom ever since the sighting of the American, suddenly was inspired into action. He $a1shouted an order down to his first mate in the waist, which brought a chorus of bosuns' pipes and a rush of men. Emmie heard the concerted rumble of heavy wheels on the deck below as the guns were run out.

Michelsen turned to his passengers assembled on the poop.

"If the American frigate try to take *Peder Wessel,* I shall resist," he said calmly. "All take shelter below deck, please."

One of the maiden ladies began to cry, and was comforted by her companion. Suzie let out a wail of terror. Emmie took her by the hand and dragged her down the companionway and into her own cabin. There she pointed at the bunk.

"Lie down there, Suzie," she said. "If you feel the need, pull the bedclothes over your head. But stop that infernal keening, do you hear?"

"Yes'm, milady," wailed Suzie, wild-eyed.

"Do that, then," said Emmie, and crossed over to the windows, where she could clearly see the American frigate closing in on them fast. Indeed, by that time, one could discern the figures grouped upon her decks, and several men on the yardarms in readiness to take in sail and slow down the speedy vessel when she came up with the big merchantman.

With a dryness in the mouth, Emmie speculated on the possible outcome of the encounter. In common with most large merchantmen, the *Peder Wessel* carried a complement of defensive cannon, not enough to tackle an armed naval vessel of any size, but sufficient weight of metal to deter, say, an armed schooner with a captain of piratical bent, or a corsair dhow off the Algiers coast. On the face of it, Michelsen's determination to prevent his ship from possible capture was an act of folly; Emmie was well aware—as was all England—of the potency of the Yankee privateer frigates that were likened to hunting leopards of the sea. She devoutly hoped that the Norwegian captain's stance was mere bravado. But if it was, and if the Americans really intended to take the neutral ship upon some pretext, what then? What of the passengers?

"Milady, oh milady, we's all going to be raped!" wailed Suzie, who had sized up the situation and arrived at *her* conclusions.

"Be quiet!" snapped Emmie.

The frigate was gaining space, and now she could see the bronzed faces of the men on her decks, and distinguish between seamen and officers by reason of the latter's blue coats. A group of three officers stood on the quarter deck. One of them, taller than his fellows, was hatless, revealing a head of dark hair with a streak of startling white in it. As she looked, he raised a telescope to his eye and swept the length of the *Peder Wessel*. As the glass pointed at her, Emmie instinctively drew back out of sight. When she looked again, the man had lowered his instrument. And even in that short space of time, the American had come appreciably closer.

As she watched, the man with the white streak in his hair moved the whole length of his deck, till he was in the bows of the flying frigate and that much nearer to his quarry, and there he lifted to his lips a speaking trumpet.

"Ahoy there! What ship?"

Emmie's hand flew to open the window, the better to hear what followed.

An answering cry came from above her head: "*Peder Wessel*, of Bergen. Neutral ship. Norwegian."

"I read your ensign, sir," replied the American. "What was your last port of call and where are you bound?"

There was some delay before Captain Michelsen made his grudging admission: "Bristol. Bound for Quebec."

"What cargo?"

Another pause, and then: "That is my business!"

"I am putting a party aboard to search you, sir," replied the American. "Heave-to and lower a line."

"I go on my way," shouted Michelsen. "Stand off from me, or I shall open fire."

"You would be ill-advised to do that, sir," came the stern answer. "Put your helm up and heave-to."

"I tell you to stand off. If you do not turn away by the count of five, I give the order to fire!"

Breathless, Emmie waited for the effect that Captain Michelsen's stern determination—or was it merely bluff?—would have upon the American captain. She had not long to wait. The man with the white streak in his hair turned and shouted something down the deck, with the almost immediate result that the frigate, far from turning away from the Norwegian, pointed its long bowsprit even closer to its quarry.

A couple of heartbeats later, a thunderous crash broke from the *Peder Wessel*, and the deck shook beneath Emmie's feet. Suzie screamed and continued to scream. A billowing of white smoke momentarily obliterated the frigate from Emmie's view, and when it cleared, she saw a blossoming of small waterspouts far astern of the American. Across the intervening distance, she heard a chorus of mocking cheers from her crowded decks. Captain Michelsen's gunners had missed—and missed badly.

An instant later, there was a single brief orange flash, followed by a wreath of smoke, from the frigate's bow. Emmie distinctly heard the cannonball thundering through the air above her head. There was a mighty impact. A rending and a tearing. Men's screams from the poop deck above. The sound of something crashing down and splintering to fragments. And then silence.

The American ship slid swiftly across her vision, as the *Peder Wessel* turned sharply on her beam ends. Suzie was hurled, shrieking, from the bunk, and Emmie only kept her feet by holding onto the window frame with both hands. The rush of passing water ceased as the Norwegian ship came to a halt, wallowing lamely in the trough of each passing wave. The American went about with a flapping and a gathering-in of sail by the seamen on the yards. She lay still in the water close by her stricken quarry. Moments later, a boat appeared from under her stern and was rowed smartly toward the *Peder Wessel*.

"Suzie, will you stop that terrible racket?" said Emmie. "It's all over now and I am going up on deck. You may stay here, or you may come with me. Please yourself."

"Milady, oh milady, you's'll be raped!" cried the black girl. "We's'll both be raped."

It was on the tip of Emmie's tongue to make the tart retort that, considering Suzie's showing aboard the *Peder Wessel*, the comely black girl would scarcely need to be taken unwillingly by a crew of virile seamen, but refrained from the incivility. Instead, she went up the companionway to see what had happened on the poop deck, and also to put a bold face upon an imminent encounter with the enemy.

The sight that greeted her in the open air sent her reeling back against the rail of the companionway. Of the ship's mizzenmast, nothing remained but a ragged-ended stump no higher than a man and a half. The top end of the mast hung over the side and was imprisoned there by the tangle of cordage that had descended with it. White-faced and shocked, Captain Michelsen and some of his men were frantically scrabbling among the wreckage and seeking to lift a heavy yardarm from something that moaned and writhed beneath a mercifully concealing mass of tumbled canvas. When Emmie glanced downward, she saw to her horror that a thick dribble of scarlet was coming across the deck toward her feet, snaking back and forth with every movement of the ship. She closed her eyes and turned away.

The American boarding party came over in a cutter pulled by six sailors, all stripped to the waist and heavily muscled, grinning, confident. The officer was a lad of about nineteen or twenty, with a brash air about him. He was first up on deck, and doffed his hat civilly enough to Captain Michelsen.

"Compliments from my captain, sir," he said. "It was not his wish to fire upon you, and it was only with the intent of bringing down your mizzen." He cast an appreciative glance toward the severed stump. "I trust that no one was hurt in the regrettable process?"

"Two men were killed by the falling spars," said

Michelsen shortly. "Another is dying up there on the poop."

"I am sorry, sir," said the young American.

The Norwegian shrugged. "What now?" he asked.

"Your cargo, sir," said the other. "What cargo are you carrying?"

"Nothing," replied Michelsen. "I am in ballast."

"But how is that—coming from a teeming port like Bristol? Could you not find a cargo to carry to Quebec?"

"I have a contract to fulfill in Quebec at the end of the month," explained Michelsen sullenly. "It did not permit me enough time to load a cargo in Bristol. There is nothing aboard this ship for you, mister."

"Passengers?"

"A few."

"Nationality?"

"All British."

"Combatants?" The American did not wait for an answer. Looking beyond Michelsen, he saw Major Tredegar emerging from the companionway. His eyebrow rose upon seeing the other's scarlet regimentals. "I see you carry at least one combatant," he said icily.

Emmie watched Tredegar from the corner of her eye. The man's weak mouth took on an unaccustomed firmness as he squared up to the enemy officer, removed his hat and bowed stiffly.

"Major Tredegar, sir. At your service," he said.

The American performed the same salute. "Midshipman Clegg, United States Navy," he responded. "You are my prisoner, sir, but you may retain your sword."

"I thank you, sir," replied Tredegar. "Is it your intention to remove me from this ship?"

"Those are my orders," said Midshipman Clegg. "All combatants are to be brought aboard the *Delaware*."

Like two fighting cocks facing up to each other,

thought Emmie. All in their colored plumage, ducking and bowing, exchanging their false courtesies, hating each other all the time. Only men could act like this.

Tredegar said, "One thing remains to be settled, Mr. Clegg."

"And what is that, sir?" responded the other.

"I am charged with the care of Lady Devizes, wife of the military governor of Quebec," said Tredegar.

"Are you, by God?" exclaimed the American. "And is this lady present?" His gaze swept round the line of watching passengers and lighted upon Emmie, who drew herself up and eyed him with all the haughtiness she could muster.

"I am Lady Devizes, sir," she said.

Off came the American's hat again. Another bow. There was bafflement and dismay in his young, unformed face. He had come upon a problem that had never been taken into account during his training before the mast: what was the precise status of the wife of a highly placed enemy combatant? *Think fast, Mr. Clegg. Your sailors are watching you; everyone is watching you.*

"Hem! I much regret, ma'am," he said, "that you will have to accompany me back to the *Delaware*."

"Am I a prisoner, sir?" demanded Emmie.

"You must consider yourself so, ma'am," replied Clegg. He took a deep breath. "Pending my captain's decision regarding your status."

"Milady, milady!" It was Suzie. Pushing her way past the affronted archdeacon, she threw herself in Emmie's arms. "If you'se a-going, milady, don't leave me here. What'll become of me?"

"May my maid accompany me, sir?" asked Emmie.

Midshipman Clegg made the gesture of a young man who had set his foot upon a path and discovered, too late, that he had walked into a quicksand. He shrugged. "As you please, ma'am," he said. "And now, are there any more combatants aboard this ship?"

There being none, and the *Peder Wessel* carrying

no contraband, the Americans shortly left Michelsen to bury his dead and go about his business. The Norwegian captain was not to be prevailed upon by Emmie to wait for her possible return from the American frigate, but gave orders for making sail. As Emmie and her companions and their baggage were rowed away in the cutter, the crippled merchantman was making her awkward way downwind into the evening sun.

She was a prisoner. A glance at Tredegar's profile revealed that there was a small, mean smile dwelling at the corner of his lips, and she thought she knew the reason for it. Not out of duty and honor, but out of spite, had he revealed his obligation toward her. If he had kept silent, instead of blurting out her name and station, she could have gone on her way without him—and good riddance to him. Tredegar had had his revenge for the way she had spurned him.

As they drew near the frigate, she saw the line of faces looking down at them from the high deck. Most of them were grinning; some of the seamen exchanged quips with each other and pointed at the Redcoat officer and the women. When Emmie was handed up the steep ladder, they crowded to help her. A big fellow took her about the waist, lifted her over the rails and set her upon the deck. There was an equally enthusiastic rush to assist Suzie, who, upon the appearance of so many cheerful stalwarts, had quite lost her fears.

"Will you accompany me to the captain's cabin?" said Midshipman Clegg. "This way, ma'am—sir."

He led them down a companionway to the door of a stern cabin, upon which he tapped respectfully. A voice bade them to come in.

"Captain, sir, I have brought three prisoners aboard," said Clegg.

The tall figure of the frigate's captain was bowed over a chart on a table set in the middle of the cabin. He did not look up for a moment or two, and Emmie was able to confirm her earlier view of him. His hair was dark—dark as her own—and the streak of white stretched from the widow's peak to the nape, and grew from a scar that marred his hairline at the crown. His face was bronzed the color of chestnut, his hands— the long and capable-looking hands spread across the chart—also.

He looked up, and she met the gaze of the bluest eyes that she had ever beheld. They immediately sparked anger.

"Good God, Mr. Clegg—I told you to bring combatants!"

"This lady, sir, is the wife of—" began the unhappy Clegg.

"I don't give a damn if this lady is the wife of Beelzebub!" growled his captain. "Get her off this ship and back aboard the Norwegian. And look sharp about it!"

"But, sir," said Clegg. "The Norwegian is already underway and making straight downwind, which is her best point of sail, now we've rid her of her mizzen."

With a muffled curse, the captain strode across to the stern windows and looked out.

"Confound it!" he exclaimed. "She's gone, right enough, and there's no going after her now!"

Emmie gave a warning cough to attract his attention. The blue eyes flashed in her direction. One eyebrow rose quizzically.

"Did you have some observation to make, ma'am?" he demanded.

"Speaking as an unwilling guest aboard this ship, sir," responded Emmie, "I should like to request that more energetic steps be taken to return me aboard my own vessel. This frigate can far outstrip the merchantman, for I have seen it done with my own eyes. I request—indeed, I demand—that the trick be repeated!"

The blue eyes narrowed. "Do you, now, ma'am?" he said. "Do you demand it, eh?"

"I do, sir!"

She met his gaze unwaveringly. In doing so, she had the opportunity to observe that he carried his head very high, that his sea-blue gaze was directed down the side of a very straight nose, that his disfigured brow was neither too high nor too low and that his ears were well-shaped and set close to his head.

Presently he said, "Believe me, ma'am, I would gladly accede to your—demand. However, it is out of the question." He gestured toward the chart on the table. "The Norwegian is heading downwind. It is nearly dark and will be pitch black by the time we overhaul her. After we have transferred you back aboard—no easy feat in the dark, even if we can easily persuade that Norwegian captain to heave-to again—there will follow a long and time-consuming tack back into the eye of the wind. It will be dawn before we have returned to the spot where we are at this moment. I cannot spare the time, ma'am, for I have a rendezvous to keep."

"Then I am, indeed, your prisoner?" said Emmie.

"So it would appear, ma'am," he said coolly, and a glimmer of amusement appeared, for the first time, in those blue eyes. "We had best introduce ourselves, and then you will perhaps do me the honor of joining me and my officers at dinner."

He was Nathan Grant—Captain Nathan Grant, of Providence, Rhode Island—and he showed no great amazement and awe to hear of her name and position. Indeed, he seemed the sort of man who would not have turned a hair if Midshipman Clegg had come aboard with the Prince Regent himself for prisoner. He made it quite clear, by his attitude toward her, that his sole objection to her presence was on the score of her sex.

"Madam, a woman has no place aboard a ship of war," he said. "Aside from the usual sailor's superstition about the ill-luck that comes from carrying women and parsons, I have to tell you that a warship in action is likely to produce sights and sounds that should never be seen or heard by persons of the gentle sex."

"I have seen and heard a little of it already, sir," responded Emmie tartly, "when, as you will recall, you were constrained to interfere with a peaceful neutral merchantman going about its lawful business."

If her barb struck home, it produced no sign in the eyes or on the well-chiseled countenance of the *Delaware*'s captain, who merely addressed himself to the glass of wine that stood at his elbow.

They were at dinner: she and Grant, the half-dozen officers not on watch and the detestable Tredegar, of course. The wine they were drinking was theirs at third hand, having been taken from a captured British merchantman, who had in turn received it from the spoils of a captured French ship. It was the thin, dry claret of Bordeaux so beloved by the English gentry. Captain Grant appeared to appreciate it also, savoring it upon his palate, sniffing at its bouquet with every sip, rolling it around his tongue. It occurred to Emmie that Nathan Grant was a bit like Bordeaux wine: dry and austere, not to everyone's taste, an acquired predilection. . . .

They were being served at table by the captain's steward, one Gumbril, a man of middle years, who performed great feats of dexterity with piles of plates and brimming soup tureens, considering that he possessed a wooden leg, and that the frigate was proceeding through the water with a distinct heel. Gumbril was assisted by Suzie, acting as wine steward. The black girl had taken great pains with her appearance by plaiting her kinky hair in a score of tiny points, all gathered at the parting with bright red butterfly bows; she had on a purple blouse whose neckline was expanded to the full extent of its drawstring, showing her shoulders and bosom to a scandalous advantage. Emmie could not but notice that the eyes of her fellow diners were being constantly directed toward the visible charms of the pretty black girl. Once, stooping to refill Captain Grant's glass, she leaned so far as to make a momentary display of her nipples—a vision that was not lost on the captain. Nor did he seem to take the matter amiss. Perhaps, thought Emmie, he was not so dry and austere after all.

The conversation was largely directed by the ship's first lieutenant, an eager-faced redhead with an explosive laugh with which he punctuated his discourse. The talk was of the successes that the small fleet of American frigates were enjoying against the vastly superior Royal Navy. It was not boastful talk, nor in any way directed toward their English guests in an offensive manner. From fragments of the conversation Emmie gleaned that several of the officers—Grant included—had actually served in the Navy with which they were now at war; all spoke of their opponents with the respect that professionals reserve for their equals.

Tredegar maintained silence during this talk, but soon began to show signs of pent-up fury. Following one remark by the first lieutenant—to the effect that, given half a dozen frigates and two sound third-raters, the U.S. Navy could control the Atlantic—he could contain himself no longer.

"Fine talk!" he snapped. "But let your fleet of frigates and your third-raters come against an equal number of British ships, and you would see another Trafalgar in miniature!"

The first lieutenant, O'Leary, looked down into his wine glass in some embarrassment. Nor did his fellow officers seem inclined to take up the challenge. It was left to Captain Grant to make reply. This he did in flat, matter-of-fact tones, under which Emmie could discern an edge of weary contempt that was directed toward the blustering Britisher.

"There will be no second Trafalgar for you to celebrate, sir, for there can be no such battle. We do not even possess a single third-rater. But if we did have battleships, and if it came to a killing match, I think you would be surprised."

"An American victory over the Royal Navy?" sneered Tredegar. "What, after our fellows have trounced every fleet that has been set against them in the last hundred years: Dutch, Spanish, French, the lot? You presume too much, sir."

Very quietly, Grant replied, "I will tell you about the Royal Navy, sir. I took this wound while serving under Nelson at the Battle of the Nile." He lightly touched the silvery scar that stood out lividly against his bronzed brow. "It was at the Nile that Nelson not only destroyed a French fleet, but also a whole generation of trained officers and men. Since the Nile, the British navy has not fought with men of its own mettle. I do not detract one iota from the glories of Copenhagen and Trafalgar, but that's the truth of it."

"And what conclusion do you draw from that, sir?" demanded Tredegar.

"This conclusion, sir," replied the other quietly. "We are a different stamp from the seamen whom your fellows have been used to fighting in the past fifteen years. And not only are our seamen highly trained, they are volunteers, all. No pressed men, no sweepings of the prisons, serve aboard *our* ships of war."

"So you are telling me that you will win this war?" sneered Tredegar. "Your reasoning is clever, but none the less unlikely."

"Neither will win, sir," replied Grant. "We do not possess the weight of sail to bring your fleet to battle, and all the patrolling in the world will not check the activities of our frigates. I repeat, neither side will win the war at sea, but I tell you this, sir—it is we who will make the greater clatter!"

In the silence that followed Captain Grant's declaration, a knock came upon the door of the dining cabin, and an officer entered.

"Two bells of the First Watch, sir," he said. "Permission to lay over on the port tack, course sou'west by south."

"Make it so, Mr. Pearson."

"Aye, aye, sir." The officer departed.

Grant addressed Emmie. "Lady Devizes, we are beating to windward, and this entails a lot of tacking to and fro. In a few moments, the ship will go about and we shall lay over on the other side. I mention this in order that you take a firm hold of your wine glass, so as not to spill claret down your exceedingly handsome gown."

"I thank you, sir," responded Emmie, who looked upon the *Delaware*'s captain with considerably more favor after his trouncing of the unspeakable Tredegar.

"Here we go, Lady Devizes," said Lieutenant O'Leary.

The whole ship seemed to give a sigh. Woodwork creaked all about them. A barely perceptible movement toward the upright increased in velocity. The lamp that had hung in an inclined position above the dining table now hung straight. Suddenly, and with a frenzied and concerted creaking of every piece of timber and strand of cordage in the vessel, the U.S.S. *Delaware* inclined over on her opposite beam, and there was no sound but the rushing of water past the thick timbers outside.

"Maneuver completed," said Captain Grant. "And now, may I suggest that we change the subject of the general conversation and discuss, say, the theater? What plays are being performed in London this season, Lady Devizes? Is it true, as they tell me, that the incomparable Mrs. Siddons has at last retired from the stage?"

"It was last July," replied Emmie. "She played Lady Macbeth at Covent Garden and the audience would not permit the play to proceed further than her sleepwalking scene. In fact—"

"What was that?" exclaimed Lieutenant O'Leary, rising with such force that his chair overturned behind him with a clatter.

"Did someone shout fire?" cried another.

Fire! Emmie chilled at the thought. To be caught in a wooden hull in the ocean's midst, there to be burned alive. . . .

Suzie dropped the wine bottle she was holding and proceeded to scream continuously, only stopping when the officer of the watch burst unceremoniously in through the door.

"Well, what is it, Mr. Pearson?" demanded Grant.

"Sir, we are holed below the waterline on the port side!" cried the other.

"Holed, you say? Holed by what?"

"By a ball from that Norwegian, sir!" said Pearson. "By a fluke, they caught us between wind and water, and it didn't show till we put over on the port tack. We've already shipped a ton of water below deck!"

"You're putting the ship about again?"

"She's already going over on to the other tack, sir."

The *Delaware* began her creaking again, and the sound was accompanied by a sneering laugh from Tredegar, which ceased abruptly as Nathan Grant flashed him a savage glance.

So, thought Emmie, Captain Michelsen's gunners had not bungled after all, and the dead of the *Peder Wessel* had been in some small way avenged.

The damage was inspected, and Grant made his dispositions upon the dining table, on a chart spread amid the remains of the abandoned meal. The *Delaware* was now unable to make her rendezvous with her sister ship, the *Constitution,* and would be obliged to continue to the starboard tack, carrying her in the direction of Portland, which, opined Grant, would likely be their destination if the wind remained in the same quarter.

"In any event, Lady Devizes," he said with a wry smile, "the arrangement will benefit your interests, for we are more likely to run across a neutral merchantman in the more northerly latitudes. I promise you that, weather permitting, you and your maid will be transferred to the first such ship we encounter."

What followed had to be said. "What if you come across a ship of the Royal Navy, sir?" she asked quietly.

"That would be a matter for some regret," he said. "If a British frigate came in sight, I should be caught like a lame duck with a fox on her tail, with no means to maneuver. Nevertheless, I promise you that, in the event of a battle, I will first have you put aboard the enemy ship, from whose decks you will have the pleasure of watching the *Delaware* go down with her flag still flying."

"That would give me no pleasure at all, sir," said Emmie gravely.

"That I can believe, ma'am," replied Grant, giving her a long and thoughtful look with his brilliant blue eyes. "And I am most obliged to you."

That night, Grant turned out of his cabin and Emmie moved in. It was, next to the dining cabin, which doubled as wardroom and sleeping quarters for the ship's officers, the most commodious compartment aboard the *Delaware*, with a let-down cot and an extremely comfortable ducks' down mattress and pillows.

Peg-legged Gumbril assisted Suzie in carrying in her mistress's traps, and he showed Emmie the workings of the washstand and the rest of the very efficient plumbing arrangements. As a bell on deck struck six times, which she presumed was six bells, or eleven o'clock in common parlance, Emmie turned into Captain Grant's ducks' down bower and composed herself for sleep. It was not long in coming, and she was dreaming of her childhood days at Flaxham, with strawberries and cream, pony rides and high summer, when a sharp cry awakened her. She sat up.

"What was that—is someone there?" she whispered.

By the light of the single tallow dip that illuminated the cabin, she saw that she was quite alone. The sound—whatever it may have been—had come from beyond her door.

She strained her ears to listen. Nothing but the gentle creak of woodwork, and the faint sound of the sea hissing past outside.

And then it came again, a sharp, anguished cry—the cry of a woman in agony.

Suzie . . . !

She was out of bed on the instant and feverishly throwing her peignoir over her night shift. Rushing to the door, she threw it open and went out into the small lobby beyond. To her right was the tiny cabin, scarcely larger than the cot and chest of drawers that it contained, which had been given to her maid. A light shone through the slats in the closed door.

As she reached out to take the handle, Suzie uttered the cry again, but with subtle differences of tone and volume. No longer a cry of agony, this was more a moan of something like pleasure. Some inner prompting restrained Emmie from flinging open the door and rushing in; instead, she opened it quietly and peered cautiously into the dimly lit interior.

A breath-catching tableau met her astonished gaze. By the shifting light of a tallow dip, the body of her maid gleamed like polished ebony: shoulders, breasts, thighs, the long and suavely tapering legs. Save for one white stocking, Suzie was entirely nude, and her head was thrown back on the pillow, eyes closed in rapture, full lips parted to show her perfect teeth.

A man was straddling her nakedness, and he was stripped buff, his white buttocks enclosed within the girl's entwined legs. The two of them were still, their passions spent. His head—Emmie could not see his head—was bent over Suzie's breast, and whatever his lips were doing there caused her to make small moans of rapturous contentment.

With a shudder of nameless emotion, Emmie quietly closed the door upon the scene.

Who, then, was Suzie's lover? One of the ship's officers, no doubt. Well, the girl had displayed her wares with some success, and she wished her well of her conquest. Each to her own tastes.

Turning to approach her own door, Emmie then saw that the door of the cabin opposite Suzie's was open. A faint light inside disclosed that it was a compartment of like smallness, with an empty bed and tumbled sheets. Above it there hung a brass-buttoned coat with gold lace and epaulets: the coat that she had last seen upon the back of the *Delaware*'s captain.

She flashed a glance at the closed door where the two of them lay: the semi-slave girl and the strangely dry and austere American. Dry and austere, fiddlesticks! He was just like all the rest! Rub a man and reveal a goat!

Emmie wrenched open her own door and slammed it behind her, uncaring of whether the embracing pair heard her or no. Ripping off her peignoir, she threw herself back upon the bed. It was hours before she was able to go back to sleep. Her whole mind was upon the pair in the cabin next door. And, surely, it was absurd to let oneself be upset by a matter so vulgar and trivial.

Chapter Three

Daylight streamed through the long windows of the stern cabin, and the sun obliged her to narrow her eyes. Touched by a strange feeling of eagerness, she leaped from the cot, and, filling the washbasin from a copper ewer, she dashed cold fresh water on her face till her cheeks tingled.

Ten minutes later, cloaked and bonneted against the fresh breeze, she went up on deck. The *Delaware* was lying over on the same tack, with the spread sails thrumming a deep-voiced chorus overhead and the wake rushing past. Every so often, an especially large wave struck the bow and rose in a fan of diamond spray above the white deck. All around, the horizon was empty: a waste of shimmering blueness under tumbled clouds and clear sky mixed in riotous confusion.

"Good morning to you, ma'am." First Lieutenant O'Leary stood, straddle-legged, on the quarterdeck, a telescope tucked under his arm. "I trust you slept well, your ladyship."

"Very well, thank you, Mr. O'Leary," replied Emmie demurely.

"She's thrusting well," said the officer, patting the ship's bulwark affectionately. "We spent the whole night pumping water out of her bottom—that which was taken in when we went on the other tack. You never saw the like. The bilges were overflowing. All the long night it took us, and every man lent a hand, the captain included. But she's not taking in much water now, and sailing like a bird."

Something prompted Emmie to say: "Captain Grant was pumping out water last night?"

"That's right, ma'am. Cap'n Grant will never ask a man to do anything he wouldn't tackle himself. You'll not find many captains in the British navy as will spend the first half of the middle watch in his shirtsleeves, swinging at the handle of a bilge pump with the rest of 'em. Begging your pardon for the comparison, your ladyship."

"The middle watch, you say?" Emmie paused for a moment. "At what hour would that be, Mr. O'Leary—the first half of the middle watch? I ask merely out of—er—curiosity."

"Why, ma'am, that would be from midnight to nigh on two in the morning," replied the first lieutenant.

"I see. Thank you, Mr. O'Leary," said Emmie.

Upon her return to bed, she had noticed, from her fob watch that hung above her pillow, that it was exactly a quarter past one. Whoever Suzie's lover of the night had been, it could certainly not have been the captain of the *Delaware*. Grant had doubtless snatched a couple of hours' sleep before going below in his shirtsleeves to do a trick at the pump. Odd, how the realization cheered her, since the man meant nothing to her at all, and it scarcely mattered to her if her maid bestowed her nubile charms upon the entire ship's company, from captain to cabin boy and back again.

"A day like this, ma'am," said First Lieutenant O'Leary, narrowing his eyes to squint up at the sea of taut canvas above their heads. "A day like this, with the wind in the right quarter, and the old ship going like a bird, it sure makes you glad to be alive."

"It does, it does," agreed Emmie feelingly. "It is most—most *exhilarating!*"

By noontime the tumbled clouds took over from the patches of limpid blueness, and white horses rode the tips of the waves as far as the horizon. Bosuns' pipes brought the watch on deck to shorten canvas, and the *Delaware* was soon dipping her long beak into the mounting waves, catching them up, tossing them on high and sending them down her decks, into the brimming scuppers and out back from whence they came.

Suzie predictably fell sick with the motion, and Emmie, finding that unaccountably she had lost all the dislike and contempt that she had nourished for the girl the previous night, tended her like a mother.

In the midafternoon, with all hell let loose outside, and the frigate riding out the gale on a sea anchor, there came a rap on Emmie's door. It was Gumbril. Compliments of the cap'n, and would her ladyship please attend the cap'n in the great cabin? A glance at Suzie told her that the black girl, weakened from vomiting, had slipped into a sleep of utter weariness and would scarcely need her ministrations for some time to come. Emmie obeyed the summons.

All the officers who were not on watch, and the detestable Tredegar, were in the great cabin. Upon the table that served as a dining table had been nailed a chart of the eastern seaboard of America. Captain Grant, clinging to a beam above his head, gave a brief nod at Emmie when she entered. The rest of the company were likewise clinging to what they could, for the pitch and toss of the frigate against her sea anchor was of considerable violence. Someone gave Emmie a hand and held her safe.

Grant addressed them all without preamble.

"Wind and weather have confounded us. We'll not

make Portland in these conditions. Moreover, she is taking in more water than we can remove with the pumps going round the clock. I propose to make a dash for the nearest land and careen. Any questions?''

Careen? Emmie looked for guidance at the man next to her. It was Midshipman Clegg. Stooping, he put his mouth close to her ear.

''Careen means to deliberately run the ship ashore on a sandy beach at high tide,'' he whispered. ''At low tide, she is high and dry, so you can repair her in time to float off at the next high tide.''

Emmie nodded, still confused. Everyone was talking at once now. Expressions such as ''spring tide,'' ''lay out a kedge anchor to haul her off'' and ''a copper patch and a quick caulking will do her'' were being bandied about. Only the detestable Tredegar was silent. The British army officer clung to an upright stanchion, eyeing the *Delaware*'s captain like a rabbit regarding a snake, his mouth twitching, naked terror written in every line of his countenance. When a mighty wave brought the *Delaware*'s bow high into the air, so that one of the officers, losing his foothold, was carried right along the cabin to land in a bruised heap, Tredegar gave a hoarse cry of horror.

The brief conference having been completed, and all matters settled, Captain Grant gave orders for the sea anchor to be brought in and for the *Delaware* to set course for the nearest land. That done, he made his way across the cabin to the door, passing close by Emmie on the way. Unconsciously, her lips assumed a tight smile of greeting in anticipation of meeting his eye; she was even composing a short phrase of good wishes for his coming enterprise. To her surprise and dismay, however, he went by with not so much as a word or a glance; indeed, he seemed to avert his face from her.

Emmie was on deck, taking shelter by the companionway, huddled in cloak and hood, when the *Delaware* got underway again. Freed of her sea anchor,

the raking bows swung across wind and water, the
reefed sails bellowed, the lofty masts bowed before
the tempest, and the gallant ship began her race
against time and circumstance.

Emmie remained above deck till nightfall, while the
ship clawed her way shoreward, and the tall figure of
her captain loomed like a dark ghost alone on his quarterdeck. His white-streaked mane streamed free, his
eyes were narrowed against the gales of wind, as they
plowed onward, ever onward.

Emmie watched him and wondered. Would he bring
them safely to land? She put the question to herself a
score of times.

There was another question at the far edge of her
mind, but she could bring herself to ask it only once:
why had Nathan Grant so pointedly snubbed her?

She slept a fitful few hours, with the wretched Suzie
huddled beside her in the narrow cot. Gumbril woke
them, still in the dark hours, bidding them to rise and
dress, and take whatever portable valuables they
could easily carry onto the deck. They were approaching land, he said, and the careen was about to begin.

Suzie was as helpless as a child; she crouched, sobbing with helpless terror, while Emmie dressed her
and chided her to be brave. The ship was rolling most
alarmingly, with the sluggish, slow roll that, did the
two females but know, told of a vessel that is all but
swamped with the weight of water within her. The
Delaware had but a short while to live, unless Captain
Grant brought her ashore.

Thrusting a few pieces of her favorite trinkets into
the pocket of her cloak, and taking the whimpering
black girl by the hand, Emmie fought her way out of
the cabin to the companionway. Out on deck, the
steely light of the new dawn was just beginning to
pierce the gloom, and she could pick out the high
hump of a wooded island directly ahead, with a wide
bay and a long strip of white sandy beach. The ship

was wallowing unsteadily toward the bay, her masts swaying with every great comber that passed under her keel.

"Away the cutter!" The voice of First Lieutenant O'Leary blared from the quarterdeck through a speaking trumpet.

"This way, ma'am." Midshipman Clegg took her elbow and guided her to the ship's rail, where, looking down, she saw the boat that had brought them aboard the *Delaware* pitching and plunging in the waste of water alongside her parent ship.

"Am I—are we—to go down *there?*" exclaimed Emmie, appalled. And Suzie resumed her pitiful wailing.

"There's nothing to it, ma'am," Clegg assured her. "You'll be down in a trice, and safely ashore, to watch our coming in, before you know where you are."

Indeed, somehow, they were lowered safely into the waiting cutter, and then began the long and alarming row for the distant beach, with the *Delaware* wallowing after them, her gun ports almost under water, and the waves breaking over her proud bows, and the dark figure of her captain, standing where he had stood the long night through.

The roar of the breakers presaged a violent arrival on the shore—that, and the line of white water that marked the end of their hazardous voyage. As they drew closer to the shore, the control of the stout cutter passed from the hands of the sailors at the oars to the wild grasp of the sea. Oars were raised and brought inboard. Standing in the stern, Midshipman Clegg guided her through the maelstrom as best he was able, fighting two-handed with the tiller. Through three lines of breakers they passed, lifted on high as the combers passed beneath them. At the last moments, Clegg lost control, and the craft swung broadside to the waves. It seemed that she must be swamped. Emmie clung to the gunwale with one hand and hung tightly to the screaming black girl with her other.

And then—suddenly, unbelievably—it was all over. The cutter was deposited with scarcely a jolt upon the soft sand. The waters receded. The sailors, leaping over the side, dragged their craft high onto the beach.

"Home and dry," commented Clegg smugly. "Let's hope to God that the old *Delaware* fares as well."

The frigate was close inshore and coming in fast as the combers took her. Her yardarms were festooned with sailors, hanging up there, scrabbling with numbed fingers to gather in the reluctant sails. One by one, they were furled in, till only her foresail remained, and it was on this last rag of canvas that Nathan Grant brought his ship to safety. An instant before she struck bottom, the foresail was gathered up.

"She's aground, and the kedge anchor is holding her!" cried Clegg. This was a signal for the cutter's crew to cheer and throw up their caps, embrace each other.

"He's saved the old *Delaware!*" they shouted. "No skipper but our Nat could have done it!"

Her arms around Suzie, Emmie looked out across the waters to the grounded frigate, and felt the tears of relief flowing, unbidden and unexpected, down her cheeks.

Two hours later, the spring tide being on the ebb, the *Delaware*'s high masts were beginning to lean over as the ship's hull rolled onto its beam ends. An hour after that, they were able to walk out to her, almost dry, now. And already the ship's carpenters were at work upon the ugly gash that the Norwegian's ball had made below the waterline on her port side.

Emmie was there when the first group came ashore, with the tall figure of Grant leading. He splashed through the knee-high shallows toward her, his face set and expressionless.

"May I offer my congratulations, Captain Grant," murmured Emmie, fearful as she spoke that he might walk straight past and cut her dead.

"I thank you, Lady Devizes," replied Grant in a voice as cold as charity.

And, with that, he walked on past.

"Brought you an easy chair, ma'am," came a voice at her elbow, taking her by surprise as she gazed after the retreating figure of the *Delaware*'s captain, stalking, long-legged, up the beach.

"Oh! Yes?"

She turned to see the grinning, walnut-wrinkled face of the captain's steward. "Brought you a chair, ma'am," he repeated. "An' a length of old sailcloth for to make you a shelter, for the sun will be powerful strong when she gets up."

"Thank you, Gumbril," she murmured.

"It's a pleasure, ma'am. Are you all right, ma'am? Is anything the matter?"

"No, nothing's the matter, Gumbril," she said, turning away. "Thank you for bringing the things for me."

They set up a shelter for her and her maid at the top of the beach: a canvas awning slung from the spreading branch of a tall tree. While Suzie slept in the soft sand close by, Emmie sat and watched the proceedings below.

The tide, now fully out to the limit of the headlands at each side of the bay, had left the *Delaware* totally stranded in a wide, flat sea of gleaming sand. Behind the frigate stretched a long, stout cable connected to an anchor driven deep in the sand. It was by hauling upon this that she would eventually draw herself out of the bay, stern-first. Meantime, between tides, the carpenters and blacksmiths were repairing the damaged hull. Emmie had been informed by Gumbril that the damage was worse than had been feared: instead of making a clean hole in the planking, the unlucky ball had smashed one of the main ribs, causing extensive hurt along much of the port side. It might take two tides, possibly three, before the work could be completed. The island—an unnamed and uninhabited

strip of sand and rock off the American seaboard—
might well be their home for two days and more.

She watched all that morning, and was still watching
when the tide crept back in again across the sand,
slowly enveloping the *Delaware* in its clutches, bearing her up and setting her masts skyward again, till
she rode true in the water upon her safe anchors,
awaiting the next ebb.

Gumbril brought Emmie and her maid a hot meal
of boiled hard tack and biscuit from the alfresco galley
that the ship's cook and his minions had set up among
the trees. Emmie ate sparingly, and sipped a little of
the Bordeaux wine that had known so many masters.
From time to time, she could not help but let her gaze
stray to the shoreline. It was there that, seated upon
an upturned chest, facing out across the bay where his
vessel rolled gently to her anchor in the now peaceful
sea, Captain Grant ate his fare. He must have been
aware of her, but made no sign, giving not so much as
a glance in her direction. It was obvious that she had
done, or said, something to give him offense, but what
it could have been was beyond her imagining. Only
once had she insulted him, and that was when she had
accused him of lying with her maid—but the accusa-
tion had only been in her mind.

Through the long afternoon she pondered upon the
strangeness of his behavior, and received no enlight-
enment; she could not understand why the thought of
him obsessed her, a man she had known only for a
few days, and with whom she had had the briefest of
converse.

Suzie, now that she had recovered from her fright
and her seasickness, was showing signs of restless-
ness. Her dark-eyed gaze strayed longingly toward
those of the ship's crew who formed the shore party.
These men, numbering about a dozen, had stripped to
their breeches and were playing rough games along
the shore: wrestling with each other and indulging in
the sort of lighthearted horseplay enjoyed by school-

boys the world over, laughing and joshing, exercising
their lean, strong bodies, heedless of the two women
up by the trees. Still heedless, and in unselfconscious
innocence, they stripped to the skin and plunged into
the boiling surf, chasing each other like young seals,
climbing upon each other's shoulders and leaping high
over the oncoming waves. Moved, despite her modesty, by the grace and beauty of their naked bodies,
Emmie felt obliged to avert her gaze, and the more so
when, coming out of the water, the sailors dried themselves by racing up and down the beach like a herd of
colts. Suzie missed not a moment of the sight, but
follqwed their every move with her longing eyes, her
hands ever straying to ensure that the neckline of her
blouse was displaying her smooth shoulders and
bosom to the best advantage. And so the afternoon
wore on.

It may have been that something of the black girl's
restlessness communicated itself to her mistress, for,
when the sun had sunk lower and a cool breeze set
the leaves rustling above her head, Emmie was seized
with a desire to take a walk. This she did, leaving
Suzie to enjoy her nude sailors. Emmie set off through
the trees toward the gentle slope of a rocky escarpment that encircled the bay.

Beyond the trees, the breeze took her hair and blew
it in abandon, molded the muslin gown to her body,
caressed her arms and shoulders. She kicked off her
slippers and left them behind to be picked up on her
return, walked barefoot on turf that was as soft as an
Eastern carpet.

Halfway up the slope, she turned to look back
across the bay, The frigate, like a toy boat in a pond,
lay in a shimmering sheet of glassy stillness, displaying
no sign of life till, clearly across the intervening space,
there came the shrill call of a bosun's pipe. Below, on
the beach, the sailors were sprawled in attitudes of
sleep, their nude bodies dark against the startling
white sand. Of Captain Grant there was no sign; his

sea chest lay close by the shoreline with his uniform coat draped across it.

Emmie went on her way, resolving to reach the highest point of the escarpment and see what lay on the other side of the island. The slope became steeper toward the summit, and she grew hot and breathless. Being well beyond the scrutiny of the men on the shore, she paused and peeled off her silk stockings, and then her gown, leaving the garments on a rock. She would take them up on her return. Clad only in her thin shift, she felt a curious sense of freedom from physical restraint, at one with the elements of sun and air that played upon her body, alone and untrammeled.

She came to the crest of the escarpment and saw that her journey was not yet over, for a screen of trees obscured the view ahead and below. She walked toward them and entered the thicket, out of the sunlight and into the shade, till all ahead was blue sky and sea, and she was looking down a steep slope like the one she had just ascended, into just such another bay as the one in which lay the *Delaware*.

And the bay was not empty. . . .

Four ships lay at anchor. Three she recognized easily as frigates like the *Delaware:* long and lean and rakish-looking, with one line of gun ports along their sides. The fourth vessel was twice their size and more, and it had two lines of gun ports: a battleship. She gazed in dawning recognition at the flags that curled lazily at their mizzenheads, the insignia of her own country, the White Ensign of His Britannic Majesty's Navy. The *Delaware* was not alone in her sheltered isle!

A score of ideas teemed into Emmie's mind. What she should do, of course, was to make her presence immediately known to her countrymen down below. The simplest method would be to go back and retrieve her gown, and, waving it like a flag, attract their attention. Someone on those crowded decks—one of the sailors, or one of the red-coated Marines—would spot her. In no time a boat would be sent ashore. She would give them the news that a disabled American privateer lay within their grasp just round the other side of the island, half of her crew and her captain ashore, a sitting duck for their guns.

Why, then, did she tarry? Why, when she had only to step out of the thicket into the sunlight, where her stark white shift would surely be picked out, did she shrink from sight behind a tree, gazing out and down with the greatest caution, as if—*as if she did not want to be seen?*

She faced the self-accusation, and found herself guilty. Moreover, her guilt once admitted, it was easier to compound her crime. She admitted to herself that, not only did she not intend—had never intended—to betray the Americans to her countrymen, but her one and most pressing desire was to return to the beach with all haste and warn Nathan Grant of his peril. And that having been admitted, she crept quietly away.

Half a dozen paces through the thicket, she heard a twig snap underfoot a few paces distant, and, turning, she came face to face with the captain of the *Delaware*.

Nathan Grant was shirt-sleeved, his lawn shirt unbuttoned to the waist, revealing his well-muscled breast and the neat pelt of fine black hair that stretched from throat to waistband. He was hatless, as ever, and one lock of hair hung across the cruel scar that marred his brow.

She met his gaze, uncaring that the exiguity of the flimsy shift revealed the most intimate contours of her body to those searching blue eyes, aware that her heart was beating a wild tattoo and that her lightly-draped bosom was rising and falling to her quickened breath and that, surely, he must divine the reason for it.

"I watched you," he said evenly. "From first to last, you never had any intention of betraying the *Delaware*."

She shook her head. "Never."

He took the few paces that separated them, looked down into her eyes. The whole of her world, the sun-blessed island where they stood, the lark that sang overhead, the wind in the top branches, the grass beneath her bare feet, all nature and all life were gathered into one, and became part of the hands that he extended toward her bare shoulders to draw her to him.

There was a steep gully leading down from the copse at the top of the escarpment. It descended like a cleft in the flank of the island, separating the two wide bays. At the base of it, far below, the sea lapped the shore of a tiny beach of white sand, a secret and inaccessible place locked by the sea. Hand in hand, with Nathan Grant leading, they descended the natural steps that led down the gully, barefoot, both, upon the warm rock. When they reached the bottom, he held her at arm's length and feasted his eyes upon her.

"You are so beautiful," he said. "Do you know that?"

"I would wish to be anything that would please you," she whispered in reply.

His hands stole gently over her shoulders, drawing down the shift over her breasts, her belly, her smooth hips, till it fell in a silken pool about her feet. With a small moan, she pressed herself to him, her fingers stealing inside his opened shirt front, questing the firmness of his flesh, the male-scented richness of his taut skin.

Taking her up in his arms, he brought her to the side of the gully that lay in cool shadow, close by the edge of the sea, where the sand was still warm from the sun that had just left it; there he laid her down, with his bundled shirt as a pillow for her head. She waited, her arms spread to receive him, and watched

him unfasten his waistband and let his breeches fall,
and her heart cried out for tenderness at the sight of
his male nakedness.

He stooped over her, taking her small face between
his hands and raining kisses upon her eyes, her lips,
her ears, the soft places of her neck, her shoulders,
nipples. She responded in kind, her mouth seeking to
know every part of him. And in these tender devices,
the two lovers delighted themselves in gentle innocence, till their mutual yearnings became more urgent
and abandoned. . . .

It was as if she were being borne shoreward on the
breast of a giant comber, lying just beneath the surface
in a world apart. It was as if a great power had entered
into her and she were able to exist out of time and
place, neither breathing nor thinking, merely existing.
The rhythm of the deep became part of her, and she
of the deep, and in her iridescent world beneath the
surface, she let herself—willed herself, with savage
eagerness, stinting nothing in her total abandonment—
be carried on and ever on by the great power that had
entered within her, till the waters broke, and she was
triumphantly borne into the sunshine and the living
air, to lie gasping and replete.

"I love you so much." She breathed the words in
his ear.

"And I you," he said. "From the first. There was
never a moment's doubt but that I wanted you above
all others."

She made a small *moue*. "One would not have
thought so from the offhand way you have been treating me since last evening."

He dropped his gaze, frowned. "That was—nothing. A misunderstanding."

"But why—why?"

He met her eyes again, reached and stroked her
cheek with his fingertip. "You won't like it."

"Then I shall have to dislike it," she said. "I won't
have any secrets between us, Nat."

"It concerned Tredegar," he said. "Last night, after dinner, he was boasting in his cups."

"About me?"

"Yes. About you—and your maid."

"What did he say?"

"I wasn't present. I had it only at second hand, from O'Leary. Tredegar boasted before them all that he regularly bedded both mistress and maid."

"And you believed the story?"

Grant drew a deep breath and said, "I knew he was having his way with your black girl, for I saw him coming out of her cabin at two in the morning."

"That would be the night you worked on the pumps?" she said quietly.

"Yes."

"I see. And on that evidence, you believed that I, also, was taking Tredegar as my lover?" Her voice was steady, her eyes watchful. Only by a slight tremor of the nether lip did she betray the importance of that vital question.

"In my jealousy, I both believed and disbelieved," he said. "The question of proof hardly entered into my thoughts. In the words of your national poet:

> 'Trifles light as air,
> Are to the jealous confirmations strong,
> As proofs of holy writ.'

My only concern was that, if it was true, could I go on loving you? I decided to put the question to the test. I shut you out of my mind. Ignored your presence as much as I was able. Treated you with scant civility, so that you would avoid my company."

"And? You found the answer to your question?" she asked.

"A day and a night have gone past," he said. "In the effort of shutting you out of my mind, I have carried your face, your name, the sound of your voice, the scent of you with me all the time. You have never been further from me than the next breath. Down there on the beach, when I saw you walking up the hill, it was as if you were walking out of my life. So I came after you."

She lowered her eyes modestly. "And you found your answer."

"I found you, in love and joy, to be chaste," he murmured against her ear.

"You took my maidenhead," she said. "And I rejoice that it was you—the only man I have ever truly loved, or will ever love."

"Emmie. Oh, Emmie."

He rained kisses upon her anew, till she was crazed with ecstasy and moaning with pure delight to the touch of his lips and hands. And then she was being gathered up in the maw of the great waters and carried along in triumph to a distant shore.

Their two bodies, his so dark and hard, hers yielding and pale rose, coupled in splendor on the bone-white sand, with the sea lapping at their bare feet with every incoming wavelet, alone in their private paradise.

And when he had taken her a second time, they lay and talked, their arms entwined, head to head, gazing up at the illimitable blueness of the sea and sky.

"What are we going to do, Nat?" she asked. "What are we going to do?"

"I don't know," he admitted.

"You are married also?"

"Yes."

"Children?"

"There was a girl. She died in infancy."

"I'm sorry."

"Everything passes," he said.

"What's she like—your wife?"

"Rather small. Delicate. I want you to know, Emmie, that we have never shared a bed since the child was taken. In fact, we scarcely know each other anymore. I haven't set foot in Providence since war was declared. When it's over, I don't think she will want me back. We shall live apart for the rest of our days. And what about you, Emmie?"

"As you know, I am married by proxy to the military governor of Quebec," she said bitterly. "He is sixty years of age to my twenty-four. A marriage, you might say, between summer and wintertime."

"Why, Emmie, why?" he asked.

"Why did I marry him? Because I had no choice. My uncle the marquess said it was either that or the streets. My husband paid a very large sum of money for me, and, if Tredegar is to be believed, I was chosen because I am young and have nice breasts. Do you think I have nice breasts, Nathan Grant, Captain, United States Navy?"

Rolling over, he beat his fists, impotently, into the yielding sand.

"Stop it, for God's sake, Emmie!" he cried out.

"My darling!" She reached out and took his hand in hers. "I'm sorry. Forgive me for hurting you. But it has to be said. I am another man's chattel, like his house and his coach, his silverplate and his horses. In law, he may do with me as he wills. If I displease him, he may whip me. My body is his to use as the fancy takes him. That is the law. That is what it means to be an Englishwoman in this year of grace, eighteen hundred and thirteen."

"Emmie—dearest Emmie." He stroked back her raven hair.

"But, though his chattel, my darling," she said, "and though he may use my body as he wills, I shall never cease to be yours. You, the first man I have ever known, will own me and be part of me for as long as I live."

They kissed. There was no more talk. They dressed, she in the flimsy shift that was no concealment from his admiring eyes as they walked, hand in hand, up the steep gully to the copse at the top of the escarpment.

They looked to see the British squadron, but saw

only four sails on the horizon, and two of the frigates were already hull-down.

"They've gone," she said.

"And to the southwest," he said. "That leaves me clear for a run to Portland with the news of their whereabouts."

Their eyes met, the same question in both.

"I shall put you on the first suitable ship we encounter," he said. "Be she British or neutral, I'll let her go on her way in peace, provided the captain pledges to take you direct to a Canadian port. There's nothing else for it, Emmie."

"Nothing else at all," she whispered. "Oh, my darling."

The repairing of the *Delaware* was completed on the next ebb. Grant himself inspected the repairs from both inside and outside the hull, walking around her, criticizing the work, displaying more than his usual persnicketiness, so that the anxious carpenters and blacksmiths were for a time afraid that he would demand that the work be done all over again. It was as if, said one of them afterward—and only in jest—old Nat wanted them all to spend the rest of their lives on the damned island.

They left on the evening ebb, with Emmie standing a discreet distance from Grant on his quarterdeck, watching with an elaborate display of casualness as he gave the orders for the helmsman and for the topmen on the highyards, loving him in her mind and sensing the touch of his hands upon her body, the feel of him possessing her. Casual still, she bade him good night and went down to her cabin, where the girl Suzie had laid her supper. By an unspoken agreement, she and Grant had ceased to take their meals at the same table as the unspeakable Tredegar, but ate in their own separate quarters. It was Emmie's great fear that Grant would abandon discretion and take the Englishman to task for befouling her reputation in front of his officers; for that reason, she had feared to disclose to her lover that the blackguard had also attempted to rape her. For that, she guessed, the captain of the *Delaware* would possibly have killed his prisoner.

So, in discretion, they parted on the quarterdeck, and Emmie ate her supper in solitude. When six bells of the first watch rang out, she stripped naked and bathed herself all over, afterward scenting herself with rose water. For her lover's further delight—though she was never one for the artifices of the toilette—she touched the corners of her eyes with a little kohl to give a look of mystery; that done, she put the slightest possible trace of rouge to her lips, and, after a moment's thought, to her nipples. And then she lay down on her cot—and waited.

He came to her quietly after midnight, closing the cabin door behind him and shutting the bolt. There must have been some rain, for his boat cloak was sparkling with droplets in the candlelight. He threw it off and stripped himself to the skin. Soundlessly, she stretched out her hands to take his as he approached her.

The good *Delaware* made a calm passage throughout that night, sailing through light airs with not a sail or a lamp sighted; there was no call for the captain to be sought out and brought on deck. The calmness above was not matched by the storms of passion that raged on and off in the cabin below, as Emmie and her lover matched ardor for ardor throughout the long night. Not that all was wild abandonment; their mutual passion took many guises, and, as lovers will, they made up delicious improvisations. Sometimes she feigned indifference to him, and he was obliged to employ the most elaborate and extensive caresses as inducement to her responding to his attentions. Emmie continued to display coolness and detachment, while inwardly screaming for release, so that he redoubled his attentions till in the end the dam burst, and she totally abandoned herself to him, moaning and writhing with the torment of her unbearable delight. Sometimes they changed roles, and it would be he who assumed a monkish contempt for her female charms, frowning disapproval as she flaunted herself before him, offering lips, breasts, thighs in shameless abandonment till he could contain himself no more, and they collapsed with laughter, and laughing still, mouth to mouth, gave themselves up to passion.

He left her in the dawn light, and she slept till nearly noon, at which time she was awakened by the sharp crack of a pistol shot. The sound was repeated, and, rising, she swiftly washed and dressed herself and went up on deck, anxious to learn the cause of the shooting.

Grant was on the quarterdeck and with him two of his officers. All three carried pistols and seemed to be in high good humor.

"Good morning, ma'am," said the *Delaware*'s captain blandly. "I trust you slept well."

"And also overslept, sir," replied she, giving him a Roland for his Oliver. "So persuasive to slumber was the gentle rolling of the ship. But why the shooting?"

"Ma'am, we are at pistol practice," said one of the officers. "One of the men is throwing empty bottles from up in the bows, and we attempt to shoot them at a dollar a hit. So far, we have won five dollars between us from Captain Grant."

Grant scowled and looked severe. "I am not, perhaps, the best pistol shot on the ship," he said. "A fact of which these gentlemen seek to remind me on every possible occasion."

"Would you care for a shot, ma'am?" asked O'Leary.

"I have never fired a pistol in my life," said Emmie.

"It is simplicity itself," said Nathan Grant, handing her his weapon. "See, the hammer is at half cock and

is perfectly safe, for you cannot pull the trigger till it
is brought fully back, and that you do not do till the
moment you fire."

He was standing close to her, his firm hand steady-
ing hers that held the pistol. So close to him that she
could smell his maleness: the amalgam of leather and
gun oil—and something else, something she recognized with amusement to be the rose water scent that
had rubbed off her naked body in close contact with
his.

"And how do you take aim, sir?" she asked.

"I do not speak as an expert shot, not like these
other gentlemen present," said her lover. "But I am
told—and pray correct me if I am wrong, gentlemen—
that, rather than squinting, one-eyed, down the barrel,
one should point the pistol as one would point a finger
at an object. It's a matter, you see, of being good at
pointing. Do I have it right, gentlemen?"

"Quite correct, sir," said O'Leary, enjoying his
captain's good-humored irony. "I have never heard
the theory expressed better."

"Thank you, Mr. O'Leary," said Grant. "And
now, Lady Devizes, we will see how you fare with
your first shot. Pull back the hammer to full cock—so.
Now you are ready to fire." He turned and shouted
to the man standing on the forecastle. *"Throw!"*

The green bottle came past her at a quite surprising
speed, and the man had thrown it well clear of the
ship. It seemed impossible that she could hit so small
a target as the bobbing neck of a bottle. Remembering
her lover's words of advice, she imagined that she was
pointing her finger at it—and pulled the trigger. There
came a flash from the pan, an instant's pause, and the
weapon discharged its ball with a jolt that made her
hand fly up.

"By God, that was a clean hit!" exclaimed one of
her companions. "Well done, ma'am!"

"It was a fluke," said Emmie, feeling unaccountably pleased. "Beginner's luck."

"Try again," said Nathan Grant. "Another loaded pistol for the lady."

A bottle was thrown. Once again, she took swift aim at the bobbing speck of green as it swept past. Pulled the trigger.

"Another hit!"

"We have a natural-born marksman in our midst!"

They were all smiling at her, full of unstinted admiration at her prowess. Someone slyly suggested that she and the captain should have a shooting match together for a purse of five dollars, but he shook his head and said he would never live down the shame of being bested by a lady on his own quarterdeck.

The episode was brought to a close with good-natured laughter, and Emmie thought little of her unexpected prowess then. But she was to remember it in the time ahead.

Each day they shared together was a day snatched from life, a stolen twenty-four hours to which they had no right by the laws of God and men. Blessedly, the *Delaware* made slow progress in the lightest possible airs. Indeed, one day passed with a wind like the doldrums, when the topsails barely stirred and the ensign hung like a damp rag from morn till sunset. That night, as if to mock the two lovers with the impermanence of their idyll, a great wind blew up, and the *Delaware* lay over on her beam ends and was driven through the water at such a rate that she made up for the distance that she had lost during the day of calm—and more. That night, Emmie lay alone and waiting for her lover, but the flying frigate's captain was needed on deck at every watch, to be consulted as to how much canvas could safely be carried. By dawn, when the wind had died once more, there was a constant passing to and fro in the lobby and companionway outside her cabin, and she knew that he would not risk destroying her reputation by coming to her. It was the first night she had spent unloved and unfulfilled since they had come together—and a doleful presage of the empty years that lay ahead for her.

Every day, now, they were sighting ships. All turned out to be carrying the American flag: merchantmen and fishermen. To each of them, the *Delaware* gave news that a powerful British squadron was operating to the southwest and that they must amend their courses accordingly. No neutral vessel came in sight, and from Canadian waters no Britisher. The *Delaware* sailed on, and the lovers' idyll continued.

"For love of you, my Emmie, I am neglecting my duty to my country in time of war."

This he admitted to her the night after the storm, as they lay together in her cot, bodies entwined, slippery with the sweat of their expended passion.

"How so?" she asked him.

"My clear duty is to put back in the direction of New York," he said. "Instead, I sent that merchantman we came across this morning to give news of the British. I have changed course even further north. To my officers, I have justified my change of plan on the grounds that it is more likely that other frigates—the *Constitution* and perhaps the *Chesapeake*—will be in Canadian waters, and we can join forces and make a foray against the enemy. But, while admitting to myself the wisdom of this plan, I tell myself that we are heading north for one reason and one reason only. To give us more time together, my Emmie."

"You are unjust to yourself, my darling," she told him. "I know you. I know you well, and you would not be going north if it were not your best course of action."

"Tell that to my conscience," he murmured.

"Your conscience wouldn't listen," she said. "And I wouldn't wish it any other way. I love you for everything you are. For being, among other things, the sort of man who would wrestle with his conscience on a matter of principle as to whether his best course of action in going north is less worthy because it also gives him the opportunity to sleep with his mistress."

"Mistress," he repeated. "Mmm, well, it's not a word I've thought of in connection with you, Emmie, but I suppose that's what you are. My mistress."

"I like it," she said. "It has a wicked, sinful ring about it, and I'm proud to claim the title. 'Mistress of Captain Nathan Grant.' How does that sound?"

He gazed down at her, lying with her arms pillowed behind her head, nude and open to his gaze. He saw the few touches of paint and powder that told of her concern to please him, and his own sense of future emptiness was driven away by an overwhelming compassion for the lovely creature at his side. Young, inexpressibly beautiful in face and figure, innocently sensual and ardent to a degree that he, who had known many women, had never before experienced. Yet condemned to the pawing attentions of a rich old man who might live for decades, till all that loveliness grew blowsy and withered, the sensuousness perished in bitterness and the ardor died with memories.

"I think it sounds very fine," he said. "And I hold my head up more proudly for knowing that you acknowledge yourself to be my mistress. And I'm glad as hell that we're going north."

Her slim arms came up and, entwining about his neck, drew his face down to her bosom.

"Then why waste the precious time in repining?" she asked softly. "Every moment we have left should be savored like old wine, or the last echo of a lovely melody. Take me again, my darling, for it's nearly dawn, and I must spend all of tomorrow being civil and formal to you, while counting the hours and the minutes till you are back in my bed again."

With a murmur of delight, he advanced his hands and his lips to devour her with ardor. Emmie was gathered up on the crest of a mighty comber, and all was set for another of their mutual voyages into ecstasy, when a sound broke in upon their great stillness.

"The cap'n—he's wanted on deck!" It was the voice of First Lieutenant O'Leary, harsh and urgent, from the lobby outside.

"I'll rouse him, sir. Leave him to me." Peg-legged Gumbril's voice.

Emmie, gathered rudely from the blissful waves of passion, felt Nathan's hand tighten on her shoulder.

"Well, don't stand there, man!" shouted O'Leary. "Hammer on his cabin door. Go in to him. Tell him that we've just sighted the lights of a ship, and, unless a trick of the British, she's identified herself as the *Constitution*."

"I'll do that right away, sir. But I'll rouse him gently. He's not one to take kindly to being aroused roughly."

"Well, see about it quickly."

"Yessir."

The first lieutenent's footsteps clattered away down the lobby and up the companionway. Nathan was out of the cot and halfway to the door before there came a gentle scratching on the far side of the panels.

"Cap'n, are you awake? Did you hear all that?"

"Yes, Gumbril. I'll be on deck at once."

"Aye, aye, Cap'n."

He struggled into his breeches and shirt by the light of the candle, and Emmie handed him his boots.

"Gumbril knows about us," she said.

"Not from my lips," said Nathan. "But he'll not betray us. You heard how he kept O'Leary away from my cabin door."

"Yes, he's on our side," she whispered. "He's our friend. Dear Gumbril."

He gathered up his boat cloak. Arms about her nude waist, he kissed her lips. One last kiss for her taut breast.

"I may not be back tonight," he whispered. "Good night, my love."

Then he was gone, and a shudder ran through Emmie's frame, for as surely as if she had stared down into her own grave, she knew that their idyll was ended.

It was the *Constitution*. The *Delaware*'s night encounter with her sister ship set in train a disposition of American warships to counter the threat of the British squadron. Because the *Constitution*'s captain was senior to Grant, it was upon the *Constitution*'s captain to make the immediate decisions. The brief conference took place on the *Constitution* after Grant had crossed over the dark waves that separated the two halted frigates. So Grant carried women aboard? That was bad. If the worst happened, if they were not able to wean the British frigates from that battleship, if the *Delaware* suffered a broadside from that sixty-four gunner and was smashed to coffin wood . . .

Get rid of the woman if it was at all possible! Let the Redcoat officer go with her, the servant too. Make toward the shore in the hope of finding a coaster. Any coaster. But tarry no longer than midday.

"At midday, if we don't sight a sail, I must turn back and follow after the *Constitution* to the southwest," said Grant.

They stood together on the quarterdeck, next morning, side by side, their expressions set in the polite masks which they had learned adopt in public. No sign of the turmoil in their minds.

"I pray to God that we sight nothing," breathed Emmie. "I want to go with you. If you're killed, I want to die with you."

"It may come to it," said Nathan. "Death may be our destiny."

Unseen by anyone on deck or in the high rigging, their fingertips met briefly; then he strode to the opposite side of the deck and shouted an order to the topmen.

Let nothing appear on the horizon, prayed Emmie. *Let us turn at midday and go after the other frigate.*

Never let this end. Let this dear, dear ship carry us both to whatever destiny awaits us. . . .

"Sail in sight on the port bow!"

It was the meanest-looking ketch, with kipper-brown sails patched like a scarecrow's second-best coat. A fisherman: they could catch the stink of her at five cables' length downwind. A bearded pirate of a man lolled against her tiller, and a half-breed Indian lay asleep on her hatchway. They comprised her crew. The bearded skipper was persuaded to down sail and come alongside the frigate. He was a French-Canadian and did not give a damn about the war. He had fished off Grand Manan since he was a *garçon*, and had let *les Anglais et les Yanquis* cut their throats as they pleased; he would continue to do so.

But for fifty dollars, sure, he would take madame to the Canadian shore; you could see the good will bursting out from behind the truculence.

"That's settled, then, ma'am," said Nathan Grant, turning to address Emmie. "I don't think you will have any trouble with this rogue. And you, sir"—glancing coldly at Tredegar—"you will be armed, and are charged in the name of the United States Navy with bringing Lady Devizes safely home to her people." The British officer bowed stiffly in reply.

By a hideous mischance (for they had not even foreseen the possibility), there was not even a moment alone to say goodbye. No last kiss. No brief embrace. Without an order from her mistress, the girl Suzie, immediately upon hearing of the fisher boat's approach, had packed Emmie's few belongings and brought them on deck. They were already being lowered down into the ketch.

"It only remains for me . . ."

"I would like to . . ."

"Please, ma'am—after you."

"I was going to say," faltered Emmie, "that I would like to extend my thanks, Captain Grant, to you and your crew, for all your kindness and courtesy."

"It has been an honor, ma'am."

Of course, she could give him her hand, and who could see anything wrong in him kissing her fingertips? One last kiss of fingertips to suffice for a lifetime.

"I hope we may meet again, ma'am, and in happier circumstances."

"Yes," she breathed. And surely everyone must see her tears.

They helped her over the ship's side. Old peg-legged Gumbril was the last to release her hand. There was no one within earshot when he whispered: "God bless you, ma'am. I'll watch over the Cap'n and keep him safe, never fear. And I hope you two may meet up with each other again."

"Thank you . . ." she choked.

The cord that bound her to her lover and the ship and that had nourished their brief idyll was broken. Blinded by tears, she waved to the tall figure that she knew to be standing on the quarterdeck, looking back at her with an emptiness in his heart that matched her own.

Part Two

The Wilderness

Chapter One

The skipper of the fishing ketch, one Lefevre, showed an early disinclination to be agreeable. From the brooding manner with which he regarded Tredegar, it seemed possible that he was contemplating the means to rid the Englishman of the pistol in his belt and then of the twenty-five dollars—the second half of the payment to be made upon their safe arrival on Canadian soil.

There was one all-purpose cabin aboard the ketch, and it stank so vilely of Lefevre and his half-breed that Emmie much preferred the deck, where there was only the stench of rotting fish guts to contend with. She seated herself upon the hatch cover and composed herself for an eternity of emptiness, till she reached Canada—and whatever fate awaited her there.

Tredegar, with whom she had not exchanged a word all the time they had been aboard the *Delaware*, chose the bows for his perch, and squatted down beside the inboard end of the bowsprit, from whence he flashed occasional, sly glances in Emmie's direction. And so the ketch made her way to Canada.

The first night, Emmie shared the hatch cover with Suzie, with only her cloak for cover. The second night, it rained, and she was obliged to take shelter, along with Suzie and the three men, in the narrow cabin. Lefevre had lashed the tiller, and the old ketch made what way she could against the weather. Overcome with nausea at the stench—a nausea compounded by the effects of the supper of boiled fish, which was the sole diet aboard the ketch—Emmie slept fitfully in an upright posture, seated on the end of an unmade bunk, her head lolling against the hard bulwarks. Tredegar sat beside her, Lefevre and the half-breed opposite, and Suzie was curled up on the deck between them.

Emmie was simultaneously awakened and thrown bodily to the deck by the impact of the ketch's keel against rock. The second jolt, which tore out the small vessel's underside and sent the water rushing in, also dashed Lefevre's head against the iron cooking stove and brained him. Suzie was underneath her and screaming. The single tallow dip that lit the noisome compartment had fallen out of its socket and had been extinguished by the sea water that already lapped, ankle deep, on the deck. Someone put a booted foot in the small of Emmie's back and strode over her. It was Tredegar: she saw him silhouetted against the night sky as he wrenched open the cabin door and clawed his way out.

Next instant, the ketch struck rock again and rolled on her beam ends. A further inrush of water goaded Emmie to action. Seizing the screeching Suzie by her wrist, she dragged the black girl on all fours toward the door. There she was met by a wall of white water that rushed the length of the small craft's deck and wasted itself inside the cabin.

"Milady, oh milady, we's gonna be drownded!" wailed Suzie.

"Shut up, and hang on to me!" snapped Emmie.

Now, the boat's keel was snagging bottom with every onward lurch. Gaining the deck, she was able to see white surf along a coastline; a fang of glistening black rock swept past them close by. Tredegar was clinging to the mainmast, like a man at a whipping block, head bent, eyes closed. Through a gap in the ragged clouds, a full moon lit the scene as light as day. And the rain still streamed down.

The shore seemed deceptively close, and the temptation was to leap over the side, abandon the doomed vessel, and swim to safety. Emmie resisted the impulse, and was grateful for resisting it when, after what seemed an age of their wild onrush, the breakers seemed no closer.

Their arrival at the shore was announced by continuous jarring crashes as the craft's keel came into contact with the bottom. One almighty impact, and the ketch would go no further, but bowed over before the incoming combers that broke over her decks. The masthead came crashing down, shattering the bulwark a foot from where Emmie and the black girl crouched. From all around came the sound of breaking timbers. The sea, unable to swallow the ketch whole, was devouring her piecemeal.

Stark against a white wavecrest loomed the figure of Tredegar. With a crazed cry, he leaped over the side and disappeared in the tortured waters. And Emmie knew that her only chance of life, and the black girl's only chance of life, was to follow him. The ketch had become a coffin ship.

"Come, Suzie," she shouted in the other's ear. "We're going to swim to land."

"Eeeeh! I can't swim, milady!" shrieked the wretched girl. "Is'll drown in there, milady."

"Not with me at hand you won't!"

There was no call but for her to leap over the side, pushing the panic-stricken Suzie before her. The ketch gave a mighty roll before an oncoming comber, top-

pling on her beam ends and sending both women into
the trough of the previous wave. As the waters closed
over Emmie's head, she thought—quite calmly and
with detachment—*and now, I am going to die*. Instants later, her head broke the surface close by the
staring eyes and the plastered hair of the black girl.
Something jarred against her shoulder. It was the
ketch's hatch cover. She seized hold of it, screaming
to Suzie to do likewise. In this manner, clinging to
their lifesaver, they were washed ashore on a pebbly
beach, where they fell, face downward, coughing the
salt water from their lungs as they slept from total
exhaustion.

Emmie woke at dawn to the tang of wood smoke. At
the top of the beach the half-breed Indian had made
a fire and was crouched before it, head bowed as if in
prayer. Tredegar was standing over the fire, holding
his uniform coat close by the flames, so that a thin
plume of steam arose from the scarlet material. Suzie
lay asleep close by her, her splendid bosom rising and
falling steadily.

Tredegar looked around as Emmie got up and approached him, but the half-breed continued to stare
expressionlessly into the flames.

"We're in Canada," said Tredegar harshly. "That
much I can get from this damned heathen. We must
be pretty near the frontier, so there will be army out-
posts hereabouts. God, I crave a drink."

Emmie sank on her knees by the fire, stretching out
her hands toward the comforting flames. In doing so,
she became aware that she was displaying the deep
cleft of her breasts to Tredegar's gaze and that he was
glancing covertly down at her. With one hand, she
drew the edges of her bodice closer together.

"I've tried to get this brute to go and find water,"
growled Tredegar, "but I might as well talk to myself."

Emmie did not reply. After a while, he put on his uniform coat and buttoned it to the neck. It occurred to Emmie that, despite the fire, she was shivering with cold, having on only a velvet bodice and skirt with a shift underneath. Her cloak was back aboard the wreck.

"What's more, I've lost the damned pistol," said Tredegar. "Or I could hold it under this animal's nose and make him jump-to and fetch water."

There was no sign of the wreck. Looking out to sea, she was able to trace the course that the ketch must have taken on her last voyage to destruction. They must have passed close by a tangled mass of rocks about a mile offshore, and the first blow had been sustained there. Now as calm as a millpond, with tiny wavelets lapping on the beach, it was hard to imagine how it had been a few brief hours ago.

"I'll go and look for damned water myself," said Tredegar peevishly.

She did not spare him a glance as he turned and strode toward the dense woodland that started at the top of the beach. She glanced up sharply when he cried out: "By heaven! I am glad to see you fellows!"

Three men had come out of the thicket. Two were in scarlet regimentals of the British army; the other was in Rifle green. All were hatless, but wore filthy cloths knotted about their brows as sweat rags. They carried short carbines, and pistols were stuck in their belts. Their once-white breeches were stained with ancient filth, and one of them walked barefoot. All three men were looking straight past the officer who had addressed them, and were regarding the woman by the fire with lustful leers on their unshaven faces.

"What formation are you from, men!" demanded Tredegar harshly. "Speak up, now. You, the sergeant. Answer me!"

The man who wore sergeant's chevrons on his scarlet sleeve slowly transferred his gaze to the officer, and the grin never left his face.

"Do you hear what the major says, lads? He wants to know what formation we're from."

"You could call it Hell's Brigade," sniggered one of his companions.

"Or the Devil's Company," supplied another, baring his mouth in a wide grin to show blackened stumps of teeth.

"Stand to attention when you address a field officer!" snapped Tredegar. "By God, I'll have the three of you flogged when we reach the outpost!"

"Did you hear that, lads?" said the sergeant, who was tall and rangy, with a thatch of red hair hanging in tangled locks beneath his sweat rag. "The major's going to have us flogged when we get back to the outpost."

"Be silent!" raved Tredegar. But a shrill edge had entered his voice, and his weak face fell apart when his outburst only served to send the three men into a wild chorus of mocking laughter, so that they clung to each other and wiped their streaming eyes with the backs of their grimed hands.

Watching them, Emmie was seized with a great dread, and her dread increased when, pausing in his mirth, the man in the Rifle green nudged one of his fellows and pointed down the beach to where Suzie, roused from her sleep by their noise, was sitting up and staring at the newcomers, bemused.

"By all that's holy, the major's got *two* wenches with him!" exclaimed the sergeant. "This must be our lucky day, lads."

"I fancy the blackie!" observed the rifleman.

"You'll take what's given you," declared the sergeant. "Fetch her up here and let's take a closer look. Myself, I've a taste for that raven-haired morsel by the fire."

"Now see here, men . . ." Tredegar made a last attempt to impose his authority. It won him a cut across the mouth from the back of the sergeant's hand.

He staggered and nearly fell, blood splattered across his weak chin.

The rifleman dragged Suzie up the beach, laughing at her screams and aiming playful slaps at her shapely rump.

"Milady, milady, save me!" wailed the black girl.

The sergeant cocked an eye toward Emmie. "Milady is it?" he commented, and mouthed an obscenity. "I've always fancied throwing my leg over a nob of the aristocracy. I'll attend to you later, milady."

The torment of the terrified black girl was greatly protracted. It was watched by Tredegar, who made not the slightest attempt to intercede on her behalf; some of it was watched by Emmie, who knew that to intercede would only hasten the moment when she, also, would be subjected to their combined lusts. Only the half-breed Indian remained with his head bowed, impassively gazing into the flames.

Two of them held Suzie's arms while the third stripped her nude, tearing blouse and skirts to rags and ripping away her shift in one piece. Then her first tormentor, the sergeant, handled her body as if he were buying a horse at a fair. She screamed when he roughly kneaded her full breasts, but her screams turned to a piteous whimper as his hands sought out her loins. Emmie closed her eyes and tried to will her mind to shut out the thought of the obscenities that were being wrought upon the soft body of poor Suzie, the young woman who so loved to be gently bedded by a vigorous swain. They took her, one after another, and when they had finished they shamelessly fastened their breeches and exchanged coarse-mouthed comments upon their individual performances. They totally ignored Suzie, who, sobbing brokenly, dragged herself away to the fire and flung her arms about Emmie, who smoothed her kinky locks and wiped away the sweat and tears from her face.

"Here come Black Crow and his fellers," said the sergeant.

Out of the forest strode half a dozen Indians, their shaven heads and near-nude bodies glistening with oil, their faces daubed with ocher. At the sight of them, the half-breed by the fire cried out with alarm, and, leaping to his feet, raced off along the shoreline. This won a guffaw from the soldiers, and, at a nod from the sergeant, the rifleman raised his carbine to his shoulder, took swift aim at the fleeing figure and fired. Without checking his stride, the half-breed hurtled forward onto his face. His legs continued running for a few moments as he lay in the sand, and presently they were still.

"Back to camp, lads," said the sergeant. "Come on, milady, you will walk alonger me."

Emmie walked beside the sergeant as he loped through the greenwood. She did not pause for an instant, lest his hand reach out to take her. After her stumbled Suzie, clutching the rags of her shift to the front of her body, yelping every time the men behind her slapped at her bare buttocks. Next came Tredegar, his face a mask of horror and apprehension. After him padded the silent and impassive Indians.

It was clear that they had had the misfortune to be taken by a party of British deserters who had allied themselves with a band of savages. It was not a combination that boded well for the future of the two helpless women and the hated officer. Emmie speculated in dread upon that possible future. It was certain that she herself would share Suzie's fate, though whether she would suffer concerted violation or be reserved as the personal concubine of the sergeant and ringleader was a matter for speculation. She guessed the latter. From time to time he cast her a sidelong—and apparently appraising—glance. Helpless as she was, vulnerable as she was, and possessing a body whose charms her wet velvet gown did little to conceal, it was odd that she had not yet even been stripped, or partly stripped, for their lustful inspection. Perhaps the sergeant, intent upon possessing those charms for himself alone, had refrained from exposing them to his men for fear of arousing their lusts beyond the call of obedience. Taken all in all, Emmie decided that this must be the case. She had been chosen by the leader. Fearfully, reluctantly, she came to the conclusion that it was a circumstance which, if handled carefully by herself, might lead to her advantage. . . .

They came at length to a clearing in the forest in which stood a cluster of rude, log-built huts set around a campfire. Two other deserters came forward to greet them, and their eyes feasted upon the beautiful woman at the sergeant's side, and upon the nude black girl. When one of them tried to paw at Emmie's bosom, the sergeant rebuked him with a foul oath—more proof of his intent toward her.

"We'll have a meal," announced the sergeant, "and while we're eating, we'll have some sport with the gallant major. You, milady, will sit alonger me." Taking Emmie by the wrist, he pulled her down onto the ground. The others, Indians included, formed a seated circle about the campfire. Pieces of roast meat were taken from a long spit above the fire and handed around. The sergeant offered a haunch to Emmie, who refused with a shudder.

"What about the wenches?" shouted one of the men who had remained in the camp. "When are we going to have a taste of the wenches?"

"You'll have your piece of handy dandy all in good time," declared the sergeant. "I've a mind to tickle my appetite by putting the gallant major through his paces. Bring him forth, there!"

Two of the grinning deserters dragged Tredegar into the seated circle. Not that he made any struggle, but came willingly enough, his expression washed of all hope. His eyes fixed for a moment, pleadingly, upon Emmie. She looked away, ashamed of the contempt that his wretchedness aroused in her.

"You see before you," said the sergeant, pointing to Tredegar with his haunch of meat, "you see before you a major of Foot. The Twentieth, if I read his facings aright. You know his kind, lads. At the orders of such as he, you have hurled yourselves against fences of bright bayonets, into the sabers of charging cavalry, walked toward the great black cannon balls that come bounding across the battlefield, taking off heads and limbs along the way. Worse than that, at the orders of such as he, you have been tied to the tail of a cart and whipped till the flesh hung off you in bloody rags. At the orders of his like, you have formed a hollow square and stood to watch one of your comrades hanged for the outrageous crime of striking an officer."

"That's right enough!" shouted someone at the other side of the circle. He had an arm round Suzie's bare shoulders and was forcing the black girl to eat from his haunch of meat. "You have a right silver tongue in your head, Sarge, and no mistake."

"String him up!" shouted another. "Let's see him dance a jig from a treetop!"

"We'll think of something better than that," declared the sergeant. "First, we'll see what manner of man lies beneath all that braid and those epaulets. You there"—pointing to the shrinking figure before him—"take off that fine coat."

Tremulously, Tredegar did as he was bidden, dropping the uniform coat in a scarlet pool at his feet.

"Off with your shirt!" commanded the sergeant. "Ah, not a bad pair of shoulders on him. They feed 'em well in the officers' mess. It's the nourishment as makes the difference. They eat like pigs. Drop your breeches, pig!"

Tredegar's hunted eyes sought out Emmie's, as if entreating her to intercede with the brutes about her and spare his shame. Again, she lowered her glance from him. When she looked up again, he was entirely nude.

"Very fine," commented the sergeant. "For a namby-pamby kind of feller you ain't badly hung-about, bless me if you ain't. When did you last pleasure a woman, hey? Answer up smartly."

"On—on shipboard," mumured Tredegar in a dying voice.

"Speak up loudly, so all can hear you, pig," commanded his tormentor. "On shipboard, you say. When on shipboard, and who did you pleasure? Was it milady here?"

"It was the b-black woman," stammered Tredegar. "I—I have not had—congress with Lady Devizes."

"And it's a blessing for you that you ain't laid hands on milady, or by my oath I'd geld you with my own clasp knife," shouted the sergeant. "So you pleasured the blackamoor wench, eh? Bring her forth, there. Stand her in the center."

The frightened Suzie was dragged to her feet, her pathetic rag of clothing was snatched from her, and she was pushed into the middle of the circle. They stood together: he, tall, pale and straight; she, small, black, rounded and comely. Both in terror.

"Bring a whip," commanded the sergeant. And Suzie screamed.

A grinning deserter came back with a six-foot hide whip of the sort used by army mule drivers. "Who do I give it to, Sarge?" he demanded. "To the major?"

"Damn you, no!" shouted the sergeant. "Would I spoil a good woman when you lads have still to work your lusty ways on her? No, give it to her. Set to, wench! Flog the pig, and keep flogging him till I tell you to stop. And if you don't lay on hard enough, I'll step out there and give *you* a taste of the lash."

The girl Suzie looked to her mistress for guidance, but Emmie had no counsel for her. The wretched Tredegar was staring at the whip in the black girl's hand as if its dark coils were those of a snake. He was trembling from head to foot.

"Set to, black-a-moor!" bellowed the sergeant,

making as if to rise, "or I'll flog the hide off you where you stand!"

Wild-eyed with terror and apprehension, Suzie drew back her whip arm. The action lifted her right breast, subtly altering its contours in a manner that was not lost upon the vile and debased men who gazed upon her nakedness, but drew an appreciative murmur from all sides.

Emmie closed her eyes before the lash fell. When she heard the thwack of leather on flesh and the scream of agony it drew from Tredegar, she clasped her hands over her ears. Blessedly, it shut out the sound of the protracted torture that followed, the more so because the audience was howling encouragement to the black girl and applauding every whiplash. Emmie crouched for an eternity, eyes shut, ears blocked, while the hideous clamor went on all about her. When at last it died down, and she removed her hands and looked about her, the afternoon sun had lengthened the shadows across the clearing. Three of the deserters were dragging Suzie away toward one of the huts and the rest of them, some Indians included, followed after. Of Tredegar there was no sign.

A protracted belch at her side announced that the sergeant was still with her. He cast her a sidelong glance, tossed aside a gnawed-at bone and wiped his mouth on the sleeve of his coat.

"And now it's you and me, milady," he said. "Unless it's your taste to join the black-a-moor wench and be tumbled by all of 'em."

She shuddered. "No," she whispered.

"There's wisdom in you, milady," he said. "Now I'll tell you about those lads of mine, and how they treat a wench. What they like best is to have a wench tied up by her wrists to the branch of a handy tree in the camp, and there they keep her, day and night, convenient-like for to go and cut themselves a piece of the handy dandy whenever the spirit moves 'em." He reached and, taking Emmie's arm at the softness above the elbow, drove his horny-ended fingers into the yielding flesh till she cried out with pain. "Tell me straight, milady, is that what you'd like for yourself— to be strung up for all comers to take when they fancy? Answer me now."

"No-o-o-o!" breathed Emmie.

He grinned with pure pleasure, as will a schoolmaster who, by application of logic, example, precept and exposition, has brought the light of truth to the mind of a dull pupil.

"There, you see, milady," he said. "I knowed there was wisdom in you. You've been reared gentle and know how many beans make five." He winked. "I've another question for you now. Consider in your mind—how can you best avoid being strung up for all comers to take, like yon black-a-moor wench? Answer me directly."

"I . . ." Emmie choked on the unspeakable.

"Yes?" Again he squeezed her arm in a pincer grip, and his foul breath fanned her face. "I ain't one who likes to be kept a-waiting. And I'm a great one for changing my mind. . . ."

"I—I must submit to you," whispered Emmie.

"You must do one hell of a lot better than that, milady," leered the other. "Oh yes, by the devil! If you've a mind to be Sarn't Dick Mendigo's wench, and his alone, you'll have to do one hell of a lot better than play the sacrificial ewe." He bared his broken teeth in a lustful grin and leaned forward to whisper (and surely not for reasons of moral delicacy) a suggestion so blatant in lewdness and explicitness as to make Emmie draw breath in horror and lower her eyes.

He was still addressing her, pouring evil over her. It seemed to Emmie that she was back in the dark street behind Drury Lane, with the latter-day Mohocks preparing her for defilement with the same hideous devotion; she was hearing the brute called Snakey cataloging her charms in the same drooling and licentious terms as the creature beside her, while pawing at her flesh.

And then she saw—*it*. . . .

The pistol stuck into his belt was very similar to the one that Nathan Grant had pressed into her hand on the *Delaware*'s quarterdeck that unforgettable morning after their night of sublime passion. . . .

Quiet. Think. Forget this creature's mouth that is spewing filth, forget his questing, lewd hands.

What was it Nathan had told her? *"The hammer of a pistol, when at half-cock, is perfectly safe."*

So, to carry a loaded pistol in one's belt (and would any of these human animals carry a weapon that was not available for an instant killing?), one had it at half-cock, which is to say that the flint on the hammer was safely clear of the priming powder in the pan—safe, that is, from a spark caused by accidental jolting. Was this creature's pistol loaded or unloaded . . . ?

"Hey? What do you say to that, milady?" He was addressing her in a manner that demanded an answer, chucking her roughly under the chin and forcing her eyes to meet his. But what had been his question?

"Y-yes," faltered Emmie by way of reply. And for good measure: "Of course."

" *'Of course.'* " Sergeant Dick Mendigo flung back his head and gave a riot of laughter. "She says, 'Of course'! Weel, in all me life, I never heard the like, s'welp me." He went into another paroxysm of unholy mirth.

Emmie's eyes slid cautiously toward his waistbelt, fled away when he recovered his composure and fixed her gaze.

"By the devil's own hell-brew," he declared, "I never knew a tuppence-ha'penny barrack-gate doxy as would agree to pleasure a poor soldier after *that* manner. My, you're a shameless lot, you gentlefolk, when it comes to saving your precious skins, strike me dead if you ain't." And he went off into another round of laughter.

She looked quickly. The hammer of his pistol was clear of the priming pan by a clear inch, and the pan was closed. Her heart ceased its frantic pounding, and she felt a curious sense of peace.

"Well then, milady," said Mendigo at length, "we'll to the handy dandy, which promises to be a memorable contest." He seized her by the wrist and led her toward one of the huts that surrounded the campfire, and Emmie went unresistingly. "And to think," he declared, "that a nob of the aristocracy will be a-pleasuring me in a manner that a tuppence-ha'penny barrack-gate doxy would be ashamed to consider."

From the other side of the camp, a woman's scream died away in a whimper that was drowned by a chorus of brutal laughter. Poor Suzie was not suffering unwatched, or unmocked.

There was a rough pallet in the center of the earth floor of the hut, and it was there that Sergeant Mendigo thrust Emmie, and grinned down at her while he divested himself of his belt and pistol, his heavy uniform coat, and kicked off his boots. The coat he slung down at the foot of the pallet, the belt and pistol lying beneath its scarlet folds. Mendigo's knobbly fingers then went to the buttons of his breeches.

Emmie swallowed hard. "Would you, please—might I have a drink?" she whispered.

He looked knowing. "A drink, eh?"

She forced what felt to her to be the merest travesty of a coquettish smile, and contrived to let her bodice slip from one smooth shoulder—no difficult feat after the rendings it had received. The sight of her would have turned an anchorite to lusting.

"If you please—Dick," she said.

He licked his lips and went about the task of pouring a stiff measure of stolen army rum from a stone pitcher into a tin mug—this he performed at a rough table in a corner of the hut, his back to her. When he turned again, the muzzle of the pistol was pointed directly at his thickly pelted chest. Hefting the weapon two-handed, she brought it to full cock. The harsh click of the lock sounded surprisingly loud in the airless hovel.

"You wouldn't dare!" he growled. A man who had faced death in the field a score of times, and was in no way dismayed by a frightened, trembling girl with a pistol that was too heavy for her to hold properly.

"Don't try me," whispered Emmie. "I have never been so scared to desperation in my whole life—save once. If you take a step toward me, I'll fire."

"And miss!" he sneered.

She shook her head firmly. "No, I would not," she promised him with conviction.

His grin faded before her assurance, so he tried another tack. "And what'll you do, milady, if I don't step toward you?" he demanded. "Shall you, perhaps, blast me in cold blood, as the saying is, and then run for the forest, to escape?"

Emmie did not reply. In truth, she had thought no further than to arm herself against violation, to prevent which she would have killed the brute before her— would still kill if he came at her—without hesitation.

"For I have to tell you, milady," continued Sergeant Mendigo, "that you'd get no further than the tree line afore one of my fellows brought you down with a carbine ball clean through the back of the head."

Emmie shuddered. She had seen it happen. The memory of the wretched half-breed on the beach was too close for comfort.

"Or," resumed her tormentor, "suppose the lads didn't hear the pistol shot that did for me, and you got clear away unseen? Come nightfall, they'd find me cold and stiff in here. Did you but put five miles— twenty—between you and this camp, Black Crow and his fellers would track you down before dawn, moon or no moon. Those Iroquois scouts can follow a woman by her scent. And they've a great taste for the scent of womanflesh, have those fellers. I tell you, I would never be able to look my poor old mother in the face again if I were ever party to delivering a maid like you into the hands of the Iroquois. And may I be struck dead if I lie.''

The pistol was heavy in Emmie's hands, and tiredness made her lower it to her lap, though still keeping the muzzle pointed at the man before her. Taking the action as a sign of irresolution, Mendigo, like a keen advocate who sees the witness faltering before his forensic skills, hastened to press home his supposed advantage.

''See here, milady,'' he said in a no-nonsense, let's-get-down-to-brass-tacks, good-fellowship sort of voice, ''you've been treated ill, and I'd be the last to deny it. But escape is hopeless. We can't afford to let you run into an army patrol and bring 'em down upon our camp. One step beyond the tree line and you have to die. So why attempt it? Why not stay here?''

''As your concubine?'' she asked bitterly. ''Thank you—no. I would rather die.''

He spread his horny hands wide, all sweet reasonableness. ''Who spoke of a concubine?'' he asked. ''There's no shortage of the handy dandy, not in our trade. Not with frontier families fleeing either from the redcoats or the Yankees. Not to mention the Iroquois squaws who're always willin'. No, milady, what I offer you—since you can't be allowed to leave—is the respectable position of housekeeper.'' He gestured about him, to the earth floor, the ceiling of rough thatch, the tumbled pallet where Emmie still crouched.

Housekeeper! The idea almost brought a smile to her lips. *Chatelaine of a cutthroat's hovel!* The marquesses of Beechborough must be stirring and groaning in their marble catafalques at the notion!

Taking her silence for consent, he turned back to the table and reached for the rum pitcher. ''Be in no hurry to make up your mind, milady,'' he advised her. ''But let us pledge a toast on it, you and me. To our

future fellowship! For you're as lively and spunky a
lass as I ever clasped eyes on, strike me dead if you
ain't."

She stared at him in disbelief as, turning, he raised
the pitcher to his lips, winking at her the while over
the rim of the vessel. Was he really serious in sup-
posing that she would accept his offer? Or was it simply a trick?

It was a trick. . . .

She saw the knife in his hand the instant he produced it from behind his back, having picked it up
from the table. The sinewy arm went back and was
flung forward before she had time to think, let alone
to scream, or to fire the pistol. And he did not take
the pitcher from his lips.

The impact of heavy blade and handle knocked her
backward on the pallet with the force of a mule's kick.
Oddly, there was scarcely any pain, only that terrible,
never-to-be-forgotten experience of being struck. That,
and the awful shock of seeing a knife sticking out of
one's own bruised and bleeding flesh.

She heard his voice, cursing, triumphant, telling
how he would have his way with her while life was
still in her. She saw him coming at her, hands grab-
bing.

She pointed. Pressed the trigger. Saw the splutter
of the priming powder. Felt the weapon come alive in
her hand and obliterate the sight of Sergeant Dick
Mendigo's face in a sudden blossoming of stinking
white smoke.

Finally, the unbearable pain struck at her, and she
escaped it into a sudden pit of blackness.

They were shouting for Mendigo across the camp,
calling to him to know what was amiss, and had he
shot the wench? Drunken, careless voices from men
too bemused to comprehend.

Emmie rolled off the pallet and sobbed with the
stabbing return of the pain. The knife had entered her

right shoulder just below the bony protrusion of the joint and at the outer limit of the slope of the breast. There was some blood, but not a lot. She touched the hilt of the weapon and felt the shock of her trembling fingertips transmitted through the length of the blade and deep into her flesh.

The knife must remain. To induce any further pain must be to render herself unconscious again. How long had she been senseless already? Obviously not more than a few moments. No one had come in response to the shot. Not yet. But they would soon be on their way, though not—if the far-off, drunken laughter was anything to go by—very soon.

Escape . . .

To reach the door was to pass by the sprawled form lying in her path, and she had not yet brought herself to look at the upturned, dead face. There was a compulsion to do so as she stepped over the body. Sergeant Dick Mendigo was staring up at her with an expression of mingled disfavor and mild surprise, while a hole the size of a marble in the center of his forehead bubbled a small fountain of bright carmine.

Emmie peered out of the door and across the campfire. There was no sign of the band, neither deserters nor Indians, only the laughter from beyond the huts opposite where they had earlier been tormenting poor Suzie, now silent. Emmie stole out into the afternoon sunlight. Looked this way and that. Ran for the nearest line of pine trees that masked everything beyond in secret shadows. Dry leaves and dead pine cones rustled under her bare feet, and accented the dreadful stillness of the forest. With no notion of which way to head, Emmie took the straightforward option of going directly away from the camp. She advanced at a stumbling, painful run, right hand pressed against her wound and in a small way supporting the weight of the cruel knife, which tugged heavily upon her tender flesh. And her senses were reeling already.

Neither by sight nor by sound did she detect her

pursuer; only the dread sense for menace inborn in all living creatures alerted her to her peril. Reeling against a tree trunk, supporting herself there and looking back, she perceived a tall figure stalking her with not much regard for concealment some twenty yards away. Dressed in a coat and leggings of skins and carrying a long rifle, he had the looks, in the shadowed forest, of an Iroquois, but his head was unshaven, and his hair, worn in two plaits, was as white as bleached bone. She could see him in no further particular than that. Whether friend or foe, she had no way of telling. She slumped back against the tree and awaited her fate.

"*Qui va là?* Who are you?" His voice was deep and harshly inflected, gravelly, accented. Not one of the late Sergeant Mendigo's fellows, nor an Indian.

Emmie summoned the last of her strength and all the wiles she had left to secure the stranger as an ally before the stunning pain drove her back again to black oblivion.

"I—I am an English lady of title," she said. "I beg you to render assistance to my companion and myself. You will be . . . well rewarded. . . ."

English lady of title. Echoes of Flaxham Palace in the screaming wilderness of North America. Tea on the lawn and peacocks strutting. Obsequious footmen (*oh! my darling Toby Stocker of yesteryear!*). All of it sounded so incongruous, so risible, that Emmie was half-laughing, half-crying, as she slipped to the ground in a deep swoon.

A fast stream ran through a narrow gorge scored by passing boulders of ancient time. It was a secret sort of place, greatly overhung by trees and thick with undergrowth, the home of fox, beaver, otter, marten, fisher, mink and skunk—though not all at once. At that present time, it stank of man—one particular man who had made it his temporary abode—and all the larger animals had abandoned it. A sole marten was

witness to the return of the man carrying his unconscious burden. The marten remained for a fraction
longer than it might when it scented blood. Short legs
poised to take flight, lithe and slender body arched,
and every tip of its dense and lustrous pelt bristled
with anticipation. It was gone in a flurry of bushy tail
before the white-haired man broke out of the shadows
and into the sunlight by the stream, where he laid his
limp burden on a bed of yielding, thick moss and
squatted on his hunkers beside her.

The cruel knife first commanded his attention. His
dark eyes narrowed and he drew breath sharply, suck-
ing it in between very even teeth, shaking his white-
maned head as he made a grim assessment that
directed his hand to the knife. The blade came out
readily enough, and there was some fresh bleeding,
which he staunched with his neckerchief, afterward
cleaning the wound with the chill, pellucid water of
the stream.

From one side of the gorge, a rocky crag had deposited a tumbled mass of scree, and it was among
this that the man had made a cache of his few belongings: a sleeping bag made of soft deerskin lined with
fox fur, a cooking pot, some jerked meat, powder and
ball for his long rifle. He took out the sleeping bag and
laid it like a counterpane over the unconscious girl.
Then, lifting his white-maned head, he gave a high-
pitched whistle. Minutes later, with a loose-jointed,
ambling gait, a lurcher dog came out of the undergrowth and stiffened when he scented and saw the still
form by the edge of the stream; the stiff hair stood up
like a cockscomb all along his spine, and his mouth
gaped in a soundless snarl.

The man stilled the dog's suspicions with a word
and tousled the shaggy head fondly. At a word of command, the animal seated himself close by the unconscious girl—but not too close—and cast doubtful
glances toward the pale, immobile countenance.

He was still sitting there when his master gathered

up his long rifle and ammunition pouch and disappeared into the forest. And there he remained, guardian over the lost scion of the noble Beechboroughs.

Emmie's eyes flickered open and she gasped with pain. A strange face, a man's face, filled her vision. He was touching her right shoulder, which was bare. An imp of modesty prompted her to draw the edge of her bodice over her partly uncovered right breast.

"Are you hurting very badly?" he asked. And with the repetition of the gravelly, accented voice, she remembered him, as the man to whom she had appealed in the forest.

"The pain—comes and goes," she whispered.

"It is nearly night," he said. "I have brewed you a little *tisane,* a concoction of herbs, which will make you sleep."

"Who are you?" asked Emmie.

"My name is Yves," he replied. "And yours?"

She told him.

"Emmie Devizes," he repeated. His lips—he had curiously long and mobile lips—twisted in a smile of recollection. "And an English lady of title, yes? Or so you said."

Emmie nodded.

"Ma foi! We are honored!" The man Yves made a gesture toward something just out of Emmie's vision. She turned her head to see the big black lurcher dog crouched close by her elbow. He blinked and licked his lips encouragingly.

"This is Raoul," said Yves. "And now I will attend to the *tisane."*

There was a campfire, a small heart of intense flame that gave off not a discernible puff of telltale smoke. He tended it with a tiny bellows that he worked between finger and thumb, exciting the little pile of pine wood chippings to white heat. As she watched, he added a pinch of dried herbs to a pannikin that was suspended over the fire at the end of a sapling. A curiously sweet-sour aroma played at her nostrils.

"Soon it will be ready," he said.

The sky above her—a small patch of blueness bounded by the ring of trees encompassing the gorge and the rocky bluffs on both sides—was darkening. An evening star glittered coldly. Beyond the pain, the weakness that held her down, the confusion of mind, Emmie was aware of an urgency to act, a need to give shape and substance to something that must be accomplished now, straight away, before it was dark, before she slipped back into unconsciousness again and it was too late.

She remembered. . . .

"Monsieur . . ." she began.

"Yes," he said. "Call me Yves."

"Please, you must rescue my companions," she begged him. "Now! Tonight! Heaven knows what agonies they've endured already. We were captured, you see, by a band of English deserters and some Indians. Iroquois . . ." The effort of speech sapped the strength from her like water from out of a hand. His face before her lost shape, crazed, broke, faded.

She emerged from the darkness of mind again, to find him dabbing her brow with his dampened neckerchief.

"I will give you the *tisane* now," he said. "You must sleep, for you are very weak from shock and loss of blood. In the state that you are in, you could easily be stricken of the fever and your wound go sour."

"Please," she whispered. "There is a girl back there. A black maidservant. Her name is Suzie and she must have suffered the torments of the damned. If she's still alive, if those deserters and savages haven't done for her, I beg you to try and . . ."

"The deserters," he said, "they are the worst. What the Indians do in their untutored savagery, the

Englishmen do in calculated malevolence, knowing full well what evil they are about. Here is your *tisane*."

She feebly brushed aside the pannikin as he advanced it toward her lips. "And there's a man," she whispered. "An English major. Heaven knows, I owe him no regard, but no human being deserves to be treated the way they were treating him, the way some children will pull the legs and wings off flies. . . ."

"The *tisane*—drink," he said quietly.

Feeble still, she continued to resist him.

"You must help them!" she pleaded. "There will be danger for you—yes. But I will see that you are well rewarded. My husband, you see, is the military governor of Quebec Province. You must have heard of him—Sir Claude Devizes. General Sir Claude Devizes."

"To Quebec I do not go often," he replied.

Feeling that she was making no headway against his wooden imperturbability, she nevertheless persisted: "Monsieur—Yves—you are a hunter, or something of that sort, I suppose?" she asked.

"I hunt—yes," he replied.

"You are not a rich man, I guess."

He shrugged. The wide and expressive mouth answered her without words.

"Then," she said, "even if, in human charity, you will not raise a finger to aid that wretched pair, you will surely make *some* attempt for money. More money, I promise you, than you would earn in a year's hunting."

Again that Gallic shrug. "It would not need to be much, at that," he declared.

"*Two* years'!" she cried. "*Ten* years' wages—if only you will go back there and make *some* attempt." Her voice rose almost to a scream. "If only to find out if they are alive or dead!"

"Lady, they are dead," he replied.

She stared at him.

"You—*know?*"

He nodded.

"How do you know?" She began to tremble.

"Lady, I have just come from there," he said. And wearily, laconically, he told her how, while she had been unconscious, he had left her in the dog Raoul's charge and retraced his steps toward the deserters' camp. And as he spoke, he gently raised up her head against his lean and sinewy arm and placed the pannikin of *tisane* against her lips. She drank the ill-tasting brew as meekly as any child, listening to his every word, with slow tears coursing down her smooth cheeks as the horror unfolded.

He had not discharged his mission without risk— that much was obvious, though he did not make much of it. He had run into an Iroquois sentry on the edge of the camp. They had fought, and the outcome of the duel was that Yves lived; he did not dwell upon the fate of the redskin.

So potent was the *tisane* that Emmie's eyelids were drooping despite all her efforts to stay alert. And he had the wisdom to protract his account so that she was more asleep than awake when he came to speak of her former companions' ends. He did not particularize about the manner of their dying, nor did she dare to ask him, but shed more tears of compassion and, weeping still, passed into a profound and dreamless sleep.

He watched over her till the moon came up and illuminated the secret bower by the tumbling stream. By its light he removed the crude bandage from her shoulder and inspected the knife wound. It had stopped bleeding, but the flesh was bruised over an area the size of a man's hand, and the mouth of the wound itself had an inflamed and puffy appearance that caused Yves to shake his head and purse his lips.

Toward midnight she grew feverish. A dew of pearly sweat stood out upon her brow and formed rivulets in the dimpled hollows of her neck and in the deep cleft of her bosom. He damped his neckerchief in the cool stream, wrung it out, and gently, so as not to waken her, wiped away the sweat through all that long night. When the dawn chorus of birds in the high treetops awoke the echoes of the forest, he was still there, sleepless, alert, attentive.

By daylight, it was clear that Yves's worst fears had come to pass. The harsh privations that Emmie had suffered had left her with no reserve of strength with which to combat the cruel effects of her terrible wound. A severe fever had struck at her, and the wound was mortified. Yves had no other medicines save the herbs known to forest dwellers, no instruments save his own hunting knife with which to bleed the girl and expel the evil humors. Bleed her he did, and of some six ounces, after which the heated flust left her cheeks and her agonized threshing was quieted. She slept like a babe till noonday, when he gave her a few sips of the *tisane* and was concerned to note that she did not recognize him, nor did she have any awareness of her surroundings, but called like a small child for her "mama."

That night came the crisis in the fever. At times, her agonies were so great that he was constrained to pinion her arms for fear that she would tear the rough bandage from her wound in her mindless exertions. One moment she was all afire and slippery with sweat, the next she shivered as if with the ague. It was during one of the latter conditions—and shortly after midnight—that Yves, desperate for means to keep her warm, lay down under the sleeping bag and wrapped his strong arms about the tormented girl, nourishing her soft body with his own body's warmth. He did not take the slightest advantage of the circumstance to make lustful excursions against the helpless, beautiful creature imprisoned in his arms, but lay quietly with her, she with her head upon his breast, till the warmth of the morning sun permitted him to quit his patient's side and prepare a fresh *tisane* for her.

Emmie made some progress that day, but did not completely recover consciousness. Yves washed her wound and was satisfied to see that no pus had formed within it and that the angry inflammation had subsided. As she lay quietly and at peace in the warm sunlight, he removed her rent and blood-caked bodice, likewise the skirt and petticoats that had suffered the depredations of sea and forest, washed them all in the stream and laid them out to dry. He then addressed himself to the task of bathing the dried sweat and blood from the nude body of the unconscious girl, which he did with gentleness and with the devotion of a mother.

Late that afternoon Emmie stirred and opened her eyes, looked about her in puzzlement. The yielding mattress upon which she lay proved itself to be a bank of moss and white clover, and her counterpane to be of deerskin. She felt curiously lightheaded, bewildered in her mind, and, oddly enough, very hungry. A delicious scent of cooking prickled at her nostrils and caused her to raise her head and investigate the source.

A few paces from her the man with bone-white hair was crouched over his small fire, working the bellows with one hand, stirring the suspended pannikin with the other. He looked around upon perceiving her slight movement.

"I think you are better," he said. "So I am making you some soup. Very mild. Nothing but herbs and the yolk of a lapwing's egg. What you smell is the clove of wild garlic I have just put into it."

"How long have I been—ill?" asked Emmie.

"Two days and two nights," replied the other. "Do you remember what happened?"

"Yes," whispered Emmie. "Your name is Yves. You brought me here. And . . ." Another memory touched the edges of her mind, but she thrust it away from her.

"How is your shoulder?"

"Not so painful as it was. I . . ." Emmie drew a sharp intake of breath as, fingering the bandaged wound, she became aware that her shoulder was bare and—horrors!—her breasts also. Furthermore, the briefest of probing revealed to her that she was entirely nude under the deerskin sleeping bag. Her eyes flared wide with alarm and met his steady gaze.

"Your clothes are drying on the bushes over there," he said with a careless gesture in their direction. "They will be bone-dry by the time the sun goes down. Would you like your soup now?"

"Yes, please," breathed Emmie.

"Can you sit up unsupported?"

"Yes!" she said hastily.

But she was weaker than she would have believed, and when she was seated upright and he was crouched beside her, she very soon found it impossible to remain erect without the buttress of his shoulder. To her profound relief, Yves held the pannikin and spooned the warm soup between her lips, leaving her hands free to hold the deerskin in place across her bosom. The soup was excellent.

When he had fed her, she lay back again and drew the covering up to her chin, her dark kitten's eyes regarding him warily, this man who—there was really no other explanation—had almost certainly stripped her mother-naked and (by the feel of her skin: dry and smooth after being sticky with blood) washed her all over. By hand! And was now sitting as calm as you please on his hunkers and chewing away on a knob of dried meat of singularly unappetizing appearance which he had produced from a leather sack hidden under a nearby fall of rock. And casually regarding her, from time to time, as if she were no more than an appendage, like his dog. She had to say something to break the—for her—strained silence.

"Where's your dog?" she asked. "Raoul, isn't that his name?"

Yves pointed to the heights above them, across the stream. "Raoul is keeping watch," he said. "If anyone ventures this way, he will warn me in good time. And silently."

"Anyone? *Who* might come this way?" she demanded in sudden alarm.

"The Iroquois," he replied. Biting the end of the knob of jerked meat, he sawed with his hunting knife, severed its connection with the remainder held in his hand, chewed upon it thoughtfully for a full minute and continued: "Chief Black Crow knows me, knows my handiwork. He will want revenge for the spirit of that brave I sent to the last happy hunting grounds beyond the setting sun."

"They'll find us here!" Emmie sat bolt upright in alarm, but not so alarmed as to forget to keep herself covered.

He shook his head. "No," he said. "This gorge is a forbidden place to the Iroquois. 'Bad medicine,' they call it. They will not venture down here; they do not believe that anyone who did could possibly leave this place alive. Convenient—for you and me."

In her relief, she was able to bear the long silence that followed his declaration, which gave her the opportunity to scrutinize her companion covertly as he ate. The question of his age was a puzzlement, for the unnaturally white hair laid more years upon him than he could possibly have possessed, since he had the physique of a man in his prime. His countenance, though weather-beaten and scored with lines of character, was markedly agreeable to look upon. The white hair apart, his eyes were his most striking feature, being of the deepest possible blue, like lapiz lazuli, and with a reflective gaze that was disconcerting to meet. Now, when he glanced her way, he caught her looking at him and sent her eyes scurrying to the sight of her bare toes peeping from beneath the end of the deerskin cover.

"So it is to Quebec that you want to go?" he said.

She nodded. "Yes. If you take me there, you will be well rewarded, I promise you."

"Quebec is a long way."

"Then perhaps you could guide me to the nearest British army fort. I can be escorted on from there."

He shrugged. "The only fort in the territory is at Fredericton, but that has been abandoned and the soldiers moved to the frontier and beyond. There will be much fighting. It is not a good time to be traveling in these parts."

"But I must get to my husband!" cried Emmie. "I should have been in Quebec weeks ago. With no word of me after all this while, he will think the worst."

And if he does, she thought, *will he greatly grieve for the young wife he bought at such a high price and never saw? Ten thousand for the best pair of bubs in Oxfordshire, and never to have laid a finger on them. Poor Sir Claude Devizes, poor old rake!*

The disconcerting eyes lingered upon her as if probing her thoughts, which Emmie certainly did not wish to share. She looked away.

"It would take two, three weeks to reach to St. Lawrence," said Yves. "Even by canoe. But you are in no condition to travel. And the frontier is all aflame with war. You will rest here for a week, perhaps a little longer."

He put the last piece of meat into his mouth and carefully cleaned his knife by driving it in and out of the soft turf.

"And then you will take me to Quebec?" asked Emmie.

"Your clothes are dry now," he said. "You can put them on."

She avoided his eye, making no move. When she looked up again, he was walking away from her; he did not turn, but disappeared into the undergrowth that skirted the stream.

Chapter Two

"Have you always been a hunter, Yves?"

It was evening. He had moved her under a tree, where she was able to sit up with her back supported by the trunk. Dressed once more, with her linen clean and—though unironed—sweet smelling from running water and sunshine. For supper he had prepared a simple omelette of lapwings' eggs spiced with a sprinkling of basil and a pinch of rock salt, all served on maple leaves and eaten with the fingers. A far cry indeed from the gargantuan repasts in far-off Flaxham Palace, but Emmie decided she had never enjoyed a meal more in her life. The feeling of a gratified appetite, of well-being after sickness, quite dispersed the memories that had preyed upon her dreams and waking hours, so that even the recollection of her brief idyll with Nathan Grant seemed no more than a delicate sweetness, far-off and insubstantial, like the trace of basil that had informed the omelette. In her mood of tranquillity, she felt disposed to learn more about her companion.

He did not answer her for quite some time, and then he said guardedly, "My father was the hunter. I learned everything from him. Everything." For once, his eyes avoided hers.

"And where is your home, Yves?" she asked.

"My home is here," he replied. And he smote the turf with the flat of his hand. "Wherever I stand in the wilderness is my home. Here. Now."

Emmie felt disposed to probe him further. "Have you never felt the need to settle down?" she asked. "Have you never thought to marry and raise a family?"

He ate the last of his omelette, balled the maple leaf in his fist and threw it far into the undergrowth.

"I have been married," he said at length. "And I have raised a family." He got to his feet. "And now you will sleep. There is a frost in the air tonight and it will be cold. Get right inside the sleeping bag and you will be well protected."

"But—what about you?" asked Emmie in all innocence. "Surely you'll need some protection from the frost."

"There is not room for the two of us *inside* the sleeping bag," was his disconcerting reply. "Though it served well enough as a cover for us both last night."

And with that even more discomfiting observation, he turned on his heel and walked away into the undergrowth.

Emmie's young, well-nourished body was bounding its way to a swift recovery. On the night of the frost, she slept in the cosseting envelope of the fur-lined deerskin and woke refreshed. Yves was already awake and about. She was bathing her face and hands in the tangy waters of the stream when he stumbled out of the undergrowth with a young buck slung across his back, antlered head lolling. They breakfasted off its liver, broiled with herbs and washed down with stream water. All day Emmie rested.

That was the pattern of their life together in the secret gorge. Yves was frequently away, but seemingly never very far away, for on two or three occasions when she strayed only a short distance from their small encampment, he stole upon her, long rifle in hand, she having betrayed her presence to him by no more than a twig snapped underfoot, a tumbled pebble.

They ate well, but simply. The lurcher Raoul made an appearance after every meal and uncomplainingly ate up all the scraps, bone, hide and all. The rest of his days and nights were spent, so his master explained, in keeping watch from the heights above.

On the fifth day of their sojourn in the secret gorge, the orderly pattern of their existence was rudely disrupted. It happened shortly after their evening meal. Raoul had returned to his vigil, carrying with him the bone from a leg of venison that his master had slow-roasted in a casing of baked clay. He returned within a few minutes, his bone abandoned. By his demeanor, by the way the coarse hairs stood up in a crest along his back, by the soundless snarl he directed to the heights above, the lurcher spoke his warning plainly.

"The Iroquois are here," said Yves. "He cannot abide even the scent of a redman. So—they are still searching for me after all these days. They must have cast a wide net and convinced themselves that I had not gone so very far. They may have decided, indeed, that there is only one place where I can be hiding. Here."

He was not directly addressing Emmie, but speaking as if to himself, his dark eyes scanning the heights.

"I'm sorry I brought you to this," faltered Emmie. "If it hadn't been for me . . ."

"Black Crow is very determined to track me down," said Yves, disregarding her remark. "That brave I killed must have been very close to him. Perhaps one of his own sons.'' He gestured to the lurcher and snapped his fingers, upon the receipt of which Raoul bounded away, leaped from boulder to boulder across the stream and went back to his post.

''What—what do we do now?'' whispered Emmie.

''We hide,'' replied the hunter. ''That is all we need to do. The Iroquois will not come down into the forbidden gorge. Not knowing for sure that we are here, Black Crow will leave two or three warriors, only, to keep watch—just in case we evade the evil spirits and come out of here alive. Raoul will know where they are. When you are strong enough to travel, we can simply walk out of here. Come.'' Taking her by the elbow, he guided her to a high bank of ferns, whose broad leaves formed a curtain above their heads, through which they were able to see the craggy heights above the gorge, yet remain unseen by anyone up there.

They crouched side by side, shoulders touching, eyes fixed upon the crest. All of a sudden, a flock of wild geese rose into the air, high above the treetops, calling loudly.

''They are here,'' said Yves.

Almost immediately, a dark figure was etched against the skyline high above them. Shaven headed, half-naked, alarmingly menacing. He was immediately joined by others, similarly attired, and accoutered with firearms and bows.

''They're looking down here,'' breathed Emmie.

''Hush! Still!'' whispered Yves. ''The game is all ours. They will not dare to come down. Watch—they will soon be gone.''

But the redskins showed no sign of departing. Indeed, they were gesticulating to each other and pointing down into the gorge. Their guttural voices, raised in animation, carried quite clearly down to the two watchers.

"Something's amiss," said Yves. "They've de-cided that we must be here. But how could they know that?"

And then, a light of understanding burst in upon Emmie's mind, and she knew the answer to her com-panion's question.

"Oh, my God!" she faltered. "It was I who . . ."

'Who did *what?*' The blue eyes burned into her.

"I—I washed out a petticoat this afternoon," said Emmie, "and left it—left it over the bushes down by the stream to dry."

"And they have seen it," he said flatly.

There was no doubt about it. By following the di-rection in which the Iroquois were pointing, and by craning his head through the fern branches, Yves was able to see a splash of white down by the water's edge, and he cursed himself aloud for not having noticed it before.

"I—I'm sorry, Yves," she said.

"We are both sorry," he replied, "and may become sorrier yet."

The Indians' excited chatter had ceased. They stood in line on the lip of the gorge, looking down, a dozen bronzed statues in attitudes of contemplation. One of their number—he was the tallest among them by a head—stepped forward to the very brink and, raising his arms above his head in a gesture reminis-cent of supplication, proceeded to declaim in his own tongue, and the echoes of his voice were reflected from wall to wall of the gorge.

"What's he saying, I wonder?" whispered Emmie.

"He speaks of me," said Yves. "Using the name the Iroquois give me, which is White Water. He also refers to a paleface squaw, and he means you. Black Crow—for that is he—is calling upon the spirits of the forbidden gorge to deliver us up to the Iroquois for vengeance. As I had feared, the brave I killed was close to him: his brother's only son. And if the spirits

will not give us up, he asks them to give us an agonizing death, so that the Iroquois up there can hear
our dying screams and rejoice. . . ."

"Oh, no . . ." cried Emmie.

The terrifying peroration gave its last echo and fell
silent.

". . . and so that the nephew of Chief Black Crow
may also hear in the last happy hunting grounds and
rejoice," added the hunter.

His address concluded, the Iroquois chief made a
brusque gesture to his followers and they quit the skyline.

"What will they do now, Yves?" asked Emmie,
slack-mouthed, staring-eyed with horror.

"They will wait," said Yves. "They will wait in
force, in the hope of hearing our death agonies. As
Black Crow said, even if they have to wait till the
snows come."

"And what shall *we* do?"

The other smiled, tight-lipped, wry. "If we evade
the attentions of the evil spirits . . ."

"Please!" said Emmie. "I beg you, don't *speak* of
such things!"

Yves shrugged. "Very well. We shall move as soon
as you have regained your strength. From now on, I
can no longer hunt game beyond the gorge, and I
would not put it past the Iroquois to make sure that
no game enter the gorge. Or to spread nets upstream
and downstream to deny us any fish." He smiled,
again that wry, mirthless smile. "The Indians, for all
their superstitions, are a very *practical* people, and
see nothing inconsistent in aiding and abetting super-
natural forces with any workaday measures that come
to hand."

Before Emmie could reply to that, the dull, insistent
beat of a tom-tom came from the heights above, accompanied by a hoarse and tuneless chanting from
many throats.

"I had thought they would make the night hideous,"

said Yves. "You will have to stuff your ears with something, or there will be no sleep for you. It will go on till dawn: a prudent precaution on their part, to drive away the evil spirits in case they venture beyond the limits of the gorge."

Night was falling fast. Above the skyline of the gorge, they could see the rosy loom of a campfire. Away in the distance, there came the harsh cough of some predatory animal. The chanting continued.

And then, from near at hand, the high crack of a firearm.

"*Raoul!*" The name sprang to the hunter's lips, and his hand closed about Emmie's wrist as he stared up to the heights.

They listened in silence. Presently, the tom-tom ceased to sound. There came a chorus of laughter— mirthful, jaunty, but disquieteningly off-key—from up there.

"They have got Raoul!" cried Yves.

"How can you be sure?" ventured Emmie, by way of comfort.

"They have him," was the reply. "They know Raoul well, know he is my comrade, and hate him for it. I pray they have not taken him alive."

Another peal of unholy mirth, this time counterpointed by wild whoops, came from above. Yves the hunter snatched up his long rifle, saw to the priming, brought the lock to half-cock, eyes questing the heights. Emmie shrank back against the bowl of a tree, conscious, in that moment of stress, of how weak she was, how ill-equipped, still, to make shift in the wilderness.

By the sun's dying light, and framed in the glow of the campfire above, a figure ran into view, drew back his arm in the action of throwing. The arm went forward and something flew from the thrower's hand. In that same instant the priming of Yves's long rifle spurted to life and the weapon discharged skyward. Emmie clearly heard the impact of the lead bullet striking flesh and bone, saw the redman throw up his arms and fall backward without a sound. And something slammed to earth in the ferns close by. Laying his rifle on the ground, the hunter went to investigate.

He went slowly. Waist high in ferns, he parted the leaves and looked down at what was there. The watching girl saw the sudden agony in his face. He returned even more slowly, and empty-handed.

"What—is it?" she whispered.

"The head of Raoul," said Yves.

The secret cache in the scree contained not only the simple requirements of a hunter's life, but also a squat black bottle. Emmie watched as, not meeting her eye, Yves unearthed the bottle, held it close to his breast as a mother might hold a suckling and took it down to the stream to a spot where an overhang of bluff afforded him protection from the sight—and bullets and arrows—of the Iroquois. He squatted down on his hunkers, drew the cork from the bottle with his teeth, spat it out and, putting the neck to his lips, threw back his head and took a protracted draught that made him cough, choke, retch, gasp. He then essayed another assault upon the spirit.

The hunter consumed the contents of the bottle in four swallows, whereupon he rose, none too steadily, to his feet. He retraced his steps to the scree, searched and took forth another bottle. The performance was repeated. Four or ve swallows, and he threw the second empty bottle into the tumbling waters of the stream, cursing as he did so. An attempt to—presumably—fetch yet another bottle was thwarted by his tripping over his feet and falling face downward upon the turf.

Emmie lay back, pillowed her head in her arms and looked up at the stars. Presently, the Iroquois' tom-toms resumed their insistent rhythm. She would have stopped up her ears with her fingers had not the sound aroused Yves to drunken ramblings.

She listened. . . .

His slurred voice rose above the barbaric drums on the clifftop, calling upon his dead lurcher by name and cursing those men who had slain him. And then he called out another name repeatedly. . . .

The name Marie.

Emmie slept soundly despite the dreadful noise from the top of the gorge and the insane ramblings of her companion. Her healthy constitution reassembled her whole in mind and body and delivered her awake in the first light of dawn. Yves had risen earlier. While she sat combing out her tangled dark mane with her fingers, he came out of the undergrowth carrying a jack rabbit he had trapped in the night.

She greeted him civilly and he responded, hanging his catch upon a tree branch and proceeding to skin and gut it. They spoke not a word as they breakfasted together off some of the last of the jerked meat washed down with a cool draught of water from the stream. The meal over, he then pointed out that area at the bottom of the gorge which, because of treetop and rocky overhang, was rendered safe from the sight— and the missiles—of the redskins above. They were still there; the tom-toms had ceased with the dawn, but the smoke of their campfire rose in the clear blue sky like a challenge.

The safe area that the hunter had indicated included a fair stretch of the stream and its bank. Emmie, who had grown accustomed to bathing herself every morning and washing one or more items of her vestigial wardrobe, lifted her skirts to her knees and stepped into the ankle-deep, crystal-clear water. When she looked around, her companion had quitted the camp. Unhesitatingly, she stripped to her skin and lay down in the stream, so that the cool, mountain-fed benison of the wilderness swirled and eddied over her taut skin, prickling it to gooseflesh.

Did Yves watch her from the fringe of the trees, she

asked herself. She thought not. Nothing in the hunter's behavior had ever prompted her to suppose that he would do anything so underhanded. But as she lay there, drinking in the boisterous refreshment of the torrent, Emmie recalled that an old nursemaid of hers—a cynical old biddy who had wet-nursed, potted, nose-wiped, and taught the rudiments of civilized behavior to half the Beechborough brood then extant—had always drummed into her young female charges that men (who were all animals) were affected by the quarters of the moon (so that all men were lunatics), and were affected in carnal matters by drink. With the example of the orangery before them (brandywine flowed freely throughout the debaucheries), Nanny's young charges had accepted this without question as coming from one who had observed life as closely as they.

Having turned to strong spirits as solace for the cruel killing of his lurcher, might Yves not do it again? And next time, thought Emmie, might not the demon drink inflame his mind to notions of carnality? Nanny would have considered it to be as certain as night following day. It was an alarming prospect for a gel. The question was, did any bottles of drink remain hidden among the rocks?

The question was no sooner asked than Emmie was drying herself upon the petticoat she had set aside to wash that day. She made all haste to the scree, still buttoning up her bodice, with the question still hanging in the air.

There was one further bottle remaining. She took it out of the cache and, uncorking it, sniffed the contents. From whatever hell's brew the stuff had been distilled, it had the capacity to take one's breath away by its stench alone. And the hunter had tossed back two bottles as neatly as a lamplighter! Upon an impulse of disgust, Emmie upturned the bottle and let the contents drain away among the rocks. Her resolve then suffered a setback when she speculated on what might happen if Yves found it gone. In a clumsy effort to restore her credit, she refilled the bottle from the pure waters of the stream, and was washing her small clothes as docilely as you please when the hunter returned. They did not exchange a word, neither then nor at the midday meal nor at supper, but Emmie essayed a "good night" when the Iroquois' tom-toms commenced their nocturnal thrumming. Yves grunted an acknowledgment and settled himself down a respectful distance from her.

Emmie was composing herself for rest when she heard him give a snort of something like exasperation, and she was dismayed to see him striding toward the scree. Reaching the cache, he stooped, took out the bottle, tucked it under his arm and went down to the water's edge, where, in the thin moonlight, he appeared to be weighing something in his mind. Dry-mouthed, the girl watched him uncork the bottle and slowly put it halfway to his lips. A pause—and then, with a loud exclamation, he drove home the cork with a blow of his fist and threw the bottle into the stream.

Emmie heard his approaching footfalls over the ragged beat of the tom-toms and closed her eyes, feigning sleep.

"Lady Devizes," he said. (He had never so addressed her before.)

"Yes, what is it?"

"I owe you an apology for my behavior last night. For getting drunk."

"Let's not speak of it, Yves," she said. "Forget it happened."

"What? Do we live in silence, as we have done all day? Is that how it must be? No, this thing must be spoken of."

"You had cause to get drunk," she said.

"No, no!" he cried. "There is no excuse. It is my ruin. Even out here in the wilderness, I drag myself back to the bottle like a dog goes back to its own vomit. I am like an animal. No better."

"Yves," she said, "I have known you for so short a time, but already I know you are better than that."

"Lady Devizes," he said, "I think I will tell you a story."

Emmie felt a prickle of unease. "I'm not so sure I want to listen," she replied.

"You must listen!" he cried, adding more calmly, "It will explain everything. The drink. My solitude."

"This story, does it concern—Marie?" she asked.

The dark eyes flared with surprise. "What do *you* know of Marie?" he whispered.

"You called out her name last night. Many times."

"Aaaah!"

He sat down, but not very close to her, and began his tale.

He came of good French settler stock, he told her with a note of pride. Those who left the mother country and came to live in what used to be known as "New France" were not the rebels and religious dissidents of the Old World, as was so often the case in the rest of the Americas, but loyal Frenchmen. As such, Yves told her, his forebears had dwelled in Quebec since the days of Samuel de Champlain, founder of the city and province, had fought against the English under the Comte de Frontenac and Montcalm, and against Benedict Arnold and his Americans. Indeed, they had fought too well, striven too hard, protested too loudly and too long. No longer citizens of New France, there was no place in British Canada for the likes of them. The family, which had once owned elegant country mansions in broad acres above the St. Lawrence and stately townhouses in the capital, had pledged its riches for love of country—as well as sacrificing the best and the bravest of its blood. By the time Yves was born, his parents were reduced to scratching a mean living from a small holding rented from an English landlord, where man, wife and children labored from dawn to sundown, winter and summer, merely to stay alive. They got further into debt with every passing season.

His father, Yves told her, was a gentleman in the true sense of the word: civilized, rich with Gallic style, his spirit untouched by successive disasters. When his wife and all but Yves perished in a plague that ripped the province one appalling winter, he buried his dead, gave his slender savings to have masses sung for them and went back to cultivating the narrow field, with himself in the shafts and the eight-year-old lad at the plow handle.

Through his father (whose own father had graduated with distinction from the Sorbonne), Yves learned the elegancies of his own language and of English, by way of Montaigne, Corneille, Pascal and Racine; Shakespeare, Milton and Dryden. Thanks to his father, also, the boy grew up without bitterness or envy toward any man, not even toward the English landlord, a coarse creature of no breeding who rode horse and hound over the lovingly tilled small holdings of his tenants and demanded payment of his rents no matter how disastrous the harvest. "Monsieur Hoskins is not *un gentilhomme,* Yves," Papa would say, "and is not to be judged by *our* standards."

To Emmie, Yves conceded wryly that his father may have been something of a snob and a little of a prig. Papa's head also rested in the high clouds. To his son he confided the notion that his, Yves's, concern in life must be to restore the family fortunes, make enough money to buy back the family *hôtel* in Quebec and the country houses that gazed down so elegantly upon the wide St. Lawrence. Having so confided, Papa would return to his rare and beloved leisure pursuit, the works of Montaigne, Corneille, Pascal and Racine; Shakespeare, Milton and Dryden. There was always the plow awaiting at dawn.

After a trio of particularly hard winters, half-starvation and the consumption took Papa. Yves told how

he buried his sire beside the rest of the family, paid
for a mass and took stock. The road back to family
fortune did not lie in the small holding. Nor was the
sword likely to bring advancement to a young man of
French extraction in the British colony of Canada.
Trade and commerce were the thing. From the dilap-
idated log cabin and half-hectare of bad earth in near-
swampland, the next step must be a small business in
Quebec. But businesses, however small, require
premises, stock, working capital.

In the years that followed, he told Emmie, he made
himself a jack-of-all-trades. After a day's toil on the
small holding, he would work as a tapman in a tavern,
or hire himself out as a laborer. Best of all, he hunted.
His father had been a great hunter—a tradition of the
family dating back to the old days in their motherland
where, as aristocrats, they had enjoyed the rights of
la chasse denied to the lower orders. But it was not
the art of hunting the noble stag on horseback that
Yves had learned from his sire; it was instead the infinitely more subtle business of snaring and trapping,
working with the ferret, the terrier and lurcher, even
with the poor man's falcon, the sparrowhawk. The
youth, his eyes fixed firmly upon a small business in
Quebec as the first step in realizing his father's dream,
hunted meat for the army—any man's army—and
trapped furs that were currently being worn upon the
befrogged dolmans and pelisses of both British and
French hussars opposed in Spain and Portugal.

His enterprise, his single-minded devotion to his
father's dream, suffered the setbacks of the seasons'
vagaries. A bad harvest could wipe out the profits of
a good winter's fur-trapping. Too poor to employ la-
bor, Yves had recourse to no other means than that
employed by peasants the world over: to marry and
produce children, more hands for the plow.

His bride was Marie, the child of a family as good
as his own. She brought no dowry save the work of

her hands and the fruits of her womb. Alas for those fruits! Narrow-hipped, nervous, frightened, she perished in childbirth nine months after the frugal nuptials, leaving Yves—as he described it to Emmie—"the better for God's gift of a girl-baby, no idea of how to raise her, and nothing but a moody and recalcitrant nanny goat to provide her with milk." He named the baby after her dead mother.

The next fifteen years were hard indeed. An aged Iroquois squaw, widowed and cast out by her tribe because her mate had died a coward, served as nursemaid for her food and a pittance, and stayed with them till the child was old enough to join her father out in the narrow field. The child did so as soon as she could reach the handles of the plow and was strong enough to wield a mattock and work the rudimentary treadmill that carried away the water and rendered that sour half-hectare just capable of cultivation.

In Marie's fifteenth winter, it seemed that their luck had changed at last. A good harvest in the previous year had enabled Yves to augment considerably the small nest egg, which, by dint of scrimping and scraping since his father's death, he had always added to, no matter how great the self-denial. The fecund year was followed by a mild winter, with the forests teeming with fur and feather. By the thaw, Yves had amassed a stock of fine pelts, which he sold that Easter in Quebec. While in the city, he took the opportunity of making inquiries regarding cheap business property, and found to his delight that, due to the buoyant effect of the French war upon the economics of British Canada, trade was booming and real estate changing hands at very competitive prices. He and Marie had just about enough money to open a modest store in the city suburbs.

That night, when he returned to the log cabin in the small holding, he took with him a bottle of wine—the first that had been seen in that humble dwelling for many a year. They toasted their success, father and daughter, and pledged to the future. No more would the ordering of their lives be at the whim of the seasons and the rapacity of a landlord. From the day they set foot on their own property—however mean—they would be working for themselves and their own future. Marie, close to sixteen and, despite her hard life, possessing a delicate loveliness that betokened her aristocratic lineage, could hope to possess in a short time a dowry that would enable her to marry well.

And then, *they* came—the spoilers.

They were not evil men, not as the world judges evil men. They were the product of their times. Given influences other than those inspired by his father, Yves might have gone the same way. This much he conceded to Emmie. Like him, they were men of a ruined and disheartened people, but without even the meager blessing of a sour half-hectare. For them there were only the sleazy byways of a teeming city: low taverns, cheap drink, cheaper women.

Somehow, they had heard about the peasant farmer who had been inquiring about property in the city—an unusual state of affairs, but one from which it was possible to construct a simple equation. A peasant prepared to spend a considerable sum of money equals a peasant with a considerable sum of money stuffed into his mattress. Or under the floorboards. Or somewhere.

It was simply a matter of persuading him to talk. . . .

At this point in his narrative, Yves leaped to his feet and walked away from Emmie, so that she thought he had finished telling her all he wished to tell her. She watched him go down to that same spot by the water's edge where he had thrown away the bottle, and there he stood, head bowed, silhouetted against the white water, as the tom-toms thrummed above.

It was a long time before he returned. When he did,

he plunged straight back into his story without any preamble, any breast-beating. . . .

"I knew something was wrong," he said, "as soon as I drew near the cabin. I had been fishing down by the river. It was Sunday. Marie kept a few chickens for their eggs. Chickens have a way of making themselves known when they are uneasy. They were smelling blood. My terrier bitch Alphonsine, who had elected to stay at home with Marie, was lying dead by the door, brained. I burst in to see it all. There were three of them. One of them I actually knew by sight and by name, though he did not know me.

"Already they had started to manhandle Marie. Her clothing was torn and she was crying. Her young, little breasts . . ."

"Stop! Stop!" screamed Emmie, hands pressed to her ears. "No more—no more!"

The sound of the Iroquois tom-toms penetrated through her muffled hearing. His face was in deep shadow, so she could not tell if he was still speaking. She lowered her hands. There was only the drumming.

He said, "I beg you to hear me out."

She nodded. "Yes, if it will help you." What else to say, what else to do, in the face of a tragedy that from a first prompting stretched ahead with a terrible inevitability.

He drew a deep breath and began to pace up and down: five steps one way, five the other, but always within earshot. His voice was counterpointed by the barbaric clamor above.

"They were armed only with cudgels," he said, "but one had a knife, and he was holding Marie. Because of that, I did not struggle when they tied my wrists together and looped the rope over a roof beam, jerking it tightly so as to raise me up, helpless, almost on my toes. And then they told me what they were about. They had come for the money—our nest egg.

"I am not a fool. I knew that certain cards lay in my hand, and I played them with great dexterity, I thought. Oh, yes, I had been making inquiries about property in Quebec, I told them, but on the instructions of my landlord Monsieur Hoskins, who was wishing to invest some capital in real estate. Two of them believed my story; I saw the disappointment in their faces. But the third, the one I knew by sight and name—and the name was Jacques Martin—was more subtle. Said he, 'We will test the truth of your words, man.' And turning to his fellows, he said, 'Strip the girl.' "

"Oh, no!" breathed Emmie. *"No-o-o-o!"*

"Did I tell you she was a lovely, unspoiled thing?" asked Yves, speaking to her from the limit of his pacing, only a dark form in the shadows. "For she was, and I had never seen her nude before. So modest was she that she had never disrobed in my presence, and not after early childhood would she allow the old squaw to be there when she undressed.

"I will say this: they were not harsh with her, but permitted her to remove her own clothes, which she did, frightened, ashamed. But they looked on. And still they looked on, drinking in her young body, as she cowered by the wall, covering herself as best she was able with her hands.

"Then the questioner, this Jacques Martin, turned back to me again. 'I think you are lying, man. Why should your landlord, who has lawyers, bailiffs, notaries to act for him, send a common peasant to do his business in Quebec, hey? Answer that.' And I replied to him, 'I am not a common peasant, but a man of breeding. My grandfather held a commission under Montcalm and was a graduate of the Sorbonne. See, over the fireplace yonder is his sword and a diploma to prove the same. Monsieur Hoskins, who cannot read a word and signs his name with a cross, regards me very highly. Often when I go to Quebec, I perform small commissions for him.'

"And all the time, my mind was racing ahead. And I was weighing the options. On the one hand, the money—our money, Marie's and mine—which lay in a secret cache in the yard, of which only two of us were aware, Marie and I. The proceeds of nineteen years' drudgery in which, since she was old enough to work the treadmill from dawn till dusk, Marie had played her part. Was all this to be given away to a trio of city loafers? Would Marie wish this—she who could hope for a handsome *dot* in a few years' time when our business prospered? I thought not. In my blindness, I told myself that both she and I shared the option: to tell, or not to tell. And I was sure that my quick wits, my ready tongue, would convince these men that they were on a fools' errand. Marie could rely on me.''

Yves ceased his restless pacing, sank down upon his hunkers and was silent for some time. Emmie, who was shedding silent, uncontrollable tears, could not bring herself to speak.

He continued in an oddly brisk tone, as if he could excise the horror by making the narrative busy and matter-of-fact.

''Jacques Martin's companions looked to him, as ringleader, to comment upon my newest affirmation. They were older men than he, less assured, perhaps already half regretting the enterprise upon which they were engaged. Said they, 'Is he telling the truth, and how can we prove him true or false?'

''Jacques Martin had the answer. He looked up at me, cocking his shrewd eye at me hanging there, and said, 'I think you are lying, man, but we shall see.' And to his companions: 'One of you, take the girl. Have your way with her. Over there—where he can see everything.''

Emmie moaned . . .

Yves continued. ''I will say that he treated her gently, the man who took her maidenhead. A strong fellow, about my own age. He did not need to exercise any force. She was like a doe being led to the slaughter. Lifted her up and laid her on the bearskin by the hearth. She whimpered a little, and I said to myself, "We both know what we are about, Marie and I. One word from either of us and this nightmare can cease. Marie knows where her future lies. If I speak, or if she speaks, she will spend the rest of her life in this cabin. Grow old and toothless before her time. Married, perhaps, to some drunken sot who will beat her and give her a child every year, till her shoulders stoop from bearing them and her shriveled dugs hang on her stomach. Is this what she wishes?'

"When he had had his way with her, this man, he was ashamed to meet my eye as I hung there. Marie just lay where he had left her, sobbing quietly and no longer making any attempt to cover herself, no longer caring.

"And then Jacques Martin resumed his questioning. 'Man, I still think you are lying,' he told me. 'So I will listen to no more explanations, but will assume that you have the money and in time will reveal where it is.' I answered him that it was not so, but how could I prove a negative? Why did he not make a search of the place and prove it himself? Let him tear the cabin apart and he would find nothing, I told him. I thought my argument was good, my reasoning sound. God help me!

"And then Jacques Martin turned to his other companion and told him also to have his way with Marie."

The hunter fell silent. The moon had come up over the tall pines, and through her own tears Emmie could see that he too was silently weeping, the droplets coursing down his lean cheek.

He continued, voice still steady despite the profundity of his anguish. "The second man was coarser-grained than the first. A brute. I shut my eyes when Marie screamed, but I could not stop up my ears. I could have told them then, but again my reason intruded. 'Is Marie's torment not a thousand times worse than mine?' I asked myself. 'Yet still she does not speak. It must be that her mind is fixed upon the vision of the future. Our future, as it will be when we leave this hovel. Knowing Marie as I do, knowing her loving unselfishness, it is certain that her entire regard is for me. She sees me as a man who has slaved in the small holding all his life and who will soon be old. If she speaks—she tells herself—Papa will be slaving till he drops.'

"Knowing this, reasoning the cause of her silence, how could I fail her? For myself, I cared nothing. Rather than tell them, they could have plunged the knife between my ribs. And all for Marie. So that she would not spend the rest of her life as a drudge, but marry some worthy young *garçon* of good family. A worthy young *garçon*—it had to be said—who loved her so dearly that he was willing to overlook the fact that she came spoiled to their marriage bed.

"Those were my thoughts. That was why I remained silent while she—my Marie—was screaming into the face of her brutish impaler.

"There is worse to come, Lady Devizes," said Yves. "You show great generosity of heart in listening to me. It is an intolerable intrusion upon your sensibility."

"I wonder that you can tell it," whispered Emmie. "It must be torture for you."

"It is like being torn to pieces," said Yves. "But it has to be done. I can escape no longer. Someone has to hear the echo of the screams that resound inside my head, and I am afraid that you, who have done nothing to deserve such a horror, are that someone. Shall I go on? I warn you, the rest is—appalling!"

"For your sake—continue," breathed Emmie.

"The second man," said Yves, "unlike the first who had had the grace to be ashamed of deflowering my daughter before my eyes, grinned in his pride when he had done with her, buttoned up his lappet and winked at me. I swore on oath to his face that I would pursue him and kill him if it took me all my life. It may be then that Jacques Martin knew that he had

brought me to the brink of my rea on. One more push
and I would crack. And the truth would out.

"I looked toward Jacques Martin. He was looking
at me. Did I describe him to you, Lady Devizes? I
should tell you that he was young—twenty-seven,
twenty-eight. Previously, though knowing him only
from afar, I had formed a certain opinion about him.
His manner during that hellish ordeal confirmed me in
that opinion. I knew that it would not be to his . . .
taste . . . to slake his lust upon my child, for his taste
followed another persuasion. What then had he in
mind? Or had I convinced him, by my silence, that
there was no money after all?

" 'Man, I still think you are lying,' he said. 'Either
that, or this girl is no daughter of yours.' 'She is my
daughter and my only child,' I told him. 'How then
can you watch these lusty fellows have their ways with
her when all you have to do is tell where the money
is?' asked he. 'Because there is no money,' I answered.

"I really thought, Lady Devizes," said the hunter,
"that I had convinced him at last. But this devil incarnate, this degenerate—for such I knew him to be—
had not finished with me, or with Marie. 'Bring the
girl,' he said to his companions. 'Seize hold of her and
bring her over here.'

"You may be sure that my heart turned over with
foreboding as I watched them dragging Marie before
me—not that she offered any resistance, but came like
a lamb. Trembling, whimpering, her eyes lowered
from me in hurt and shame of her state.

" 'You say this is your daughter?' demanded Jacques
Martin. And I told him 'yes.'

" 'Do you love her?' And I said 'yes'—and was
that not proof positive that there was no money? I had
hopes, then, that my logic had confounded him at last.
"My logic—ha . . . !

" 'Then what you love, man, you shall enjoy!' said
he. Whereupon he reached for the belt that sustained

my deerskin breeches and unfastened it. In horror, I saw him peel down the garment and render me naked from the waist down, my manhood and all—exposed to the gaze of my own daughter. And still I did not—could not—divine his foul, his beastly intent.

" 'Bring her closer,' said Jacques Martin. 'Make her kneel.'

"His companions comprehended his design at once, and so did I. Even as I cried out for him to desist, Marie must have had some inkling of what they were about to force upon her. She began to scream and shake her head.

" 'Where is the money, man?' demanded the implacable Jacques Martin.

"All that had gone before, all that I had allowed Marie to suffer—for *my* sake—could not be cast aside without one last throw of the dice. And I swear to you, Lady Devizes, my sincere intent was to retract and confess before the final outrage was committed upon my Marie.

" *'There is no money!'* I cried.

There followed a silence so profound that the very war drums on the clifftop were eclipsed. Emmie held her breath, fearful to disturb the delicate balance between madness and reality upon which she and this strange man were poised. Yet soundlessly she called to him to break the intolerable suspense that encompassed the night.

"And then . . . ?" she prompted him, and instantly clasped her hand across her mouth, shocked at her own presumption.

"And then," he said, "it was all over. Or nearly over. Jacques Martin shrugged his shoulders and, turning to his companions, he said, 'We were mistaken. He is clearly telling the truth. There is no money here. No matter, my friends, you have had your amusement with the girl.' "

"And then they left us without a backward glance. Just as we were. Just as they had rendered us, the two of us: helpless, unclothed, violated. And alone together with our shared tragedy.''

To Emmie, the account had been appalling, as insupportable as drawing one's fingernails down a roughcast wall. There was even worse to follow. . . .

Said Yves, ''Marie did not cut me down till she had put on her clothes. She averted her eyes from my nakedness when she severed the rope with a kitchen knife. Not a word passed between us till I had made myself decent. Then I laid a hand on her shoulder and asked her if she was all right. By that I meant was she in pain, and did she wish me to fetch a physician? I did not have the sensibility—but I tell you, Lady Devizes, I have it now!—to guess at the hurt to her mind.

''Gently, so that I scarcely noticed it, she eased herself from my hold, murmuring that she was all right. I said to her, 'Marie, my girl, you have suffered greatly, but you have won in the end.' 'Yes, Papa,' she replied, and went outside without another word or a backward glance.

''I buried my poor terrier Alphonsine, and contemplating what they had done to that poor, dumb animal aroused my fury anew. Would I pursue them and take my vengeance? It would be easy to track down Jacques Martin. Kill them, all three? What profit there? I would let some time pass, I told myself. Healing the hurt to Marie was more important than vengeance.

''I addressed myself to preparing our evening meal of baked coney, which was Marie's favorite, and took more than the usual care over my task. I laid the table and placed there the remainder of the bottle of wine that I had brought from Quebec. I set candles and a vase of spring flowers, freshly picked. I told myself that we would make a small celebration of our tragedy, an affirmation of our resolve to start a new life together.

''Dusk came. I went to the door and called Marie,

but she did not come. The supper grew cold, and I warmed it through again. I took a sip of the wine; it had turned sour in the bottle.

"I went to look for Marie, and found her a stone's throw from our threshold. She had hanged herself from a branch of a maple tree. She was quite dead."

Chapter Three

Emmie knew at that instant that he had tried himself too far. It had been a hideous mistake to retrace his steps into the past and uncover again the tragedy of Marie.

"Yves, Yves, don't go. Listen. Stay here and let's talk of something else. . . ." She reached out and took his hand when he rose up, staring-eyed and close to madness.

"No, no!" he breathed. "Spare no sympathy for me, Lady Devizes. I killed her! I, the father, killed my own child as surely as if I had put the rope about her neck and kicked away the log upon which she had stood. I need a drink! What did I do with that damned bottle?"

Shaking free of Emmie, he staggered away, looking about him wildly. She heard him stumbling among the scree, kicking over the stones, cursing, mouthing wild and incomprehensible French.

Presently he was quieter. There was only the deep, wrung-out and most awful sound that a woman can endure: the sound of a weeping man. Emmie's heart melted with an ineffable compassion, as presently, also, the night grew chill, and upon every blade of grass and still leaf there grew a lacy garment of hoar-frost. Upon a sudden resolve, she arose, took the deerskin sleeping blanket and went in search of where he lay.

He was huddled at the foot of the bluff, face to the rock wall, knees drawn up, arms folded tightly across his chest. The frost was already forming on the wild hairs that stood out from his white mane and upon the fringes of his buckskin tunic. She knelt and touched his shoulder. Instantly he was awake, and his long hunting knife glinting in his fist. The habits of the wilderness die hard.

"Oh, it is you," he said. "Never do that again. You nearly had this between your ribs. Why have you come here?" He was shivering, whether from cold or from anguish she could not guess.

Emmie was entirely matter-of-fact, brooking no resistance. She spread out the sleeping bag, opening up the soft envelope to display the sleek fur lining. She then slid inside and reached out to take the hunter's hand.

"Come in, Yves," she said. "If I let you perish of the cold, how shall I ever get to Quebec? Come—you've slept with me before. You told me so in no mean terms."

"Underneath it," he said. "Not inside it. There's no room for two inside it."

"There would be," she said, "if you took off that leather tunic and those ridiculous high boots. Come, now. Hurry! I'm freezing cold."

And so, joshingly, making small complaints about his tardiness, encouraging him all the while, Emmie succeeded in getting him to remove his outer clothing and the thick deerskin buskins that reached to his knees. And he crawled into the cosseting warmth of the fur-lined sleeping bag, whose narrow confines dic-

tated that he be brought into close and continuous
contact with her soft body.

"There—you see?" declared Emmie. "Plenty of
room for us both and to spare. Are you quite comfortable? This arm's rather in the way. Why don't you
put it around my waist? Like that. So. Better?"

"Why are you doing this?" he growled in her ear.
He still smelled vilely of spirits, though not as vilely
as before.

"Would you not be more comfortable," said Emmie, "if, instead of leaving your head and most of your
neck out there in the cold, you brought it inside and
laid it against my bosom?" Like a baby he was brought
to nestle against the cleft of her breasts, with her small
hand encompassing his neck, holding him there.

"I have never lain with a woman since that day,"
he said. "The day that . . ."

"You slept with me," she interrupted firmly.

"But not with any desire," he replied. "Since the
day of my chil's ravishment and death, I have been
incapable of pleasuring any woman. I am like—a eu-
nuch!"

"Do you desire me now, Yves?" she whispered.
"Not just a little?"

"Yes. Strangely, I do—but it is useless to hope."

"Mmmm."

Far off, an owl hooted. Near at hand, a gust of night
wind rattled the treetops. He felt her hand move upward to her bodice. A moment later, when he shifted
his head, her bare nipple hardened against his cheek.

"I wonder," said Emmie, "if you would please
scratch my back? That's nice. And now a little further
down. Under the material, please. Heavenly."

Gently encouraged by her purring contentment, the
hunter persisted in his attentions, growing ever more
bold in the pursuit. In the doing, they both became
aware that his emotions had become involved in that
lighthearted game of dalliance she had extemporized,
and that a palpable miracle had taken place within that

fur-lined chrysalis they shared in the frosty wilderness. Step by step, she leading all the time, guiding his hands and lips, whispering sweet encouragement when he seemed to falter, breathing delighted reassurances in his eager ear, Yves the hunter and the lovely young aristocrat soared, in spirit, from their warm chrysalis, mounted up to the eternal glory of the night sky and out into the sunlight beyond imagining, where dreams take shape and become reality. They returned at one and the same time, still joined, mouth to mouth, breathless, replete, spent and satiated beyond all belief.

"In all my life," he whispered against her flesh, "I shall never be able to thank you enough, or repay you, for what you have given me."

"I gave you so very little," said Emmie. "A small part of myself, some affection. Small return for all you've done for me already—such as saving my life."

"What you have given me is my manhood," said Yves. "The manhood that fled from me before the frozen stare of my dead child. My hair used to be jet black, do you know. It turned white the eve that Marie hanged herself because of me, and I have been like a gelding."

"Not because of *you*," she chided gently. "You persisted in silence for her sake, not your own. It was they—the men who ravished her—who drove her to what she did."

Silence.

And then he was weeping against her breast. She felt the moistness gather and form a hot rivulet down the deep cleft to her belly. The wind moaned in the high trees.

Emmie slept till noon, and Yves examined her wound. The healthy young flesh was healing nicely (their exertions of the previous night had not done it any ill); the simple, nourishing diet she had enjoyed in the gorge had built up her strength. The hunter nodded and covered her up again.

"We will leave," he said. "I must get you to the St. Lawrence before the snows start."

Emmie glanced upward to the ragged pencil line of the Iroquois' campfire scratched across the blueness.

"What about—*them?*" she asked.

"We must outthink Black Crow," he said. "The mind of the redman is very subtle. Black Crow will already have decided that we have so far escaped the ministrations of the evil spirits, since our departure from this life was not accompanied by the legendary screams of agony. He will have reckoned that we shall do such and such. We must, therefore, be careful to do no such thing." Yves was not to be drawn out on any further particulars, save that their escape bid would be made during the coming night.

When the sun was high, Emmie bathed in that part of the stream which was out of sight of their enemies above. Serenely conscious that the hunter's admiring glances were constantly directed upon her, she crouched waist-deep in the boisterous shallows, scooping up handfuls of the pure coldness and pouring it over her head and shoulders. She knew that he was desiring her with his regained manhood, and she was happy in the knowledge that, by her body's beauty and the practicing of her allurement, she had freed him from the past horrors that had so diminished him.

She fell to wondering, then, what had brought him to live in the wilderness. The answer did not seem hard to find: neither the small holding nor life in the city would have been tolerable for him after Marie had killed herself. He had said to Emmie once that his home was wherever he stood in the wilderness. When she had gone from him, when she was settled into her role of an old man's plaything in Quebec, Yves would still be stalking the trackless forests: silent, austere, frighteningly alone. Yet no longer completely alone, for he would have memories of Emmie Devizes to warm his solitude and color his dreams. And Emmie was glad in her generous heart.

"Yves, if you've nothing better to do, would you please wash my back?" she asked him.

The day sped by quickly. Well before dusk, Yves muttered something about reconnoitering their escape route, picked up his long rifle and plunged into the undergrowth. About an hour passed.

Emmie looked about her. Soon, they would be gone. During their stay in the friendly gorge, the roles of Yves and herself had been turned entirely topsy-turvy. At first rescuer and rescued, now it was she who had snatched him from the imprisonment of his memories. All the same, she still remained greatly dependent on him. As, for instance—now.

The bottom of the gorge, with the ever-chattering stream, the mossy banks, the luxury of foliage—always so friendly—had grown indefinably sinister with the approach of dusk. Up till then, Yves had never left her alone so late in the day. Usually, he was back with her and preparing their evening meal. She hoped that he would soon return. Very soon. Before those hideous tom-toms began their nightly thrumming from on high. Emmie shivered as if someone had just walked over her grave. She hastily thrust the thought from her.

What could be keeping him? He had never stayed away so late. Had he, perhaps, been ambushed by the Indians? Fallen foul of one of the larger predators that stalked the forest? A bear, perhaps? Yves had told her about the great black bear, dweller of the forest wilderness. He had told her how, though of a retiring disposition, it was a powerful and potentially dangerous creature, given to stalking its prey and overpowering the same with a quick, merciless charge. . . .

"Oh, hurry, Yves—hurry!" she breathed.

The dying daylight drew the long fingers of trees

upon the darkening greensward. A breath of wind rustled the leaves. Even the friendly river's bright chatter seemed to have turned to the hostile whispering about one that the ill-disposed make behind the cover of their hands.

Emmie shivered, drew the sleeping bag across her lightly clad shoulders and huddled back against the bole of her favorite tree for comfort.

Alas for comfort! She felt, rather than saw, the presence of the *thing* in the undergrowth. She was aware of its eyes upon her before she turned her head to regard it, before it padded out of the shadows and stood regarding her balefully. Emmie felt her hair prickle and stand up on her scalp with pure horror. Next, she drew breath to scream. The breath would not come. Shocked to stupefaction, she could only stare. And die inside.

The thing had the semblance of humanity, since, nude from the waist down, it displayed the characteristic appendages of a well-formed male, though its legs and loins were streaked with something that looked like dried blood. Above the waist, the torso was covered in shaggy hair, goatlike, and the creature was grotesquely hunchbacked. From where the shoulder blades should have been, there rose an ugly, domed shape, itself covered with a thick pelt.

But it was the head, craned forward upon the stooping shoulders, that beggared all imagination. It was the head of a black hellhound, with pricked ears, a savage snout, cavernous eye sockets and gleaming white canine teeth below which was nothing but a gaping maw. It was not till the apparition began to move toward the petrified girl that she was able to assemble the means to scream. To rise and run was out of the question; she had lost the power to move. But scream she did. Loud and long, rousing the far echoes of the gorge, causing the roosting birds to ascend, flapping and cawing into the evening sky.

And still the creature came on. Bereft of the will to

direct her limbs, Emmie closed her eyes, and, still screaming, waited for her end.

A hand closed on her shoulder—gently.

"Well done, my dear. That will give the Iroquois something to think about. You may stop now."

Slowly, hesitantly, she permitted herself to look. Below that hideous, gaping upper jaw with its cruel canine fangs was the mouth and chin of Yves the hunter. And the eyes that looked down on her through the eyeless sockets of the head were those same searching eyes that she had come to know so intimately.

"*You?*" she breathed.

Raising his hand, he removed the hellish head, which he had been wearing on top of his own head like a cap. He looked down at it, turning it over and over, reflectively.

"Poor Raoul," he murmured. "Faithful to the end and beyond. He serves me in death as he served me in life."

"Oh, my God!" cried Emmie. "The dog's *head*— all bloody and stinking! But why—*why?* And how *could* you do that to me? My heart nearly stopped beating!"

The hunter gave his mirthless, thin-lipped grin. "I am an evil spirit," he said. "And I have just devoured you alive. That, at least, is the construction Black Crow and his followers will put upon that extremely convincing display of yours, every note of which they will have heard with dread. Later, when it is dark, we shall leave the gorge by way of their encampment; I shall approach their campfire and show myself as I am now. There will not be a brave who will leave the safety of that campfire and the protection of the drumming this night. By dawn, we shall be miles from here."

Emmie backed away. "No!" she cried. "I won't do it—I can't! Go up there—where they are? I'd rather stay here in the gorge till the day I die."

"And die you soon would," he retorted. "Come the snows there'll be nothing for you here but frostbite and starvation."

"Any other way, but not up there!" she pleaded. "Why not downstream, keeping to the bank?"

"That's the way Black Crow expects us to go," said Yves. "There's a camp—a bigger camp with twice as many warriors—downstream just beyond the gorge."

"Upstream—that way!" She pointed.

"That way leads back to the deserters' camp. You want them to get their hands on you? After they found what you had done to their ringleader, they shot that black girl out of hand, pinioned as she was to a tree. You could not expect such a merciful end, not you."

"How much better would I fare if I were taken alive by the Indians?" she cried. "I've heard what *they* do to women captives!"

Yves shrugged his shoulders and spread his hands. "Not a pleasant fate," he conceded, "but infinitely better than mine if I were captured. They would all rape you, of course, every man. That is to be expected. After that, you would be auctioned off to the warrior who was willing to pay the most in tobacco, firewater, gunpowder and the like into the common fund. You would then become his chattel. His house slave. His whore."

"I have been your whore!" blazed Emmie, "so I am well trained to the task of pleasuring a stinking savage!"

"I am sure you will suit admirably well!" he shouted.

In a relationship that had seldom been discolored by the clash of wills, they were having their first quarrel since becoming lovers.

"Anyhow—what would they do to *you?*" demanded Emmie, sulkily.

"In order that I may touch your heart, I will tell you," said Yves. "Like your late and unlamented

friend Tredegar, I should be turned over to the
squaws, who live extremely boring lives, fraught with
childbirth, drudgery and total subservience to their
menfolk. Apart from a little singing and dancing of the
less colorful sort reserved for members of their sex,
they find their only amusement in torturing male captives to death—a task the warriors delegate to them.
Friend Tredegar, after they had derived protracted
entertainment by means of unspeakable practices
handed down from mother to daughter since time immemorial, they flayed alive. I found him skinned and
slow-roasting over a low fire. He was still alive when
I put a bullet through his brain. By now they will have
fed him to the dogs. Not a suitable end for an officer
and gentleman."

"*No! No-o-o-o!*" Emmie pressed her hands to her
ears. "Don't tell me any more, I beg you!"

He put his arm around her. In a gentle voice he
murmured, "Up there, Emmie, is our best chance—
to take advantage of their superstitions and win a
night's march. Tomorrow, when it is light, they will
pick up our tracks, but, with luck, we will reach my
canoe before they catch up with us, even though Black
Crow will send on ahead his youngest warriors, the
ones most fleet of foot. Believe me, Emmie. And trust
me."

She nodded, sniffed, wished she had a handkerchief
and felt incredibly foolish and helpless.

"You look so silly without your breeches," she
said, by way of retaliation. "And what's that awful-
looking hump on your back?"

"My breeches," he said. "And my buskins. Do you
not think it effective, Emmie, and also my winter
sheepskin jerkin worn inside out?"

"I don't know if you will scare the Iroquois tonight," she replied. "I only know you took years off
my life. What time do we leave the gorge?"

"After the moon has gone down. Just after midnight."

"Mmmm. Hours yet. What do we do till then?"

He pulled her closer to him. "The sleeping bag looks very inviting."

"Not with you in *that* state!" she retorted. "All smeared with dried mud and stinking of dead dog!"

"I will bathe in the stream," he said. "Wait for me in the sleeping bag, Emmie."

He turned and strode swiftly toward the stream, peeling off his upper garment and rendering himself as nude above as he had been below throughout the encounter. She watched him go and shook her head.

"Emmie, my girl, how can you be so?" she murmured. "How can you love one man so dearly and play the abandoned strumpet with another? By God, you're a thoroughgoing Cradock of Beechborough right through, you are, Emmie. No better than Uncle Eustace!"

Before the moon was down, Yves had again vested himself in the hideous get-up. Emmie herself, at his direction, smeared his bare legs, loins and buttocks with red sandstone mixed to a paste with water, which dried like splattered blood upon his skin. Next the sheepskin jerkin and hump, and last the cranium and upper jaw of his dead and faithful lurcher. Emmie averted her eyes from the sight.

"You must take my rifle. Do you know the action of a flintlock?"

She nodded. "I killed a man with one such," she whispered.

"Then you will know what to do in the unlikely event that the redskins see through my stratagem. All you will have to do is put the muzzle against your heart and . . ."

"I will do no such thing!" declared Emmie. "That one shot shall end the life of one of those damned savages—and they may do with me as they please!"

"Spoken like a true lady of title!" said Yves.

"Emmie, there is no one else like you. You are unique. Matchless."

They left the gorge, Yves leading. . . .

She followed in his footsteps up the scree. She was careful, as he had instructed her, not to disturb any stones in her ascent. Beyond and above the scree, the climb became simpler: the ascent of a steep ridge in which the fingers of time and weather had scratched away what amounted to a staircase. He moved slowly, making allowances for her, but Emmie had no difficulty in keeping up with him, even though she was burdened with the rifle and other impediments. Then they reached the lip of the gorge and the plateau where the Iroquois held camp.

He put his head close to hers, whispered into her ear, "Stay here. Our line of retreat is that way—along the edge of the gorge. As soon as I have reduced the Iroquois to a state of terror, move down there and I will follow. If I fail—if they recognize me for who I really am—shoot! And, since you are determined to spend the rest of your life as a drudge and a whore rather than die, I commend you to aim for Chief Black Crow, the tall fellow yonder, who, in addition to being as low and treacherous a fellow as I ever set eyes on, is also your country's inveterate enemy. But I hope it does not come to that, Emmie."

"And I!" she whispered with fervor.

"One last kiss—just in case."

"Then take off that awful head."

He obeyed. Their mouths met.

"One thing more," said Yves. "Do not join in the caterwauling with which I am going to entertain the redskins. If they hear a woman's voice they will know we are not evil spirits."

"Why?"

"Because in the religious canon of the redman, all evil spirits are male. Let's go. Keep well back out of sight, Emmie."

By the glow of the firelight, they could see about a dozen forms squatting around the blaze, with the commanding figure of their chief taller than the rest, even on his hunkers. At opposite sides of the fire were two drummers, each with a tall tom-tom between his knees upon which he smote an ever-changing rhythm in counterpoint to that of his partner. The effect, from Emmie's viewpoint on the edge of the gorge—dark, humped forms silhouetted in searing redness, the insistent pulse beat of the drums—was nakedly barbaric. She took a firmer grip of the long rifle, sighted along the barrel to the broad chest of the Iroquois chief.

Scarcely less disquieting was the outrageous form that was creeping up on the gathering: ears pricked, stooping, moving almost on all fours, the firelight etched in a halo of brightness around its hairy body. The watching girl felt her skin prickle anew.

Some ten paces from the campfire the figure paused, rose to its full, humpbacked height, threw back the awful head and gave tongue to a piercing, tremulous shriek, a drawn-out ululation that stilled the drums and brought every last horrified pair of dark eyes probing the blackness beyond the campfire's loom. Some rose to their feet—slowly, like men woken from a nightmare. The rest remained seated, huddled close by the sanctuary of the fire. Guttural monosyllables were exchanged: "Who . . . ? What . . . ? Where . . . ?" Not a single warrior thought to go out into the darkness and seek out the source of the appalling cry.

Emmie saw Yves move forward again. Slowly. A pace at a time, gauging his distance from the edge of the firelight's loom, so that to the observers there he would appear out of the blackness quite suddenly, like an apparition.

And so he did. One last quavering ululation, a raising of the arms, a flinging back of the head with its ears pricked was all he needed. Seeing the apparition, the redskins chorused their terror and fell to their knees. Chief Black Crow was the last to kneel, but kneel he did—slowly, reluctantly, a proud man bowing to the call of religious observance. Emmie's aim followed him down, and her finger was tight against the trigger.

There was silence. Nothing but the crackle of the blazing brushwood. Soft-footed, Yves rejoined her.

"They will not shift this night," he whispered. "Come, Emmie. The way is open to us—till dawn."

They moved quickly along the edge of the gorge. He was leading. Downstream. They had traveled for about half an hour, unspeaking, when the tom-toms resumed their beating—a faster and more convoluted rhythm than before.

"The Iroquois will be praying for the dawn," said the hunter. "And for fire and drums to keep at bay the evil spirit."

A mile or so further on, the gorge grew wider, and the dark ribbon of the stream far below them grew wider also. The light of another campfire appeared through the trees below, a flickering firefly reflected in the fast-flowing waters. Yves pointed down.

"That camp marks the end of the gorge and the limit of the forbidden territory," he said. "There will be a redskin behind every bush down there, crouched in every gully, for that is the way Black Crow decided we must come if we evaded the evil spirits."

Emmie peered down. The sides of the bluff were sheer beyond the vertical and quite unscalable. It was easy to see how they had been caught like rats in a trap, obvious at a glance how Yves's stratagem had been the only option open to them.

She took his arm.

"I should have trusted you unquestioningly from the first," she said. "You've saved us."

"Not yet," he replied. "Wait till dawn. Wait till they find our tracks and Black Crow realizes how we've fooled him. No rest for us this night, Emmie. No dalliance in the sleeping bag. We march through the night. And we march fast, or tomorrow eve will see me flayed and roasting over a slow fire, and you a concubine in the teepee of some Iroquois buck.''

Two hours further on, they were descending rapidly to a forest-covered plain through which the stream— now broadened to the stature of a river, though still shallow and rock-studded—drove straight as an arrow. They kept close to its bank, moving at a swift walk. At least the hunter walked; Emmie was reduced to a stumbling run to keep up with him. At the first indication of a greenish blue light in the sky to the east, Yves called a halt. Taking Emmie by the hand, he led her into the shallows and told her to sit upon a flat rock there, and rest till his return. He then plunged on downstream, knee-deep in water, till he was out on sight. He did not return for some time, and Emmie saw that he had bathed and dressed himself in clean breeches and buskins again.

"Are you rested, and ready to go on, Emmie?'' asked Yves.

"Yes, Yves,'' she said. "The Iroquois—are they far behind?''

"They may not yet have picked up our tracks, since it is barely daylight,'' he replied. "As soon as they have done so—yes, they will be after us as fast as they can run, and some of those young bucks can outstrip a deer over a long stretch. However,'' he continued, handing Emmie down from the rock into the water, "I have laid a false trail ahead that might delay them for a further hour or so. Come!''

By noon they had left the river and were heading north. The river had taken a sharp right-hand turn and would reappear, Yves explained, directly in their path sometime in the late afternoon. By then it would be a broad flood leading as a tributary straight into the River St. John, which in its turn would carry the canoe toward the mighty St. Lawrence, gateway to the

northernmost Americas, and high above whose wide
waters stood the city of Quebec. The canoe was hidden at the spot to which they were heading, he told
her. And he hoped no one had found it.

He allowed her a brief rest shortly after noon, and
gave her a piece of jerked meat to chew upon. Scorn-
ing rest, he climbed a low hill nearby and looked back
the way they had come, back to the heights above the
gorge, still in sight above the treetops. He soon returned on the run. She saw the urgency in his face.

"Are they—close behind?" she asked.

"Nearer than I had dreamed," he said. "They must
have sighted our tracks at first light. Just now, I saw
a flight of alarmed crows ascending not a mile back.
That means they rejected my false trail and are on our
heels."

Emmie's fingers, scurrying like small mice, were
hastily buttoning up her bodice.

"What are we going to *do*, Yves?" she asked.

"Do? We are going to run like hell, Emmie!" he
responded.

So they ran, she with her skirts held waist-high, he
carrying the long rifle, powder horn and ammunition
pouch—all else they had discarded, including the
sleeping bag of sweet memory. After an eternity of
exhaustion, the hunter called a halt, and it was then
that Emmie, reeling against a tree where she clung to
support herself, all but swooned with utter fatigue.

Yves was on his knees, ear held close to the ground.
He stood up. Their eyes met.

"There are two of them," he said. "Perhaps three,
but no more. The rest will be far behind. These fellows
will be the youngest, the fastest, the bravest. How are
you feeling, Emmie?"

"I—I can't go another step," she whispered.

"Then we must make our stand here," he said.
"For better or for worse. Take the rifle, Emmie."
And he handed it to her. "Hide behind the tree. You

must account for one of the devils. Shoot to kill. There will be no time to reload. Good luck.''

Lying on the soft turf, the rotten-sweet smell of dead wood in her nostrils, still panting from her lung-bursting run, Emmie experienced a curious feeling of being back at Flaxham in the fall of the year, with one of old Grandpa Beechborough's shooting parties going on.

It was Flaxham home park reborn. The smell of it. The very sounds of it: a woodpecker juddering away, the whisper of wind in high branches. If she closed her eyes, she would surely hear old Grandpa Beechborough's admonishing voice, Uncle Eustace's sly snigger, the delighted squeals of his current doxy when she was pinched in the undergrowth.

"Here they come, Emmie!" It was no more than a whisper from across a narrow glade. Yves was ten paces from her, standing, shoulder against a tree, broad-bladed hunting knife hefted.

Emmie brought the hammer of the long rifle to full cock. He came, the first of them, and Emmie almost vomited with fright at the sight of him. . . .

Young he was, not a day over eighteen for certain. Muscularly built. Naked save for a long strip of deerskin tucked under his loins and secured by a thong around his waist. Head shaved all but for a long tuft across the crown. Face daubed with bands of red and white paint. He carried a light ax and wore a knife at his hip. At the sight of the hunter, he stopped in his tracks.

Emmie sighted along the barrel of the rifle, aiming straight at the bronzed chest of the young warrior.

"Save powder and shot, Emmie," murmured Yves, without looking in her direction. "Leave *this* one to me!"

If the redskin understood the import of the remark, or realized to whom it had been addressed, he gave no sign, but continued to regard the white-haired man for some moments, chest heaving with the exertion of his long run.

And then, with a piercing scream, he leaped.

The first bound took him three paces, ax upraised. Upon his leading foot touching the ground, the ax came forward and sent the weapon spinning through the air toward his opponent. At such short range—another five paces at most—it was scarcely credible that the ax would not find its mark in the hunter's skull.

It did not. . . .

Even as the scream was forming in Emmie's mouth, Yves had dived forward out of the path of the hurtling ax, which passed close over his bent head and buried its blade deeply in the tree trunk behind him. He and the redskin met in a jarring collision of bone and muscle. And both had knives in their hands.

Their duel was incredibly fast, violent and brutal. Neither party eschewed the most blatant of dirty tricks. When they were face to face for an instant, the young redskin drove his shaved brow hard against the hunter's nose; Emmie heard the bone crack and witnessed the sudden torrent of carmine. But Yves was not so put out as to miss the opportunity of kicking his opponent in the loins, sending him staggering back, lurching and choking, but swift to recover.

The end, when it came, was sudden and shocking, as it had to be, given that both were fighting with broad-bladed hunting knives without shield or protection save their own dexterity. With a wild war whoop, the redskin aimed a vicious slash at Yves's throat that should have half-decapitated the hunter. The move was mistimed by an inch and an instant, and the effort put the Iroquois off balance for the brief span of time that ordained he would not grow old and wise in the councils of his people. Yves's knife, point first and jerking upward, rent the youth's bare belly from groin to breastbone, spilling steaming guts into the youth's open hands, down at which he stared in wide-eyed surprise. Staring still, he stumbled, tripped and fell.

"Emmie—for God's sake—*shoot!*"

She was shocked out of her horrified torpor by Yves's urgent cry, and followed the direction in which he was pointing. Another redskin had appeared. Young, brutal and well-made, like the other who lay kicking out the last moments of his life at the feet of his killer. The newcomer was aiming a bow at the hunter, was drawing back the feathered barb to his painted cheek. Emmie acted by no conscious direction of will, but out of pure instinct. She pointed the rifle and pulled the trigger. When the report had died away and the smoke cloud had dispersed, the bowman was staring at her from across the glade, mingled surprise and hatred written large across his young, unformed countenance. Still staring, he fell dead.

"I—I've killed another man!" whispered Emmie.

"And I am mightily grateful to you for it," was the hunter's wry response. He wiped his bloodied knife on the turf and sheathed it. "These two were the advance party, but the rest will not be far behind. Come, Emmie."

He took her by the hand, and they moved as quickly as she was able. In less than an hour they saw the glint of bright water through the trees ahead. There was the river, broader now than a flung stone could span, deeper and smoother flowing. There was a giant cedar close by the bank, its spreading branches overhanging the water and its gnarled roots bared to form a deep cavern. Yves swung himself down and splashed, waist deep, into this natural hiding place. He emerged, smiling, with his hand clasped about the prow of a canoe.

It was late afternoon. Long shadows and not a breath of wind. They took the flood, gliding downriver, the hunter directing the frail craft with simple, dexterous strokes of his paddle.

To Emmie, it could have been any autumn evening

at Flaxham, in a punt on the river and light mist rising. In her imagination, she could see Toby Stocker, nude and beautiful among the reeds.

They journeyed through the night. As Yves said, it was easy going with the current in their favor. Later, when they joined with the St. John river, it would be upstream all the way.

He stayed at the paddle, while Emmie lay on his sheepskin coat spread at the bottom of the canoe. She slept little, and that fitfully. The call of night birds in the forest around them, the hiss of water at the prow— these sounds intruded upon her to a quite astonishing degree, robbing her of easeful sleep. Yves's presence, his nearness in the narrow craft, the fact that his leg was touching her bare shoulder were a distraction. Upon her lying down, he had wished her good night and offered a brief, intimate caress—an entirely inconclusive gesture that nevertheless had the power to arouse her. Her sensibilities, heightened by her recent terrors, sharpened by accumulated horrors and a blessed release, were prey to the lightest impressions. From where she lay, she could look up and see the hunter kneeling at the stern, looming above her, his eyes fixed ahead, the cap of bone-white hair ghostly in the moonlight. His deerskin tunic was unfastened, baring his lean torso to the navel. That and the gamy, male smell of him served further to enflame her.

She shifted restlessly and sighed, wishing to command his attention, but he paddled stolidly on, bowing with every stroke, his muscled leg pressing gently against her shoulder each time. Her intentions thwarted, her desire fed upon itself and waxed exceedingly, so that her threshings grew ever more frenzied, her sighs more heated. Still he seemed not to notice, but continued to ply the paddle.

Finally there had to be an end to subterfuge and evasion, for her needs demanded it. Without raising herself up, Emmie unbuttoned her bodice, tugged free the bow of her waistband, and in one pure movement peeled off her clothing, uncovering breasts, belly, hips, thighs, tapering legs. And then, tightly closing her eyes, she lay quiet—and waited.

She did not have long to wait. The steady rhythm of the paddle ceased. Then there was only the slight hiss of the water slicing past the prow. Soon that was silent, as the canoe slackened its pace to the speed of the current. Then there was only the call of the night birds in the forest.

Emmie felt him move. She caught her breath, clenched her small fist in anticipation of his first touch upon her body. The touch, when it came, was inexpressibly tender: the gentlest of kisses upon her brow. She reached up, clasped him about the neck, and brought his mouth down upon hers, moaned ecstatically as his questing fingers molded her breasts, waist, loins.

A birch bark canoe is not the best of vehicles in which to venture upon the classic transports of passion. Furthermore, it was quite impossible for him—without standing up and overturning the craft—to insinuate himself beside her, head to head. But the demands of unleashed desire, though mindless and frenzied in expression, have a certain makeshift logic of their own, a capacity to extemporize, to discover new modes of expression. It is truly said that "love will find a way."

By one means and another, Emmie and her lover made shift to serve all their mutual needs that night, while the birch bark canoe, borne on the breast of the current, made fair progress downriver, under the benevolent eye of the watchful moon.

Dawn was a delight of newness. A crisp frost announced the day, but did not waken Emmie, who slept for one pure, dreamless hour after she and the hunter, all ardor quenched by the delights of excess, had drawn apart at last.

They breakfasted on jerked meat and pure water sucked from the palm of the hand dipped straight over the side of the canoe. Their eyes met as they sucked, and there was mischief and amused recollection in both their glances.

At noon, the river—*their* river, formerly *their* stream—joined the St. John, and easeful living was over, for every inch of progress to the northwest had to be fought for with muscle and skill, upstream against the current. Yves gave Emmie some rudimentary instruction in the handling of the paddle, but directing a birch bark canoe is a difficult art and not one to be picked up in a short time. In truth, the theoretical advantages—never realized—of having a second pair of hands to direct the canoe were greatly offset by the hazards inherent upon the tuition. For instance, the hunter, while guiding Emmie's hands and arms to the correct angle at which the blade of the paddle must enter the water, was so entranced by the wild disparity between the slenderness of his pupil's waist and the fullness of her bosom that he felt constrained to offer caresses to both. Noontime found the canoe tied up to an overhanging tree branch, with master and pupil lying on the mossy bank, together entwined, nude and satiated, enjoying their first real sleep since they left the gorge.

On the second day up the St. John river, they heard far-off gunfire: the sharp rattle of musketry, the heavy thud of cannon. Yves immediately pulled in to the bank and, dragging the canoe out of the water, upturned it and slid it into the concealment of the undergrowth.

"There is a skirmish going on," he said. "We do not want to get involved."

"But there will be English soldiers," said Emmie. "Surely this is our opportunity to make contact with them."

"If there are English troops, there will also be Yankees," replied Yves. "Or maybe there will be English deserters of the sort you have already met. Or red-skins, perhaps, taking what advantage they can of the war in loot and women. Do you still want to make contact with them, Emmie?''

Contrite, she whispered, "Anything you say, Yves."
Their hands met.

"Stay with me, and me alone, Emmie. Trust no one else. I will bring you to your goal, to Quebec."

To Quebec. Did she really want to achieve the goal of Quebec? Lady of title. Wife of the military governor of Quebec, himself a millionaire fleet owner of Bristol, able to purchase a nubile little wife with hard cash. It seemed a very far cry from the comforting benison of the wilderness, with this odd and exciting man close to her, and the true, the real, love of her life gone from her perhaps forever. . . .

The time would soon come—how soon?—when she and the hunter must part. Emmie knew, sensed it with certainty, that Yves would try to persuade her to re-main with him when that time came. What would be her answer? The options were clear-cut: be an old man's plaything, or be cherished by a good, brave man still in his prime of life. To her surprise, Emmie was able to answer herself without hesitation. She would choose the former option, but not out of a sense of duty to the man with whom she had entered into the solemn contract of marriage. The reason she would not, could not, remain with Yves was that she did not love him. Not as she had come to know love through Nathan. And she liked and respected the hunter too much to condemn him to—what? A lifetime of half-measures.

But all that lay in the future, Emmie told herself. There was a long way, yet, to the St. Lawrence River and Quebec. The decision having been made, she would not be called upon, yet, to carry it out. Mean-while it was uncommonly nice to be admired, to be cosseted and pleasured so satisfyingly. And to have the time and opportunities to enjoy her lover.

Alas, for time. Did Emmie and her lover but know it, the sands had all but run out.

"Who goes there? *Qui va là?*"

The challenge came from their left side, from the west bank and was clearly directed across the water to them. In the darkness someone had spotted the creaming of white foam at the canoe's prow. Yves cursed himself for the oversight of going too fast, and plied his paddle even harder.

"We'll make a run for it, Emmie," he said. "If they are that side of the river, it's odds on that they are Yankees from over the border, in which case they likely will not have boats. Head down, Emmie. We are going to move!"

The hunter drove his paddle home with ferocity, and the prow of the canoe rose as the current strove against the forward motion of the light craft. Emmie did as she was bidden. She lay low, peering out into the night in the direction from which the challenge had come. There was nothing to be seen. No lights. And the call was not repeated.

"We are well out of their sight now," said Yves, who had not only redoubled his efforts but was edging the craft toward the east bank. "Rest easy, Emmie, we are—"

The hunter never finished his observation. They came out of the darkness ahead: two rowboats the size of naval cutters, with six men apiece at the oars. And musketeers at their prows.

A sharp order rang out. "Prepare to give fire!"

"No!" yelled Yves. "There's a woman . . ."

"Give fire!"

A splutter of frizzens. A ragged thunder of discharges. Emmie distinctly heard and felt a ball slash close to her ear. Yves, kneeling at his paddle, gave a cry and, clutching his chest, folded slowly over like a broken woodentop doll. Screaming his name, Emmie clasped hold of him and felt the sticky wetness of welling blood.

The boats were on each side of them, and she could see the scarlet uniforms and white crossbelts of British soldiery.

"Bastards! Bastards!" she screamed. "You've killed him!"

"By George—a woman!" A drawling, affected voice. "Help them both into the cutter. Egad, what's a woman doin' in this outlandish spot? Surely not a Yankee camp follower so far from home."

The officer was a Captain Forbes-Rufford. He introduced himself to Emmie in the British encampment on the west bank. Forbes-Rufford was mightily pleased with himself, for, as he was at pains to explain to Emmie, he had repulsed a powerful Yankee thrust that night and sent the damned renegade colonials packing off back the way they had come. It was regrettable, of course, that he had been obliged to fire upon the canoe, but the lady and her companion had ignored the challenge, and if civilians will go wandering around in a theater of war they must expect to get hurt. Luckily the young lady's companion was now in the hands of one of the finest surgeons in the army, though Forbes-Rufford gloomily opined that chest wounds could be the very devil.

It was at this point in his monologue that Emmie spoke for the first time, interrupting him with the declaration of who she was and what she was, coupled with a promise that if her companion were to die as a result of his wound, he—Captain Forbes-Rufford—would answer personally to her husband the military governor of Quebec Province.

Forbes-Rufford was alarmed—and amazed. All Canada knew of her disappearance, he informed Emmie. Sir Claude Devizes had made the highest representations to the American government, sending an emissary under flag of truce to Washington, with a letter of protest to President Madison himself, demanding the return of his wife. And Mr. Madison had had the grace to reply. Lady Devizes, he informed the distraught husband, had been released from the U.S.S. *Delaware* and had last been seen continuing her journey by fishing boat. Since then—nothing. What had happened to her ladyship? asked Forbes-Rufford, who had become mightily deflated.

Emmie gave him a brief account of her adventures, omitting much. Again the gallant captain expressed amazement. Why, he put it to her ladyship, had her companion and guide not brought her directly to the safety of an army stronghold? There were plenty much nearer to hand than Quebec. There was Fredericton and St. George. There was even Eastport, captured from the Yankees. Emmie was digesting this gobbet of information when the army surgeon entered the tent and showed by his expression that he was the harbinger of ill tidings.

"Ma'am, the man is asking for you," he said.

"Sir, is he . . . ?"

"He cannot live for much longer, ma'am," said the surgeon. "Indeed, though I have dosed him with tincture of opium, he is suffering grave pain and a swift release would be a mercy. The ball, you see, is buried deeply in the lung, and I could not possibly probe for it with any hope of success. This way, ma'am."

The surgical tent was at the far end of the camp. Emmie followed her guide with her heart weeping silently within her. The tent was small. Yves lay on a pallet covered with an army blanket. His face was chalk-white like his hair, and his eyes were open. He smiled to see Emmie and held out a hand. There were three men standing over him, all officers. They exchanged glances when they saw the warmth of the dying man's greeting, and one of them muttered something under his breath.

"Would you please leave us alone together?" whispered Emmie, falling to her knees beside the stricken hunter.

They left. An owl hooted in the distance, a poignant reminder of their nights together in the wilderness.

"I wanted to keep you for always, Emmie," he murmured. "From the very first. You were my Marie brought to womanhood. I could have taken you straight to Fredericton or Eastport, but . . ."

"I'm glad you didn't, Yves," she whispered, pressing his hand.

A paroxysm of agonized coughing seized the hunter, but presently he fell quiet. Emmie dabbed away a thin trickle of bright blood that issued from the corner of his mouth.

"You brought me alive again, Emmie," he said, in a voice so faint that she was constrained to put her ear close to his lips. "After I had buried my Marie, I threw away the money—threw it into the river, that accursed, tainted money that had destroyed us both—and looked for oblivion in drink. I never found it . . ."

"Hush," whispered Emmie. "Don't tire yourself. See, I'll put my arm around your shoulders and you can pillow your head against my breast, the way you did that first time."

"Darling Emmie . . ."

"Shhhh . . ."

"I—I have not told you all . . ."

"It doesn't matter, No more need be said between us, Yves. We understand each other perfectly."

He shivered and made a small moan. "Emmie, I am going. Hold tightly to me."

"Of course." She slipped her bodice from her shoulders, baring her breasts upon which his head was resting. "There—is that nice?" she whispered.

"Blissful. Oh, Emmie, Emmie—goodbye . . ."

"Goodbye, Yves. Goodbye, dear, dear Yves!"

She pulled him closely to her, pressing his face between the deep cleft of her breasts, and felt his manhood stir. He gave a deep, shuddering breath, and went limp in her arms.

Yves the hunter had departed into eternity.

Emmie laid him down, closed his eyes, kissed him for the last time and pulled the edge of the blanket over his dead face.

Captain Forbes-Rufford's demeanor had undergone a marked change during Emmie's absence. Gone was the anxious deference to the lady of title and influential connection; in its place was a certain slyness and an air of having made a considerable recovery of lost ground. Emmie was soon to learn the reason for it.

"So he's dead, eh?" said Forbes-Rufford. "Well, I have to tell you, ma'am, that he was recognized a short while ago by some of my officers. Broadsheets bearing the description of that fellow have been circulating these eighteen months or more. The fellow was an outlaw."

"An outlaw?" Emmie stared at him, uncomprehendingly.

"Murder, ma'am. He was wanted for murder. Shot three fellers out of hand in Quebec."

"Aaaaah!"

Forbes-Rufford smirked and examined his well-kept fingernails. "I fancy," he said, "that your husband will have little complaint with my conduct of the affair. You were kidnapped by this fellow, there's no doubt. All unawares, you were being taken to some secret lair of his up in the headwaters of the St. John."

"Do you think so, Captain?" asked Emmie.

"Undoubtedly, ma'am. A desperate fellow."

"Oh, I'm sure."

"Stands to reason, ma'am. Capable of anything. For who but such a fellow would kill three perfect strangers in cold blood? And for no reason."

"No reason, you say?"

"None that has ever been divined, ma'am."

"I see." She turned away to hide the treacherous

tears that prickled her eyes. So that was Yves's last
secret. He had taken his revenge, but he had not
shouted from the rooftops his reason for killing the
brutes who had encompassed the deflowering and destruction of his innocent child. Marie lay in her grave
with name and memory unsullied. For all the world
knew, Marie was a virgin still.

As chance had it, Forbes-Rufford was dispatching
three of his fleet of cutters upriver a few days hence,
on the first stage of a journey to Quebec. Lady Devizes should travel with the party, he advised her.
And—felicitously—she herself would carry the dis-
patches to her husband Sir Claude telling how, by
skillful and inspired leadership, an enemy force had
been routed on the St. John, and a notorious outlaw
and murderer killed while attempting to escape.

Emmie agreed to the proposal when it was put to
her the following morning, but the greater part of her
attention lay elsewhere. That morning she was confirmed in her mind regarding a matter that had nagged
at one small corner of it for some little time: she was
almost certainly with child.

But—*whose* child?

Part Three

The Shadow of the Gallows

Chapter One

It poured rain in Quebec, Canada's oldest city, founded and named by the French explorer and colonizer Samuel de Champlain. Water dripped from every eave and pediment, gathered itself into miniature lakes in the rutted streets of the upper town and was disgorged down the steep, narrow alleyways descending to the lower town at the foot of the cliffs. From there the rainwater flowed into the basin of St. Charles river, where, in that October eve of 1813, warships and merchantmen made a forest of masts and spars. The rain was vomited from the stone mouths of gargoyles above the nave of the ancient basilica, and sluiced down the gullies and ravines of the historic Heights of Abraham. It soaked the scarlet-coated sentries outside the residence of the military governor and made them wish they were serving with Wellington in what they supposed was the eternal sun and wine of Portugal and Spain.

The residence of the military governor was newly built to designs by Smirke, architect of Covent Garden

Theater, London, and was aggressively theatrical in
style and pretensions. It stood in the center of a fine,
long promenade overlooking the St. Lawrence, where
a handsome and inoffensive mansion dating from
French colonial days had been knocked down to accommodate it. The present military governor, General
Sir Claude Devizes, Knight of the Bath, had paid for
the building of the residence out of his own pocket—
and had learned to regret every penny.

To return to the sentries: they were two in number,
one on each side of the pretentious entrance gateway.
At the approaching clatter of hooves and the rumble
of iron tires, they exchanged glances and nodded.
Both brought their Brown Bess muskets to the shoulder and awaited events. When the vehicle, a closed
carriage, made to turn in through the gateway, one
winked at the other, and both presented arms. The
carriage swept past, drenching both soldiers' lower
extremities with muddy water. They cursed quietly
but without venom, for both were trying to steal a
sight of the vehicle's passenger, who was none other
than the governor's lady, presumed lost these weeks
past on the way from England, but who had that morning set the military hierarchy of Quebec on its ear by
turning up in a commandeered river boat from God
knows where.

"Did you mark her looks?" asked one of the sentries when they had ordered their muskets.

"That I did," responded the other. "Fresh as a
daisy and twice as toothsome. I tell you there is no
justice in a world where the likes o' you and me must
take our pleasures with tavern whores and be glad to
find one with teeth, while the likes of His Nibs can
afford such as that little black-haired quean we saluted
just now."

"One day it will all be changed," declared the other.
"When the fruits o' the earth—the comely queans included—will be properly shared out 'twixt Us and

Them, and in this manner: One for you, two for me. One for you, three for me."

They guffawed together. . . .

Meanwhile, the carriage containing the object of their philosophizing had drawn to a halt before the ornate entrance portico of the mansion. The vehicle's door was opened by an earnest young man carrying an umbrella, who handed down the beautiful occupant and gave her cover from the streaming rain till they were both up the steps and under the severe Doric entablature, where a double row of footmen, white-wigged, powdered and patched, formed a guard of honor at the portals.

"Your ladyship, I am Gareth Hemmings, private secretary to Sir Claude, at your service." The earnest young man stooped awkwardly, when he took Emmie's proffered hand, and colored like a schoolgirl. His crisp, curly hair was becomingly russet, and his eyes were of a fugitive hazel tint. Secretary-like, he was clad in black, with a spotless white stock at neck and ruffles at the cuffs.

"How do you do, Mr. Hemmings." Emmie looked about her with awe and a considerable nervousness, as well she might; the entrance hall of the residence had not greatly taxed the architect's imagination, for he had provided the military governor's builders with drawings of the entrance hall and staircase of Covent Garden. However, it was not the overpowering surroundings that occasioned her nervousness. "My husb—Sir Claude—is he about?" she asked.

"Sir Claude is gone to York, ma'am," replied the secretary, "to inquire of the progress of the fighting. You will no doubt have heard of the recent disasters which have befallen our arms?"

"Don't tell me that we have lost this war with the Americans?" cried Emmie.

"Beyond question, we have not, ma'am," replied the other. "Nor shall we. But our naval squadron on

Lake Erie was compelled to surrender last month, and Colonel Proctor's soldiers and their Red Indian allies have been beaten by the American Harrison, leaving all upper Canada exposed to a Yankee advance.''

"My husb—Sir Claude—is he in personal danger?" asked Emmie.

"Not so, ma'am," replied Hemmings. "He has merely gone to confer with the government and general officers about how best the threat may be contained. News of your arrival was sent to him by fastest boat as soon as the message reached us. I am sure Sir Claude will return posthaste as soon as the glad tidings reach him—contingent upon the military situation, of course. But I fail in my duty, ma'am. Would you care for some refreshment? Sherry wine, perhaps?"

"No wine, Mr. Hemmings," said Emmie. "But—but I should greatly like a cup of chocolate, please. Very hot and sweet."

Hemmings looked baffled. Clearly, hot chocolate was not much called for at the residence.

"Yes, ma'am," he said, nevertheless. "Very hot and sweet."

"And, Mr. Hemmings, I crave a large green apple. Do you have such a thing?"

"An apple, ma'am?" The young secretary's smooth brow furrowed with worries far heavier than the weight of his years. "Yes, I fancy we have apples. In the orchard, you know. Um—would you care to step into the drawing room, ma'am?"

Hemmings made Emmie's wants known to the double row of footmen, giving rise to many surprised looks and raised eyebrows, after which at least half a dozen bewigged servitors departed to accommodate her ladyship's wishes. Then the secretary escorted his master's bride into a large chamber off the lofty entrance hall, where Emmie's ears were assaulted by a— for her—pleasant and homey sound that immediately transported her back to England and Flaxham.

Plip-plop-pleep-plop-plop . . .

All around a hexagonal-shaped chamber of extreme elegance as to proportion, decoration and furnishings, stood buckets, handbasins, chamber pots and other receptacles—all receiving drops of water that descended from the ceiling in a random cacophony.

"I'm afraid, ma'am," said Hemmings, "that we have a lot of trouble with the roof here. Whenever it rains—anything more than a light shower . . . We have done everything in our power, but to no avail." He assumed the mien of a man who is willing to accept total responsibility for disaster.

"I beg you, don't worry yourself on my account," said Emmie. "Where I was brought up, we had to put out crocks and pans the whole year round. The family seat of my ancestors leaked water during a drought— or so the saying went."

Perceiving that she had delivered a witticism, Hemmings gave an austere smile and blushed crimson. A long silence followed, as they sat facing each other on fashionably uncomfortable chairs that aped the style of Chippendale.

Presently, he cleared his throat and said, "Hem— did you have a comfortable journey from England, ma'am?"

"Very uncomfortable, Mr. Hemmings," replied Emmie. "And I think the last part was the most uncomfortable of all, for it rained all the time we were sailing up the St. Lawrence in that small brig, with everyone crammed in a single cabin, all smelling like wet spaniels."

"Ah, here we are with your refreshments, ma'am," said Hemmings, rising, as a sextet of footmen filed into the drawing room. Those in the center file bore, respectively, a silver salver containing cup, saucer and steaming jug, and a large green apple on a plate. Emmie felt her spirits revive.

They set salver and plate upon a side table by her chair, bowed in perfect unison and filed out. Emmie nodded approval.

"A few thousand drilled as well as they, Mr. Hemmings," she said, "and you would soon have the Yankees running."

Secretary Hemmings looked by turn baffled, surprised, enlightened and tentatively amused.

"Yes, ma am," he said.

"Well, tell me about the domestic arrangements here, Mr. Hemmings," said Emmie, "while I set about my chocolate and apple."

The chocolate was delicious. She sipped it scalding hot, savoring the burning sensation as it passed over her tongue, rolling it around her mouth and allowing it to set up nervous echoes in her teeth, so that she could feel the size and shape of them, every one. And then—to sink one's teeth into the firm flesh of the green apple, allowing the tart, cool juice to fill and overflow the mouth and pour, unchecked, over one's chin and bosom. And, really, she must get some fresh clothes before Sir Claude—her husband—returned to Quebec. No wonder the secretary fellow looked at her so queerly, and she half out of her bodice and her knees showing through her skirts. Oh, but the apple was delicious! Why had she never before experienced this simply divine craving? And what was the secretary fellow (he was really quite nice, and terribly handsome in a brash, boyish kind of way) going on about . . . ?

"And, finally, ma'am," said Hemmings, "Sir Claude instructed me to obtain for you a lady's maid, whom I hope will meet with your approval. She is the widow of a good fellow: a corporal-of-horse, Inniskillin Dragoons. Her name is Agnes Reilly. Shall I summon her, ma'am?"

"Mmmm!" replied Emmie, mouth full, gesticulating assent.

Agnes Reilly proved to be an agreeable enough woman in her mid-thirties. She was of good appearance: apple-cheeked, trim of waist and wide of bosom and hips, with a slant-eyed, greeny-eyed glance that would have been more proper in a wench ten years her junior. Irish as Galway Bay. And she did not so much as turn a hair at her new mistress's appearance, raggedy clothing and all, but dipped a curtsy and waited meekly for her instructions.

"And what would you like to do now, ma'am?" asked secretary Hemmings. "Dinner is at your command, whenever you wish it."

Emmie licked the rest of the apple juice from her fingers with a feeling of sinful repletion. "Dinner I shall not require, Mr. Hemmings," she said. "What I need most of all now is a hot bath and a night's sleep in a proper bed."

"Agnes, see to it," said Hemmings.

The lady's maid curtsied again and withdrew.

"Ma'am, I will show you to your quarters," said Hemmings, "when you are ready."

"I am ready, Mr. Hemmings," said Emmie.

At the door, he turned to her. "Ma'am, do I have it correctly?" he asked. "You *are*—or formerly were—Miss Emmie Laetitia Dashwood, daughter of the late Lady Jane Dashwood, formerly Cradock, herself daughter of the third marquess of Beechborough—do I have it right, ma'am?"

"Quite right, sir," replied Emmie, rather puzzled.

Hemmings blushed. He really was a most charmingly boyish creature, thought Emmie. One would like to keep him in a pretty, pink box and feed him on strawberries and cream.

"Ma'am, I must straightway write my mother and tell her that I have met you," he said. "Mother keeps a complete record of the English aristocracy and their relations, right down to the most obscure third cousin thrice removed, and it will make her day to read that I have walked and talked with the granddaughter of a marquess."

"Will it now?" said Emmie, amused. "Then pray convey my kind regards to your mother."

Together they ascended the great staircase, a fac-

simile of the one at Covent Garden, with a ceiling
painting by a local French-Canadian artist depicting
the rape of the Sabines in some interest of detail but
rather shaky drawing. The principal suites of bed-
chambers and dressing rooms led immediately off the
upper corridor, and most of the windows looked out
on breathtaking views over the St. Lawrence river,
with its unending, two-way stream of boating traffic.

Agnes Reilly had already seen to her mistress's
bath. Half a dozen strapping lasses from the kitchen
department had just completed the filling of a large
copper hip bath placed in the center of the dressing
room. The whole line of them dropped curtsies and
departed with their empty water ewers, chattering like
magpies, and no doubt the burden of their discourse
was her ladyship's appearance: the disparity between
her extreme beauty and the wild disorder of her dress.

Alone with Agnes Reilly, Emmie slipped out of her
bodice, dropped her skirts, kicked the pile of torn and
crumpled material across the room, stood nude with
arms akimbo.

"Reilly," she said, "I put those clothes on aboard
a Norwegian merchantman more weeks ago than I
care to remember. Since then I have worn them, day
in and day out, unceasingly. Get rid of them. Burn
them or give them to the deserving poor."

"Yes, m' lady," replied the maid, green eyes atwin-
kle. "Will y' ladyship be taking her bath now?"

"That I will, Reilly," declared Emmie, and suited
the word by climbing into the high-sided vessel of
highly polished copper and luxuriating in the hot,
scented water. "Soap my back, will you, please?"

"Yes, y' ladyship." Having no doubt that it was
better to perform the task and at the same time keep
her clothing dry, the maid shrugged out of her bodice
and let it fall to her waist. She wore no shift under;
her generous, dark-nippled breasts jounced freely as,
stooping, she took up soap and sponge and com-

menced to wash her young mistress's shapely back.

Giving a small sigh of contentment, Emmie addressed herself to the problem that had been bedeviling her waking hours for the past week and more: the question of her "condition."

She was with child—that much was now quite definite. That Nathan was the father of the unborn infant was scarcely in doubt. It was he, and not poor dead Yves, since Nathan had been—as Grandpa Beechborough used to say—"first past the post."

There remained the question of her husband, who had paid out a considerable fortune for what he must surely have expected to be unsoiled goods. A child of candor, Emmie's first thought had been to speak out frankly to Sir Claude and let him know about her condition; with second thoughts came prudence—better to wait and see. In practical terms—and as a married woman with no personal fortune, she must be practical above all else—the producing of a healthy babe in somewhat rapid order (how rapid? eight months, a little less?) would pass almost without comment. In moral terms, the very notion was just about as wrong as it could be. But prudence dictated that she must consider the option. The alternative: to declare the truth out of moral pride, to be sent back to England on the next boat, disgraced, to arrive at Flaxham and be allowed to remain there only under the condition that she comply with Uncle Eustace's vile goings-on. Or else she could sell her body in order to feed herself and the child, starting as a high-priced courtesan of the sort who drives out in carriage and four with liveried coachmen and grooms, and ending as a twopenny drab in dark doorways of the city slums.

Wait and see. That should be her motto. If, when Sir Claude returned (and if the progress of the war kept him away for another month or more, his credibility as father of the child would be somewhat strained), she found him to be of amiable, easygoing disposition and fond of children, she might tell him the truth of it. On the other hand, if he were proud and high-stomached, jealous of his lineage and not tremendously attracted to the young, it might be more prudent to hold her tongue and let matters take their own course.

That settled, her most pressing problem set aside with the same airy practicality that had moved her to cast away the garments that she had worn during her adventures since leaving the *Peder Wessel* (with all their amatory, and other, connections), Emmie relaxed in the soothing warmth and Agnes Reilly's ministrations. The woman was quite a treasure, and one scarcely needed to do anything but lie and luxuriate. Agnes had a very handsome figure, too, for her age, though she had obviously given suck in her time.

"I understand you are a widow, Reilly," said Emmie. "How many children do you have?"

Having soaped and rinsed her mistress's back, the maid was doing likewise with her belly and breasts. "Six, y' ladyship," she replied. "But none o' the little innocents lived long enough to walk on their own two feet, but was taken of the fever or the consumption, God rest their souls."

"That's very sad," said Emmie. "And to lose your husband also—what a tragedy."

"Bless you, y' ladyship, the day that a Yankee cannonball carried away Seamus Reilly's head was the best day that happened to me since I was wed, for wasn't he the drunkard and the bully boy? And didn't he beat me like any old army mule?" The woman laughed. "Sure, with a little encouragement and a drop o' porter inside me, wouldn't I dance on the grave o' Corporal Seamus Reilly, so I would! Will you be wanting the massage, y' ladyship?"

"A massage—that would be heavenly!"

Emmie's personal chambers comprised, apart from the dressing room, a handsome sitting room and adjoining bedchamber. It was to the latter that she and the lady's maid retired. By then it was dark. A fine log fire burned merrily in the huge grate. Through the unshuttered windows, the top branches of a tall yew tree formed a fine tracery of lacework through which could be perceived the constellations of the stars and, below them, the lights of ships passing up and down the broad river. Emmie lay down, still nude, upon the counterpane of a handsome four-poster bed and, arms pillowed behind her head, closed her eyes and awaited her maid's ministrations.

The first touch of Agnes Reilly's hand upon her newly dried skin was like a lover's caress. Emmie drew a sharp intake of breath and her eyelids snapped open.

"Did I hurt you, m' lady?" asked the woman with some concern. She was still naked to the waist, and her green eyes were shaded and inscrutable.

"No, not at all," replied Emmie. "It was—quite nice. Please continue." She shut her eyes again and made a deliberate effort to let her senses slip away toward sleep.

The hands were upon her again, as gentle and coaxing as a lover's hands, molding her body with long, firm strokes, glissading over the skin, sometimes with firmness, sometimes like the touch of eyelashes.

"I always say," murmured the voice beyond the hands, "that when all's said and done, 'tis a warm heart that wins through in the end. And sure 'tis a warm heart that you have, m' lady. It shines out o' your eyes like a candle out o' the darkness. . . ."

The voice droned on, far off on the edge of reality, which was fast slipping away. And then Emmie was lying in the secret gully close by the sea, with the wavelets lapping her feet and her lover pleasuring her with his questing fingers and his adoring lips. And surely it was so. Surely only Nathan's hands and lips could communicate such ecstasy? The moist mouth upon hers, the darting, piercing tongue that mingled with her tongue, meeting, crossing, joining—whose else but her lover's?

Mounting skyward in rapture, she was at the same time succumbing to a sweet languor that was halfway between sleep and imagination. Visions burst in her mind, cracked, crazed, fell apart and were reunited again. And always the vision was of Nathan. She cried out his name at the instant of her release, held him tightly to her till her energy was totally drained and she fell back, prostrate and panting, eyes closed.

The lady's maid Agnes Reilly straightened herself up, swept back a stray lock of hair, drew her bodice back on and rebuttoned it. She smiled down at the nude girl upon the bed.

"Bless you, y' ladyship, but there's thin times ahead for one with such a warm heart as yourself, and that's the truth of it," she whispered to herself. And then, snuffing the candles, she tiptoed silently from the bed-chamber and closed the door.

Outside, a dark figure, who had been witness to it all, carefully lowered itself down from the high branches of the yew tree that afforded such a favored prospect into the secrets of the residence's new chatelaine. Gaining the ground, the trespasser first looked this way and that for fear of having been observed, then, reassured, walked swiftly away.

Secretary Gareth Hemmings occupied a narrow room, a garret high in the rooftops hidden by the noble pediment of the residence. Late, by candlelight, he sat in shirtsleeves and wrote a long letter addressed to his mother in far-off Gloucester. For a loving son, and for a man who made his living by plying the pen, Mr. Hemmings took an unconscionable while to compose the communication, frowning and biting the end of his pen for long periods at a time, constantly scratching out words with his knife, even tearing up a whole sheet of writing and beginning again.

One principal theme ran through the letter: his new mistress, described in most acclamatory terms . . .

. . . of exceedingly pleasant appearance and an ARISTOCRAT to her fingertips, Mother. But much YOUNGER than we had been led to suppose, and it is certain that Sir Claude will DOTE on her, as indeed I confide that we ALL shall.

Sir Claude has been apprised of Ldy. Devizes's arrival and is expected to return to Quebec as soon as the exigencies of the war permit. There is no doubt in my mind that if my master could but see the MANIFEST EXCELLENCES of his bride, he would hasten all the more. . . .

Closing with the conventional filial elegancies, Hemmings sealed the letter and laid it aside for delivery; that being done, he prepared himself for bed. It was past midnight when the young secretary laid his head upon the pillow; by then, his russet hair was set in rag curlers and the smooth skin of his face gleamed with white-lead cream.

He allowed the candle to burn itself down to extinction, lay looking up at the ceiling and smiling quietly to himself.

"Oh, yes, milady," he murmured, when the flame guttered and died. "I think that, when you perceive the manner of husband you have gotten for yourself, you will quite easily become mine."

The next few days were, for Emmie, a riot of frenzied activity. First she must obtain a complete wardrobe. Thanks to the assistance and advice of the indispensable Agnes Reilly, this enterprise posed no difficulty save that of *l'embarras de richesse*. The doughty Reilly had been lady's maid to the wives of other senior officers of the Quebec garrison and knew the ins and outs of all of the many excellent French dressmakers, milliners, glovers, corsetmakers and shoe-

makers of the smart upper town. There was no question but that the most select of these would lay aside
even the most important of work in progress to complete an order for the wife of the military governor.
And as for the minor matter of cash or credit—it simply was not mentioned. Within a week of her arrival
in Quebec in rags and tatters, Emmie was arguably
the best dressed woman there—thanks to Reilly. Emmie was a girl of simple tastes (life and upbringing at
Flaxham inculcated simple tastes, with one new costume per year, and that usually handed down from an
older sibling or relation), and was quite horrified by
her maid's insistence that "y' ladyship" must dem-
onstrate her station in the city and province by out-
shining all other wives of the establishment. Reilly
accompanied her mistress on all the shopping expe-
ditions, sat through the fittings, was vociferous for
better workmanship, swifter service, and took as
much delight over Emmie's new wardrobe as if she
had been her own child. Or her lover.

Ten days after Emmie's arrival in Quebec came
news that General Sir Claude Devizes and his entourage were half a day's distance up the St. Lawrence
and were to be expected by the evening. In a fine old
tizzy, Emmie riffled through her brand-new wardrobe
and settled—after much heart-searching as to the propriety of *décolleté* depth and skirt width—for a simple
straight-skirted afternoon gown in the current Grecian
mode, offset by a single osprey feather worn high in
her sleek, sable hair. Reilly attended to dressing her
mistress and piling her hair into the fashionable chignon, dusting the lightest suspicion of rice powder on
her smooth cheeks and touching her full lips with a
fingertip briefly dipped in carmine, her eyelashes with
kohl. At the end of it, regarding herself in a tall pier
glass, Emmie remarked, in her no-nonsense, matter-
of-fact way, that she "didn't look at all half bad." The
susceptible Reilly was by this time close to tears of
pride and joy at her mistress's appearance.

Emmie fretted in the vast, downstairs drawing room of the residence, with its long windows fronting the promenade where soldiers of the 21st Foot, who were at that time stationed in the barracks close by, were drawn up to receive the military governor as guard of honor. Shortly after sunset—the last strains of bugles were dying in the seasonably chill air and the Union flag was being hauled down outside the residence—an officer of light dragoons clattered to a halt before the guard commander and informed him that His Excellency's coach was on its way from the harbor.

Emmie saw the soldiers bring their weapons to the present, heard the roll of drums heralding the arrival of her bridegroom, but was greatly put out when, after a while, an old gentleman in a rusty black greatcoat and tall hat was carried through the scarlet ranks, seated in the crossed arms of two kilted Highlanders.

"Have a care! Damnation, I'll have the hide off your backs if you jolt me again like that! A plague on both your houses, and may you both be struck with the gout—as I am—but afore you are thirty. Devil take all Scots, and here's a shilling apiece for your pains. Now be off with you." The grinning Highlanders, having carried the military governor into the drawing room and carefully deposited him in a wing chair, took their rewards, saluted brightly, glanced speculatively at the lovely creature in the Grecian gown, and departed.

"So you are Emmie. . . . Come here, my dear child." Sir Claude Devizes extended his hands to his bride.

Tremulously, Emmie obeyed. He was old-looking—more so than she had reckoned. Apart from the bandage-swathed right foot stretched on the stool before him, infirmity had laid other, more telling, marks upon the military governor of Quebec Province. Grave pain had scored deep lines upon his face, at the corners of his mouth and about the eyes. And an unhealthy tinge of blueness, a certain puffiness of flesh at the jowls,

suggested an even more serious disorder to his health.
And yet the man she remembered from the portrait
was still there behind the crumbling facade of age and
infirmity. The proud beak of nose was still held high,
the mouth set in a firm line. And the eyes—rheumatic
and red-rimmed, but still dancing with good humor—
explained why the Highlanders who had borne him in
had responded so well to his rough, joshing manner.

"As pretty as a picture," murmured Claude Devizes, reaching up to touch her cheek. "Kiss me here,
child." He touched his own cheek.

Emmie obeyed. In an instant, her dismay at her
husband's appearance—which had been considerable—
faded to nothingness. Whatever Claude Devizes
lacked, it was not character—that emanated from him
as from the painted representation of his prime. Age,
illness—these had made their marks, but the essential
man was still there beneath it all.

"I'm—I'm sorry to see you unable to get about unaided, sir," said Emmie, and wished she had left it
unsaid.

"The gout—nothing," responded her spouse. "That
will be gone, given rest, within the week. As for everything else"—he shrugged his lean shoulders and flashed
her a grin that was not far from boyish—"I tell you,
Emmie, I greatly fancy a brandy, which, because I
have had my footsteps dogged by my physician ever
since I left Quebec, has been forbidden me. I beg you,
dear child—it is over there on the console table. That's
it. A little more. There's a dear. And a drop of water
to eke it out. Not too much. Aaaah!"

She smiled down at him as he took a deep quaff of
the glass and winked at her over its rim.

"And now, tell me," he said, wiping his lips, "how
have you fared? The message I had was exiguous to
the extreme, merely stating that you had arrived after
many vicissitudes. Tell me, I beg you, what happened
after you were released from that Yankee frigate?"

This Emmie did—as well as she was able in the circumstances—eschewing the intimate details of her congress with Yves the hunter, but dwelling upon the part he had played in her escape from the hazards of the wilderness. Devizes listened attentively, occasionally interjecting a remark or exclamation, particularly when she touched upon Yves's death.

"A great pity," he declared. "I would greatly have wished to reward the fellow with a pension. You have been lucky, my dear, to have fallen in with such a commendable pair as your hunter and the Yankee frigate captain. The latter's report—sent to me by President Madison, in reply to my protest at your capture—speaks volumes for that gentleman's humanity and decency."

"You—you have a report, sir?" cried Emmie. "Written by Nathan—by Captain Grant himself?"

"Not in his own hand. A copy, merely," replied Devizes.

"You—you have it here, sir?"

"Why, yes, my dear. It is among my papers in the bureau yonder."

"May—may I see it, sir?"

"But of course. You will find it at the top of the right-hand drawer."

Emmie found the document. It had been transcribed by some clerk or other in the Navy Office in Washington, penned in a prim, clerkish hand with a lot of flourishes. At the head of the first page was dashed off the brief instruction from the American president: *Send this to Gen. Devizes—J. Madison.*

Through sudden tears, Emmie read the opening paragraph, and relived the reality behind the formal prose:

. . . we chanced upon the *Peder Wessel,* a Norwegian out of Bristol, who, declining to heave-to when so ordered, fired upon the *Delaware,* who

returned fire. By an excess of zeal, to which no
blame attaches, Mr. Midshipman Josiah Clegg
brought back aboard Lady Devizes, wife of the
British military governor of Quebec. . .

(*"Excess of zeal!" Oh, dear, dear Midshipman
Clegg, I shall treasure your memory, and your zeal-
ousness, till the end of my days! And so will your
captain—I know it!*)

There were six pages of the report. Impossible to
read it under the watchful eyes of her husband, particularly since even the first few lines had affected her
so deeply. But she must see the end of Nathan's account, even if it broke her heart. She riffled over the
sheets, and, through her tears, read his closing words:

. . . upon which I consigned Lady Devizes and
her companions to the fisher boat, with a profound reluctance, but in the fervent hope that her
ladyship, who is a gentlewoman of most admirable parts, would come to the safe haven she de-
served.

                    sgd. N. Grant, Capt, U.S.N.

(*Oh, my darling! Did you intend that I should see
this? But how could you? This tender love story,
dressed up to read like a sober report, destined for
some dusty repository, to be read once and then forgotten, the bare truth of an idyll past and gone forever. "A gentlewoman of most admirable parts."
Thank you, my darling, for the saucy little double-
entendre!*)

"Well, my dear, does the gallant captain's account
match up to the truth of it?" Her husband's voice
brought Emmie back to the then and there.

She blinked away her tears, avoiding his glance.
"As far as I can judge at a glance, sir. May I take it
away and read it more closely?"

"By all means do," replied Devizes. "Keep it, if

you will. A keepsake—in memory of what I take to
have been a most significant experience for a young
gel.''

She met his eye. Surely there was no hidden meaning in his comment? Of course not. Nothing she had
done, nothing she had said, could ever make him sus-
pect. One so old, so out of touch with the passions of
the flesh, could not possibly discern so clearly.

To amuse her, Devizes had himself divested of the
seedy suit of civilian clothes and installed in the scarlet
full-dress of a British general. They dined together in
the great hall of the residence, a commodious chamber
that, in its original conception, had been the audito-
rium of the Covent Garden Theater. They were seated
facing each other at the two ends of a thirty-foot-long
refectory table, with a dozen servitors in attendance,
and a menu comprising three courses with *entrées,*
dessert and removes. Emmie, whose quite considerable appetite seemed to have gone oddly awry, declined all but the third course, which included goslings
removed by college pudding, and most thoroughly enjoyed no less than three large green apples at the end
of it. Her spouse, seated in his scarlet glory in the
distance, pecked half-heartedly at everything put before him, at the same time carrying on a lively monologue which absolved Emmie from the need to say
very much, and allowed her to ruminate upon the contents of Nathan's report, which she had devoured
while Agnes Reilly was dressing her for dinner.

Sir Claude Devizes, it seemed, was carrying the
biggest part of the blame for the disastrous course of
the American war; whereas the true villain of the
piece, according to Devizes, was Canada's governor,
Sir George Prevost. . . .

"An incompetent, dastardly swine, my dear," declared Devizes. "There's no more to be said about
him. . . . Yes, give me more of the boiled mackerel,
fellow; even my rotten teeth can make shift with it. I

will give you an example, my dear. On Lake Erie, the American flotilla was vastly superior to ours. Captain Barclay, who commanded our little squadron, and as brave a man as ever sailed, and had lost an arm in the service of the king—I see him now, just as he sat at this table many a time—urged Prevost to send him more sailors, or our few vessels must be captured or destroyed. What response from that swine Prevost? I will tell you. Prevost, who takes care to keep out of harm's way himself, sends messages to Captain Barclay telling him that the valor of his men will more than compensate for their lack of numbers and that he must take courage and attack the Yankees. In the end, Barclay was stung to give battle. I will tell you the odds, for they are burned into my brain as if with a red-hot iron: three hundred and fifty-six men and forty-six guns on our side, five hundred and eighty men and fifty-four guns with the Americans.

"Our fellows fought—God, how they fought!" Sir Claude was speaking with mounting choler, the unhealthy tinge of his complexion darkening to a purplish hue and his bloodshot eyes almost starting from their sockets. "Barclay fought till he had taken the flagship of the American commodore Percy, and lost his remaining arm. But it was not enough.

"Not enough!" Emmie started with alarm as her husband rose unsteadily to his feet, supporting himself heavily on the table. "Flesh and blood cannot fight against weight of metal! Not enough for one hundred and thirty-five good men to fall. Not enough for brave Barclay to lose another arm! In the end, our vessels were compelled to strike their colors!

"They were compelled to . . . *aaaaah!*"

"Sir!" cried Emmie, horrified.

He swayed and fell. Before the nearest footman could reach him, the scarlet-coated figure toppled like a puppet whose strings have been severed. He clutched at the tablecloth as he went, bringing down a chaos of serving dishes, silverware and glassware, spilled wine, candelabrum, finger bowl, cutlery—all in a sorry heap.

Four footmen, with Emmie coming after, carried him to his bedchamber. His personal physician was sent for, leaving his own dinner table in the officers' mess of the 21st Foot in the adjacent barracks. Massive and lugubrious in undress regimentals, he took the pulse of the unconscious man, turned back the unresponsive eyelids and shook his head gravely.

"Sir Claude is killing himself, ma'am," he said, addressing Emmie. "If he were back in England, resting on his estate, doing no more than walking a hound or taking a gun around a copse, I would still say he was doing too much. And to think of all he is expected to do here in Canada!"

"I will try to see to it that he rests, Doctor," said Emmie.

"Do that, my lady, I beg you," said the physician. "Do that, or, to state it bluntly, you will become a widow hard on the heels of becoming a bride. There— I have said enough. Here are some opium pills to relieve the pain in the chest when it recurs, as recur it will, for the heart is severely put upon. I bid you goodnight, ma'am. Do not hesitate to summon me if Sir Claude's condition worsens."

"Doctor, I will not," replied Emmie with fervor.

Alone with her spouse, and he in a sick torpor in his great canopied bed, Emmie looked about her. Her own bedchamber was close by, but could as lief have been on the far side of the moon. No congress would ever, could ever, take place between her and the old man in the four-poster bed. For whatever reason Sir Claude Devizes had purchased his girl bride, it could not have been for the pleasures of carnality, since it was obvious that even the slightest venture into the courts of Venus must lay an intolerable burden upon her bridegroom's ailing heart. In short, she was destined to be a wife in name only, not even an old man's plaything, but one with the chattels that lay around the residence. She would be prettier than most, perhaps, a better than average piece of furniture.

Over the chimney piece she discerned a dark painting which on closer inspection proved to be a portrait of a young girl in a gray frock. She looked to be about twenty, fair and delicate, quite lovely. Emmie was speculating upon the possible identity of the sitter when a low moan from the bed brought her to her husband's side again.

"Emmie—is that you, Emmie?" The rheumy eyes flickered open.

"Sir, you have tried yourself too much tonight," said Emmie.

"I know it, child," he said. "The mere mention of that swine Prevost is enough to bring about an attack. But how can I dismiss him from my life, seeing that he is bent upon destroying me? The defeat of which I spoke has been laid at my door. I am accused of having neglected to bring the matter of reinforcing Barclay's squadron to Prevost's attention. Ye gods! I am military governor of Quebec Province, not naval attaché to that swine!"

"Sir, don't upset yourself again," said Emmie.

"They are all intriguing against me," said Devizes. "The lot of them—excepting young Hemmings, whom I trust as a son. That fellow Tredegar, he whom I sent to fetch you from England—do you know, he had no sooner left here than I learned he had been conniving with Prevost for my downfall."

"Major Tredegar paid dearly for his shortcomings," said Emmie. "He paid in very hard coin, sir." She had told him of Tredegar's hideous end.

The thought seemed to calm her husband. "That he did, Emmie," he affirmed. "That he did indeed." The old man's breathing became less labored, and presently his hand stole across the counterpane and closed on Emmie's.

"You are a good lass," he said. "I told them I wanted the pick of the Beechborough litter, and you are she. Do you feel diminished on that score? Are you angry with me for having bought you like some palfrey at a fair? Tell me true, Emmie."

"I have been angry," admitted Emmie. "But now that I have met you, sir, I cannot find it in my heart to be other than grateful to you for taking me away from Flaxham and my awful family."

"Youth and beauty I love above all," said Devizes. "How I would have wished to have filled my life with children. Alas, that can never be, Emmie. My first wife, my dearest Mary—that is her portrait yonder— was brought to bed of no less than five children, but all were stillborn or died in infancy. And my Mary, alas, she died of the fever after bearing the fifth. So you will have to be all the children I never had, Emmie. Do you see?"

"Yes, sir." Emmie thought she saw very well. "And now, I think you had best go to sleep. Are you in pain?"

He shook his head. "No."

"Then good night, sir."

"Good night, child. Kiss me here." He touched his cheek.

Emmie chastely kissed him and departed. Agnes Reilly was attending upon her when she reached her own rooms. The maid had put out night attire and provided a basin of hot water scented with rose petals. The watchful green eyes regarded Emmie with amused calculation as she reached out to unfasten the back of her mistress's gown. But Emmie brushed her hand away, irritably.

"I can undress myself!" she snapped.

The woman's smile did not fade. "Shall I help you to wash, y' ladyship?" she asked.

"No, I am not quite helpless," replied Emmie.

"The massage, perhaps, y' ladyship? 'Tis a sure

way o' getting a good night's sleep, is the massage."

"I have no difficulty in getting to sleep."

"Well then, you'll not be needing me, y' ladyship."

"No, I will not. Good night, Reilly."

"Good night, y' ladyship. Just pull the bell cord if you need me."

Emmie waited till the door had closed behind her maid before she unfastened her dress and stepped out of it. The woman's presumption bordered on impertinence and she would possibly have to be gotten rid of. However, that consideration could wait. There remained the question of her condition, of being with child. . . .

Her husband's declaration put a very different complexion upon the case. Indeed, his words and actions had amply demonstrated that the most favorable of all options was open to her, since he was clearly incapable of making any carnal demands, yet at the same time he craved to have children of his own. Soaping her breasts, Emmie had the suspicion that her nipples were a mite sore—a phenomenon which she had heard innumerable mothers-to-be among her relations at Flaxham comment upon. A month hence, two months—at least before her condition became obvious—she would confess all to Sir Claude. By that time they would know each other better and the confession would come easier. In any event, she thought, and with some candor, it was always pleasant to postpone an awkward scene. . . .

The silk nightshift slipped over her head and whispered down her body in liquid kisses, setting up a strange arousal in her mind. The feeling persisted when she crept between the sheets and reached out to snuff her candle. Odd, how, without any warning, one's body could assert itself and make dictates upon one's mind. She had come from Sir Claude's bedside in a testy, thin-skinned sort of mood, quick to rebuff her maid's importunities. How she missed the woman now!

Emmie toyed with the notion of pulling the bell cord, which was close by her hand, and which would summon, at one touch, Agnes Reilly, whose room was just down the corridor. The woman would come straight from her bed, dressed in her coarse linen nightshift, hair plaited in a single pigtail, green eyes insolently amused. One could say, simply: "Damme, I can't sleep, Reilly. Talk to me if you will. It's cold now that the fire has gone down, so get into bed with me if you please. . . ."

The notion aroused her the more. She stayed her hand from touching the bell cord. Instead, inspired by a wayward wantonness, she shrugged the silk night-shift from her shoulders, peeled it over breasts, belly, hips, legs, trampled it down into a knot at her feet. Nude, now, she allowed her hands to make a new exploration of her body—as if they were not her own, as if they were the hands of her lover, of the far-off man who owned her heart.

Still searching, high on a mountain crest of blissful self-knowledge, she drifted from sublimity into slumber.

Two days later, Sir Claude was sitting up in bed and demanding gargantuan meals of broiled meats washed down with copious draughts of small beer and brandy. His bout of malaise appeared to have given him a new lease on life, and from it he emerged strengthened in body, stiffened in resolve. Let that swine Prevost beware, he told Emmie, he—Devizes—was not without influence in the halls of power, nor was he averse to applying the levers of intrigue, not if it meant tumbling a swine like Prevost, not if it meant winning the war. . . .

On the fourth day after his attack, Devizes was on his feet and walking. Walking, still—though leaning heavily on Emmie's arm—he took her to meet the officers of the 21st Foot, who lived only just across her back yard, in the barracks that formed the other two sides of a handsome square containing a bronze statue of General Wolfe, victor of Quebec, set high upon a plinth.

The colonel of the 21st and his officers were enchanted by the lovely young wife of the military governor of Quebec Province and straightway extended to the governor and his lady an invitation to a ball they were holding the following Tuesday eve. It was by way of a farewell party, for the regiment was relinquishing garrison duties in the city to the Argyll and Sutherland Highlanders and marching to upper Canada and the stern business of fighting the Yankees. Fortuitously, the occasion also coincided with the anniversary of some minor skirmish in which the regiment had gained distinction under Marlborough during the wars in the Low Countries.

On the day before the ball—Monday—came news that the Americans under their General Harrison were marching on Kingston and Montreal, had killed the chief of Britain's Indian allies, one Tecumthé, flayed him and cut up his skin into razor strops and sent them to various prominent Congressmen. No less than three Yankee armies were closing in. Sir George Prevost had—typically—lost his head and ordered the scanty British forces on the spot to fall back on Kingston, leaving all Upper Canada exposed to the invaders.

"I shall have go back there posthaste, Emmie," said her spouse. "Someone has to stiffen that swine's backbone. And I thank the Lord that he will be too busy trying to save his own skin to waste any time in stabbing me in the back."

"But, sir, you have been so ill," protested Emmie. "Such a long journey, not to mention the strains and anxieties of war. Your country demands too much of you."

"Dear Emmie, sweet child," he murmured, patting her cheek. "I declare that you are the most tenderhearted creature I have ever known. But you plead in vain, my dear. Without me to hold the center, Kingston and Montreal must surely fall."

"I shall come with you!" declared Emmie, inspired with the sudden notion.

"No, my dear, you will not." He was gentle, but implacable. "You will remain here and look after my establishment, entertain my guests, and write to me often. And tomorrow night you will represent me as guest of honor at the ball of the 21st Foot. They deserve you, poor devils, for they march back to the war the day after, and you may be sure they will be thrust into the worst of the fighting as soon as they arrive."

" 'Pon my word, Lady Devizes, you present a vision to gladden the eye!"

Colonel Charteris of the 21st had a not entirely unwarranted reputation as a lady killer, in addition to being a firebrand in battle and an inspiration to his men. Tall, massively made, with a thatch of unruly red hair, he seemed about to burst out of the constricting scarlet coat and doeskin breeches.

"You are too kind, Colonel," smiled Emmie, giving him her hand to kiss, well aware that every eye in the room—both male and female—was upon her. She was wearing one of the Grecian gowns—deceptively simple in appearance, yet owing everything to the subtle cutting of the fabric on the bias to achieve the effect of the garment having *grown* on her, partaking of every nuance of her shapely form, though not to the point of scandal, and certainly not to the contrivance of having been damped the better to cling—which had been made for her by one of the skillful little French dressmakers in the upper town.

The colonel beamed down at her from his great height, from which vantage point he was able to reflect upon the admirable structure of her bosom.

"I trust, ma'am, that Sir Claude made a good departure this morning."

"That he did, sir," said Emmie.

"Well, the Twenty-First will be hard on his heels

tomorrow," declared Charteris. "And with Sir George's
good counsel being heard in Montreal, I don't doubt
but that we shall be in the thick of it before another
week is out. Lady Devizes, your hand, ma'am. The
time has come for you and me to take the floor and
start the proceedings."

The first dance was a lively gavotte, the music supplied by the regimental string orchestra of some fifteen
pieces, who occupied an outward-curving balcony
above the dance floor. Emmie and the colonel did
three solo circuits of the floor in very brisk manner
and then the remainder joined in. Officers and their
wives and local sweethearts, a sprinkling of city dig-
nitaries.

There were some who did not take the floor for the
first dance. One who did not—a dark-haired, dark-
eyed young subaltern—lolled against a pillar with an
awkward grace, made a gauche attempt to stand to
attention in time to meet his colonel's eye, and blushed
like a schoolgirl when Emmie smiled at him in passing.

"They're sendin' some pretty rum officer material
out from England nowadays," said Charteris loudly—
certainly loud enough for the boy to have heard. "The
cream of the newly commissioned fellers are being
sent to the Peninsula, and that's right enough, I
s'pose, for it's Bonaparte who really holds the pistol
to our vitals and 'tis only a matter of time before we
lick those demned renegade colonials, the Yankees."

"I'm sure you're right, sir," murmured Emmie.

On the next turn around the floor, Colonel Charteris
paused by the dark-haired boy officer and pointed a
commanding finger.

"See here, Mr. Morris, my lad," he said. "I'm told
that you ain't walked the plank yet."

"Nu-no, Colonel," was the faltering response.

"Then you shall walk the plank tonight, Mr. Morris," declared the colonel.

"Yes, sir." The boy bit his lip.

"Demned namby-pamby!" growled Charteris, as he

guided Emmie around the floor again. "I'll not countenance back-sliding from my subalterns. Tradition—
that's the ticket. Unwritten rule of the mess says that
all junior officers must perform such tasks as the president of the mess ordains. That young feller had his
orders a week since and ain't carried 'em out yet. But
he will do so tonight, by gad!"

The gavotte ended with a brisk flourish of violin
pizzicato. Charteris bowed and handed Emmie toward
her seat.

"And what, pray, does walking the plank involve,
Colonel?" she asked.

Charteris grinned down at his guest of honor's generous *décolletage*. "Ah, you will see, ma'am, you will
see," he replied. He would not be drawn further.

Emmie, new to regimental functions, was surprised at
the rapidity with which the ball of the 21st Foot de-
teriorated from a quite formal occasion, by way of a
mild romp, to the kind of thoroughgoing Saturnalia so
beloved of army messes and the common rooms of the
senior universities. A very great deal of champagne
was drunk at the buffet table, its effect aggravated by
a hot negus produced, with a great deal of ceremony,
in the vast silver regimental punchbowl. What was not
drunk of the negus, the younger officers proceeded to
throw over each other. Colonel Charteris did not appear to see anything amiss in their behavior, but called
out encouragement to the more riotous of his subalterns.

It drew near to midnight. Emmie, smothering a
yawn, began to assemble in her mind the most quick
and easy means by which she could excuse herself and
slip away across the square to the residence and her
comfortable bed. The older and more staid guests had
already taken their leave, and there remained only the
regimental officers, the younger of the wives and the
sweethearts. Some of the latter had so forgotten their
decorum as to be behaving as badly as the subalterns;

one chit of a thing in *tissue d'or* was riding piggyback upon her drunken swain and had all but overspilled her bodice during her exertions. Someone had produced a hunting horn and was sketching his way hesitantly through "Gone to earth," "Gone Away" and so forth.

Emmie laid a hand on Charteris's arm. "Colonel, do you greatly mind if I . . . ?" she murmured.

He beamed down at her, not hearing a word she said. "All in good time, ma'am, all in good time," was his obscure response, patting her hand. Then, addressing the company: "Silence, all of you! Have a care! Cease that caterwauling, Pendennis! Leave that lady be, Marjoribanks! Listen, all of you—our young Mr. Ensign Morris is goin' to walk the plank!"

Loud whoops followed his announcement. The hornblower essayed another blast and was silenced by a glare from his commanding officer.

"Step forth, Mr. Morris!" bawled Charteris.

More whoops. The lines parted, and the dark-haired boy was shoved forward to face his colonel. Emmie's heart went out to him immediately, for his countenance had that damp pallor that accompanies extreme terror, his mouth hung slackly, his eyes were haunted. Notwithstanding, he bore himself tolerably well, with shoulders squared, chest out, fingers aligned with the stripes of gold braid that ran down each side of his overalls.

Colonel Charteris pointed upward to the gallery that ran around the upper part of the mess; partaking of the wide staircase and the orchestra balcony, it was bounded by a handsomely carved wooden balustrade some twenty feet above the parquet dance floor.

"You will walk the plank, Mr. Morris, as you have been so ordered by the president of the mess," said Charteris. "Somewhat *belatedly*, I may add. However"—he treated the youth to a bare-toothed, vulpine grin—"I am willing to overlook your tardiness, not to say your unwillingness to carry out the order, providing you perform the feat with style, dispatch and coolness. Be off with you!"

"Yessir . . ." It was no more than a whisper. The boy's haunted eyes circled the ring of faces as if seeking for assistance. They held Emmie's for a moment, then sped on—for her hand was still resting upon the colonel's arm, secured there by Charteris's massive paw.

"Then why do you tarry, boy?"

Turning about, the youth walked toward the staircase, and the ring of spectators parted to let him through. Emmie watched him go, with something inside her screaming aloud to her brain that she must stop whatever cruelty was about to be enacted.

"This will be interesting, ma'am," confided Charteris.

"What exactly is he going to attempt?" she whispered.

Charteris pointed. "He will climb up onto the capping of the balustrade, which, as you see, is about as wide as a man's boot. He will then walk along it from the staircase to the balcony. Not very far—about twenty yards, as you see, ma'am. That is what we call 'walking the plank.' "

"But—if he should fall?" breathed Emmie, horrified.

Again that vulpine grin. "Consider, ma'am," said Charteris, with the air of a teacher reciting a lesson, "yonder capping. If it were placed two inches above the ground, a man could walk it—*would* walk it—without hesitation, carrying a hundredweight sack of coal on his back and both his boots on the wrong feet. Raise it by twenty feet, ma'am, and there you have the difference. There *is* no difference, save in the mind. But it is a *distinction* that separates the soldier from the namby-pamby. We shall see, ma'am, into which category comes Mr. Ensign Morris."

"But—Colonel—what if he *did* fall?" persisted Emmie.

"He would break an arm, or a leg, or his neck, or all three," replied Charteris, and by the steely deadness in his eyes, she could see that he was very drunk and completely uncaring. "In which case, I am rid of an officer who will be nothing but a liability when next we march to the sound of the Yankee guns!"

"Oh, my God!" said Emmie under her breath.

The boy officer had reached the top of the staircase. A moment's hesitation, only, and he hauled himself to a seated position on top of the balustrade. In a silence that could be felt, he slowly rose to his knees, and then, slower yet, he stood up with arms extended, one foot slightly advanced along the capping. Below him, the unaccommodating wooden floor; ahead, twenty paces to the orchestra balcony and safety.

He took a shuffling pace forward—swayed—almost lost his balance.

A woman screamed.

"Have silence!" roared Charteris. "Carry øn, Mr. Morris!"

Another cautious step, this time achieved with steadiness. And then he paused for quite some moments. Emmie bit her lip and clenched her teeth.

"Get on with it, do, lad!" ordered Charteris.

Young Morris took a quick pace. And then another. By this time, his face was bathed in sweat, as was his whole head, the black hair being plastered across his brow; and there were rivulets pouring down his cheeks, bedewing his upper lip and chin, blinding him. He paused again to wipe his eyes.

"Don't cry, Bo-Peep!" mocked his colonel. Everyone laughed. Charteris grinned at Emmie. "I had a notion that the feller was nothing more than a namby-pamby of the girlish persuasion," he declared. "And I'm being proven right."

"I would not say that, Colonel!" retorted Emmie. "I would say that up there is a gallant young man obeying a stupid, utterly pointless and criminally dangerous order. And doing not too badly.'' Her splendid bosom rose and fell with the fury of her passion.

Charteris's essentially stupid, beef-red face turned toward her, the pale blue eyes incredulous. " 'P-pon my word, ma'am!'' he stammered.

Emmie raised her voice. She had a high, clear voice when aroused to anger, and with a very good cutting edge. "Mr. Morris!'' she called. "Don't look down. This is Lady Devizes speaking. I greatly admire your courage and expertise, but I beg you to cut short this exhibition. Your audience is getting bored and restive and I for one am wanting to go home to bed.''

In the silence that followed her astonishing outburst, young Morris seemed to undergo a change of spirit. He swallowed hard, blinked the sweat from his eyes, shook his head free of the excess droplets, extended his arms widely, took a very deep breath.

And walked twenty-odd swift paces to his goal!

Quickly, unhesitatingly, as if—in Charteris's phrase—the balustrade had been two inches above the ground!

A chorus of acclaim greeted his feat, and they clustered around him as he descended the stairs. A young girl kissed him on the cheek. A glass was pressed into his hand, and a frothing gush of champagne poured into it. He met Emmie's eyes over and through a sea of heads. She smiled.

"My dear boy,'' said Colonel Charteris, "I am proud and happy for you. Well done! Up to the standard of the Twenty-first!''

"Thank you, Colonel,'' responded the boy, unsmiling.

"And I'll tell you what, young feller. To you shall go the honor of leading the first patrol into the Yankee positions. What d'you think of that, hey? Chance of glory for you, my lad. Make your mother proud o' you, hey?'' He clapped Morris on the back.

"Thank you, sir,'' responded the boy officer, handing his glass to a comrade. "Will you excuse me, please. I must go and . . ."

Bowing briefly, he walked quickly away out of the mess.

"Well, that had a happy conclusion," declared Colonel Charteris. "I had my doubts about young Morris, and I don't deny it, but I was entirely confounded." His eyes met Emmie's and he smiled. "Ah, ma'am, ma'am!" he said, chidingly.

"Sir?" Emmie's chin went up.

But he was placatory, all male condescension. He took her soft upper arm between finger and thumb and squeezed, while gazing with yearning at the rich cleft of her bosom.

"You have judged us harshly, Lady Devizes," he said. "We men of the sword. Harshly, but perhaps not unjustly. Ah, yes, our codes, practices, shibboleths are often incomprehensible to the world outside, but they all serve a great design, are directed to a glorious conclusion."

"Indeed, sir?"

He mauled her upper arm, put his beef-red face close to her face, so that she could smell the wine and spirits on his breath. "But we are not composed entirely of hardness and violence, ma'am," he confided. "There is in every soldier's breast a heart that beats for love of beauty and gentleness. Do I make myself plain?"

Emmie thought he made himself—and his aspirations—very plain indeed. Gently extricating her arm from his fondling grasp, she said brightly, "Well, it has been a most enjoyable evening, Colonel. You will excuse me, but I must retire."

"Quite so, ma'am. Quite so." He rocked back on his heels. Hiccuped. Gave her a very close approximation to a wink. "I will have the honor to escort you personally to your—*quarters*."

"How kind," said Emmie, her mind racing. "Ah—

will you be so good as to attend while I fetch my shawl from the cloakroom?"

"The wait will seem an eternity, but worth every instant," breathed her would-be seducer.

There was, she supposed, a rear exit from the mess building, and the residence was only a half-minute's walk—or run—across the square. She obtained her paisley shawl from the attendant in the ladies' cloakroom and, upon inquiry, learned that the egress she sought lay through the mess anteroom and beyond the billiard room. She directed her steps toward the same.

There was no one about. The lofty rooms, smelling of polished leather and Macassar oil, were dimly candlelit. Pushing open a screen door beyond the room where stood a billiard table, she encountered night air and a hint of frost. Nor was that all. A humped form was pressed against the wall hard by the door. And to her ears came a sound that evoked a bitter memory: the sound of a weeping man.

He stopped at the noise of her footfall.

"Who—who's that?" Tremulous. Defensive. Frightened.

Emmie thought she knew the voice. "Is that Mr. Morris?" she asked.

"Oh, my God—Lady Devizes!" He groaned. "That it should come to this! I wish I had the courage to put a bullet in my brain!"

"But why—*why?*" cried Emmie. "You have passed the test. You have satisfied the stupid, wicked dictates of your caste—all of which, I am assured, are intended to serve a grand design and a glorious conclusion. Why do you not dry your eyes, blow your nose and go back in there—where I am sure you will find some adoring and complaisant wench to dote on you for the brave boy you are?"

"How can I go back in this state?" he said. "I can't stop trembling. And—I have wet myself."

Emmie's heart turned over. "Oh, you poor, silly

boy!'' she cried. ''Look—come with me.'' She seized him by the hand.

''But—Lady Devizes. Ma'am . . .''

''Come. Quickly. Before somebody sees us.''

Leading him by the hand, she ran across the moonlit square, under the—no doubt disapproving—bronze eyes of the Victor of Quebec, to the small formal garden of the residence and a garden door that led, by way of a staircase, directly to the upper corridor and her suite of rooms.

''Tread quietly,'' she whispered. ''My maid will be waiting up for me and she mustn't hear you.''

Tiptoeing along the carpeted corridor with Morris after her, Emmie reached her door, dragged him inside, shut and locked it. Agnes Reilly must have heard the sound. . . .

Tap, tap. ''Is there anything you require, m' lady?''

''Thank you, no, Reilly.''

''I hope as you enjoyed the ball, m' lady.''

''Tolerably well, Reilly. Good night.''

''Good night, y' ladyship.''

Footsteps receding down the corridor, the quiet closing of a door at the far end. Emmie exhaled noisily. ''Ha, well, that's settled for her. Now, young man, what am I going to do about you?''

He stared at her wildly. ''Ma'am, I am compromising your reputation. I must leave here. I must . . .''

''You must strip off your clothes and have an all-over wash for a start,'' declared Emmie. ''Come into my dressing room. There'll be a hip bath and a ewer of hot water laid out. I'll go and fetch one of my husband's dressing gowns for you to change into. Don't stand gawping at me, young man. Attend to yourself, or must I bath you as if you were a babe?''

She found a voluminous woolen dressing gown in her spouse's adjoining quarters and tossed it in through the door beyond which she could hear Morris splashing in her hip bath. Returning to the sitting room, she poured herself a large measure of brandy, adding seltzer. The night's events, the heat of the over-crowded mess had together contributed to a restless-ness of spirit, a fretfulness that was quite foreign to her. Why else should she pace about the room, panth-erine, glass in one hand, plumping cushions, setting ornaments in order, straightening pictures.

What was she going to do with that ridiculous, pretty boy? She was certainly insane to bring him here. What if it were to get about that the lady wife of the military governor of Quebec had entertained a young subaltern in her quarters during her aged hus-band's absence at the war? Let his wet small-clothes be dried before her bedroom fire and she would send him packing, bathed and dressed.

Emmie downed the rest of her brandy in a gulp, poured herself another, without seltzer, and threw herself down into a chaise longue witt a flurry of dia-phanous silks and a sulky expression.

How long was that boy going to be in there—how long?

He came out. Her husband's voluminous dressing gown reached only to his knees and revealed that his lower calves were well-shaped and covered with a fine pelt of black hair. Likewise his chest, disclosed by the buttonless front opening of the garment, was smoothly formed and darkly fleeced. The head, neatly set upon the man's body, still looked incredibly boyish.

"Put your things to dry in front of the fire," said Emmie, pointing. "In there—in my bedroom."

He nodded, and came back when he had performed the task.

"Well now," said Emmie briskly. "Do you feel bet-ter?"

"Somewhat better, ma'am," he replied. "At least I know what I must now do."

"And what is that—if one may ask?"

"I must resign my commission and return to Eng-land," he said.

"Resign?"

His dark, brooding and melancholy eyes avoided hers. "I cannot leave with the regiment tomorrow," he said. "Tonight has proved it. I am—a coward."

"That you are not!" responded Emmie heatedly. "A mite of encouragement from me and you stepped it out like a man."

A bitter, self-mocking smile touched the corners of his lips. " 'A mite of encouragement'—I'm grateful to you for that, ma'am. But—regrettably—you'll not be at hand to offer encouragement when I have to march to the sound of the guns, and—" He broke off, buried his face in his hands. "The thought of it has haunted my dreams and my waking hours ever since I arrived in Canada: the thought of meeting my baptism of fire!"

"You have never been under fire before?"

He lowered his hands, shook his head. "No, ma'am. I am—straight from school. My widowed mother bought me my commission because she thought I would cut a fine dash in uniform. Indeed, I did cut a fine dash—in the assembly rooms at Bath!"

"And so you will when you meet the enemy!" Emmie promised him. "You have no idea of what your feelings will be, never having had the experience."

He exhaled a shuddering breath. "Ma'am, it's well said that a coward dies a hundred times and a brave man only once. My fellow officers, considering me to be—effeminate . . ."

"Oh, no!" cried Emmie. "I'll not have *that!*"

"Considering me to be effeminate, and having no wish to spare the feelings of a 'namby-pamby,' regaled me in some detail with what it's like to be under fire. There is a Lieutenant Marjoribanks—you must have met him tonight—who told me how he led a patrol, one dawn, against a Yankee outpost on the shore of Lake Erie—a position of honor, which, you will recall, I earned for myself by walking the plank tonight. Marjoribanks, who is not a bad fellow at heart and who holds me in utter contempt for what I am . . ."

"You are what you *wish* to be, what you *will* yourself to be!" cried Emmie. "Not what other people *thrust* upon you!"

Morris closed his eyes and continued. "Marjoribanks, who also has a good turn of phrase and tells a vivid story, particularly after his second bottle of mess claret, said how the patrol approached the Yankee position in extended line, bayonets outthrust. It was pitch dark. Ahead lay half a hundred men—asleep. And sentries, with eyes probing the darkness. The object of our patrol: to capture a sentry and bring him back for interrogation.

"Picture now the scene, ma'am. Darkness and silence. Moving forward to one's own heartbeat.

"And then, says Marjoribanks, a row of cannons gave fire ahead of them. Bombs spluttered in the air, lighting the scene in a ruddy glow of hell. Men screamed. Marjoribanks distinctly saw a man's head being taken off and explode like a melon. . . ."

"*Stop it!*" cried Emmie.

"And the company sergeant-major, he was cut clean in half by a shell. Marjoribanks told how the upper part of the torso landed squarely on the ground. Upright. And still screaming from the dead mouth. . . ."

"No more. Don't torture yourself further," pleaded Emmie, taking his hands and drawing him to her. "Put it out of your mind, or you'll go mad!"

"There was more—worse!" he cried. "I was spared nothing of what war is all about. And, oh! What a fine figure I cut in the assembly rooms at Bath! My God, if they could all see me now!"

"Hush, hush!" she whispered.

"Ma'am, what am I going to do?" He fell on his knees before her, and she, still seated on the chaise longue, drew his head onto her lap. "I dare not march to the sound of the guns. I cannot go back to my mother and confess that her brave soldier boy is a coward and a namby-pamby." He looked up at her, pleadingly.

"You are neither of those things, my dear," she

whispered, pressing him to her bosom and immediately receiving his eager, thirsting lips. "You are a complete man, but all unaware—as I will shortly prove."

So saying, she tugged gently at the sash of his borrowed dressing gown so that it fell apart, revealing him nude underneath.

Chapter Two

A church clock in the upper town tolled the hour of
seven. Emmie counted every stroke and stretched herself, luxuriating in the feeling of being alive to the
extremities of her toes. It was still dark. She could see
the branches of the yew tree outside her bedroom window wavering in the night wind, and the lights on the
river beyond. Her slight movement half-roused the
boy at her side; he mumbled in his sleep, turned over,
flung out an arm, found her there. Woke with a start.

"Hello," she whispered.

"Hello. What time is it?"

"Seven o'clock."

"The candle has burned out."

"Hours and hours ago," said Emmie. "It guttered
and died. I watched it happen. So did you."

"When?" he asked. "When was that?"

"Young man," said Emmie, tracing her finger, in
the darkness, down his chest to the firm recess of his
navel, "you are fishing for compliments."

"When?" he persisted.

"And such a bully!" she declared. Fingers splayed, her small hand stole across his firm, flat belly. "You know well enough the candle died just after you had pleasured me for the second time."

"The second time—ah!"

"Not only a bully," she said, "But also demanding to a degree, and intolerably smug withal. Do you like what I am doing to you, or shall I stop?"

"If you stop," he said, "I shall throw wide the window and call out the guard to arrest you, Lady Devizes."

They laughed, mouth to mouth, each tongue exploring the other, the whole length of their bodies pressed each to each. A long quietness followed. And then began a mounting of their concerted passions. Slowly at first, then gathering momentum, true as waves beating on a shore and as irresistible.

Emmie, alone, maintained a degree of detachment. To her, the delight of knowing her boy-lover was part of a great pattern whose shape, form, texture, colorings had been dictated for all time by the loving craftsmanship of Nathan Grant. To the youth in whose strong arms she was clasped, the encounter was clearly as pristine as a gambol over virgin snow, in which he delighted to skip, hop and cavort with no regard save that of discovering new means. And his very abandonment, his warm vivacity, won her completely, so that she allowed herself to be gathered up with the fierce current of his passion and finally delivered, breathless upon the shore of fulfillment.

A cock crowed in the distance. Cold dawn showed through the branches of the yew tree outside. Her boy-lover, spent, was sleeping with his tousled, dark head pillowed on her shoulder, his lips close against the generous swell of her breast.

Sleep for another hour, my little soldier, she thought. *And then I'm sure you will know what you have to do. No namby-pamby you, but a man like all the others— only in a prettier wrapping.*

But I beg you, she thought, *never in your swaggering, manlike way, boast to your comrades that you seduced the wife of the military governor of Quebec Province. Nor (and this is the truth of the matter) that you were seduced by her.*

Rather, tell them that, long ago, with the name and the place forgotten after the uncounted women who have enjoyed your favors since, you lost your manly virginity to a total stranger—a lady of title and of tremendous discrimination, who, bored to distraction by the attentions of princes, poets, painters and prelates, looked upon you in favor.

She stroked his sable brow fondly.

The departure from Quebec of the 21st Foot was enlivened by a glorious day of high blue skies and bracing wind, with the last of the old year's golden leaves showering the long, scarlet columns. Emmie watched it all from the balcony of the residence with the obsequious Gareth Hemmings a respectful two paces behind her elbow. The young secretary opined that the soldiers looked very fine—as indeed they did.

Colonel Charteris rode at the head of his regiment on a spirited black charger. Upon passing the residency, he called for an "eyes left" in a stentorian bellow that sent the turtle doves flying in alarm from the rooftop and brought five hundred and fifty pairs of lustful glances to bear upon the beautiful brunette up high on the balcony. She acknowledged the tribute with a gracious wave. There were many among that brave company who would greatly have preferred to stay in Quebec and try their mettle with the wife of the military governor rather than march to meet the Yankees—Colonel Charteris not excepted. Notwithstanding the tribute of the salute, there was a gleam of resentment in his eye that could be discerned at the thirty paces that separated them. Emmie wondered, with a twinge of conscience, how long he had waited for her to return to the mess with her cape the previous night.

"Yes, a very fine body of men, ma'am," repeated the voice at her elbow.

"Indeed, yes," said Emmie.

"The Second Company is very smart," said Hemmings. "Mark them when they go past, ma'am."

"Yes, I will," said Emmie. "Would you please point them out to me when they come abreast of us?"

"That will scarcely be necessary, ma'am," was the secretary's curious response. "Suffice to say that the Second Company is Ensign Morris's company. And that gentleman will be marching at their head."

Emmie gave a start of surprise and met the other's gaze.

"Indeed?" she murmured.

"And your ladyship is familiar with Mr. Morris, of course," continued Hemmings with a smile of mockery. "Not to say—*intimate*."

Emmie felt a hot flush rise from her throat and suffuse her cheeks, and by this was hideously aware that she was exhibiting guilt.

What to say? The remark was clearly barbed and aimed to wound. To ignore it was to invite further insinuations. Here was a nettle that must be grasped boldly and uprooted.

"What exactly are you trying to imply, Hemmings?" she demanded with a fine edge of hauteur.

He did not reply at once, but continued to outstare her, eyes narrowed, the ugly smile playing on his lips. Somewhere far off on the edge of reality, a fife and drum band tooted and rattled past, and the *stamp-stamp* of nailed boots on cobblestones went on ceaselessly.

"Come, ma'am," Hemmings said at length. "We know, do we not, that your ladyship's congress with the officers of the Twenty-first was not entirely confined to matters social? Nor did your ladyship extend her gracious favors generally, as a guest of honor should, but particularly—and to one particular party. And that party was Ensign Morris."

She almost hit him across the mouth then, but curbed herself in time.

"You have been spying on me, Hemmings," she said.

"Yes, ma'am." The smile persisted.

Emmie felt some of her assurance dribble away before his imperturbable glance, but was far from throwing away the game. After all, she told herself, what could he possibly *know* for sure?

"Listen to me, Hemmings," she said with a calmness that she certainly did not feel. "I do not have to explain or excuse my conduct to the likes of you, but I will, nevertheless, illuminate your grubby little mind about the happenings of last night."

"Oh, pray do, ma'am," said Hemmings, still grinning. "That will be most instructive."

Again resisting the impulse to strike him, Emmie continued. "Mr. Morris very kindly offered himself as escort from the officers' mess to the residence. That is all. That is the beginning, the middle and the ending of the story."

"In return for which, ma'am, you entertained the gallant gentleman in your quarters," replied Hemmings.

Emmie took a deep breath. "It may seem incomprehensible to the likes of you, Hemmings," she said, "but in the enlightened society in which I was reared, a lady may offer a gentleman a glass of wine in her own quarters without fear of jeopardizing her reputation to any save the low-bred, mealy-mouthed, puritanical rabble."

He flushed darkly at her thrust. A Roland for his Oliver there, thought Emmie.

"Quite so, ma'am," he retorted at length. "But I fancy that even within your ladyship's exalted set—

and I include your ladyship's husband—it is deemed a trifle too *enlightened* for a married lady to take a young gentleman to her bed upon first acquaintance.''

For the third time, secretary Hemmings stood within an ace of being struck across the face in full view of all, but, again, Emmie restrained herself.

"Hemmings," she said. "I have been unbelievably patient with you. I have tried to enlighten you as to the behavior of persons belonging to a higher station than your own. But you persist in offering me gratuitous insult. Here is what you will do: you will immediately pack your traps and depart from my house this day. I will explain your departure to Sir Claude when he returns—and I shall omit nothing in the telling!''

"Shall you tell him perhaps, my lady, that you played the game of handy dandy not once but twice with young Morris? And all with the candle burning— shameless as you are!''

Emmie had no response, no armor against that killing thrust. She could only stare and mouth a silent question. And that question was: *how?* . . .

Hemmings divined the question. He pointed along the southern facade of the building, from which the windows of Emmie's quarters looked out, to the spreading branches of the great yew tree that grew outside her bedroom.

"From the yew," he said simply.

"You—you were *watching* us?" breathed Emmie, all thoughts of denial gone.

"Until the candle burned down," said Hemmings. "Your performance I found most instructive. You are a born teacher, my lady. Many would like to receive tuition in the arts of Venus from your hands.''

In that instant, the last vestiges of the earnest, deferential functionary died in Emmie's imagination, and she saw Hemmings plainly.

"You disgusting swine!" she breathed. "Are you blackmailing me, then?''

He spread his hands, shrugged. "Shall we say, rather, ma'am, that I am making a bid for a debt of gratitude. Your—encounter—with Ensign Morris is a safe secret with me, likewise the somewhat curious goings-on that take place between you and your lady's maid . . ."

"My God!" cried Emmie. "Is nothing sacred from your prying eyes?"

He tried, without much success, to look pious and holier-than-thou. "I do not seek to pry," he said. "We all have our foibles. Some pursue the innocent beasts of the field with horse and hound and gun. Others"— and he cocked a meaningful eye at Emmie—"others pursue their own kind, in lechery and lust, intent upon fornication. My vice, if vice it can be called, is to enlarge my knowledge of my fellow beings by observing them in moments when they are not aware of being watched."

"You are a dirty-minded Peeping Tom!" cried Emmie. "That's what you are!"

"As you choose, my lady," responded Hemmings. "However, as I said, your secret is safe with me, and all I lay claim to is your gratitude. I am sure you will not require me to leave today, after all."

"Get out of my sight!" hissed Emmie.

"As your ladyship pleases," said Hemmings, smiling. "A pity, is it not, that the parade has gone past? You have been so busy declaring your innocence that the object of your guilt has gone by without so much as a farewell glance passing between you. I will take my leave, ma'am." A mocking bow and he was gone.

With a small wrench of anguish, Emmie turned and gazed down the promenade to the tail end of the 21st Foot: the broad backs of the bearded pioneers with their shouldered axes, the sutlers' carts bringing up the rear, and the sound of fifes and drums as faint and far away as a memory.

She closed her eyes. A sweet sadness gave way to self-anger.

"Fool! Fool!" she whispered. "You deceived yourself that you were helping a frightened boy to discover his manhood; but it was only your damned, lecherous Cradock blood, Emmie my girl!

"You've delivered yourself into the hands of a pervert and a blackmailer, that's what you've done, Emmie. And make blackmailing demands upon you he will, have no doubts on that score.

"But—what *sort* of demands?"

She gave an involuntary shudder, as if someone had just walked over her grave.

Gareth Hemmings wrote to his mother that evening, as usual taking tremendous care over the letter's composition. As he wrote, a smile played upon his lips and he occasionally glanced up from his task to meet his own reflection in a mirror on the wall opposite, and then the grin of triumph turned to a smirk of self-satisfaction, so that it was almost with reluctance that he readdressed himself to his work.

The day following the departure of the 21st brought a flurry of snow to the province. Though quickly dispersed by the midday sun, pockets of it remained on the hillsides, in the hedgerows and the eaves, and in the bronze ears of General Wolfe's statue in the square behind the residence. On that day, also, Emmie felt so sick and wretched that she could not bring herself to eat her breakfast when Agnes Reilly brought her tray to her in bed. The lady's maid formed her own opinion of the occurrence but kept prudent counsel. Not till a week later (and the morning nausea had continued), when, during her daily massage, Emmie winced and cried out in pain when the questing hands brushed against her nipples, did the woman speak her mind.

"Y' ladyship," she said, "speaking as one who's borne six, I'm thinking that you're with child."

"Yes, Reilly, I am," replied Emmie. "I think"—
she made, surely for the hundredth time, a rough count
of the weeks since the idyll aboard the *Delaware*—"I
think I'm just about two months gone."

"Quite so, y' ladyship." The green eyes were unwavering. "Sure, that would be about right for the
condition you're in. Well, 'tis a lovely blessing for Sir
Claude, so it is."

"Sir Claude doesn't know," said Emmie. "Not
yet."

"Well, there's no use in making the dear gentleman
anxious before 'tis necessary," replied the imperturbable lady's maid. "But sure, 'tis with a joyful heart
that he'll hear the news. When you tell him."

Silence. On Emmie's part, a long and thoughtful
silence . . .

"Are you *sure* of that, Reilly?" she asked.

"Yes, y' ladyship, I am so!" The reply was instant
and unequivocal. There was no need to bandy dates
and places. The woman could add up as well as she.

"I hope so," said Emmie. "Oh, how I hope so!"

"Y' ladyship"—the green eyes were entreating and
treacherously close to tears—"you need have no fear
about Sir Claude, God bless him for the lovely gentleman he is. Why, a child would bring sunshine into his
life to brighten his days."

"He told me," said Emmie, remembering, "that he
would like to have filled his life with children."

"And when he heard that my poor six innocent
mites were taken from me a babbies," said the other,
"Sir Claude, he all but broke down and cried. Says
he, 'Reilly, we are joined together by the bond of experience. Never to have had children of one's own,
that's a sad thing, but to have known the delight—
even for so short a time—and then to have lost the
loved life, is half joy, half bitterness.' "

"I shall tell him," said Emmie, full of resolve, "just
as soon as he returns to Quebec."

"Ah, you do that, y' ladyship," said Agnes Reilly

fervently, "and I swear to you that you'll not regret it."

Having secured by tacit, unspoken agreement an ally in her lady's maid, Emmie felt greatly raised in spirits, and the more so because Agnes Reilly's summation of her husband's worthy character confirmed her own opinion. As the days lengthened into weeks and the signs and portents of her confinement grew ever more marked, she fretted for Sir Claude's return so that—as she hoped and earnestly prayed—he might, at worst, accept the unborn child without undue repining, and, at best, with joy and love.

The winter days drew in, and the province lay under a counterpane of the first snows. Emmie received not a word from her husband, but many-tongued rumor breathed in every corner of the city, gained credence in alehouses and taprooms galore, spread, even, to the mess of the Seaforth Highlanders, newly established in the barracks behind the residence.

The war, said rumor, was going well for the British. The cowardly order from Sir George Prevost for the defenders to fall back on Kingston had—some said at the instigation of Sir Claude Devizes—been disobeyed. This move was the salvation of Upper Canada. Standing firm, the British had met the invaders head-on and routed them—or so the stories went. Somewhere about the shores of Lakes Erie and Ontario, scattered armies were locked in desperate struggles for supremacy. Redcoat and Yankee, redman and Canadian militiaman, all slept rough in the freezing subarctic nights and rose to stand-to at every dawn. Few prisoners were taken. Emmie listened to it all— and prayed for her husband's safe return.

Of Gareth Hemmings, she saw nothing. The secretary had no business to perform in the private rooms of the residence, and for obvious reasons Emmie never extended any social invitations to the man whose very presence nauseated her. On a very few occasions, only, they accidentally met on the great staircase, when Hemmings would pause to let her pass, bowing low so that she could see neither his face nor the expression it bore—even if she had deigned to look.

Shut off from company (she refused an invitation to a *soirée* in the Seaforths' mess, together with numerous requests from prominent matrons of the city for the pleasure of her presence), Emmie was thrown back, more and more, upon her new rapport with Agnes Reilly. As with the earlier stage of the intimacy, when she had countenanced—even invited—physical manifestations of the most familiar nature, the relationship between mistress and servant was never sundered. The mistress remained, formally, "y' ladyship," "m' lady," or—*very* informally—"ma'am;" the lady's maid was always "Reilly," a style of addressing servants to which Emmie had been brought up and from which she would as lief depart as address Almighty God, in her prayers, as plain "you."

To while away the empty hours of the increasingly shortening days, Emmie would sit in her drawing room at her petit point, with "Reilly" sitting opposite, the latter engaged upon the more mundane task of patching and mending (for the domestic life of the residency was run on aristocratic—that is to say, cheeseparing—lines). During these hours, the mistress drew out the maid upon the facts of her life.

The facts of Reilly's early life—viewed from the standpoint of someone reared in the cosseted security of a palatial piggery such as Flaxham Palace—were as foreign to Emmie as those of a Hottentot. Born in County Mayo of a scrubwoman and an itinerant knife grinder who had taken his leave shortly after the birth of this, the twelfth fruit of his loins, Agnes Reilly had watched the rest of her siblings perish in a potato famine. She had been saved only because her mother and she smuggled themselves aboard a ship to England, where both earned a precarious living as cross-ing-sweepers, till the mother died. Reilly was curiously reticent regarding the circumstances of her mother's demise, and Emmie never pressed the point.

Alone, friendless and sixteen, the Irish waif had but three courses open to her, as she frankly admitted: to remain a crossing-sweeper, to go whoring or to wed. She took the worst option of the three by marrying a drunken corporal-of-horse who beat her daily and kept her continuously with child for the six years of their conjugal life, till the happy chance of a Yankee cannonball terminated the relationship. For the second time cast adrift on a foreign shore, Reilly had then managed to obtain employment as a scullery maid in the establishment of a British general, from which she had risen, by way of upstairs maid and nursery maid, to her present eminence at the residency.

The bald outline of the woman's life was a revelation to Emmie. She had known, but never before at first hand, how close to penury and starvation the lower classes stood, and how near to whoredom their wives and daughters were. That Reilly should have survived such a fate to become the woman who sat before her—still plumply pretty, pippin-cheeked and cheerful, tender and loving to a fault—spoke volumes for her worth of character.

It was the day following Reilly's account of her life that Sir Claude Devizes came back to Quebec.

Emmie watched her husband's arrival from the window of her drawing room and went halfway to greet him when Sir Claude Devizes was assisted across the threshold by two grooms. One glance sufficed to tell her that for all his walking on two feet, here was a man who in a few brief weeks had moved a considerable distance toward the grave. The unhealthy hue of complexion had increased and the eyes—though lively, still—were yellowed with jaundice. And over him like a pall—in his manner and bearing, in the way

he carried his once-proud beak of a nose—there hung
an air of defeat.

"Emmie, my dear, how lovely you look. Like a
rose, newly opened."

The tired face lit up, the jaundiced eyes brightened.
He took hold of her hands and kissed both her cheeks.

"Sir, you are not well, I think," said Emmie.

Devizes shrugged, took her arm and allowed her to
assist him to his favorite chair in the drawing room.
"I have not suffered the way those brave fellows are
suffering in the battle line," he said, "but war takes
its toll in other ways than blood-letting. Let us say
that I am one of the wounded of this present campaign,
but that I hope soon to be healed of my hurts. Pour
me a brandy, I beg you, Emmie."

This Emmie did. By the time she had turned around
the console table with the brimming glass in her hand,
Devizes's head had lolled, his mouth hung slackly
open and he was snoring noisily.

The surgeon of the Seaforths was summoned. A dour,
straight-speaking Scot from the western isles, he was
brutally unequivocal in his declaration: the military
governor's best hope of survival was to resign his appointment and commission and return to England,
where, if he were willing to submit himself to the life
of a semi-invalid, he might well live for another five
years. So much for the long term. In the short term
(and here the canny eyes lingered thoughtfully upon
the blooming charms of the military governor's nubile
young wife), the patient must rest on his back for at
least a week, perhaps more. And suffer no excitement.
No excitement of *any kind*. He stressed the last words
so forcefully that Emmie was half inclined to confide
in the surgeon that she and Sir Claude had no physical
cohabitation.

Alone again with her sleeping spouse, Emmie
gloomily realized that the surgeon's interdict quite
prevented her from breaking the news about her state.

In either case—whether Sir Claude was overjoyed or whether he was furious—the excitement would be too much for him. It would have to wait till he was strong enough to bear the news. She, also, would have to wait.

Emmie left her husband's bedchamber, nodding amiably to the two armed sentries of the Seaforths who stood guard at his door. This was a new departure: to keep so close a watch over the person of the military governor. Emmie was at a loss to know why it should have been considered necessary.

She was soon to learn the reason. . . .

A tap on her private sitting room door announced the immediate entry of none other than Gareth Hemmings. Emmie rose with the pale fury of boiling milk to order his instant departure, but the secretary merely closed the door behind him, and, brushing aside her demand, crossed over to the occasional table where stood a decanter of sherry wine and glasses. Pouring himself a bumper measure, he drained half of it and turned to regard his master's wife.

"You insolent, ill-bred swine!" hissed Emmie, her hackles well-raised by his cool assumption of proprietorship.

"My lady," he responded, "restrain your aristocratic contempt, for it is like water off a duck's back. I am come to demand the discharge of the debt of gratitude that you owe me."

"Debt—of *gratitude*—what do you *mean?*" asked Emmie, knowing full well what he meant, and dreading the outcome.

Hemmings drained the glass and poured himself another. "I have not had the opportunity to speak with Sir Claude," he said. "When I do, you may be sure that I shall not allude to your recent—how to put it?— peccadillo."

"You are very kind," breathed Emmie.

"This is subject to a certain condition."

"I thought it might be!"

He laughed shortly, placed the wine glass back upon the occasional table, stroked the side of his nose, laughed again. Emmie stiffened as he took the three strides that separated them, reached out his hand and offered her bosom a brusque, insolent caress.

Emmie shrank from him, fighting to quell the sudden assault of trembling that racked her, stripping her of dignity, of poise, of self-respect.

Hemmings sneered. "You fear for your chastity, Lady Devizes? I wonder that you remember such a divine quality. Have no fear, I have no designs upon your body, even though it may be lusted after by the entire Quebec garrison. You will be relieved to hear that I am not of that—persuasion." He gave her breasts a contemptuous slap. "To me the beautiful, the desirable Lady Devizes, is just a—a milch cow."

Relief mingled with a remaining unease, Emmie watched him warily. "Then what do you demand of me in return for your silence?" she asked. "What kind of blackmailer *are* you?"

Hemmings was in no way put out by the brutal frankness of her question, but nodded approvingly. "By all means let us get down to business, my lady," he said. "I require of you a certain service. A service not related to your undoubted—but for me elusive— charms. A simple matter of—acquisition."

"Acquisition?" She stared at him in puzzlement.

"Sir Claude was brought in here today," said Hemmings. "With him came aides-de-camp, equerries, military secretaries galore. At present he is incommunicado in his bedchamber, guarded night and day by a pair of brawny Highlanders. Though his secretary, I could as lief gain admission to that room as enter the Kingdom of Heaven unshriven. And I have a special need to enter, ma'am."

"Why?" demanded Emmie.

"There is a dispatch box with him," said Hem-

mings. "I saw it taken into the bedchamber. Red it
is, of red leather, with a lock. I know it well. Sir
Claude uses it to carry only the most secret of military
documents, which, as a civilian secretary, I am never
privileged to see.

"The documents at present locked within that dispatch box, Lady Devizes, guarded by Highlanders—
a circumstance which in itself is highly suggestive, for
I can never recall a previous occasion when Sir
Claude's person has been so closely attended—must
be of the highest importance."

"And what is this to do with me?" demanded Emmie. "Or, for that matter, *you?*"

The secretary smiled thinly. "As to myself," he
said, "I wish to view those documents. As to you,
Lady Devizes, you will obtain them for me—or I will
apprise your husband of your late encounter with Ensign Morris, omitting nothing in the way of corrobo-
rative detail, however prurient."

Emmie's hand went to her throat. She stared at
Hemmings in disbelief. "You—you are a *spy!*" she
breathed.

He shrugged. "I have told you my philosophy of
life, ma'am," he said. "I seek to enlarge my knowledge of mankind by devious and wayward paths that
the common ruck scorn to use. You call me Peeping
Tom; you call me a spy. In doing so, you simply follow
your own philosophy, which is that of the ordinary
mortal."

"I won't do it!" blazed Emmie.

"Your pardon, ma'am—but you will!" he responded.

"You cannot make me!"

"Oh, yes I can!"

"Never!"

He crossed over to the occasional table and poured
himself more sherry. The hateful, mirthless smile was
fixed when he turned to face her again.

"I am privy to the surgeon's report on Sir Claude,"

he said. "Let us consider the effect upon that poor old man if, having gained admittance to his bedchamber on the pretext of urgent personal business, I were roughly to arouse him and . . ."

"You wouldn't dare do such a thing!"

"Oh, yes, I would!" he said. And she knew he would.

"What are you going to do with the documents?" she asked.

Hemmings knew that he had won. His attitude immediately became brisk, businesslike, matter-of-fact, even friendly. "I shall need them for a short while only," he said. "If you extract them from the dispatch box and bring them straight to me, I will peruse them and give them back to you within the hour. You can replace them in the dispatch box and no one will be any the wiser."

"You, Hemmings, will be somewhat the wiser," said Emmie tartly.

He grinned. "True, your ladyship. But you, ma'am, will be safe from exposure as an adulteress. Your husband will not die of a seizure tonight, which would render you a widow. In short, there will be advantages a-plenty for all."

Emmie avoided his glance. "How shall I gain entrance to this locked dispatch case?" she whispered.

Hemmings looked puzzled, but only for a moment. "Ah, I had forgotten that you do not share a bed with Sir Claude," he said, "or you would know that he keeps the key on a length of silk cord tied about his waist, next to his skin. I have seen him produce it many times. I would try to obtain it myself, but it would greatly tax my ingenuity to explain to Sir Claude, if he woke up, why I had pulled up his nightgown to the waist. On the other hand, you, as his dutiful wife . . ." He sneered.

"I will do it," whispered Emmie, closing her eyes.

*   *   *

Sentries the world over, from time immemorial and for evermore, play a game of make-believe with the world of reality. When they are being watched, sentries are automatons: mindless, rigid, disciplined, uncomplaining. As soon as the regarding eyes have gone, they become like everyone else. The two stalwart Highlanders on picket duty outside the bedchamber of the military governor were no different from any other in this respect. Safe from sight and sound in that vast, echoing upper floor, they had leaned their bayoneted muskets against the wall and were squatting on their hunkers (bare-arsed under their kilts of tartan), playing a wordless, soundless game of cards for money.

The first *tap-tap* of dainty slippers brought them to their feet. The cards and stakes were scooped up. Bayoneted muskets were swiftly taken in hand. When Emmie came in sight at the head of the staircase the two Highlanders were frozen at each side of the military governor's door in an immobility that rivaled the great monolithic statuary of ancient Egypt.

Emmie was carrying a small tray upon which stood a cup, saucer and a pot of steaming hot chocolate. The delicate aroma of the beverage touched the sentries' nostrils, mingled with the scent that Emmie wore. She smiled at them both, and neither barred her way, but stamped to the position of attention as she laid her hand on the door latch, opened it and went inside.

"Och, but I wish I had yon lassie to bring me chocolate in bed!" declared one of the Highlanders with fervor.

"Aye, and to hell wi' the chocolate, Jock!" responded his comrade.

It was very still, dimly lit, smelling of old man in the room. Emmie laid the tray on a side table. The chocolate was a subterfuge.

He looked very, very old, very ill. The thinning gray locks spread over the lawn pillow produced an insubstantial appearance, which, coupled with the unnatural hue of his complexion, gave him the look of a man already dead. Only the gentle rise and fall of the breast and the thin whine of his breathing showed that life was still there.

Emmie steeled herself. It had taken her two hours—even after her agreement with Hemmings—to bring herself to the task before her. There was so much at stake. And the stake that she held in highest regard was the life of the old man who had bought her, had wed her and had treated her with naught but sweet kindness. That was the sticking point: that, the consideration which had brought her to the decision.

Emmie took a deep breath, and advanced her hand toward her husband.

Emmie brought a sheaf of papers to Gareth Hemmings's narrow garret under the eaves. He had insisted upon it, and she, now that she knew he had no designs upon her body, acceded to his demand.

"You've been a long while, my lady," said he.

"I have had a long fight with my conscience," said Emmie.

"All this while? It is nearly two in the morning."

"Both before and after I took the papers," said she.

He grinned. "But you finally resolved the argument with your conscience, I take it?"

"Yes, to my entire satisfaction," responded Emmie. "When shall you have finished with the documents?"

He took them from her: a dozen or so sheets of foolscap penned upon in a spiky, clerkish hand. He riffled them through. "Two hours—a little less," he said. "I will bring them to your quarters when I have examined them."

"Tap upon my door three times," said Emmie. "And I will open."

"Yes, my lady. Thank you, my lady." When she turned to go, he added, "You call me blackmailer, my lady. You call me Peeping Tom. Spy. But I promise you that our transaction is now at an end. I will make no further demands upon you.''

"You are lying, Hemmings," replied Emmie. "However, that is no longer of any consequence." With that cryptic assertion she quitted the room.

Alone, Hemmings frowned in puzzlement. But presently addressing himself to the sheaf of papers, he dismissed all thoughts of the young woman who had been his catspaw in the enterprise. With many an exclamation of astonishment, awe, triumph, he first skip-read the documents for their general sense, then re-read the pages more closely. When he had finished reading, he took up his pen and proceeded to make a very accurate précis of their contents, reducing the dozen pages to half that number without forfeiting any part of the essential whole. The task took him a little over an hour and a half—timed by the watch that he propped up against his candlestick. When he had finished work, he folded the précis into a packet, sealed it and addressed the outside. Then, taking the original documents, he made his way to Emmie's apartments.

No sound in the great house. The eyes in the painted ceiling looked down on the dark-clad figure as he descended the stair to the principal floor. He looked left and right, and paused to listen before treading softly down the passage. Another pause. He tapped lightly on her door.

"Come in, Hemmings." Emmie's voice.

He obeyed. The room was in near darkness. A single candle burned on a table in the center, but it was shielded by a large book propped open and upright beside it, plunging half the chamber into a patchwork of shadows. Hemmings peered about him and saw Emmie.

"The documents," he said.

"Lay them on the table."

He obeyed. Emmie stepped forward and took them up. At the same time, she knocked over the book that

screened the candle. The shadows fled. And he saw—
them . . .

Two Highlanders stood like firedogs each side of
the empty fireplace, and their bayonets glinted in the
candlelight. An officer of the Seaforths stood by a
large wing chair in that part of the room that had been
most deeply shadowed. Huddled in the chair, his
proud beak of a nose held high, eyes glinting with
loathing, was the military governor of Quebec Province.

"Seize him! Bind the scoundrel!"

Hemmings cried out and ran for the door. His hand,
scrabbling for the latch, was pierced through and
pinned there to the woodwork by a lunge of a High-
lander's needle-ended bayonet.

Gareth Hemmings was tried for treason against His
Sovereign Majesty's arms the following morning, at
an *ad hoc* drumhead court-martial presided over by
the military governor's principal aide-de-camp, the
colonel of the Seaforths, and a justice of the peace of
Quebec City. The plea of "not guilty" entered by the
accused had a hollow ring about it that was accented
by the sound of carpenters' hammers erecting a gallows in the square outside the officers' mess where
the trial was being held.

One piece of evidence, alone, was sufficient to condemn the prisoner: a copy, or précis, in his own hand,
of a document entitled *An Appreciation of the State
of the War, together with a Plan of Campaign for the
Coming Spring of 1814, to Include a Landing in Chesapeake Bay and the Investment of Washington City,*
whose author was Sir Claude Devizes, and whose
contents had been approved by a council of war in
Montreal a week previously. The précis, addressed to
a Mrs. Maria Hemmings of Dock Street in the lower
town (no denizen of far-off, fair Gloucester, she)
caused also a squad of soldiers to be dispatched to the
address of Mrs. Hemmings. The wretched woman,

upon hearing the hammering upon her door, blew the top of her head off with a pistol. In her house were found letters written in a crude code from he who was discovered to be her illegitimate son, together with communications from a Yankee spy-master in the British-occupied border town of Eastport. Puzzling to the searchers was a complete compilation of the British aristocracy, lovingly penned in the dead woman's hand, giving the names of those exalted beings down to the merest third cousin twice removed.

The verdict was never in doubt, the sentence so predictable as to have got the carpenters hammering since dawn. Hemmings, pale-faced, haggard-eyed, his hand bandaged, was told that he would immediately be led out from that place and summarily executed by hanging.

As soon as the gallows was properly erected.

Sir Claude dined alone in bed. He was propped up against a mountain of pillows, with three footmen to pour his claret and brandy, assist him with his soup, spoon out his half lobster and cut up his lamb chops. The military governor of Quebec Province was far removed from the tired old man who had returned home the previous day. In spirits and in appetite—if not in strength of limbs—he was as hale as a man in his prime.

Having consumed five courses with removes, together with two bottles of Bordeaux wine, the knight settled himself back against his pillow and warmed his brandy glass between his lean hands.

"My compliments to Lady Devizes," he said. "Ask her ladyship from me if she will please be so kind as to attend me here, since I am incapable of attending upon her."

"Yes, Sir Claude." The footmen bowed their way backward out of the bedchamber.

Emmie received her husband's invitation—summons?—with some considerable misgiving, as, considering the state of her conscience, she was well entitled to do. Having awoken and found Agnes Reilly gone, she had bathed and put on an evening hostess gown, and was devising by what means she could gain admission to Sir Claude and speak with him, when the footman brought the message.

The first sight of him put her fears at rest. He greeted her with outstretched hands, bade her kiss his cheek, patted hers and told her she was a lovely child.

"It has been a trying time for you, Emmie dear," he said. "If it had not been for the pressure of events, I would have taken you to a place in the country for a few days while all this business was settled. But, there, 'tis over now. The scoundrel Hemmings is dead and buried. Though I fear the evil he has wrought is far from over."

"Why—why is that, sir?" asked Emmie.

Sir Claude pulled at his jutting nose and looked grim. "Hemmings's defection, now that it has come to light, gives my enemies the weapon they need to destroy me," he said. "But I will anticipate disgrace and dismissal by relinquishing my appointment as military governor and resigning my army commission."

"Oh, no, sir—no!" cried Emmie, appalled.

He smiled fondly at her and stroked her cheek. "Will that be so awful, little Emmie?" he asked. "To have your husband around the house all day?"

"Sir, I didn't mean . . ."

"Of course not. I merely tease. No, I beg you not to repine for me. I am as you see me: a man grown old and broken in the King's service. Time for me to step back into the shadows and make way for the young, the whole, the fleet of foot."

"Sir, I've brought this upon you!" cried Emmie. "By betraying Hemmings, I sealed your downfall!"

"Not so, my dear," replied her husband. "When

you woke me last night and told me what he had urged
you to do, you plucked out a cancer that has caused
the deaths of thousands and been the primary cause
of this year's military reverses. It is I who am re-
sponsible for my fate, I who nursed that viper to my
bosom, trusting him as I trusted none of my other
aides, confiding in him about everything save matters
of the highest degree of secrecy. Those matters, as we
now know, he sought out for himself. No, Emmie, by
taking the course you did, you may inadvertently have
revealed my lack of judgment, but you performed a
great service for your King and country.''

Emmie glanced across at her reflection in the mirror
opposite, saw her own haunted eyes, her guilt written
large—or so it seemed to her—for him to see. She took
a deep breath. . . .

''Sir, from first to last, since I woke you last night,
there is one question you are well entitled to ask, but
which you have not touched upon.''

''Yes?'' was his cryptic—and unhelpful—comment
on that.

Another deep breath, and she tried again. ''Sir, you
haven't asked me what lever Hemmings had against
me, what hold over me, that might make him suppose
I would betray both you and my country. You haven't
asked me that.''

''No, I have not,'' he replied blandly.

''But you must have realized that this—hold—that
Hemmings thought himself to have over me, was a
grave matter?''

''Perhaps.''

''Sir, I must tell you what it was.''

He inclined his head, gravely. ''As you will, Emmie.''

She had been sitting on the edge of his bed, within
touching distance; but now she rose and strode to the
far end of the chamber, turned on her heel, and walked
back. Three times she repeated this maneuver, restless as a caged leopardess, while all the time her hus-

band regarded her from his nest of high pillows, inscrutable.

Presently, steeling herself, she paused at his bedside.

"Sir, when left here, I betrayed you. I was unfaithful to you within a day and a night of your departing."

He nodded. "Is there more you wish to tell me, Emmie?" he said quietly.

"There is more, sir," she whispered. "This youth, this boy, believing that he was a coward, thought to kill himself or resign his commission, sooner than face the battlefield. I—I gave him proof of his manhood by—taking him to my bed. And we were observed by Hemmings."

"I see," said Sir Claude.

"The boy's name, since you are entitled to know it, is Morris. Ensign Morris of the Twenty-first Foot. Do you know, I never did learn his given name."

"Oh, Emmie, Emmie. You poor child!" said her husband. "Sit you down here. Hold my hands. There. Steel yourself, my dear child. I have to tell you that your young friend proved his manhood before all on the shores of Lake Erie. And at the ultimate cost."

"He's—dead?" she whispered.

"Hit while gallantly leading his patrol against a Yankee outpost. I am so sorry, Emmie. A splendid young fellow. I knew his father well. My dear, I grieve with you."

"Oh, sir!" Emmie stared at her husband with mingled wonder and disbelief. This man, so gentlemanly in the finest sense, so civilized in every sense, with his apparent disregard for his own feelings and his total concern for hers, struck down all her defenses. "Does this mean that you find it in your heart to forgive me?" she asked.

He laid a fingertip upon her lips. "There is nothing to forgive, Emmie," he said simply. "Youth calls to youth, and age must turn the cheek. I have enjoyed the pleasures of the flesh and drunk deeply of the cup

of life. Why should I—near to my dotage and released
from sensual desires—deny you the right of youth's
supreme joys?''

"Sir, you are not so old that all desire has left you
forever!'' cried Emmie. "I am your wife, your dutiful
wife, and will be your handmaiden—to summon up,
and to please." Her fingers, inspired by gratitude and
melting affection, were attacking the buttons at the
bodice of her hostess gown, beneath which her breasts
jounced freely.

His hand stayed her fingers. . . .

He shook his head. "Not that I have any doubt that
you could summon up, Emmie,'' he said, "nor that
you could give me pleasure and to spare. But, my
dear, when things are past, they had best not be recalled. The ghost of a dead refrain had best not be
played aloud again for fear that the melody is too
harsh, the harmony gone sour. Leave be, Emmie. Be
to me what you have lately learned to become: my
loving, only child."

She kissed him on the brow. "I will be that,'' she
promised. "I will be all that!"

He nodded, squeezed her hand. "I am sure of it,
my dear,'' he said. "And now—as to the morrow.
Before dinner, I dictated letters of resignation from
appointment and commission. There is nothing to
keep us here, Emmie. We can return to England. To
our country estate on the outskirts of Bristol and to
the town houses in London and Bath. Would you like
that, Emmie? You would queen all three establishments to perfection."

She looked closely at him: he who, though prema-
turely aged by illness, still had a mind as keen as a
razor's edge, who had—if rumor had it right—reversed
the recent disasters to British arms in the Great Lakes
area.

"Sir,'' she said, "are you sure you will not be totally
bored by the civilian life? You, who have worn the
King's uniform, as you have told me, since early man-

hood—to be reduced to taking the waters in Bath and being driven over your country estate."

Sir Claude smiled and shook his head. "You mistake your aged spouse, my dear Emmie," he declared. "I will take the waters, yes. I will be driven over the estate, surely. But my principal task will be to increase the fortunes of our family business, the Devizes fleet of merchantmen, which was once the leading shipping company in Bristol and which, with God's help and my application of the classic military principles of organization and logistics, will be so again.

"And besides, Emmie," he concluded, eyeing her steadily and with ineffable affection, "it is my wish that your child—I should say, *our* child—should be born in dear old England, and in the hearth and home that he, or she, will one day inherit."

Emmie was half-aware that her mouth must be sagging open in a most foolish manner, and that her heart was pounding so wildly that he must surely hear. She sought for the words to express her astonishment; they were slow in coming, and totally inadequate.

"Sir, do you mean that—you *know?* But—*how?*"

Sir Claude spread his hands. "I have told you, Emmie, that my first wife, my dearest Mary, was brought to bed of five children, all of whom God saw fit to take from us early, in consequence of which I know little—sadly little—of children and their ways. Ah, but what I do *not* know about the habits and foibles of ladies in waiting is scarce worth knowing.

"Dear Emmie, I have marked with interest your passion for large green apples, and your violent aversion to fat mutton. With mounting delight, I have observed how you have suddenly learned to dote on nutmeg, while eschewing basil and sorrel which were your favorite herbs when first you arrived. Certainty of your condition—and a great joy—came when I first saw you upon my return yesterday. I saw a woman brought to fulfillment, serene in the knowledge of the new life that she was carrying under her heart.

"And now, my dear, I think I should like another brandy before I go to sleep."

Agnes Reilly protested loud and long about her mistress sailing across the wide ocean in her condition, pointing out with true Celtic vehemence that the third month of carrying a babe rendered the mother-to-be most vulnerable to miscarrying. In answer to this, Emmie pointed out that it was merely one of three bad options, of which the other two were, respectively, to travel later on in her pregnancy and run the risk of perhaps giving birth in a storm at sea, with equally disastrous consequences, or to wait till the babe was born and then subject the little mite to the rigors of the crossing. What Emmie did not confide in her lady's maid was the hourly danger that Sir Claude stood to be arrested, through the machinations of his enemies—principally the despicable Prevost—for dereliction of his duty in employing, and keeping in his employment, a spy of the enemy.

So it was to England that the Devizes set sail within a week of Sir Claude's resignation. They sailed in the *Sauntress*, a full-rigged ship and pride of the Devizes line, commanded by one Captain Harry Vanbrough. And Agnes Reilly went with her mistress.

On passage down the broad St. Lawrence, they saw little of the shoreline, since a violent snowstorm shut out all visiblity beyond the end of the ship's bowsprit, so that the *Sauntress* was obliged to proceed under foresails and mizzen only, with her brass bell loudly clanging a warning to all others in the vicinity. Out beyond the wide estuary, past Newfoundland, the skies cleared to an icy, illimitable blueness, and every line and shroud, every last piece of canvas and woodwork on the upper deck, was crusted with a fine covering of frost, delicate as lace. Captain Vanbrough probed at it with his finger and shook his head. He opined—and frequently—that they were in for a rough crossing, and he would cast Lady Devizes a searching, sidelong glance.

Vanbrough was given to glancing sidelong at his owner's wife, particularly at table. Emmie was well aware of the captain's sly attentions; as a woman grown in loveliness, she was used to being ogled. But something in Vanbrough's manner she found oddly unnerving. He was a man of less than medium height, but strongly built, with a ruffle of black hairs extending below the sleeve of his blue broadcloth coat and growing thickly upon the phalanx of each finger. Black, also, was his hair, which was scrupulously clean and carefully brushed and combed. His eyes were dark and devious, despite which, Emmie was obliged to concede—for all that she instinctively disliked and distrusted the fellow—he was undoubtedly good-looking, with a firm mouth, a short and well-shaped nose, excellent teeth, and nicely-tended fingernails. The trouble was, he was sly in his ogling of his beautiful passenger. No woman objects to being a source of admiration. But for admiration to be *furtive* is a matter of unease.

Emmie and her maid shared a handsome suite of cabins under the poop deck, with a row of windows looking out upon the ship's wake. There was one large and one small sleeping cabin, together with a dressing room-cum-bathroom, all originally constructed for the master and his wife, if any. Vanbrough, so Emmie gleaned from the remarks he let drop, was unmarried.

On the third night after leaving Canadian waters, the *Sauntress* bit her sharp stem into an oncoming comber that, striking her with the force of a giant's fist, sent a shudder throughout the length of the vessel and caused everything movable to be thrown to the decks—people included. The passengers were in their bunks at the time and escaped injury, but three crewmen were badly injured and one topman was hurled by the jolt from the foremast and disappeared over the side, never to be seen again. Before the mass of icy green water had broken over the foredecks and dispersed itself, foaming, down the flooded scuppers, the second wave struck the ship.

And so it continued, constantly, for two days and nights.

Emmie suffered not too badly from the hideous discomforts of the gale; not so Agnes Reilly. The sturdy Irishwoman, for all her solid worth, was not blessed with the quality of being a good sailor and remained in her bunk most of the time. Emmie had makeshift collations brought to her by the stewards. These she doggedly ate in her bunk, clinging to the raised side with one hand and spooning down lukewarm soup, stew or similar, with the other. On the second night of the tempest (and Agnes Reilly had taken no nourishment since it began), Emmie was so concerned for her maid's health that she felt constrained to urge her to eat. Accordingly, with shuffling, careful steps, handhold by handhold, she went into the older woman's cabin bearing a basin of stew.

"Reilly, are you awake? I've brought you something to eat."

A muffled voice from under a blanket gave her to understand that the maid had no desire for food, nor, indeed, for anything but immediate oblivion.

"Don't be silly, Reilly. Pull yourself together, woman. Here," she said, whipping off the blanket to disclose Agnes Reilly in a crumpled shift, her hair in rats' tails and her usual bucolic countenance turned ashen, "sit up and I'll help you."

The stricken woman was constrained by her mistress's firmness to do as she was bidden. Reilly sat up against her pillow and, with much verbal and facial expression of nausea and distaste, suffered a little of the stew to pass her lips.

"You see?" declared Emmie, "you were really hungry all the time. Seasickness is really an attitude of mind, or at least that has always been my—"

And then—it happened! . . .

The heavy, rhythmic pitching and tossing of the vessel was violently broken by a catastrophic roll. Emmie was taken from her feet and carried the length of the small cabin, to land against a protruding bulwark with a force that staved in her ribs. She screamed in agony, and was still screaming when the *Sauntress*, swallowed in by another mountainous wave, was hurled upon her beam ends once more. Upon the return roll, Emmie was thrown back to the opposite end of the cabin, where she lay in a crumpled, silent heap.

It had happened in less time than it took for Agnes Reilly to struggle up from her bunk, and, sickness forgotten, rush to her mistress's side. There was a ring bolt set into the bulwark close by where Emmie lay. Clinging to it for support, the Irishwoman turned the still form over and cried out in horror to see a trickle of bright blood coming from the corner of the mouth. Blood also stained the left side of the nightshift from armpit to waist. Sobbing, praying, frantic with concern, Agnes Reilly tore at the thin cambric to examine her mistress's hurts, and moaned with despair to see a cruel contusion on her left side, just beneath the breast, where the white ends of two severed ribs protruded from a red mouth of punctured flesh.

What to do? One-handed, it was all she could do to retain hold of her unconscious mistress and prevent her from being thrown back and forth across the cabin like a broken doll. To carry her and secure her to the bunk was out of the question. She had to fetch help. The ring bolt supplied her with the means. Frantically, she tore away the skirt of her own shift. Twisting the coarse calico into the semblance of a rope, she secured one end of it round the victim's slender middle and the other to the ring bolt. That being done, the Irishwoman clawed her way out of the small cabin in search of assistance.

The images shifted with the intensity of the pain, which waxed and waned with the slightest movement. During the worst of it, she was back in the forest wilderness with the hunter, with painted redmen on their heels. Once, she was caught by them and subjected to the most vile handling. On that occasion, the sheer agony caused her to ascend to near-consciousness, and she sat up to find a strange woman with green eyes urging her in loving tones to be still and not fret herself—a gentle admonition that somehow allayed the pain and allowed her to drift back into blessed oblivion again.

At other times, when a certain numbness intruded, she was lying in her lover's arms, and it was always Nathan. Even when they were lying naked together in a birch-bark canoe and drifting under the stars, it was still Nathan. In her canopied bed back in the residence at Quebec, it was Nathan, yet, who carried her up to the heights of unimaginable ecstasy. When, waist-deep among the bullrushes in far-off Flaxham great park, she first looked upon the exquisite beauty of a nude man, it was Nathan who displayed himself before her hidden eyes.

Gradually, the worst of the pain came less frequently, and she came to recognize the woman who watched over her day and night, untiring. She was aware, also, that the ship had ceased its dreadful motion; there was now only a gentle movement to and fro, accompanied by a lazy creaking of woodwork that was curiously restful to the ear.

One day she awoke to another face that had joined the watcher by her side. . . .

"Dear little Emmie, how are you?"

"Sir, I'm much better, thank you." She felt her husband's hand close over hers.

"The ribs are mending nicely, so the surgeon said

this morning," supplied Agnes Reilly, "and sure that's a blessing. But there's better to come." She smiled down at Emmie.

"Your baby is all right, Emmie," said Sir Claude. "Despite the injury you received, you are not parted from that precious, small life. And we're due in Bristol on tomorrow's tide, Emmie. Your little one will be born in the old country—just as we had hoped. And all thanks to Reilly, here."

Smiling through the sudden tears, Emmie contrived to squeeze both their hands.

The *Sauntress,* after what old hands were unanimous in declaring to be the worst Atlantic crossing of their experience, docked in Bristol on a blustery, wintry morn just before Christmas, and Emmie was carried ashore on a litter. At the gangway, Captain Vanbrough bade his beautiful passenger farewell, and this in his habitual, slyly ogling manner that spoke volumes for what he might have added to his valediction, if their respective circumstances had not been so disparate. Emmie was relieved to see the last of him and hoped that their paths would not cross again—a hope that, unhappily for her, was not to be fulfilled.

She and Sir Claude, with Agnes Reilly seated opposite and beaming with delight upon her beloved patient, were driven straight to Avon Park, which was the Devizes' country seat south of the city. Set in a landscaped area, a mansion less like the ramshackle ostentation of Flaxham Palace would have been difficult to find, since Avon Park had been built in the previous century to the classically restrained designs of Beau Nash, with an elegance of proportion that gulled the delighted eye into believing that the edifice was smaller and more cozy than was actually the case. In fact, Avon Park's great hall was larger than that of Flaxham, but it contrived to be of proportions that were manageable to the sensibilities. Emmie fell in love with the place on sight.

The Devizes spent Christmas quietly, with no other junketing save a party in the great hall for the staff and tenant farmers of the estate and their families. Emmie celebrated her first day on her feet, at that occasion, by presenting every child there with a half guinea. And the couple spent the New Year in Bath— a matter of a half-day drive by coach.

The Devizes' town house in this, surely the most perfect city in Northern Europe, was situated in the center of the noble sweep of Royal Crescent, whose high windows and balconies command views of the great amphitheater, the staggering basin in which the city rises, tier upon tier, crescent above crescent, with squares and circuses abounding, towers, steeples and colonnades, and the slow Avon gliding past below.

Emmie was brought to bed of her babe in the Royal Crescent on a June morn at lark-rise. It was a girl-child. Her lusty cries were instantly quenched at her mother's breast. As Agnes Reilly proudly declared, there never was a better trencherman than little Annabel Devizes.

Annabel had been Emmie's choice of name. Sir Claude's sole wish in the matter was for the child to bear, also, one of the traditional Devizes appellations that had been handed down the distaff side, generation after generation: Harriet. Well-aware of the import of this wish on her husband's part—the desire to set a seal of acceptance upon the child—Emmie joyfully conceded. So Annabel Harriet Emmie Devizes she became.

From first to last, Sir Claude had made no inquiry as to the man from whose loins Emmie had been made fruitful; indeed, on the many occasions that she, by carefully steering the conversation to a point where he might logically have posed the question, her husband had seemed to shy away from the topic, till eventually she had desisted in the attempt. And with some re-lief—for there had been from the first a nagging doubt in her mind: that it might have been Yves the hunter and not her beloved Nathan Grant who had fathered her infant.

Blessedly, safe at Emmie's breast in the high-ceilinged nursery in Royal Crescent, after all the tribulations attendant upon her entry into the world, Annabel Harriet Emmie was a living, breathing witness to her parentage. The riot of dark hair and the glorious complexion were from her mother.

But the eyes—those deep blue and unforgettable eyes—belonged to Captain Nathan Grant, United States Navy.

The infant Annabel's arrival into the world coincided with the downfall of the Emperor Napoleon, who, after defeats in the Peninsula, Russia and elsewhere in Europe, formally abdicated and was allowed to king it over the tiny Mediterranean island of Elba (he who might have been master of the world!), where he lived on a grant of two million francs a year and thought of what might have been.

Sir Claude Devizes rejoiced in the return of peace, telling his lovely young wife that the heaven-sent opportunity had come to expand the fortunes of his shipping line. Round the clock, the yards of Bristol and Liverpool resounded to the carpenters' hammers, the thud of adze on prime oak, the stench of hot, hammered brass and copper—as Devizes's ships rose from keel to maintop, to ply the seven seas on Devizes's business. Seemingly rich beyond reckoning, the shipowner and his girl-wife were seen in the highest circles of society in Bristol, Bath and London. "Beau" Brummell was a frequent guest at Emmie's table, and through his friendship with that arbiter of good taste, the Prince of Wales, now Prince Regent, received Sir Claude and Lady Devizes. The royal voluptuary's eyes lit favorably upon Emmie's nubile charms, though, happily, without complication of entanglement, for albeit a fervent admirer of a pretty young face and a pert bosom, "Prinny's" vast connoisseurship in this department was merely of the academic sort; in practice, he preferred the attentions, the company—and the beds—of women a piece older than himself.

At the end of that year, the mutually destructive conflict known forever after as The War of 1812—of which it must be said that the composing of the American national anthem was the only happy outcome—ground to an inconclusive halt with the signing of the Treaty of Ghent, by which the Americans relinquished the western lands that had been sequestered from Britain's Indian allies, and not much else was changed.

One afternoon following an all-night party in the Bath assembly rooms, at which Emmie and Sir Claude had sat at "Prinny's" supper table, Emmie, rising after luncheon to go riding on fashionable Lansdown common, had first called into the nursery to see Annabel. The child was fast asleep and in the care of two nursemaids, who, in their turn, were rigorously kept up to the mark by the doughty Agnes Reilly, whose adoration of Annabel was not far short of idolatry. Emmie lingered long enough to touch the velvet cheek and to smooth back a wayward curl from the tiny brow, as the two young nursemaids watched with wistful envy. Then, with an instruction to them that the babe was to be brought into dinner that evening to say "good night" to her fond parents, the proud mother descended to the hallway.

Halfway down, she paused, suddenly struck by a most curious and pressing premonition. It was as if she had trodden that selfsame path before, dressed, as she then was, in a riding habit of rifle green velvet frogged with black cord, a truncated top hat perched jauntily forward over her veiled brow, a riding cane in her gloved hand, dainty Hessian boots reaching to the knee. And halfway down the staircase of her beautiful Bath town house on a clear winter's afternoon.

Someone was in the hall below: a man in a gray

frock coat and pale pantaloons. He stood with his back to her, looking out of the window onto the cobbled street fronting the Crescent, where a pretty nursemaid strolled by pushing a hooded bassinet, followed by a sulky-faced boy in a sailor suit bowling a hoop.

He turned at the sound of her next footfall on the stair, and she was looking down in dawning wonderment into the deep blue eyes that had once filled her whole world.

"Good day to you, Lady Devizes," said Nathan Grant.

Part Four

"The Devil Is Dead!"

Chapter One

Their reunion was almost immediately interrupted by
the arrival of Devizes's new private secretary, who
informed Captain Grant that Sir Claude would be glad
to receive him in his bedchamber, and would the captain kindly step this way? Grant, with whom she had
barely exchanged a word, and that only of the most
banal and commonplace nature, bowed formally and
took his leave of her with one single glance that set
Emmie's heart leaping for pure joy. She watched him
follow the secretary up the staircase; yearning, longing
after him, her very spirit moving out to follow.

That afternoon, on Lansdown common, she drove
her groom—an ex-hussar riding master of quite advanced age—to near distraction. Riding Master Chudleigh, who, despite his years, was extremely susceptible to pretty young women and would have given
half of his pension for a night's romp with his mistress
in his narrow cot above the tack room, could not imagine what had got into the lass. That afternoon, she
rode like a mad woman, putting her mare Jezebel at

every obstacle in sight, hedges, drystone walls, five-barred gates, all with tremendous attack. On the flat, crouched low over the mare's flying mane, her own sable locks streaming in the wind (having long since lost her hat), she matched Jezebel's headlong gallop with a wild paean of thanksgiving for her lover's return.

Why and how it had happened, by what means Nathan had contrived their reunion (surely it could not have taken place merely by chance!), she neither knew nor cared. He was here. In England. In Bath. In her own house!

And Emmie Devizes, née Dashwood, with all her wayward, passionate Cradock blood, was damned if she was not going to spend the coming night in the arms of her lover and father of her child. She had been given carte blanche by her sweet and doting husband. How had he put it? "Age must turn the other cheek . . . Why should I deny you the right . . . ?"

With a *frisson* of exhilaration, Emmie threw her mare at a forbidding-looking stone wall. Lifted by her mistress's spirit, Jezebel cleared the top with a foot to spare; but Riding Master Chudleigh, coming after, drew rein and abandoned the attempt, cursing himself and Emmie.

The reality was beyond all belief. She was seated at table in her own dining room with Nathan on her left and her husband opposite. There was one other guest at dinner: Lord George Delavere, member of Parliament for Bath, whose infirmities kept him from attending at Westminster, but whose sardonic wit was much sought after by society hostesses of his constituency, for whom an unattached bachelor—even a lame bachelor on the shady side of fifty—was a considerable bonus at any gathering. Delavere was holding forth at that moment, addressing Nathan, who was giving the other his full attention, thus permitting Emmie to feast her eyes upon her lover unobserved.

" 'Pon my word, events move swiftly," said the member of Parliament. "To think that scarce three months ago, you, Captain, were an enemy. And now you are to command one of Sir Claude's merchantmen. I must say that I find your change of circumstances ironic, not to say paradoxical."

"I'm not surprised that you should think so, Lord George," responded Nathan Grant. "However, I will attempt to explain the apparent irony. I resignèd my commission at the end of the war because, having been a fighting seaman since I was thirteen and a midshipman in the King's Navy, I now seek to sail the seas as a man of peace, in the long peace which must surely lie ahead."

"Ah, but who is to keep that peace, Captain?" interposed Delavere, wagging a finger and winking at his host on his right.

Grant grinned. "I am not to be trapped by that question, sir," he replied good-humoredly. "The Royal Navy, of course. For fifty years—perhaps more—the world will live under the protection of *Pax Britannica* and some will prosper mightily—particularly Britain herself. Maybe the time of *Pax Americana* will come one day, but I do not think I shall live to see it."

"But that does not explain how you come to be employed as a commander of a Devizes merchantman, Captain Grant," said Emmie, feeling to her horror, as she posed the question, a hot flush of emotion rising from her neck to her cheeks. And surely he must notice.

The wonderful blue gaze was turned to her. "For that, my lady, I have to thank the energy and enterprise of the Devizes shipping line," he said. "Immediately on cessation of hostilities, your husband established agencies in Boston, New York and the other major ports of the eastern seaboard."

Sir Claude cracked a walnut loudly. "Ha! 'Tis the early bird who catches the worm," he declared with a touch of smugness. "I bethought me of all those navy frigates being paid off, all those fine officers unemployed, and many of 'em—like our gallant young friend here—having received their early experience in our own navy. Lord George, you may tell your colleagues in Parliament that I am building ships as fast as our yards can turn 'em out, for I have great faith in the future commercial greatness of this country. And I'll scour the four corners of the earth to find the right men to officer those ships. Hence Captain Grant." He beamed at the latter, crunched upon a walnut and washed it down with a copious draught of port wine.

"Very commendable, sir," opined Delavere.

"I may say that the contract offered to me by the Devizes line was most attractive," commented Grant, "and one which I was more than happy to accept."

He did not glance at Emmie when he made this observation, but she seized upon it and turned the implications over and over in her mind. Did it contain a secret communication for herself? Was Nathan trying to tell her (oh, the wonder of it!) that it was the prospect of being reunited with her which had attracted him?

The clock on the chimney piece struck the hour. Dinner was nearly over. Soon, she would rise and leave the men to their port and walnuts. Meanwhile, the supreme moment was closing in upon the man she loved. The testing time. She closed her eyes and sent up a brief prayer that he would not fail her. . . .

"Ah! Here comes Reilly with her entourage," declared Sir Claude. "The acolytes of a young lady to whom I now have the honor of presenting you, gentlemen."

Emmie hastily took up her wine glass and raised it to her lips, not for reason of quenching her thirst, but to hide behind and to observe, over its rim, the effect upon Nathan Grant when he saw his own image gazing up at him from the cot that the two nursemaids carried between them.

Devizes, enjoying his role, was making great play of formally introducing the babe to Lord George Delavere, who responded to his host's mood by good-humoredly rising to his feet with the aid of the two walking sticks propped against his chair, and bowing low before he reached down and took up a tiny hand, upon which he deposited a kiss. From where he was sitting at the opposite side of the table from Lord George, reckoned Emmie, all Nathan could see of his child, so far, was her little hand.

"Your devoted servant, ma'am," intoned Delavere.

Agnes Reilly sighed with pure pleasure.

"Excellent, excellent!" cried Sir Claude. "Now, bring the child this way, gels. Captain Grant, be upstanding, I beg you, to be received by Miss Annabel!"

"Damn him—damn him to hell!"

Lady Devizes hurled her satin slipper the whole length of her pale blue and silver bedchamber, where it struck a Dresden shepherdess that stood upon the chimneypiece and sent her crashing into shivered fragments upon the tiles beneath.

Her fury instantly quenched—for Emmie loved the little shepherdess, a gift from her husband—she flew across the room and, kneeling, tried to fit together two of the larger pieces, but even they made no sense one to the other, and, anyhow, her hands were trembling beyond all control, and her eyes were so glazed with tears that she could not see to perform the task. She sat back on her heels and gave way to utter despair.

"Oh, Nathan, Nathan!" she whispered. "How could you be so *blind,* so *stupid?*" And then, another thought obtruding: "Or was it merely idiotic male peevishness? Were you so piqued to be brought face to face with the reality of my poor, infirm old husband that you affected not to recognize Annabel as your undoubted child?''

Again, repeatedly, she relived the scene in the dining room: Nathan Grant standing awkwardly before the cot as the nursemaids presented the babe for his approval; his obvious embarrassment at having to find the right words of compliment; the discernible distaste with which he gingerly took the tiny fingers in his; his alarm when Agnes Reilly suggested that he might like to hold the baby for a while. . . .

"I thank you, no, ma'am! I am not—er—familiar with the method of handling infants and I fear I might drop it.''

And, again, when Reilly (and she certainly must have noticed the resemblance between them and divined that Nathan was Annabel's father) had coyly asked him did he not think that the babe resembled her mother . . . ?

"To tell you the truth of it, ma'am, all infants look alike to me.''

" 'All infants look alike to me—I fear I might drop it!' Ye gods! The man's a monster!'' cried Emmie, beating her small fists upon the parquet floor.

She had left them to their port and nuts after that, bidding them all good night. Nathan Grant, too late for the Bristol stagecoach that would take him back to his newly acquired ship command, had been given a bedchamber on the third floor. Half an hour before, Emmie had heard his footsteps and those of the footman lighting his way. She had heard him mount the staircase, pass her door and go on up to the next floor, and her heart had leaped at the sound and the nearness of him.

One option after another commended itself to her, till, finally, she seized upon the most acceptable. All was well. Nathan had contrived everything in order to be reunited with her. He had sought for, and accepted, an appointment with the Devizes fleet in order to come to England and resume his role as her lover.

The rest of it—his reticent behavior to her at the dinner table, his casual dismissal of his own daughter—had been dictated by the need for prudence. Yes, that was it!

Fired by joy and a tingling anticipation, Emmie leaped to her feet and wiped her eyes.

What next? Why, obviously, her prudent and tactful lover would have learned the whereabouts of her bed-chamber. Not, of course, by any such blatant means as bribing the footman who showed him up—that would only serve to have their liaison bruted around every servants' hall in Bath, Bristol and London. No, Nathan—the naval tactician and master mariner—would find her without raising a scandal. She had only to wait in patience; her lover would come to her. For, surely, he had so arranged it for this night. The subtlety of his design grew clearer upon contemplation: how he had so protracted his interview with her husband that Sir Claude had been obliged to invite him to dinner, thereby causing him to miss the Bristol stage, and so on. . . .

He was coming to her. She must make herself beautiful for him!

Too late, now, to summon Reilly to call the servants and prepare a bath. In any event, she had crossly sent Reilly on her way when the woman, sensing that her mistress was put out by something, had offered her usual gentle ministrations of hands, lips and eyes, which Emmie, not to be consoled, had curtly rejected. No, Reilly might well be her staunchest ally, but she was best out of the way in the circumstances. Lady Devizes would attend to her own toilette.

She unbuttoned her bodice, untied the silk sash under her bosom and allowed the high-waisted dinner gown to whisper to her feet. So sheer was the material that the lightest small-clothes would have been delineated beneath it. She was entirely nude under, save for pink silk stockings gartered at the knee.

Emmie stood before a pier glass and regarded herself with the eye of criticism—seeing not much amiss.

Childbirth had enriched her body rather than otherwise. Without the slightest increase to her waist and belly, her breasts were perhaps a mite fuller, and none the worse for that, and they had not forfeited an iota of their shape and firmness. Little Annabel had been weaned a month since, and the only signs of her late attentions were a slight enlargement of the nipples and a darkening of their pigmentation.

As for her scars, the knife wound at her shoulder had healed beautifully and was no more than a silvery shadow in the pinkness. The marks of the broken ribs, regrettably, remained clearly to be seen, and she must remember not to present her left side to Nathan's gaze for some months yet, and to keep her arm against her side whenever possible. She practiced doing it before the mirror.

The clock on the console table chimed midnight. No time for dalliance! Rushing into her dressing room, Emmie poured a basin of warm, rose-scented water from the ewer that was kept constantly replenished there, and sponged her body from brow to toes. Attar of roses touched at brow, breasts, navel and thighs. A suspicion of kohl at the corners of her eyes, a breath of rouge upon her lips and the tips of her nipples—and the beautiful, the youthful and the ardent Lady Devizes was ready for her assignation with ecstasy.

Would she wear a nightshift? She thought not, no matter how vestigial and calculated to seduce the eye. Clad only in the scent of roses, Emmie climbed into her great canopied bed of pale blue with silver cherubs up on high, snuffed all but one candle on her side table, pillowed her arms behind her head and waited with growing fervor for her lover to tap upon her door.

In the hour before dawn that claims so many souls, she began to wake. Still in her half-sleep, she reached out for her lover. He, responding, trailed a forefinger down her body from the tip of her ear, coursing down neck, across shoulder and breast, encompassing waist, buttocks, thighs. Sighing, she turned on her side, the better to accommodate her lover's importuning hand, and listened with a curious sense of detachment as her own breathing became ever more immodestly frenzied in response to the delicious things he was doing to her. She was raised up beyond reality and, carried by the magic of his name that she whispered constantly throughout the encounter, she broke out into the pure sunlight of blissful exultation.

Fully awake, now, she blinked against the daylight of reality that streamed thinly through the chinks in the window shutters. No sunlight of a distant idyll, that, but the gray gleam of an English dawn in a downpour of summer's rain. She could hear it sluicing down outside and all the gutters gurgling to overflow.

With an anguished sob, knowing the quest to be fruitless even as she essayed it, Emmie reached out again in search of her lover. Her fingers encountered only the cold sheets at the other half of her great bed, in the part where she had not lain.

In that part where no one had lain that night, *save in her imagination*.

And then the tears came. . . .

No lover had come to the beautiful, the needful Lady Devizes. The schemes and stratagems that she had devised for Nathan Grant in order that he could win his way to her bed had been founded in her mind only, not in his.

The idyll was over. Only a small life, tucked away in the nursery at the back of the house, overlooking St. James's Square and the heights beyond, remained to mark the passing of a time of great love. And with this life, Nathan Grant—whether he did not recognize the babe as the fruit of his loins, or, recognizing, chose to ignore the same—no longer had any connection.

Unable to abide her restive bed, the scene of false memories and counterfeit ecstasies, Emmie rose and, putting on a hostess gown and a lace cap, wandered like a tired wraith haunting her own house, till finally she arrived in the breakfast room, where the butler and his acolytes were already attending breakfast. Deviled kidneys, kedgeree, lamb chops, ham, bacon, cheeses of all sorts, a cold baron of beef, side of bacon, game pies, together with coffee, tea, beer, porter, and spirits for the imprudent, awaited to be consumed.

There was an empty cover at the table; a footman was in the act of removing a used plate and dusting crumbs from the polished walnut surface as Emmie entered.

Yes, the butler informed his mistress upon her inquiry, Captain Grant had taken breakfast and had departed the house not five minutes before, to attend upon the morning stage to Bristol. And no, the captain had not left any message.

Two months later, Napoleon escaped from Elba and, landing in the south of France, proceeded to raise the finest army he had ever commanded. All Europe held its breath as he marched on Brussels. A hundred days passed before the dictator's last throw of the dice ended in a bloody field near the Belgian village of Waterloo, and the ex-emperor was packed off to end his days on a windswept, wretched little island in the South Atlantic.

In August of that year, the Devizes traveled to London so that Sir Claude, who was deeply engaged in his shipping and financial interests, could be near the great merchant banks of the city. The family took up residence at their elegant town house in Sloane Street. From there, when Sir Claude was able to spare the time, they together attended balls, supper parties and divers routs. It was during a charity performance of naval persuasion entitled *Heart of Oak! or Dare All for Britannia!* that Emmie became aware of being ogled, through a quizzing glass, by an exceedingly decrepit fellow in the box opposite. It was not till the house lights were relit during the first interval that she recognized the personage in question as her Uncle Eustace.

The fourth marquess had weathered badly in two short years. His ennoblement appeared to have attacked the pillars of his physique the way that the rising damp of Flaxham was eroding the fabric of that ill-constructed pile. Or perhaps, thought Emmie uncharitably, his recently acquired wife had brought Uncle Eustace to his present decrepitude and he was languishing for lack of orgies in the orangery, Black Masses in the chapel and similar delights. Augusta, Marchioness of Beechborough, to whom her uncle introduced Emmie in the buffet, was a lady of uncompromising plainness and commanding manner whose family fortunes had been founded on the eighteenth-century slave trade. The middle-aged and ill-favored Augusta should have been one of the most eligible spinsters in England, but, her family fortune notwithstanding (the tendency for men in search of a rich prize is to require that it also be handsomely wrapped), she was not instantly overwhelmed with offers, and was glad in the end to give her hand to Eustace Beechborough, for all his rakehell reputation, poverty and ramshackle country seat. Perhaps she had thought to reform him, or at least to change him. If the latter, then she had succeeded beyond all belief, for Eustace's formerly excellent figure seemed to have shrunk within his suit of clothes so that his coat hung upon him as upon a scarecrow and his hose were wrinkled all the way down his skinny shanks like a pair of bellows. Emmie had it in her heart—in the teeth of the fact that he had virtually sold her for gold to line his own pockets—to feel sorry for her uncle. The marchioness treated him in public as some would have treated a lapdog that was in constant hazard of forgetting its house training, her basilisk gaze ever upon him and remonstration seldom far from her lips—as when he reached for a second glass of brandy from a passing footman, or looked too long and yearningly at a pretty woman.

With the summoning bell for the second act, Emmie took leave of her noble kinfolk, accepted with a pinch of salt the marchioness's half-hearted suggestion that she must, she really must, come and visit them at Flaxham, now that the place had been reroofed, entirely refurbished, and all the indigent relations and hangers-on pensioned-off and sent packing. Emmie then acquiesced to Eustace's wistful farewell glance down her décolletage as being the homage that a former voluptuary pays to past memories. She felt constrained to ask him how the egregious Mrs. Galloway was faring, she of the eternal nightshift and the *poses plastiques*—but it seemed unkind.

When she returned to her box, it was to find the door locked and the curtains drawn. Summoned by her tapping, Sir Claude, who had excused himself from accompanying her to the buffet on account of a recurrence of gout, opened the door and admitted her. In the single candle's light of the shrouded box, she discerned a seated figure, and her heart lurched treacherously to notice that, while his face was in shadow, a patch of light fell upon the skirts of a dark blue broadcloth greatcoat such as ship's officers wore. Then he leaned forward and rose to his feet in the candle's glow, and she saw that it was Captain Harry Vanbrough of the *Sauntress*.

"Good evening, Lady Devizes," said he. "I trust you are well, and fully recovered from the hurts you sustained in the gale."

She gave him her hand. "Well enough, I thank you, Captain," she responded. "And what of yourself? I see that you have been injured."

His right arm was taken out of his coat sleeve and held in place across his chest with a sling. He glanced down at it with a start of something like guilt, then looked at his employer.

"I'm afraid that Captain Vanbrough has sustained

his injury in the services of the Devizes fleet, my dear," said Emmie's husband, "which is all the more reason why I must accede to his request for an immediate, extraordinary board meeting on a matter of extreme urgency. Now. Tonight."

Emmie gathered up her cape. "Then I will accompany you, sir," she said.

Devizes shook his head. "Quite unnecessary, my dear," he declared. "And, in any event, the meeting might go on well into the early hours, which means you would be cooling your heels in a drafty anteroom by Limehouse docks till nearly morn. No, I beg you, stay and see the rest of the performance and return home in the coach when it is over. Vanbrough and I will secure a hackney carriage to take us to Limehouse. No—don't fret—" He touched her lips with his fingertips, a familiar and, to her, endearing habit of his. "Do as I advise, and make an old man happy."

From the corner of her eye, she saw Vanbrough direct her a brief bow from the waist and make his exit from the box.

"Sir, I don't like that man," she whispered when they were alone.

"Vanbrough is not to everyone's taste," admitted her husband. "But he is a good seaman, and loyal to me. As such, I have made him commodore of the Devizes fleet and appointed him to the board of directors. In the cutthroat game of world shipping, one must not only cut one's coat according to one's cloth, but one must not be too particular about the virtues of one's cloth—given certain circumstances."

Emmie thought of Nathan Grant and his virtues, both as a man and as a master mariner, and wondered how anyone so perceptive as her husband could possibly set a creature like Vanbrough (as must surely be the case) in authority over the American.

For all that her former lover had failed her. . . .

Hastily thrusting aside the image of Nathan's face, she said, "Sir, this matter that you must now attend to, this matter of extreme urgency, I hope that you will not make yourself ill with worry over it, as happened in Canada in like circumstances."

Devizes patted her cheek. "All will be well," he declared. "The matter will be settled tonight. And, as I have said, by remaining here and enjoying yourself, you have made an old man very happy, little Emmie."

"It is your persuasive tongue, and nothing else, sir, that bends me to your will, sir," said Emmie lightly. "And your age, I think, has little to do with it." She smiled at him. "Though I grieve for the many hearts you must have broken, sir, when you were younger, with that persuasive tongue of yours."

He kissed her cheek. A chaste kiss, as ever. "I should have known you in those days, dear Emmie," he said. "Such a pity. Such a pity." A kiss on her other cheek, and he was gone.

A peep through the chink of the drawn curtains of the box revealed to Emmie that the second act of the patriotic pantomime was proceeding along the same predictably tedious lines as its predecessor. With a sigh, Emmie closed the curtain. Nothing for her there. Better to return home. Her cozy boudoir on Sloane Street beckoned more invitingly than the posturings of ebullient patriotism. She took up her cape again, and was about to quit the box when there came a light tap upon the door.

"Come in," she said.

"Lady Devizes, as I believe."

"Yes?"

He was a man in his early thirties. Tall, lean as a panther, with butter-yellow hair cut *en brosse* so that it lay in tiny, tight curls at the nape and about his ears. Nose as straight as that of a head by Praxiteles, eyes as blue as the wine-dark Aegean that laps the Attic shore. A Greek god brought to life. Save for a touch of ruffled white lawn at the shirt breast and cuffs, he was clad from head to foot in black. His eyes danced with an ancient mischief, and he carried, unaccountably, a bottle of champagne and two tall glasses.

"Ma'am, I am not known to you," said the surprising visitor. "Permit me to introduce myself: Simon de Mazarin, at your service."

Emmie inclined her head, but did not feel the need to offer her hand to this stranger who so brashly intruded himself upon her acquaintance.

"How do you do, sir," she murmured. "And now, if you will excuse me, I'm just about to . . ."

"Not to leave!" His distress was so exaggerated as to be only just short of mockery. He clasped his brow, rolled his splendid eyes. It occurred to Emmie that he was perhaps rather drunk. "Ma'am, I crave your indulgence. Five minutes of your time, I beg you."

"For what purpose, sir?" she asked.

"May we be seated?"

Emmie shrugged, gestured toward the seat recently vacated by her husband, sat down in her own.

"Five minutes, Mr. de Mazarin," she said with an air of imperturbability she certainly did not feel, for the man before her gave out an aura of maleness, of animal force, that was oddly disturbing. He was not drunk, either, or at any rate there was not a tremor in the hand that reached out and placed the bottle of wine and two glasses on a low table that stood between them.

"I am obliged to you, ma'am," responded the other. "And now to the facts of the matter. You must first know that I am a member of the famous—some say notorious—Bizarre Club, of which you will have heard."

"I am not familiar with your organization, sir," replied Emmie. *And why in heaven's name does he have the effrontery to bring champagne?* she asked herself.

"We are the losers for that, ma'am," said de Mazarin. "And so I must explain that the club's aim and

object is charitable, though it has to be admitted that
a very great deal of that charity begins at home. However, once a month, we meet for the purpose of giving
support to some worthy cause or other. This month,
it is the Discharged Seamen's Fund—a *very* worthy
cause, and the sponsors of the present rather dreary
entertainment taking place onstage—happily out of
our sight and largely beyond our hearing.''

"Sir, how does this concern me?" asked Emmie,
observing with some concern that de Mazarin was
pouring champagne into the two tall glasses.

"I will tell you ma'am," replied the other. "At our
last meeting the members of the Bizarre Club placed
the sum of one thousand and eighty guineas on the
table, a not inconsiderable contribution to the finances
of the Discharged Seamen's Fund and one which will
doubtless provide innumerable old tars with the
wherewithal to buy themselves new wooden legs, get
blind drunk and reenlist, or whatever." He picked up
one of the brimming glasses and smiled watchfully at
the beautiful creature opposite.

"I still do not see—" began Emmie.

"There is, however, a condition," he interposed.
"As the title of our club suggests, our rules are somewhat bizarre. Bizarre and eccentric. The donation of
that money to the Fund is conditional upon a certain
proviso which, if not fulfilled, will divert the whole of
that one thousand and eighty guineas to the purchase
of a hot-air balloon, in which our president and honorable treasurer will ascend from Hyde Park and ha-
rangue the citizens of Westminster on the virtues of
insobriety and libertinism. You smile, ma'am. I warned
you that we are eccentric."

Indeed, de Mazarin's manner of delivery was so
droll, his self-assurance so engaging, that Emmie was
becoming quite at ease in his company and had permitted herself to smile. There still remained, however,
the matter of the champagne. . . .

"Sir, if you would be so good as to explain . . ."

"The condition," said de Mazarin, "by which the poor indigent ex-seamen will enjoy the donation is provided for by another rule of the club which says that a designated member must select a lady . . ."

"Ah!" exclaimed Emmie.

"He must be unknown to that lady," continued de Mazarin, "though he himself may have worshiped her from afar. . . ."

Emmie rose, implacable. "Good night to you, Mr. de Mazarin," she said. "You have quite used up your five minutes."

Unwavering, he continued. "Furthermore, so runs the rule, and I am quoting from memory, ma'am, but the article in question was written down by a very learned member of the legal fraternity, formerly a judge of the King's Bench Division, or he may have been a Master in Lunacy. I quite forget which . . ."

"*Mister* de Mazarin!"

"To the effect that, I quote, 'the lady in question, by general consensus of the entire membership of the Bizarre Club, must be one of the most beautiful, if not *the* most beautiful member of the female sex residing within the cities of London and Westminster at the time designate,' or words to that effect."

"Oh!" said Emmie. And again: "Oh . . ."

She stood irresolutely.

"Only a glass of champagne," said de Mazarin. "All the lady is required to do is to take a glass of champagne with the member designated."

"I see," said Emmie.

"Such a small thing," said he. "And consider those poor seamen. You, ma'am, with your maritime connections. The House of Devizes and all."

Emmie sat down again.

He handed her the glass that he held, untasted. Their fingers briefly met during the transaction.

"Ma'am, your very good health," he said, pledging her. "And the health of all discharged seamen."

They laughed.

Emmie sipped at the wine, which, despite the passing of time since de Mazarin had entered her box, was chilled to perfection. It also had been flavored with a touch of some exotic eastern herb or other after opening, in the current fad. She felt all of a sudden—and unaccountably—cared for and cosseted, though the compliment paid her was really quite considerable. "By general consensus of the Bizarre Club, one of the most beautiful, if not the most beautiful : . ." She couldn't wait to tell Sir Claude.

"I don't believe a word of what you've told me," said she. "You leave me with the impression, Mr. de Mazarin, that I have been shamelessly gulled."

Beyond the concealing curtains, a sporadic hand-clapping announced that the second act had drawn to its turgid close.

De Mazarin smiled at Emmie and replenished her glass.

"I lied about the hot-air balloon," he said.

After the third glass, it seemed to her that the walls of the box receded and became a painted backdrop of cerulean blue skies under which white pedimented temples graced the heights of lush islands fringed by the reflected blue of sea. Such an image she undoubtedly gleaned from a large painting that had hung in one of the rooms that she had shared back in Flaxham with Cousin Mary Cradock and Deidre Collingwood. The painting was a landscape of tremendous antiquity, signed *Nicholas Poussin, 1636*, and was pierced through and through with pistol balls on account of a predilection for target practice in the home on the part of the second marquess, a noted philistine.

In this painted stage setting, the figure of Simon de Mazarin fitted like a sword in its sheath. He had—and without asking her leave—snuffed all but one of the candles in the box. Moreover—and again without comment—he went over, locked the door and placed the key in his fob pocket. As for the latter incident, by the time Emmie had consumed the fourth glass of spiced champagne, she was beyond all protest. No great drinker, despite her gamy ancestry, she habitually rested on the second glass at all times. By subtle persuasion, de Mazarin seduced her into consuming all of the bottle save a few sips that he took from his own glass.

And the images that sped before her stupefied mind—no grape that ever grew in fair France had ever been fermented to produce such imagery. No sooner was de Mazarin invested with the role of an ancient Greek within the Poussin *mise en scène* than he must appear nude before her, nude as the day he was born and beautiful as a god from Mount Olympus. But why then, and entirely without protest, did she succumb to his gentle blandishments and shamelessly strip herself before his eyes, rendering herself naked save for silk stockings and ribboned garters? And by what wizardry did she dance with him to some far-off music of a string orchestra playing a popular *valse?* Naked both, breast to breast, belly to belly, close, loin to loin, mouth to mouth and tongues joined.

And, the music over, why did she make no protest, this wife of a distinguished English knight, when this man, a total stranger, had his way with her in that curtained theater box, with a thousand people just beyond the velvet drapes? And repeatedly, in every manner familiar to a licentious age and hallowed since antiquity.

He did not leave her be when, glutted, he reached his first satiety, but obliged her to perform an abandoned improvisation upon the table top, a dance of captivation to rekindle the flickering flame of his lust, which she performed like a creature in a dream of total wantonness. And when she had accomplished his design, he took her again, with her moaning with sweet enchantment, calling upon him not to desist but to bear her up even higher, faster, more recklessly.

The end—when the vile Oriental concoction with which he had defiled the wine took another turn with the workings of her mind—came swiftly. At the remote edge of a sensual transport, she fell limp in his arms, her head sagged against his breast, her scrabbling fingertips were stilled. With a curse, he laid her aside, throwing her across a chair with no more care than if she had been an unwanted puppet, and proceeded to dress himself.

Emmie, drifting between drugged sleep and a certain hideous awareness that was insinuating itself in her mind as the doctored wine began to lose its pernicious effect, was half-aware when the door was unlocked and others entered the curtained confines: men, cloaked and shadowed, with muttering voices and sneering laughs. They grouped about her closely as she lay there, nude and helpless to their eyes and hands. One of them mauled her breasts roughly, cruelly plucking at her nipples till she cried out in pain. Then they laughed among themselves, saying how neatly it had been devised, the enticement and ravishment of the beautiful Lady Devizes. And a nickname was mentioned; she heard it quite clearly. . . .

"Well planned," said someone. "A capital notion— Snakey!"

It was one of the theater's cleaners who found her the next morning when she came to sweep out the box. By that time, Emmie, woken earlier by the dawn's chill, had contrived to struggle back into her evening gown before again relapsing into unconsciousness. The cleaning woman—a phthisical crone in her early thirties, aged beyond her years by child-bearing and laudanum—was not unduly put out to find a lady of the upper classes asleep in a curtained box at six o'clock in the morning, with hair awry and her bodice unbuttoned. There was an empty bottle on the table and two glasses; she had not been in the theater business all her working life without becoming well acquainted with the carryings-on of the "nobs." Helping Emmie to her feet, she directed her unsteady footsteps to a side door of the establishment, accepting without any thanks a shilling for the service rendered.

The Devizes' crested coach stood where Emmie and her husband had left it the previous evening, in a turning off Drury Lane, close to an oyster stall, where the common working people of the city, early about, were filling their empty bellies with the cheapest food available in London: Thames oysters at a penny-ha'penny a dozen. Above the dusty skyline of high-pitched roofs was etched the rising smoke of a thousand chimneys. The coachman was asleep on his box, the horses asleep on their feet. If the fellow was surprised to see his mistress returning from the theater at such an hour, he admirably concealed it. He bade her a brisk "good morning, m' lady," while leaping down to hand her into the coach. A click of the tongue, a shake of the reins, and they clattered westward, past the ruminative stares of the oyster eaters.

Emmie sat back and closed her eyes. The events of the previous night were not entirely lost to her, though their sequence was blurred and certain details mercifully extinguished. In short terms, she had been tricked, drugged and brutally raped. That much was certain. Even if the recollection were hazy, her whole body ached with the excesses to which she had been subjected, and there were teeth marks on the soft flesh of her shoulder and on her right breast.

But that was not all. Her spirit screamed against the revelation that had come to her sometime during that night of horror: the remembrance of a name—and an event—that had first obtruded upon her life not so very far from the street through which she was now being driven.

She seemed to hear again their wild, wolf-pack cries, the lustful howls, the scabrous asides. And was

that not poor Perry Manners screaming in his agony?
Emmie shut her ears with her hands, but the sounds
went on. . . .

There was no denying the truth of it: he who had
wrought her violation on the previous night was he
who had been thwarted from accomplishing it on that
previous occasion.

Snakey . . .

Upon reaching home, Emmie called for hot bath. It
was not suitable that Agnes Reilly should attend her;
she herself must wash clean her own defilement, and
this she did, three times over. After which, she slept,
and arose at four-thirty in a tea gown to preside over
a dumbwaiter bearing teas both Indian and Chinese,
with Bath Oliver biscuits, paper-thin cucumber sand-
wiches, toasted muffins, seed cake.

Sir Claude put in an appearance for tea in her sitting
room, having arrived back at Sloane Street—as Emmie had, with relief, elicited from the servants—some
two hours after herself. The first sight of him as he
entered banished all thought of confiding in him about
the events of the previous night. He was just as he
had been on the day of his return from the battle front
in Canada: haggard and jaundiced, overhung with
coming death, defeated. His appearance notwithstanding, he kissed her cheek heartily enough, and
sank into his favorite chair.

"Sir, I think the night hasn't gone well for you,"
said Emmie, "and that Captain Vanbrough's news
was ill-omened."

Devizes passed his hand—lean and frail as the
plucked wing of a bird and trembling with ague—
across his pallid brow. "Vanbrough is a good fellow,"
he said. "Well-meaning and faithful. We are not living
in the days of the Caliphate, dear Emmie. One does
not hack off the head of the messenger bearing ill tidings."

"So the news he brought was bad?"

"Bad, yes."

"Concerning the Devizes fleet, sir?"

"Concerning the Devizes fleet, Emmie."

"Will you take Indian or Chinese tea, sir?"

"Indian, please, my dear. And do you have handy a little, er . . . ?"

"Yes, sir."

It was a ritual between them, as formal as the English tea ceremony itself. The butler always secreted a small—but none *too* small—flask of brandy in the drawer beneath the dumbwaiter. Emmie took it out and poured a generous measure into her husband's teacup, topping it up with the brew that cheers but does not inebriate, and handed cup and saucer to her spouse.

"And how is dearest Annabel?" asked Devizes.

"Reilly says that she had a good night," replied Emmie. "She was . . . sleeping when I went to the nursery, so I didn't disturb her."

(*My God, how can I lie to him so? I never went near the nursery this morning. I felt too filthied, too poisoned, to touch my own child. And as for kissing her . . .*)

Devizes drank his tea in one long sip and asked for another. As Emmie poured it out, he watched her reflectively.

"And did you enjoy the theater, my dear?" he asked.

The question unnerved her completely. Cup, saucer and teapot became inextricably tangled. The latter slipped from her nerveless fingers and crashed to the floor. She fell to her knees and made a futile attempt to mop up the mess with her scrap of lace handkerchief. Devizes reached out and calmly pulled the bell cord to summon a footman. By the time the man had put things to rights and departed, the question was still unanswered, and was not repeated.

"To return to the topic of the Devizes fleet," said Sir Claude presently, "and to strike a happier note, I have just received a letter from your old friend Captain Grant, who is in the West Indies."

"Indeed, sir," said Emmie as casually as she was able, while uncomfortably aware that her heart had quickened its beat. "And what does the good captain say?"

Devizes fumbled in his breast pocket and produced a packet, which he handed across to his young wife. "To tell the truth, I have given it only a cursory glance," he said. "I beg you, read it aloud to me, Emmie dear, for I have left my spectacles upstairs."

"Of course," murmured Emmie, unfolding the sheet of paper and instantly recognizing the handwriting of her former lover and the father of her child. And did her hand tremble? Did her husband notice the fact?

The words swam before her eyes in a haze of tears that there was no checking. Somehow she blinked them away; somehow she found her voice, and began.

" 'Dear Sir Claude . . .' "

The communication was entirely businesslike, being a sober account of an Atlantic passage and a description of cargo taken aboard in Charleston, South Carolina and shipped to Kingston, Jamaica. The letter included brief digressions concerning a minor outbreak of scurvy aboard the ship and various small injuries caused by heavy seas. It told of long and tedious hours of watch, of petty irritations, inconsiderable triumphs. All in all, Grant's letter to his employer was about as uplifting as a shopping list. To Emmie, reading it aloud in what she piously believed to be a matter-of-fact voice, the missive had all the majesty and splendor of Holy Writ.

She read the closing lines with a tremor in her voice that she could not contain: " '. . . *pray convey my kind regards to Lady Devizes. And to yourself, sir, I remain your obedient servant, Nathan Grant.*' "

Devizes blew his nose loudly. "An excellent fellow," he opined. "Quite excellent. I must ensure his speedy advancement in the fleet. Might appoint him to the general command of all our vessels in the East Indies. Have to see about that. Well, my dear, I'll leave you now. Much to be done."

Emmie watched him raise himself painfully to his feet, noting the effort it cost him, and noting how agonizing the upright posture was, when it was achieved. Here was a good man whose sands were rapidly running out. A thought came to her. . . .

"Sir, why don't you give up the work?" she asked. "Surely you've done enough to deserve a rest from all the toil and worry. You could spend your days doing all the things you've never had time for. Fishing, perhaps . . ."

He smiled at her. "Fishing is a pastime for idiots, my dear," he said, "as are most so-called pastimes. Time is best spent in the pursuit of either ambition or wealth—and I am of the opinion that the pursuit of the latter is, if anything, the most creditable." He looked wistful. "And in any event, I have set my hand to the plow and there's no turning back now. I must see it through to—to the bitter end."

He turned to go. With his departure, Emmie knew that all hope was gone of confiding in him about the events of the previous night. But one thing had to be asked. . . .

"Sir, have you ever heard of the Bizarre Club?" she blurted out.

Devizes paused at the door. "Bizarre Club?" he repeated. "Can't say that I have, my dear. Where, pray, is it situated? In St. James's? And what kind of club is it?"

"I—I don't know where the club is housed," said Emmie. "But I believe that its members pride themselves in being—eccentrics."

"Eccentrics?" Devizes chuckled. "I would have thought the House of Commons provided sufficient outlet for gentlemen of *that* persuasion without the need to form a club. Goodbye, my dear."

Alone, Emmie realized that she was still holding Grant's letter. She supposed that her husband would ask for it back. But until he did, she would keep it to herself. Folding the paper ever so carefully, she slipped it into her bodice so that it rested between her breasts, where Nathan's face had so often nuzzled in the days of that far-off idyll.

Shed a tear for that idyll, Emmie, she told herself, for there's no recalling it. And one thing I know, one thing the sight of his letter showed to me so clearly. I love Nathan and will go on loving him till I die.

And, since this is our day for frank speaking, she continued to inform herself, *there's another reason why I never told—can never tell—my husband about last night. A reason quite apart from considerations about its effect upon that poor, sick man.*

My shame . . .

The man who calls himself "Snakey" took his pleasure of me last night, and repeatedly. I remember but little of it, but this I'm prepared to swear on the head of my own child . . .

Damn my accursed, licentious Cradock blood—I reveled in it and savored every living moment of my defilement!

It was with some surprise, a fortnight after, that Emmie received an invitation, tastefully and expensively engraved as follows:

At Home
Augusta, Marchioness of Beechborough
requests the pleasure of the company of
Sir Claude and Lady Devizes
on Friday, 19th August, at 7 P.M.
Beechborough House,   Carriages at 2 A.M.
Piccadilly   R.S.V.P.

She had not formed the opinion, upon the occasion of her one and only encounter with Augusta Beechborough, that her new aunt would ever seek to extend their acquaintance. However, by making a few discreet inquiries, she discovered the truth of the matter: the Devizes had been invited for the simple reason that *all* of London Society had been invited. Including the Prince Regent.

Emmie nearly did not go to the marchioness's party because Sir Claude was called away to Bristol on business and she had no taste for attending social functions unescorted. However, her spouse prevailed upon her to go with Lord George Delavere, who accordingly called for her in his town phaeton at the appointed hour. The lame member of Parliament was in a high good mood.

"Tonight, my dear Lady Devizes," he said, urging on his fine pair of cobs at a spanking pace, "we are going to be treated to a sight that will go down in the history books—history books, I hasten to add, of the seamier sort."

"And what sight will that be, sir?" asked Emmie, amused.

"Why, Society is formally to be made aware that Prinny has taken for himself a new mistress. I should say an *extra* mistress, for he will never give up Mrs. Fitzherbert, if indeed, as rumor has it, he is not already secretly married to her."

"A new mistress—and who is the lady, sir?" asked Emmie.

Lord George chuckled. "Why, your kinswoman, ma'am."

Emmie blinked. "My—*kinswoman?*"

"Our hostess for tonight, ma'am—the marchioness." Lord George thoroughly enjoyed imparting the news to his lovely companion and seeing its effect.

Beechborough House, Piccadilly, in the days of the previous marquess, had, due to lack of funds for its

maintenance and upkeep, fallen into almost total decrepitude. Happily, the slave trade heiress had come
to the rescue and the once-splendid town mansion was
restored, regardless of expense, to its former state.
Upon Emmie's arrival with Lord George, they were
greeted by an ensign of the Scots Fusilier Guards,
who took their invitations and handed them to a liveried flunky. Guardsmen lined the wide staircase leading up to the ballroom—a sure sign that royalty was
included among the guests.

Walking with the aid of his sticks, Lord George
managed the staircase numbly enough, civilly, but
firmly, declining any assistance from Emmie. She mar-
veled at her companion's constant good humor and
uncomplaining manner, for his lameness, the result of
a terrible fall in the hunting field, was said to keep him
in continuous pain. At the top of the stairs, he
squeezed the hand of his fair companion.

A major-domo announced them. "Lord George
Delavere and Lady Devizes!"

"Now we shall see what we shall see," whispered
Delavere.

"Only then shall I believe it," responded Emmie.

The Beechboroughs greeted each guest upon enter-
ing the vast ballroom, which was already thronged
with the cream of London Society and a fair sprinkling
from the shires. Uncle Eustace looked—though it
scarcely seemed possible—even worse than he had on
the last occasion that Emmie had seen him. Augusta,
on the other hand, was positively radiant.

"Ah, my dear Emmie," she gushed, kissing her new
niece on both cheeks. "How pretty you look. Such a
shame that dear Sir Claude was unable to come. You
must bring him to Flaxham sometime."

"Thank you—er—Aunt," said Emmie dutifully,
trying hard not to stare at the other's near-scandalous
display of bosom. It is truly said that every woman,
however uncomely, has one redeeming feature, be it

only a handsomely shaped big toe. Augusta, Marchioness of Beechborough, sustained a well-filled bodice, and on this occasion was certainly making the most of it.

"Good evening, Uncle Eustace," said Emmie, dutifully kissing the wasted cheek of the fourth marquess.

"Hello, Emmie," responded the other without enthusiasm.

Nodding to various acquaintances, Emmie accompanied her escort to a line of sofas set against the wall. "Now, pay heed to me, ma'am," said Delavere. "You are not to dance attendance on this decrepit old party, but avail yourself of every partner who offers. I see several already hovering. I do not dance, but I delight in watching others. Ah, here comes the first young gentleman to claim your hand."

"Why, it's Jock Ballantree!"

"Miss Dashwood! I beg your pardon, Lady Devizes now, is it not?"

He had not changed. The same unruly thatch of ginger, cornflower-blue eyes, crinkly smile. And he was wearing guards' officers regimentals.

"How nice to see you," said Emmie, offering her hand. "Do you know Sir Jock Ballantree, my lord? He once did me—a very great service."

They addressed themselves to small talk for a while. Ballantree, it transpired, had seen service in the Peninsula and in France, and he and Delavere had many acquaintances in common. It was with mixed feelings that Emmie thought back on her own brief contact with the young baronet. The associations with the sinister Simon de Mazarin, alias Snakey, were painful, but, after all, Ballantree *had* saved her from concerted rape at the hands of Snakey and his cronies. It was amusing—and rather poignant—to recall that she had once chosen this extremely personable young man as a suitable candidate for matrimony. . . .

A stir by the entrance to the ballroom, a waving of hands in signal, a noticeable heightening of tempo, a palpable increase of whispering announced that something important was afoot.

"Here comes Prinny," said Delavere. "Now we shall see the truth of it or not, ma'am. My God, but he continues to put on weight."

The First Gentleman of Europe, voluptuary royal, that amiable spendthrift George, Prince of Wales and—since the insanity of his father George III—the Prince Regent of England, waddled into the ballroom on the arm of his friend Charles James Fox. His Highness affected evening clothes of plain black broadcloth popularized by the arbiter of good taste, Beau Brummell, with a diamond star of the Order of the Garter winking lights upon his portly chest. The prince's hair was dyed and pompadoured, with the marks of the hot iron writ large upon the preposterous wavelets, and his cheeks were rouged. Notwithstanding his obesity—which was the direct result of his drunkenness and gluttony—and forgetting his epicene mannerisms, Prinny still carried traces of the handsome devil he had been in his youth, when all was fair promise, before the lure of the flesh and an incurable hedonism destroyed him.

"My dear Marchioness! How topping you look tonight. Sir, you are to be envied." The latter observation was addressed to Uncle Eustace, who bowed and gave a sickly smile.

"There, if I ever saw one, stands a cuckold," murmured Delavere.

Indeed, Emmie had to acknowledge that the prince was paying most outrageous court to Augusta Beechborough, who responded to the royal attentions by simpering like any sixteen-year-old at her first party, while contriving all the time to present extensive views of her décolletage to her exalted admirer. Emmie had seen the prince flirting before (had she not herself been the object of his light dalliances?), but there was, in his attitude to Augusta, the intensity of his looks, the moistness of his fleshy lips, the ogling of his pouchy eyes, a heartfelt ardor that was far from mere dalliance. There was a man, said Emmie to herself, who had thoroughly convinced himself that he was in love. And did not give a damn who knew it.

Poor Uncle Eustace, thought Emmie. *Still, it's nice to have a royal favorite in the family.*

The prince took his hostess's hand. The conductor of the orchestra, who had been waiting with baton poised for just this connection, tapped his music stand to command his musicians' attention and led them into a sprightly *valse*. The prince and his hostess danced a complete circuit of the floor before the gaze of the assembled guests, among whom there was not one who any longer nourished the slightest doubt about the couple.

"My dance, I believe, ma'am." Jock Ballantree's voice at Emmie's elbow.

"Of course, Jock."

Emmie gathered up the hem of her gown and accepted her partner's hand at ter waist. At close quarters, he had a clean, no-nonsense, manly smell that heart-rendingly put her in mind of Nathan. He was also about the same height, with the same breadth of shoulder, and muscled firmly to the touch. It was like being in Nathan's arms again. She only had to close her eyes and the magic was wrought; ancient desires stirred within her.

"I called upon you at Flaxham, you know," said Ballantree. "Quite soon after we met in London. Found some pretext or other to visit your family home. But the little bird had flown to Canada. Are you happy, Emmie?" It was the first time he had addressed her by her given name.

"I have a baby girl whom I adore to distraction," replied Emmie. "And a devoted husband who is husband, father and older brother all at the same time."

"And are you also in love?"

She glanced sharply at him, this very ordinary, matter-of-fact man whom she would never have credited with the sensibility to ask such a penetrating question.

"I esteem my husband highly," she said.

"That was not what I asked, Emmie," he replied.

"Do you have the right to put the question, Jock?" she countered.

They had come to that part of the ballroom where a long line of windows were opened onto a balcony that looked out over a lamplit garden at the rear of the mansion. Disengaging his arm from around her waist, Ballantree gently took her by the hand and led her out into the warm night, where the heady scent of honeysuckle hung heavily in the air. And there he regarded her soberly for a few moments in silence.

"Well?" she asked.

"I am a plain-speaking man, Emmie," he said, "and I will answer you plainly. From the very first, my intentions toward you have been strictly honorable, and so they remain. My intention, when I visited Flaxham, was to ask for your hand in marriage. There, you have the truth of it."

She touched his hand. "Oh, Jock," she said. "And if you had come in time, I think you wouldn't have come in pain. But that's all in the past. Now it's too late by far."

"Not to beat about the bush, Emmie," he said quietly, "but there was no secret, at Flaxham or elsewhere, regarding the conditions of your marriage. How it was an arranged match, how you were wed by proxy."

"I was bought, Jock," she said. "For money. Happily, the man who bought me did so for good and honorable reasons. It was not a wife he sought—not as a man needs a wife—but a grown daughter to love and cherish. That is what I am to him. No more."

"One other consideration remains, Emmie," he said.

"True," she said. "My husband is an old man. Old and ailing. It is likely, indeed probable, that he will soon die and leave me a widow. Is that the consideration to which you refer?"

He nodded. "And what then, Emmie?"

"A widow I shall remain, Jock," she told him. "I'm sorry, my dear, but it would be sinful for me to hold out the slightest hope. I shall never marry again."

"Then you have answered my original question," said Ballantree. "You are in love."

"Yes," she whispered.

"And he is already married."

"Yes."

"Ah!" He laid his hand gently upon her shoulder. The cornflower-blue eyes were unwavering as he gazed into hers. "Then there is one thing, only, that I have a right to say, Emmie. And it is this: I would wish you to regard me as a loving and devoted friend whose service you may call upon at any time, and in any season. I will be there when you need me."

"Thank you, Jock," she whispered. And, reaching up, she kissed him gently upon the lips.

"And now I must take you back to Lord George," he said, "for I am duty-bound to have the next dance with a maiden aunt of min. But I warn you, Emmie, I shall be back to claim most of the remainder of your program."

In the event, Emmie found her escort deep in conversation with an elderly lady who was holding forth on the virtues of chamomile as a sovereign remedy against most of the ills to which the flesh is heir. Emmie wandered away in search of the buffet, and ran straight into her cousin Petronella Pallance.

"Emmie! Fancy seeing you here. My God, from the size your bubs have grown, you must have been breeding like a rabbit."

Petronella was as sylphlike as ever, as Emmie registered with a wayward twinge of envy.

"Are you still living by grace and favor at Flaxham?" she asked.

"Yes, and I'm the only one left," replied Petronella. "The Gorgon's sent everyone else packing."

"The Gorgon?"

"Aunt Augusta," said Petronella. "Times have changed in the old home, I can tell you. No more goings-on in the orangery. All the dirty old uncles have been cleared out, and she's dismissed all the female servants under fifty. I don't suppose poor old Eustace has had his hand inside a bodice for ages. I've certainly kept him out of mine. Little Petronella knows which side of her bread's buttered. The Gorgon regards me as the only worthy member of her husband's family. I've been given the use of the Leicester Square house. The aunts have died, you know. They always did everything together and they both turned up their toes on the same day, poor dears. I must say you're looking well, Emmie. Marriage must suit you."

"Surely you must miss the carryings-on in the chapel, Petronella," said Emmie, with a conscious touch of malice.

Petronella may have detected the malice, but she laughed and showed no resentment. "My dear," she said, "that particular sport was never repeated after you frightened everyone out of their wits that night. Oh, and poor Toby Stocker's dead, did you know? Killed at Waterloo."

"I'm sorry to hear that," said Emmie, and felt a sharp pang of loss for a long-gone summer morning and a sun-kissed, naked lad. "What a dreadful waste of a life."

"Toby's life was not *entirely* wasted," said Petronella dryly, "as I should have cause to know, none better. However, to return to the living, having turned her spouse into the semblance of a monk, thereby sending him into a rapid decline, the Gorgon is now shamelessly cuckolding him with Prinny."

"It's scarcely believable," said Emmie. "How long has it been going on?"

"All the season," replied Petronella. "Prinny fell as soon as he clapped eyes on the Gorgon. It's not a lover, but a mother, that he constantly seeks, you know. The Gorgon's matronly bubs won him over. Those and her bossy manner. A certain amount of discretion has been exercised so far, but after tonight it will be shouted from the rooftops, and Mrs. Fitzherbert is bound to hear."

"Do they actually—you know . . . ?"

"Prinny's certainly stayed the night in her room at Flatham," said Petronella. "I couldn't help noticing because I lay in hiding on the upstairs landing to see him come out in the morning. As to what they get up to, that's anyone's guess. He with his great belly, and the Gorgon bellowing orders all over the place."

They laughed. . . .

The conversation had taken place between them during their progress together toward the buffet, which was set up in a large antechamber beyond the ballroom. The room was filled with the parakeet chatter of a hundred or so pampered, scented bodies, the rattle and tinkle of crockery and glassware, the discreet murmuring of obsequious servitors. Emmie accepted a glass of champagne, and Petronella bit into a cold chicken leg.

"Tell me about your experiences in Canada, Emmie," she said. "One has heard the most alarming rumors about you. How you were captured by American pirates. Shipwrecked and so forth. Emmie—good heavens, girl—what ails you? What are you staring up there for?"

It was a lofty room. On high, above the great crystal chandelier whose countless candles augmented the heat of that summer night to a stifling degree, ran a balustraded gallery.

"He—he's gone," whispered Emmie.

"Who's gone?" demanded Petronella. "What *are* you talking about? Where are you off to, Emmie? Come back here. . . ."

Emmie ran. She found Lord George Delavere still talking with the elderly lady, and rudely interrupted their conversation with a request—it was more of a demand—to be taken home immediately. It was a demand to which, creditably, the lame aristocrat responded without question, but with only a surprised glance at her shocked, fear-haunted face. He did not question her during the drive back to her house in Sloane Street, but kept up a light monologue of inconsequential matters, behind the cover of which Emmie was able to look inside her head and piece together what she had seen in the buffet room, to examine it from all sides and test its truth or falsehood.

By the time they reached Sloane Street and Sir George took his leave of her, she had convinced herself that she had not been mistaken.

Chancing to look up while sipping her champagne, she had seen someone looking down at her—spying on her—from the galley above. There was not the slightest doubt of his intent, for, on meeting her eye, he had ducked behind a pillar of the balustrade and had not reappeared. But he had stayed in view long enough for her to make a shocked recognition of the man who had so vilely used her in the theater box— Simon de Mazarin, called Snakey.

Clearly, de Mazarin must be known to the Beechboroughs, or else he had come to the marchioness's party uninvited. But what was the profit in making inquiries about the man? The circumstances of her ravishment were such that society at large would lay more blame at her door than at his. She existed in a man's world and lived by man's rules. And there was no one to whom she could turn. Her only hope was that the encounter was accidental and not—as she most feared—that the tall man with the butter-yellow hair was continuing to pursue her. The prospect kept her awake till nearly dawn—and then the creature with the yellow hair became a hobgoblin of her haunted, uneasy sleep. She rose immediately upon waking—to face what was possibly one of the worst weeks of her life. . . .

Little Annabel had taken of a slight quinsy, nothing serious, and their London physician had advocated country air as the best palliative. Consequently the babe had earlier that week been sent down to Avon Park in the charge of the faithful Agnes Reilly. Alone in the house save for the servants, Emmie felt deeply uneasy and restless, and determined to place as much distance as possible between herself and London—and Snakey. She rang for a footman to have a carriage made ready to take her to Bristol, and received no response to her summons.

Nervous and irritable from lack of sleep, she pulled the bell cord again—hard and continuously. Still no footman came.

"Is everybody asleep in this place?" she cried. And went to look.

The kitchen quarters in the basement—which she had never before entered—were reached by way of a steep flight of stairs behind a green baize door off the hall. Emmie had no sooner opened the door and set a foot upon the top step, when she heard a voice—by its sound, an exceedingly tipsy voice—raised in a ballad song.

> Of all the girls that are so smart,
> There's none like pretty Sally;
> She is the darling of my heart,
> And she lives in our alley. . . .

The stanza was brought to a rude end by a rumbling belch.

A door at the foot of the stairs stood open, and through it Emmie could see the large kitchen, with a black-leaded cooking stove at the far end and a long, scrubbed table running down the center. Seated facing her was a man in a nightshirt whom she vaguely knew to perform some such function as third groom-cum-gardener. He was red-eyed, tousle-headed and exceedingly drunk. Two claret bottles were on the table before him, one of which was lying open on its side and certainly empty. As Emmie entered, the man—she remembered that he was called Pottinger—lifted the second bottle to his lips and met her horrified gaze.

"Well, if it ain't 'er lidyship!" he declared. " 'Ere, 'ave a swig, yer lidyship. What, don't want any? Let me tell you, yer lidyship, as this 'ere's some o' the finest in the cellar."

"And what are you doing at this hour of the morn?" demanded Emmie furiously. "Stupid drunk, still in your nightshirt, and guzzling your employer's claret? Speak up, man—you're not so far gone in your cups that you can't answer a simple question!"

Pottinger's slight truculence faded before Emmie's anger, and he answered whiningly, his weasel-like countenance assuming what was intended to be an ingratiating expression.

"I'm still 'ere, ain't I, yer lidyship? Not like the others, as packed their traps and walked out last night. I'm faithful to you and the master, ain't I?" He tried to get to his feet but abandoned the attempt. "An' the wine I only took in lieu o' me rightful wages."

"What are you talking about, man?" demanded Emmie. "You speak of people walking out. *Who* has walked out? And where are the rest of the servants?"

"Gorn, yer lidyship," said Pottinger. "All gorn, like I explained yer. Said they'd had enough o' workin' without wages. But me, yer lidyship"—the fellow winked and grinned tipsily—"Alf Pottinger's quite 'appy to take 'is pay in drink."

*   *   *

It was ridiculous, of course. A simple explanation would be forthcoming as soon as she reached Bristol. Emmie had never had any dealings with the running of her three establishments in Bristol, Bath and London. One had perfectly competent housekeepers at all three places and they coped with everything, including the paying of wages. Clearly the London housekeeper, a new woman named Collis, had been embezzling the money Sir Claude's secretary provided her for the servants' wages. Yes, that must be it; no other explanation filled the bill.

Out of the question, now, to travel down to Bristol in one of the family carriages; Pottinger was too fumbling drunk to harness up the horses and certainly in no condition to drive her. Best to take a stage.

This she did, arriving at Chippenham in time for dinner at the selfsame posting inn where she had stayed in the company of the late, ill-fated Major Jack Tredegar. And she was given the selfsame room in which Tredegar had attempted to force her. However, so worn out was she by a restless night and a harrowing day that she slept like a babe, notwithstanding the associations invoked by her surroundings. An early start, and she arrived in Bristol before noon, where a hired hackney carriage took her to Avon Park. Agnes Reilly was wheeling little Annabel in her bassinet when the carriage drew up before the Nash facade and Emmie hastily alighted. The expression on her mistress's face told the good Irishwoman that something was badly amiss. The fond mother first picked up her babe, and, kissing her, inquired as to the little mite's health. Upon receiving a cheering reply, Emmie fired two more questions at her companion. In answer to the first she elicited that no, Sir Claude was not at home, but was expected back for dinner at eight.

And in answering the second, the poor creature dissolved in tears.

"Sure and it's right enough, y' ladyship. The staff

in London hasn't been paid for nigh on eight weeks,
nor in Bath, nor here.''

"But you knew that this was going on, Reilly. Why
didn't you *tell* me, since you, yourself, were involved?''

More tears. "Bless you, y' ladyship, sure but I
didn't want to visit it upon you, the upset. We were
promised that the wages would be made good, but the
weeks went by, and the servants in London, they
swore they'd bear it till this week and no longer. I told
them before I left London, so help me God, that they
weren't to leave you in the lurch, but there's no trusting today's servants, that there isn't.''

"But why—*why* were you not paid?'' cried Emmie.

The other woman looked uneasy. "Sure and it's not
my place to speak out o' turn, m' lady, but I've heard
tell in the servants' hall . . .'' She paused.

"Heard *what?*'' demanded Emmie. "Oh, out with
it, woman! Why do you seek to spare me the truth, or
even the rumor? I have to know sometime, for the
cat's half out of the bag already, and I shall hear all
of it when Sir Claude arrives home tonight.''

Emmie had been holding little Annabel all this time.
Kissing the satin cheek once more, she replaced the
babe in her bassinet and tucked the blankets around
the tiny form. The child smiled up at her—and it was
Nathan's smile.

She faced the Irishwoman again. "Here, take my
handkerchief and dry your eyes, Reilly,'' she said.
"And tell me the worst of it.''

Reilly obeyed. "Well, you know, y' ladyship,'' she
began, "a man—that's to say a gentleman—will speak
out before the servants of things he'd not dream o'
telling his wife. For a gentleman looks upon a servant
waiting at table as nothing more than a piece of furniture that moves of its own accord.''

Emmie frowned and nodded. "True,'' she conceded. "It's never occurred to me before, but you're

quite right. So, my husband has been confiding in his
male friends, over the port, I shouldn't wonder."

"Yes, m' lady."

"And . . . ?"

"Sir Claude, he's admitted—the night before last it
was—that he's bankrupt, y' ladyship. Ruined . . ."

Emmie spent the rest of the day in fretful activity,
seeking to drive the worry from her mind and replace
it with the mechanics of tending her rose garden in the
quiet quadrangle at the center of the mansion. She
gave instructions concerning dinner, rode out in the
home park. The servants still remained; clearly the
stolid west-country folk were of more faithful disposition than the flighty denizens of the metropolis, but
Emmie—perhaps in her imagination—thought she detected sullen looks and a certain truculence in the
housekeeper's manner when the woman came to her
with three alternative menus from which to choose
dinner. It may have been that the housekeeper mar-
veled that three separate menus, each comprising four
courses with removes, were excessive for two persons—particularly when they were unable to pay the
staff and the tradesmen. But if those were her thoughts,
she did not express them to her mistress.

Emmie was at a complete loss. "Bankrupt" was a
word with which she simply could not conjure. Too
young to remember her widowed mother's grinding
poverty, she had known only Flaxham Palace and,
after that, marriage. There had never in her life been
any question of *denial*. One's wants, when expressed,
were always met. Flaxham, in her time, had been a
tapestry-hung slum, but one had only to snap one's
fingers and the servants came running. The prospect
of being bereft of their protection against the outside
world was quite insupportable.

But what, she asked herself, when even the delight
of tending her roses could not shut out uneasy spec-

ulations, did "bankrupt" really mean? What did it mean to be "ruined"? One had a country seat and two town houses. The former was also possessed of hundreds of acres of parkland and farmland. In harvest time, the wheat made the fields golden as far as the eye could see, to the very gates of Bristol. The houses, all three, were crammed with priceless paintings and sculpture, Persian rugs from Tabriz and Quom, Gobelins tapestries dating from the days of Louis Quatorze. How could one be said to be "ruined" with all that to fall back on? If the servants could not be paid, why did it not occur to her husband to sell a painting or two? And if—God forbid—things did really come to the pinch, one could sell one of the town houses. Or even both. She, Emmie, had pigged it in the Canadian wilderness and also at Flaxham. No one would hear her complain at being reduced to dear, dear Avon Park as her sole residence, or even at putting up with a reduction of servants to, say, twenty. At six o'clock, Emmie took a glass of sherry wine and felt much better for her deliberations. Clearly, what Sir Claude stood in need of was womanly advice.

Devizes arrived home an hour later. She saw him through the window of the drawing room as he was assisted down from his coach. The marks of defeat and impending dissolution were limned heavily on his pallid countenance and burdened his stooping shoulders. Emmie greeted her husband in the hallway and took his arm, guiding him into the drawing room, settling him in his favorite wing chair and pouring him a glass of brandy. He took the vessel between his hands, clutching it tightly, as if seeking to derive warmth and comfort from the vital spirit within.

He sought her gaze, reading what was written there.

"You—*know*, Emmie," he murmured, "don' you?"

She nodded. "The servants, all but one, walked out of Sloane Street the night before last. From a simila source, I hear that you—that's to say, we—are bank-rupt."

"Yes, Emmie. Today, I made a last bid to buy time. But failed."

"Sell Sloane Street!" she cried, hoping that he would be dazzled by her acumen.

"Mortgaged—every last stick and stone," he said.

"*Mortgaged*—what does that mean, sir?" she cried.

"It means we—that's to say, I—have borrowed, and spent, the entire value of the house, which now belongs to a firm of merchant bankers. And all in it."

"The Bath house!"

"Likewise mortgaged."

"Then," breathed Emmie, "you mean that we have nothing but Avon Park! Well, then, we must resign ourselves to . . ."

She broke off, and saw that her husband had placed a frail hand across the upper part of his face, shielding his eyes from her gaze. Presently, a tear slid down his cheek from behind the hand, and his nether lip trembled. With a cry of anguish and compassion, Emmie fell on her knees beside his chair.

"Oh, sir, sir!" she breathed. "Can it be true? Have we indeed lost everything? What torments you must have been through. And never to confide in me, but to bear it all alone!"

He reached out and took her hands in his, smiled brokenly at her. "It's all gone, Emmie," he said. "Avon Park, the contents, the lands and farms. Everything. I think we may own the clothes we stand up in, but I would need to consult learned counsel on that point. It is done, Emmie. Finished. In a few short months, I have reduced the Devizes fleet to penury. And the fault is mine, all mine. I have taken bad advice, yes. But I bear the ultimate responsibility. As a shipowner, I am a good general."

"But how, sir—*how?*" asked Emmie.

"How did it come about, my dear? Simplicity itself. With the end of the war in America and Napoleon safely on exile in Elba, shipping boomed. I built on credit. No one could lend me enough, and there were no risks. With the family properties to offer as security, the bankers fell over themselves to lend, lend, lend.

"Then came The Hundred Days, and the specter of Napoleon again stalked over Europe. My creditors panicked, so I repaid them ten shillings in the pound, further pledging the family properties in short-term loans at high rates of interest to provide the money. The weeks went by. Napoleon marched on Brussels, and my bills of exchange fell due. I think"—he drew a shuddering breath—"I think that, had the French been brought to battle and defeated two weeks earlier—even one week—I might have won through by the skin of my teeth. But it was not to be. The last throw of the dice was the selling of most of the ships to meet the bills, but since, with the threat of another long war, the penurious government was likely to commandeer all merchant ships with little or no compensation, they fetched next to nothing. A week later, Napoleon was defeated at Waterloo. And Claude Devizes, also, was the loser."

She stroked his hand, feeling the swollen veins beneath her sensitive fingertips. "Sir, what are we going to do?" she asked.

"I shall pay all my debts, every penny," said Devizes. "That done, I shall apply to the War Office for a command. I'm not so old that I could not be commander-in-chief of, say, the London Garrison. Or perhaps an appointment in India: chief-of-staff to one of the Maharajas. How's that, Emmie? You would like India."

She made no reply, knowing—and, surely, he knew it as well as she—that he would never wear a general's scarlet coat again.

Something of her inner melancholy must have touched him, for his brief optimism faded. "My greatest regret, Emmie, apart from the deprivation I have brought upon you, is the fact that by my folly I have cheated darling Annabel of her inheritance.''

She looked at him, this tired, generous, honorable man, and she knew the truth must be told.

"Do not repine, sir," she said. "Annabel isn't your child, as we both well know, though we don't speak of it. You owe her nothing. She owes you everything for what you have been to her since she was born, and before.''

He nodded, gravely acquiescing. "True, true, my dear," he said. "She is not my child, though she is so in the eyes of the law, and, as such, I would wish to have provided for her. As for her *real* father"—he fumbled in the pocket of his waistcoat and produced a letter—"I have to tell you that, in response to my summons, Captain Nathan Grant is even now on his way back to England. This letter from him came on the previous packet from Kingston.''

Emmie became aware that she was staring at her husband in blank-faced astonishment and making no attempt to take the letter that he proffered.

"Sir, I . . ." she began.

He smiled and touched her cheek. "Do you think I am so old and lost to the ways of love and youth that I did not know immediately where your heart lay when you read his dispatch about capturing you? Or only a little while back, when you quietly purloined the other letter from him? Emmie, Emmie, your love for that man informs your whole life, your appearance, everything. I'm mightily puzzled that he doesn't seem to see it for himself, for 'tis certain that he doesn't, or he would not have run off so quickly without saying goodbye to you—as I am well aware.''

"That man!" cried Emmie, with heat. "That man didn't even recognize his likeness in his own child!"

Devizes looked puzzled for a moment, then smiled with a touch of condescension.

"Oh, come, Emmie dear," he said. "The fond mother's eye and all that, what? But everyone knows that, apart from what the mother sees there with the eye of faith, all babies look alike.''

She took a few drops of laudanum, at Agnes Reilly's advice, to help her to sleep that night. Dinner, at which she and her husband had sat at opposite ends of a long refectory table and picked at the expensive food before the disapproving eyes of the servants, might have been a disaster had not Sir Claude dismissed the servants, cut himself a slice of bread and cheese, and brought it, together with a glass of wine, to sit beside Emmie and chat quietly with her about past days that they had spent together in company with Annabel. In all their marriage, they had never been closer together in spirit, and Emmie was to remember that dinner with pleasure.

Shortly after retiring, she thought she heard the baby crying in her nursery along the passage, and went to investigate. As she did so, she heard the click of a door being closed, followed by hasty, tiptoeing footfalls. By the time she reached her own bedroom door, the footsteps had faded.

Annabel was perfectly all right. Agnes was with her, nursing her and giving her comfort. She looked up at Emmie's entrance, nodded and smiled reassuringly.

"Who was that out in the passage, Reilly?" whispered Emmie.

"The master, perhaps, y' ladyship?" ventured the Irishwoman.

"I'll go and see if he's all right. Good night, Reilly."

"Good night, y' ladyship."

Further down the corridor, Emmie was met by a draft of wind, as if from an open window, and that was strange. Stranger still, the door of her husband's master suite was open, and it was through there that the draft was coming. She went inside. The sitting room door leading into the bedroom was also open, and the source of the draft could be seen, from where she stood, to be the bedroom window, whose casement was flung wide to the night.

"Sir, are you there?" she called gently.

No answer. The bedroom was in darkness save for a patch of moonlight that picked out the four-poster bed whose sheets were thrown aside as if the occupant had quitted it in some haste. With a prickle of sudden unease, Emmie saw that the bedside candlestick had been overturned; there was a circle of spilled wax on the mahogany table top; when she touched it, she found it to be still warm.

Clearly, Sir Claude had been taken ill and had gone downstairs, perhaps to fetch himself a brandy (by gentle stealth she had at last persuaded him against the temptation of keeping spirit in his suite), in which case it had clearly been he whom she had heard.

She would go and find him. First, she would close the window.

Who had opened it? Sir Claude abhorred drafts.

One hand on the window latch, she looked out and down. And screamed at what she saw.

The front of the house was in bright moonlight; the tall columns of Beau Nash's portico made striped patterns of shadow across the marble flagstones thirty feet below. One shape, alone, broke the regular symmetry of the design: a sprawled figure lying face-down.

Then she was running, the scream still on her lips, and Agnes Reilly joined her. More servants appeared in the hall, clad in night attire and sleeping caps, the women with hair braided or tied up in curling rags; they followed after as Emmie, wrenching open the massive bolts of the bronze front doors, went out onto the terrace and threw herself down beside the still form of her husband.

General Sir Claude Devizes, sometime military governor of Quebec Province and lately failed shipowner, was staring-eyed and quite dead. His unseeing gaze was fixed upon the last, agonizing enterprise of his life, which had been to dip his forefinger in the lifeblood that still issued fitfully from his partly open mouth and write with it across the marble flagstone upon which his head lay . . .

One word, one name, wine-dark against moonlit white: *S N A K E Y*.

Chapter Two

Emmie, Lady Devizes, attended as sole family mourner at the brief obsequies of her husband three days later, in the village church of Creech-in-Gordano at the edge of the Avon Park estates. She mourned in anger, dry-eyed and in the full knowledge that the open landau in which Sir Claude's coffin had been carried, together with her own carriage, were due to be sequestered by creditors' bailiffs as soon as they were returned to the mews.

They had descended like vultures upon the Avon Park estates, creditors and bailiffs. The former were well-heeled men in good broadcloth suits and handsome carriages, who stayed apart from the tearing and the rending, but contented themselves by drinking claret in the local hostelry and reading through the inventories prepared by their hard-faced bailiffs up at the "big house": lists of paintings, tapestries, carpets, silver, crystal glass, goldwork, fine inlaid furniture, *bibelots* and bric-a-brac by the ton. And stables filled with carriage horses, thoroughbreds, hunters, hacks,

fine ponies, together with coaches and carriages to
match every occasion. Most of the vultures were not
direct creditors, but shifty discount men who had purchased the mortgages, bills of exchange and so forth
from merchant bankers in the city—the kind of gentlemen who would not have dreamed of playing vulture
to the corpse of a general officer and knight of the
Bath.

Emmie loathed and despised them all with every
fiber of her passionate, arrogant Cradock blood. She
had had no scruples about hiding her own jewel box
from the prying fingers of the bailiffs. There was not
much in it, for she had never been one for peacock
adornment, but a couple of good pieces that Sir Claude
had bought her were sold by Agnes Reilly in Bristol
and provided enough cash to settle the faithful Irishwoman and her beloved charge in a cottage north of
the city.

The funeral over, Emmie departed for London to
take stock of the family fortunes there. And for another reason . . .

She arrived on Sloane Street after dark and, paying
off her carriage, hefted her carpet bag—her sole lug-
gage—up to the front door of the house. The place
was in darkness, the windows shuttered, as she had
left them. Unlocking, she went in. The place smelled
musty and airless, but everything was in its place, so
clearly the London flock of vultures had not yet descended. Having seen that particular breed of carrion
in action, Emmie did not think their arrival would be
delayed much longer.

Ascending to her suite of rooms, she set to work.
First, she made a pile of her personal belongings: silks
and laces, pretty and expensive stockings, a few
pieces of cheap jewelry, souvenirs of her childhood in
the shape of a woodentop doll, a toy canary in a cage
a dance program. The vultures would not have any of
these!

She gathered them all up in a pillowcase, and was on her way to her dead husband's quarters on a similar errand of rescue, when she quite distinctly heard the street door open and quietly close.

Someone had entered the house!

Cursing herself for having forgotten to lock the door (but, surely, she *had* locked the door!), Emmie went to the head of the stairs and looked down into the hallway.

A man was standing there, his face shadowed by the brim of the tall hat he wore. Seeing him, she distinctly felt her heart waver in its beat.

"Why, it's Lady Devizes. Good evening to you, ma'am."

He stepped forward to the foot of the staircase, and by the light of the candelabrum she carried, she saw the dark and devious eyes of Harry Vanbrough looking quizzically up at her.

"Captain Vanbrough!" she cried. "What are you doing in my house?"

He grinned and tipped his hat to the back of his head, put his hands into the pockets of his pantaloons, gazed up at her with a jaunty air. "I reckon I'm on the same game as yourself, ma'am," he said coolly. "Which is to say I've come to take my pickings of the portable valuables before the bailiffs move in—and they'll be here tomorrow or the next day, you may be sure."

Astounded and shocked by his effrontery, Emmie was speechless for a moment. But only for a moment.

"How dare you?" she cried. "*Break* into my house and . . ."

He held up a key.

"Where—where did you get that?" faltered Emmie.

"From your late husband's office in Limehouse," he said. "Already ransacked by creditors, but they missed this. As commodore of the Devizes fleet and a member of the board of directors, I reckon I'm entitled to my pickings, particularly since I've stuck my head into a noose doing your husband's dirty work, and I'll be lucky to get away with my neck."

Emmie had the distinct impression that reality was slipping away from her. "What do you mean—dirty work?" she demanded. "My late husband would never have . . ."

"Never have soiled his fingers with dirty work?" he cried. "You're right there, milady. Not while he had others to do it for him, but I tell you that your late, gallant husband was up to his neck, nevertheless, in the dirtiest game afoot!"

"What—game—are you referring to?" whispered Emmie.

"The slave trade! And it's illegal now, you know—outlawed!"

She recoiled from him. "I—I don't believe it!" she cried.

He shrugged. "Wait and see," he said. "It will be all over England by this time next week. Warrants have been issued already. Why else do you think your husband killed himself?"

"He didn't kill himself!" she cried. "He was—*murdered!*"

"Not he!" scoffed Vanbrough. "Your precious spouse felt the rope tightening around his neck, so he threw himself out of a window, or so the story goes. Well, I'm not going the same way. Tomorrow, I'm off to Bow Street to turn King's evidence. I'll tell all I know, and let the precious Captain Nathan Grant and the others swing outside Newgate jail. Harry Vanbrough will be there to laugh at their last jig!"

"No-o-o-o!"

Her cry of horror, wrenched from her very soul, and delivered with staring eyes and livid countenance, brought him up short. He looked narrowly at her for a few moments. Then he grinned.

"So that's the way it is, eh?" he said. "You'll not be fancying the idea of the fine upstanding Cap'n Nathan Grant dancing on air at the end of Jack Ketch's bowline? Well, you've only to slip Jack a half-guinea and he'll swing on the gallant captain's legs and bring him to a swifter end."

"Please!" she whispered. *"Please . . ."*

He seized her cruelly by the wrist, drew her close to him, hissed into her face: "Please—what, my lady? *What* would you please?"

"Don't . . ." she closed her eyes, choked on the words.

"Don't let the handsome Cap'n Grant hang, is that it? Ah, but that would be an act of great folly on my part," he said, "of altruism beyond all belief, for in saving Cap'n Grant I might well hang myself. I have papers here—see?" From the breast pocket of his greatcoat he took a sheaf of documents tied with pink string. "Ship's papers, bills of loading and such. It's all here: the record of every voyage made from Guinea to the West Indies, Grant's included. And the cargo every time—slaves! Slaves! Slaves! Look for yourself, milady!" Seizing her by the chin, he brutally directed her gaze toward the paper held up before her.

Emmie's eyes were filled with anguished tears. The writing swam before her.

"I will do anything, give anything," she breathed, "but don't let them hang him!"

He released her. "You ask a lot, milady," he said. "This evidence against Grant is the best I have. With this, I can make a real bargain with the Crown for my own neck. The evidence I have against the other captains is not so sound, so conclusive. I'd be taking a risk to rely on that. . . ." He paused, cocked an eye at her, "What are you offering in return, milady?"

Emmie avoided his gaze. "I've nothing of my own but the clothes I stand up in," she whispered.

He laughed shortly, and her spirit cowered within her, as his hand pawed at her shoulder and descended the rich curve of her breast.

"I reckon the clothes you stand up in will just about meet the case, gel," he leered coarsely.

Her defilement was total—he had intended that. First, the congress had to take place in her own boudoir, which, in the London house, was of jasper green and white with beautifully fashioned Wedgwood medallions set in oval-topped niches about the walls, depicting such lovers of classical mythology as Daphnis and Chlöe, Narcissus and Echo, Pyramus and Thisbe. *Un petit chambrette d'amour.*

Alas for *l'amour* . . .

Lolling back upon her silk-canopied bed, he demanded that she strip herself before his gaze, and that with a languorous dalliance, the more to inflame his passions. And with the removal of each item of attire—bodice and stays, skirts, petticoats, stockings, till she stood nude before him, head bowed and crimson-cheeked with shame—he delivered a bawdy comment upon each of the delights that were revealed: a comment upon the saucy impudence of her breasts, the dimpled belly, the discreet fleece of sable at her loins, her long and tapering legs.

Nude, she must next dance before him, to the rhythmic clapping of his hands and his bawled instruction, while he quaffed down deep drafts of his dead employer's brandy.

Dance, Emmie, Lady Devizes! Dance for the life of the only man you have ever truly loved! Give good return for your end of the bargain, lest this monster renounces his, and the man you love dies on the end of a rope to the roll of drums and the shrieks of the enthusiasts. Dance! Though the sweat pours from you, creeping over your bare breasts and belly in descending fingers, while the monster on the bed claps out the tempo you must follow. And seek not to conceal yourself from him in any way, for that must be to displease him; rather flaunt yourself, for that is his wish and his intent. . . .

Satiated, at last, with Emmie's inflammatory performance, he called her to his side and ordered her to divest him of his own clothing. This she had to accompany with caresses of hands and lips to his order, till his pride was manifest, and in that pride (because he was a man of less than normal height, and, like so many little men, overweenful of his other attributes on that account) he strutted about the room for her delectation, displaying the taut muscles of his arms and back, his deep, thickly pelted breast, the rampant pride at his loins. And she, poor Emmie—a human creature only, and a woman of ardor, with all the passion of her Cradock blood—had to fight against the temptation of succumbing, and remember that she was enduring this degradation for the sake of her love.

Like a stallion brought to a mare, and roused by a "teaser" (which is the basis on which the English thoroughbred horse arrived), he then fell upon his victim and took her in a savage, devouring onslaught, which caused her to tear ten scarlet furrows down his back with her ten sharp nails, and to scream for him never, never to let it end.

He woke her at some unearthly hour, having himself been woken by the Watch. She heard the Watch calling in the distance that it was such-and-such time and a fine night, echoing down the street outside.

"What was that you said about Sir Claude being murdered?" he demanded.

She was with her back to him, imprisoned by one of his muscular arms banding her waist, and his other hand cupping her right breast, with the whole front of his nude body pressed closely against the back of hers. She tried to wriggle free and distance herself from him, if only from skin contact, but he held her tight.

"He *was* murdered," she said at length, and gave him a brief account of the circumstances in which she had discovered her husband's end, to which he listened, interposing a couple of remarks.

"Mmmm, it's a rum tale and no mistake," was his comment when she had finished. "You say you heard someone running down the passage outside?"

"Definitely!" said Emmie. "And whatever happened in that bedroom could only have taken place minutes before I arrived on the scene."

"Because the spilled candle wax was still warm . . . ?"

"Yes."

"Mmm. This fellow Snakey—you've met him?"

"Twice—God help me!"

"And his real name is . . . ?"

"Simon de Mazarin. Are you *sure* you've never heard of him?"

"Never. Why should I give you the lie? And it's not a name you'd forget. Have you told the authorities about your belief that Sir Claude was murdered by this Snakey?"

She drew a deep breath and exhaled it slowly, in carefully controlled fury.

"When the authorities had been informed of the circumstances of my husband's death," she said, "a man—I suppose he would be called a constable—was sent from the office of the Bristol justices. I explained what had happened, how I believed that someone had gained admission to our house and had thrown my husband from his window. Unfortunately, I was unable to substantiate the detail of the last message that Sir Claude wrote in his own blood. In the early hours of the morning, a deluge of rain had quite washed it clean. The man—the constable—scarcely troubled to hide his scorn and contempt of my story. I suppose that, like you, the office of the Bristol justices assumed that my husband had killed himself to evade—whatever fate threatened him."

"So what shall you do now, milady?" he whispered into her ear.

Mindless of his proximity, heedless that he was gently teasing her right nipple with his fingertip, she said: "I shall find Snakey. Even if it takes me forever

and till the ends of the earth. And I shall kill him with
my own hands. I swore it after our first encounter. I
repeat it now."

"My, but you are a woman of some forcefulness,
milady," he said, only half-mockingly. "I said that to
myself as soon as I clapped eyes on you, and you far
gone with child—despite which, I could have tumbled
you as soon as look at you. As now . . ."

"Please!" she whispered. "Leave me be, I beg of
you. Haven't I shamed myself enough this night, that
you should want to torture me again? Stop it, for pity's
sake, if for naught else!"

"And *shall* I stop it, then—for pity's sake?" His
hands ceased their questing, their gentle, lewd teasing. . . .

She moaned: it was the protest of wronged wom-
ankind since the world began.

"Please—*please* . . !"

The cry of the Watch came in through the cracks in
the shuttered window, together with the thin sunlight.

*"Seven o'clock on a fine morn, and a-a-a-a-all's
well!"*

Her seducer was far gone in the profound sleep of
utter repletion, as well he might have been, for he had
used Emmie most unscrupulously throughout the early
hours. He had demanded of her—a gently, if aristo-
cratically-reared lass—the sort of favors to which he
had been initiated, as a young seaman, in *maisons
d'illusion* of Marseille and Toulon, bawdy houses of
Valetta's Strait Street, and had learned from the public
odalisques of the Barbary Coast from Tripoli to Al-
exandria, and in the decadent pleasure houses of Con-
stantinople, where nothing is forbidden and no refusal
is accepted—particularly from a woman.

Having abused her body in every manner conceiv-
able, and having had his fill, he had turned over to his
other side, and now lay snoring, mouth wide and reeking of brandy.

Gently, so gently that the linen scarcely rustled, Emmie eased herself from the bed and crept out of that jasper green and white boudoir-that she would never have slept easily in again, even if the bailiffs had sanctioned it. She went down into the kitchen—that same place where she had first stumbled upon the horror that had led to her present pass. There, lighting a small fire in the grate, she boiled a kettle and made herself an infusion of tea in an earthenware beaker and carried it up to the drawing room, where she curled up on a sofa, barefoot, clad only in a voluminous velvet bedspread that had fallen to the floor during the rage of passion of the previous night and which she had snatched up. With her hair awry, her small hands clutching the overlarge beaker, she looked for all the world like some outcast orphan who had been roughly used—which was substantially her condition.

She thought over what had happened. That her late husband had been engaged in the vile trade of human flesh was something she preferred to set aside for another time. What mattered was that Nathan had—with her sacrifice, and if Vanbrough kept his word—escaped the gallows. No other consideration—even that of tracking down and having her revenge upon the vile Snakey—mattered half as much as that. Even if she never saw Nathan again, if he had rejected her forever, she knew she could not live one day longer upon the earth if he were brought to the gallows. That much, with every hope, she had managed to avert; the cost to herself in physical degradation and in mangled pride was of no account compared with that.

She all but spilled her tea, as there came a brisk knock upon the front door. It was repeated.

The bailiffs . . . !

In which case, best to lie low and quietly, in the hope that they would go away. It was likely that they did not possess a set of keys, even after having ransacked the Limehouse office, as she had learned from

Vanbrough (which would account for the fact that they had not yet ransacked Sloane Street). . . .

These considerations were running through Emmie's mind, when the knock was again repeated. The caller was not taking no for an answer. The next step might be their breaking down the door, with Emmie suffering the indignity of being found shrinking like a cornered fawn awaiting the hunter's knife. Not the way for the granddaughter of an English marquess to be caught out!

Three paces to the door. She drew back the bolt and wrenched it open. Angrily.

"Who the devil are you and what do you . . . ? Oh!"

Nathan Grant stood there, face burned bronze by a tropic sun, blue eyes unwaveringly regarding her. His hand came up, took off the peaked cap that he wore, and revealed the streak of white that stretched from hairline to crown.

"Lady Devizes, I . . ."

"Nathan!" she whispered.

"Oh, Emmie . . ."

She seized his sleeve, forgetful of all else. "Come inside—quickly!" she breathed.

He obeyed. The door slammed behind them. Next instant, she was in his arms, the velvet bedspread slipping off one shoulder to bare the breast beneath. And he was kissing her, frantically brushing with his open lips her eager mouth, eyes, cheeks, shoulder, nipple.

"Emmie, oh, my Emmie!"

"Take me, Nathan—take me now! *Now!*"

It was as if they were alone together by the empty sea, with the spent wavelets curling around their feet and the sound of the combers drowning out their breathing.

Alone—but not alone . . .

"Well, damn me if it isn't gallant Cap'n Grant—playing second little pig to the trough! Ha!"

Nathan Grant's hands fell from Emmie as if she had turned red hot to the touch. Released of his support, she recoiled back a pace and nearly fell. Both their eyes were upon the specter halfway down the stairs.

Whatever had woken Vanbrough—the knocking on the door, Emmie's ecstatic cries—had not sufficiently troubled him to cover his nakedness. He was as he had been after his final assault upon Emmie: bleary-eyed and tousle-haired, half-drunk, nude as the day he was born, flaccid. He lolled against the banister and regarded the two horrified lovers with a sneering grin.

"Nathan—please, I . . ." Emmie turned to meet the cold, blue stare of contempt, and the explanation—excuse? justification?—died in her mind.

He turned, wrenched open the door and was gone, slamming it behind him.

Emmie collapsed where she stood: slowly, sinking like a rag doll whose stuffing is pouring out of a tear in the covering, lolling back against the wainscotting and burying her face in her hands, shoulders racked with bitter sobs.

Presently, Vanbrough came to her, naked still, and laid a hand on her head.

"Pity about that, milady," he said. "Never mind—you've the will and determination to get him back—particularly when you tell him that our little handy dandy together has put me in the mood to save him from swinging."

Her face jerked up and her eyes fixed on his. She wiped away a tear, and when she spoke her voice was keen, demanding.

"You *are* going to keep your end of the bargain?" she cried.

He grinned and patted her head. "This I'll promise you, lass: Grant won't hang. I'm not sure about Harry Vanbrough. You see, there was a fight with a naval cutter off the bay of the Congo River. Shots were fired both sides. I took the wound in my arm. Two Jack Tars were killed. The Navy doesn't like that. They're after someone's blood, and it may well be mine. But it won't be Grant's. Satisfied?"

She nodded.

"Then I'll be going," he said. "Considering that it's no longer your property, you'll not object to my filling my pockets with a few things of value?"

Emmie shrugged.

"Then I'll go and put my clothes on and be away," he said, and, pausing, added, "unless you're of a mind to carry on where we left off last night?"

"Get your things and get the hell out of my sight!" blazed Emmie.

"As you will, milady," he said, treating her to a mocking bow.

Emmie watched him walk, none too steadily, up the stairs. She never saw him again.

The bailiffs descended upon the Devizes' Sloane Street town house shortly before noon. They found the door unlocked. Emmie had left an hour before, together with her carpet bag, the few personal belongings she had rescued from the disaster, and a hideous memory of her lost lover's eyes.

It was Annabel's welfare, and the need to provide for her beloved daughter's future, that took Emmie to Threadneedle Street in the old city of London, heart of England's commercial and banking empire.

That night, she took lodgings at a decent hostelry off Fleet Street, close by Wine Office Court, giving the landlord to understand that she would be making an indefinite stay till she had settled her former husband's business affairs in the city. The landlord was sympathetic and demanded a week's money in advance for bed and breakfast. It was only when Emmie turned out the contents of her reticule in the privacy of her room that she discovered she had paid out somewhat more than half the ready money she possessed in the world.

That night, also, she made a list of the former busi-

ness associates, merchant bankers and others, from
whom she knew, via Sir Claude's correspondence,
that her late husband was certainly owed many debts
of gratitude. She resolved to approach them all—for
the sake of Annabel's future.

One name alone, one person, she eschewed to consider. And that was Jock Ballantree, whose oblique
proposal of marriage she had—as she saw it—thrown
back in his face. As much for his pride as for her own,
she knew that she could never—would never—go
crawling to him for help.

Emmie, during the week that followed, made an approach to each and every name on her list. The results
were catastrophic. Out of seven names in all, four
declined to see her, two claimed never to have had
any connection with her late husband, and the seventh—after keeping her waiting till all his staff had
gone home—finally summoned her to his office, where,
to her unspeakable disgust, she found him (and he a
sexagenarian and a churchwarden of impeccable rec-
titude) waiting for her with a bright smile and his
breeches about his ankles.

At the end of that disastrous week, Emmie wrote
to Agnes Reilly, sending kisses to darling Annabel,
and hoping that she (Reilly) was managing for money.
Emmie also stated that she had every hope of returning to Bristol in a few weeks' time, there to remain in
happy concord with darling Annabel and dear, faithful
Reilly forevermore.

After dispatching this letter, Emmie went to face
things out with her landlord, telling him that she was
out of funds, had no immediate prospects, but rosy
hopes for the future. And would he let her remain in
her present situation—on credit, so to speak?

The landlord had observed his beautiful lodger, who
gave the name of "Mrs. Devizes," and called herself
as a widow, and had formed certain opinions regarding
her, some of them most favorable. Yes, he informed
Mrs. Devizes, she could remain indefinitely, with not

only bed and breakfast but bed and full board, with
wages added of five and sixpence a week. All she had
to do was act as serving wench in the taproom. Appalled at first, Emmie was hard-headed and practical
enough to take only five minutes to make up her mind.
Yes, she would accept the employment, though, as
she had to warn Mr. Winkley, it was only on a strictly
temporary basis. Winkley merely nodded sympathet-
ically and bade her be down in the taproom that evening at six.

A natural sense of vulgarity, coupled with a ready
tongue and no qualms about defending herself from
questing hands and importuning lips, quickly endeared
Emmie to the clientele of the taproom, who were
mostly laborers, porters and seamen. So well did she
prosper (and so much did the patronage of the taproom
increase) that Winkley transferred her to the coffee
room by the end of that month. The coffee room, apart
from serving some coffee, was where the better class
of clientele—inside travelers on the great stagecoaches
and gentlemen from the city business houses—took
their glass of port or Madeira, brandywine or rum. In
the coffee room, Emmie prospered as well as she had
in the taproom, and the business of the coffee room
prospered likewise.

On her third evening there, she met an old acquaintance—and changed her whole life.

"It can't be, but it is! I do declare—it's the little
Emmie girl!"

Emmie, pausing in the act of replenishing a gentleman's brandy glass, turned in surprise to meet the eyes
of a well-dressed, if somewhat overdressed, woman
sitting in a corner nearby in company with two gentlemen and another woman of similar type to herself.
Emmie, who had learned more about life in postwar
London in a month than half the Londoners knew,
placed both women in the category of high-priced
whores, their escorts as solicitors or barristers, the
latter more likely, since they generally carried on the

more racketty existence. Furthermore, not to be out-
done in matters of recognition, Emmie placed the face,
figure and manner of address, and delivered up the
name pat.

"Mrs. Galloway!" she declared. "Uncle Eustace's
friend."

"The actress," supplied the other.

"*Poses plastiques*," said Emmie.

"That's right. Fancy you remembering, lovey."

Mrs. Galloway was clearly quite taken with Emmie,
which surprised the latter, since she had been instru-
mental in the abandonment of what must surely have
been the definitive theatrical performance in which
that dubious lady of Thespian persuasion had ever
taken part: the Black Mass in Flaxham Palace Chapel.
Indeed, when her companions made moves to depart,
the "actress" waved them off, saying that she wished
to talk more with her "dear young friend of long acquaintance," and that she would meet up with them
later.

"Cheapskates, like most barristers," was her summation of her former escorts when they had departed.
"And briefless, like all the young 'uns. As for her—
nothing but a cheap doxy and poxed in the bargain.
What do you earn here, Emmie girl?"

Emmie, who had lived all her life save the last
month without comparisons regarding money, replied
proudly, "Seven and sixpence a week, *and* full board.
I started at *five* and sixpence."

"Give me another brandy, lovey," said Mrs. Galloway, "and pour yourself one while you're about it.
My Gawd, what happened to bring you to this,
lovey?"

Emmie assented. It was Wednesday and a quiet
night. From his high desk at the end of the coffee
room, the landlord nodded approval as his most attractive and inviting serving wench sat down and
drank with a palpably successful member of the half-
world.

"You must quit here, Emmie," said Mrs. Galloway. "Now. Tonight. I will fix you up at Miggs's Diversions. *Poses plastiques* and added advantages like accommodating the gentlemen clients." She did not particularize the precise form of accommodation so extended, but contented herself by eyeing her young friend over the brim of her glass.

Emmie regarded Mrs. Galloway in return. The "actress" was wearing a diamond brooch at her bosom that would certainly have kept darling Annabel and Agnes Reilly for a year or more; likewise, the silks she wore were, if garish in design and color, of the most expensive sort. A far cry from seven and sixpence a week and full board.

"How much are you paid for the *poses plastiques?*" she asked.

Mrs. Galloway hedged a little. It appeared that payment was on a sliding scale depending on how far along the path of artistic truth the actress was willing to go. The speaker implied that she herself was prepared to go a very long way indeed, and became somewhat defensive when Emmie raised an eyebrow.

" 'Twas good enough for Emma Hamilton!" she declared. "And look how she rose in Society, marrying the British ambassador to Naples and all. 'Twasn't till she met up with Lord Nelson that *she* disgraced herself!"

"Tell me more about accommodating the gentlemen clients," said Emmie. "I must say that sounds to me very much like whoring."

Mrs. Galloway leaned forward and tapped her young companion on the wrist. "You and I are women of the world, my dear," she said with the air of someone about to share a confidence, "and we know that in the matter of pleasuring a man, anticipation is all, and a promise delayed is a delight for the morrow."

"I see what you mean," said Emmie. *If a whore, then a dishonest whore,* she thought.

"But there's no compulsion to pleasure the gentlemen," said Mrs. Galloway. "Not at Miggs's Diversions. You'll scarce have to lift a finger to be showered with expensive presents, Emmie. The clients who come to Miggs's, they're all rich, you see? They've done everything, been everywhere. What they're looking for is something *new*. A new, pretty face. A new, sympathetic ear to pour their troubles into. Men, they're babies, Emmie. And isn't it our place in the scheme of things to give them pleasure and comfort—to the benefit of both parties concerned?"

Emmie laughed at the shameless hedonism of her companion's philosophy.

In the end, she agreed to accompany Mrs. Galloway to Miggs's Diversions that night after the coffee room closed. In doing this, she told herself that, for Annabel's sake, she could afford to leave no avenue unexplored. In any event, by merely going to Miggs's she was in no way committing herself.

They took a carriage eastward, alighting close to a steep flight of steps leading down to the dark river, at the foot of which several wherries were waiting, with the wherrymen vying with each other to offer the cheapest rates.

"How much to go to Miggs's?" demanded Mrs. Galloway.

"Fourpence to you, sweetheart!"

"Threepence, ma'am!"

"We'll have the cheaper fellow with the civil tongue in his head. Get in, Emmie."

They stepped into the wherry, and a sweep of oars took them swiftly out into midriver, in the direction of a dark hulk whose skeletal rigging loomed nakedly against the night sky.

"That's Miggs's, Emmie," said Mrs. Galloway, pointing.

"A *ship?*"

"What better place, lovey? Like the prison hulks,

it's got the advantages of being private and inaccessible. Discreet, too. No prying neighbors to see and
report who comes and goes, and that pleases the
gentlemen clients. But, most of all, it's something—
new!"

A few more sweeps brought the wherry close alongside a gangway of wooden steps set in the steep side
of the vessel. A lantern shone above.

A voice called down from an open entry port: "Who
comes?"

"Mrs. Galloway and lady friend."

"Come up."

Emmie followed her companion up the sheer steps,
with the dark river swirling past below. Presently, a
hand came out of the lamplight and guided her to her
feet. She passed the entry port into a low-ceilinged
lobby, dimly lit by lantern. There were three men,
powerfully built, stripped to the waist and wearing
sailors' hats and bell-bottomed pantaloons. They
greeted Mrs. Galloway with affable familiarity, and
cast frankly admiring glances at Emmie.

"Is Mrs. Miggs free?" asked Mrs. Galloway. They
opined that she was.

"Come on, lovey," said Emmie's mentor. "Let's
see what impression you make upon the admiral."

The narrow corridor beyond the lobby was carpeted
with a yielding luxury of white sheepskins. White,
also, were the paneled walls, with the moldings picked
out in gold leaf, all discreetly lit by a few candles in
gilded sconces. Mrs. Galloway tapped on a door, in
answer to which she was bidden to enter by a gravelly
bass voice of exceedingly complex texture.

Mrs. Miggs—the "admiral"—was seated in a pink,
button-back armchair with a Prince Charles spaniel
puppy on her broad knee. She was the largest woman
Emmie had ever set eyes on. Not fat, particularly,
though her bare arms would not have shamed a Cum-
berland wrestler, but hugely built, with massive shoul-

ders, a bull-like neck, strong fingers. Of her countenance, it was difficult to make any judgment, likewise
her age, for the face was thickly plastered with white
lead paint and rice powder, the eyes heavily kohled,
the lips vermilion-rouged. Indeed the entire face had
been turned into an expressionless mask.

"Mrs. Galloway," she boomed. "Who is this pretty
creature you have with you?"

"I had hoped she'll find favor with you, Mrs.
Miggs," said Emmie's sponsor. "For this is little Emmie Dashwood, and she's desirous of becoming an
actress."

"Is she now?" Berry-black eyes swam over Emmie's figure. "Well, she ain't all that *little*—not in
some departments. And if she's to be an actress, she'll
be *Mrs*. Dashwood from now on, for that adds weight
and respectability."

"Will she suit, Mrs. Miggs?" asked Emmie's pre-
ceptor.

"Yes, she will suit," replied the large woman. "The
midnight presentation is about to begin. Mrs. Dashwood may mime the role of Lucrece, following your
'Birth of Venus.' Afterward she may mingle with the
gentlemen."

Emmie felt the time had come to point out that the
purpose of her visit to Miggs's Diversions was purely
exploratory.

"Mrs. Miggs," she began, "I must tell you that . . ."

"Twenty guineas!" boomed the "admiral."
"Twenty guineas each night you appear. Any other
emoluments you earn, any intramural arrangements
you may make, are your own concern. As to rules:
there *are* no rules at Miggs's Diversions. My actresses may behave as they please. If they do not behave as *I* please, they do not appear again. You may
go now, both of you."

Twenty guineas . . . !

Emmie was so bemused by the prospect, and by

doing the mental arithmetic involved in determining how many twenties went into two thousand (so as to know how many appearances she would have to make at Miggs's Diversions to provide for Annabel's upbringing and education), that she scarcely noticed by what means she presently found herself in a dressing room, where a dozen or so exceedingly pretty women and girls in divers states of dress and undress were chattering like excited magpies all about her. Mrs. Galloway, suddenly metamorphosed in a flowing shift so fine as to be almost completely transparent, was assisting her into a costume that resembled a nightgown and binding up her hair in the Greco-Roman manner, with a chignon high up and corkscrew curls falling about the ears. She was greatly relieved to discover that her own costume was of a material vastly more substantial—and opaque—than that of her mentor.

"There you are, lovey. My God, you look wonderful. All the best of luck—no, I mustn't say that, for 'tis thought ill luck in the profession to wish a fellow Thespian good luck. Best if I wish you to fall and break your leg. *Au revoir*—'tis my turn to perform."

"But—but!" cried Emmie. "What do I have to *do* as Lucrece?"

"There's nothing to it," the other assured her. " 'Tis the easiest part in the whole of the repertoire. Jack Pickersgill the stage manager will show you the ropes. Ah, there he is, beckoning me to get onstage. I must fly." And she was gone.

A young man in shirtsleeves had entered the dressing room. The unclad among the females present paid so little heed to his presence that he might as well not have been there. He approached Emmie, eyeing her critically, but without perceptible interest.

"Mrs. Dashwood?" he asked. At close quarters, his skin was as smooth as that of a girl.

"That's my—er—professional name," said Emmie. "If you're the stage manager, I should greatly appre-

ciate a little guidance regarding the role of Lucrece
which I have to play—as I understand it—just as soon
as Mrs. Galloway has finished. I must say, it seems
rather short notice to master the part.''

Pickersgill damped his forefinger and drew it carefully along his right eyebrow. ''You are familiar with
the character of Lucrece?'' he demanded. ''Subject of
the poem by William Shakespeare entitled *The Rape
of Lucrece*.''

''Of course,'' responded Emmie. ''What well-edu-
cated gel is not?''

He spread his elegant hands. ''Then you need to
know nothing else,'' he declared. ''I shall be reciting
the key lines of the poem backstage, through a speaking trumpet. All you must do is mime the lines as they
apply to you. The actor playing Tarquin has most of
the work to do. To be frank, Mrs.—er . . . ?''

''Mrs. Dashwood.''

''To be frank, Mrs. Dashwood, the female actresses
of Miggs's Diversions are not called upon to exercise
a tremendous amount of acting ability. They are simply required to look decorative. And you will manage
that, I'm *sure*. Would you care to come this way?''

Gathering up her skirts, she followed the stage manager out of the dressing room and along a barely furnished corridor that was markedly different from the
one leading to Mrs. Miggs's room. At the end of it,
they came upon a maze of curtains, scenery, ropes
and all the appurtenances of a theater's back stage.
From somewhere beyond the gloom came the tinkling
strains of a harpsichord, a strong wave of expensive
perfumes and occasional handclaps. Emmie presumed
that her friend and mentor was still struggling with the
birth pangs of Venus.

Presently, it was time. A fair riot of handclapping
and applause came out of the gloom for Mrs. Dashwood. It appeared that some exigency or other of the
plot had required Venus to remove all of her none-

too-concealing garment, for she was holding it to her bosom. She blew a kiss at Emmie and ran lightly past her to the dressing room.

Lamps were unshielded, and Emmie saw a bare stage with curtains drawn. Two large men were carrying a canopied bed, which they deposited in the center.

"Remember," came Pickersgill's voice in her ear. "Follow the lines carefully and interpret them in the character of Lucrece. Don't concern yourself with acting, but concentrate on being decorative. Let me have a look at you. . . ."

Emmie turned to face him. He frowned at her hair and fussed with it for a few moments, teasing out the corkscrew curls, patting the chignon. Next, the night-dress garment received his attention. It had a draw-string at the neck that was fastened in a bow. Before Emmie had time to protest, the stage manager tugged the bow free, and pulled the neckline down over her breasts, baring them.

"Decorative, Mrs. Dashwood," he said. "At all times concentrate on being *decorative*. That is how you earn your twenty guineas an appearance. Now, go over there and lie on the bed. The curtain is about to go up."

Pickersgill's honeyed voice, accompanied by a staccato passage from the hidden harpsichord player, stole through the darkness behind where she lay. Through the veil of her partly closed eyelids, simulating chaste sleep, Emmie could see the curve of her right breast, with the erect nipple exactly bisecting a three-tier blaze of candles acting as the footlights of the stage. Beyond that—only blackness. She relaxed. Unable to see, it scarcely mattered that one was being seen. Indeed, one could tell oneself that the audience was so unenthusiastic over the prospect of having to sit and watch a wench lying in bed with her bubs poking out of the top of her nightdress that they had all gone home. She giggled, remembered what she was supposed to be at, and changed it to a sigh, as if in restless sleep. Indeed, she embellished the mime by shifting her position—restlessly. And did it rather well, in her opinion.

"*The Roman lord marcheth to Lucrece's bed. . . .*"

Emmie scarcely felt that this declaration concerned her, as, clearly, the actor playing Tarquin was about to come upon the stage. Indeed, this was shortly confirmed by shuffling footfalls to her right. Emmie opened her eyes a mite wider, and regarded an extremely tall and well-made young man wearing a plumed helmet in the classical mode, together with some vestigial leather harness that left his arms and legs bare. He reminded her of one of the sailors who had greeted their arrival aboard the ship. As he came closer, she saw that it was, indeed, he.

"*So o'er this sleeping soul doth Tarquin stay,*
His rage of lust by gazing qualified. . . ."

The time was fast approaching, she felt, when she would be called upon to do something. If only someone would prompt her. Eyes closed, she waited.

His hand . . . marched to make his stand
On her bare breast, the heart of all her land. . . ."

She stiffened as a hand touched her right breast, drew a sharp breath as the fingers scurried across it like spiders, cried out with shock and pain when they tweaked the nipple, rather roughly.

"Sorry," whispered Tarquin. "But that was your cue to wake up and start protesting. Did I hurt you very much?"

"No, it's all right," she whispered in return.

"She, much amaz'd, breaks ope her locked-up
   eyes. . . .",

The requirement was quite simple. Emmie sprang
up into a sitting position and stared at the intruder in
what she hoped was mingled horror and disbelief. The
action caused her nightdress to slip all the way down
to her waist. In the interests of being decorative, she
let it remain there.

" 'Yield to my love; if not, enforced hate,
Instead of love's coy touch, shall rudely tear thee!' "

The swing of the argument clearly going in Tarquin's direction, Emmie quickly decided to express
virtuous resignation, since the bed, which was not of
very sound construction, would obviously not stand
up to a lot of rumbustiousness. And so, following the
line—

'The wolf hath seiz'd his prey, the poor lamb
   cries. . . ."

—she fell back and gave a piteous moan, and was
mounted by the enthusiastic Tarquin, who, with a dexterity beyond all belief, divested his victim of her
nightdress with one clean pull. Emmie heard—or
could have sworn she heard—a concerted gasp, or it
may have been a sigh, from the dark abyss beyond the
spotlights.

Tarquin had removed all, or most, of his leather
harness, together with his plumed helmet. She felt the
whole length of his near-nude body across hers, his
face seeking hers, his lips making to slake their passion
upon hers.

'O, that prone lust should stain so pure a bed!"

Said Tarquin in her ear: "I'm wildly jealous of your lovely skin, dearie. What do you do for it in this weather? Mine goes all rough and goose-pimply as soon as I step outdoors!"

"Olive oil," whispered Emmie in reply. "I had an old nurse who swore by olive oil for the skin. She had been my mother's nannie, too, and she told me that, thanks to olive oil, my mother's skin had been the wonder of the entire county. I give it to you for what it's worth."

"Very grateful, I'm sure," responded Tarquin. "Olive oil—I'll remember that. I must say, one meets a very nice class of person working at Miggs's Diversions. My name's Mr. Pritchard. Mr. Clarence Pritchard."

"How do you do, Mr. Pritchard."

"Pure Chastity is rifled of her store. . . ."

Dressed again in her own clothes, Emmie was escorted by Mrs. Galloway to "mingle with the gentlemen," and saw for the first time beyond the glare of the footlights.

The main apartment of Miggs's Diversions was a spacious supper room-cum-theater, set about with small tables *à deux* or *à quatre* in discreet nooks around the white-paneled walls, with lighting that was subdued almost to extinction. Their arrival was anticipated, obviously by prior arrangement, for two extremely personable gentlemen of middle age rose at their approach and requested the pleasure of their company, and then invited them to take wine, which proved to be champagne, and to partake of an excellent supper.

Emmie's companion—that is to say the gentleman who engaged her in conversation, leaving his friend to do likewise with Mrs. Galloway—proved to be from the north country, and spoke carelessly of broad acres and high connections. Upon a discreet prompting, yes he had heard of the Beechboroughs, and thought them to be "Johnny-come-latelys" and "jumped up." He then cut through the polite small talk and came to the subject that was obviously uppermost in his mind.

"I say, ma'am, I have to congratulate you upon your performance as Lucrece. Most—ah—how to put it . . . ?"

"Decorative?" suggested Emmie, masking a smile behind her napkin.

"Er—quite so, ma'am. But tell me—that fellow, that great husky fellow playing Tarquin. One certainly feared for your safety. Tell me, when you and he were—ah—performing on the stage up there, did you, did he, did the both of you, in reality . . . ?"

"No, sir, we did not," replied Emmie.

"Ah!" exclaimed her companion, and again: "Ah!" He then relapsed into a thoughtful silence, during which he regarded Emmie with what could have been either disbelief or disappointment.

Emmie took the opportunity of the break in conversation to look about her. There were about twenty gentleman clients present, each with an "actress" as hostess. All were eating and drinking the finest food and wines imaginable, and obviously at the sort of exalted prices as would permit Mrs. Miggs to pay an actress twenty guineas for performing an absurd and mildly licentious charade. And in all that company, no one, herself and her companions included, was behaving with anything but the most impeccable propriety—an observation that was amply borne out when her companion, having digested the truth of her stage performance, asked her if she thought that the Duke of Wellington would make a capital Prime Minister. . . .

At five A.M. exactly, Mrs. Miggs appeared in the supper room and, in the manner of a girls' boarding school headmistress, charged the gentlemen to make their departure, which they did without demur. Emmie's companion kissed her hand and expressed the hope that she would sup with him again when next he

visited Miggs's Diversions. When she recovered her
hand, she found five guineas pressed against the palm.

A wherry took Emmie and Mrs. Galloway back to
the steps in the early morning sunlight filtering down
through the dusty murk of the waking city. It was low
tide, with the stink of putrescent shellfish and rotting
seaweed. Wallowing in the mudbank below the high
walls of the warehouses that rose sheer out of the
river were gangs of people, women and children
mostly, wading knee-deep in the reeking black ooze
and plunging their skinny hands and arms into it,
searching for articles of flotsam and jetsam washed up
and deposited there by the tide of the great river. Emmie found the sight of them unaccountably disturbing,
particularly the demeanor of the small children. No
sign, on those pale, pinched faces, of the heady delight
that all children feel at being allowed to frolic in muck.
Theirs was the air of creatures aged beyond their years
by grinding poverty, where a discarded bottle, a lost
halfpenny, a few old bones, might provide a crust to
see them through to another day of toil.

Through the children of the riverbank—the
"mudlarks"—Emmie saw her own beloved child, and
resolved that, no matter at what cost, Annabel would
not be brought to any such condition.

That morning, greatly to Mr. Winkley's dismay, she
discharged herself from his employ and moved her few
belongings over to Mrs. Galloway's apartment in St.
George's Square, Pimlico.

The months that passed provided a time of spiritual
replenishment and readjustment for Emmie. She nightly
attended at Miggs's Diversions and was popular with
both clientele and staff. Her fellow Thespian and in-
terpreter of the role of Tarquin, Mr. Clarence Pritchard, came to look upon her as something between
mother, older sister and schoolma'am. On Fridays,
she would go over to his tidy attic room in Whitechap-
el and wash and trim his hair, afterward sitting down

to a supper of tripe and onions, boiled beef and carrots, or boiled bacon and pease pudding—cooked by the hand of the host. Clarence was totally illiterate, and his one ambition had always been to get what he called "a clerking job." Accordingly, over supper, Emmie taught him the rudiments of reading, writing and arithmetic—at which he proved to be an apt and eager pupil. Then, around midnight, they would walk together through the dark and narrow streets of the east end, to the steps where the wherries waited and the black hulk of the pensioned-off third-rater swung at her mooring. Soon after, in the pampered and perfumed comfort of Mrs. Miggs's establishment, the two of them would reenact the tragedy of fair Lucrece and foul Tarquin, of Narcissus and Echo. . . .

Three things remained at the center of Emmie's existence, three anchor points: the first was her love for Annabel (she wrote daily to Agnes Reilly and received an answer daily by return with news of the child's progress, listing the new words that she had learned to lisp); second, she had great regard for her late husband's last stated wish, which had been to repay his debts, on account of which, for every guinea that she earned by displaying her charms at Miggs's Diversions, she dispatched one half-guinea to one or another on the long list of Sir Claude's creditors; last, she remained true to her resolve that the man known as Snakey would not go unpunished.

Of Nathan Grant, the love of her life, she tried not to think too often.

Emmie's friendship with Mrs. Galloway was of the strange, rare sort that never progresses beyond such superficial endearments as the touch of hands and the exchange of kind words and light kisses. Emmie never addressed the other by any title other than "Mrs. Galloway," though she had been the embarrassed confidante to the secret that the latter's given name was Ermyntrude. Even though they shared the same apartment, they seldom met outside working hours. Mrs. Galloway entertained gentlemen friends occasionally, but never introduced them to Emmie.

One blustery night in late October, when the crossing by wherry to the mooring was a thing of hazard and considerable unpleasantness, Emmie and Mrs. Galloway arrived aboard to find the establishment in turmoil. They were late, and Mrs. Miggs was raving. There would be no presentations that night, for certain ladies had been hired to attend a private fancy dress party at a gentlemen's club in Mayfair at a fee of fifty guineas a head. A fleet of carriages would presently be waiting by the steps to transport them to the party. And would the lady actresses please change into fancy dress and be ready to depart almost immediately? So ran the decree from the "admiral," relayed through her various minions and underlings and delivered in the dressing room by the stage manager.

Fancy dress presented no problems, for there was a host of costumes to choose from among the extensive repertory of the establishment. Mrs. Galloway limned the tips of her breasts with vermilion and put on the gossamer-thin "Birth of Venus" attire. Emmie considered carefully and finally chose to be Sheherazade for the night, in baggy harem drawers and a short, embroidered sleeveless jacket that rendered her belly and navel bare, and an elaborate turban and veil, held in place by a hatpin.

The ladies, twenty-five of them, and all attired in costumes ranging from the exotic to the outrageous, put on their cloaks against the wild, autumnal night and trooped to board the wherries that had been summoned to take them ashore. In the lobby by the entry port, Emmie was tapped on the shoulder by Jack Pickersgill, who, largely because of her kindness and understanding toward Clarence Pritchard, had only recently unbent toward her.

"In passing, I should mention, Mrs. Dashwood,"

he said, "that a gentleman was asking after you earlier this evening."

"Indeed?" replied Emmie, and posed the names of two current admirers among the regular clientele.

No, it was neither of those, she was told. The fellow had red hair and was accompanied by a rough-looking fellow whose appearance suggested that he might have been a prizefighter. They did not stay.

On the way over to the steps, Emmie speculated, with some concern, on the fact that Jock Ballantree had run her to earth.

Six carriages had been provided to convey the ladies from the riverside steps to the heart of fashionable Mayfair, to Berkeley Square and a fine mansion set back from the pavement behind high railings, with a carriage drive going both in and out, and an army of servitors bearing flambeaux. The servitors bowed the ladies from their carriages and guided them, one lackey to each lady, up the imposing steps of the residence and in through the open portals, where a resplendently attired butler was waiting to greet them on behalf of the gentlemen members. If the ladies would care to follow him into the yellow drawing room, intoned this vision of magnificence in royal blue and gold, the gentlemen members would attend them presently.

Mrs. Galloway was at Emmie's side as she entered the room beyond the hall on the heels of the butler.

Said Mrs. Galloway: "This place smells of money, lovey. Money and power. Just look at that!"

Emmie, no stranger to magnificence, both tasteful and ramshackle, could scarcely withhold an exclamation of awe at the sight of the chamber to which the butler had conducted them. Though illuminated only by pinpoints of flame from great chandeliers high above, the entire surroundings—walls, ceiling, floors— glowed with an inner warmth. The color was yellow:

a subtle, glowing yellow like the iris of a goshawk's eye, or a cornfield at sunset when it is brushed by passing zephyrs. And all subdued: the Oriental rugs beneath their feet, soft as outworn sandals; a water fountain rising from the center of the floor and descending in myriad particles of the same fugitive yellow tint; the upholstery of the opulent sofas and deep armchairs scattered about the chamber, yellow patterned upon yellow.

If Emmie was impressed, some of her companions were enraptured. Pretty little street waifs, who had been taken up by Mrs. Miggs and schooled to the ways of entertaining rich gentlemen of the upper classes, rhapsodized to find themselves amid such opulence—they whose ideal of luxury had hitherto been the plushy vulgarity of Miggs's Diversions.

"And yet," whispered Mrs. Galloway, seizing Emmie's hand, "I've a strange sense of something wrong here, and you wouldn't have to be the seventh child of a seventh child to feel it, either. Do you feel it, Emmie—and what do you feel?"

"We—we're being *watched!*" whispered Emmie.

"You're right, my God!" murmured the other, looking about her. "I can feel eyes creeping all over me, like worms."

It was at this moment that doors at the far end of the chamber were opened by a pair of liveried footmen, to admit a file of dark-appareled figures. These, by their bearing, were the members of the club. They wore modish evening coats and pantaloons, with white shirtfronts and stocks, and as a sole concession to the event being a fancy dress party, animal masks.

There was a savage-seeming dog, an exceedingly wise owl, a hare, parakeet, rodents of all kinds. The masks were cunningly fashioned of real fur and feather and designed so as to leave the lower parts of the wearers' faces uncovered while at the same time affording a very high degree of anonymity, which is the supreme object of the masquerader. They numbered twenty-five—the same as the invited party from Miggs's Diversions.

"Ladies, your servants!" The speaker was a sleekly muzzled fox, whose own dark eyes flashed from out of the mask's hideously empty sockets in a singularly disturbing manner. "Have you not yet been offered wine? Shame on the club servants. Bring wine!" He waved a terrified footman toward Emmie. "Wine for the lady there!"

Emmie took a glass of champagne. Fox Head came up behind her and slid his arm through hers. "Come and sit over here with me, my dear," he purred. "Let us, in a few brief minutes, simulate an acquaintance of several years' standing, along with entirely fictitious—but delicious—memories of uncounted nights when we together relived ancient sorceries forgotten since Cleopatra was queen and Mark Antony her lover and slave."

"That will be nice," murmured Emmie, who was not averse to Fox Head, a man of middle years (as well as one could tell from the part of his face showing—he had all his teeth), with the easy arrogance of breeding and wealth. Emmie knew a hundred such men, and was related to at least a score.

"I pledge your health, ma'am." He raised his champagne glass and, placing it against his eye, stared at her through clear wine and crystal.

"I thank you, sir—and yours also," murmured Emmie.

"I have observed you at Miggs's," said her companion. He waved his hand fussily, encompassing her baggy harem drawers and the sleeveless jacket. "And I confess that I have not before seen you so overdressed." So saying, he reached forward and very slowly and deliberately unfastened the single button that held the edges of the jacket together against her straining bosom.

Emmie smiled, telling herself that fifty guineas, by her careful arithmetic, would provide darling Annabel 'and faithful Reilly with another two months of comfortable living *and* pay off a portion of the mountainous debt still standing to her late husband's account. Later, of course, she would need to inform Fox Head that she was not available for cash. Conversely, he might so enflame her damned Cradock blood that she might, after a few more glasses of the excellent champagne they were drinking, give him everything for nothing. One could never tell, but on his performance so far she considered it unlikely.

Emmie made no attempt to rebutton the jacket, and her first intake of breath had achieved his object.

"It seems to me—er—Mark Antony," she said, looking down at her front with a wry smile, "that you have, in your own phrase, already simulated an acquaintance of at least a week."

He laughed, delighted at her sang-froid. "The members of our distinguished club always aim to please, ma'am," he said.

"And what is the name of your club, sir?" she inquired.

"The Bizarre Club, ma'am," was his shocking reply.

Fox Head was not Snakey—that much was for sure. Simon de Mazarin was as blond as a buttercup. This man's hair, extending down below his mask, was sandy-colored and shot with gray.

Trapped . . . !

It was a trap, Emmie knew it for sure. It was all of a piece with the sensation of having been watched before the menfolk had come in. Snakey, or some of his fellow members, must have seen her performing on the stage at Miggs's, and the whole contrivance of the party was to bring her along here. But for what? She shuddered.

Escape . . . ?

Out of the question; every door in the room was

shut, each with a brawny footman standing guard, arms folded.

Emmie saw, with unease, that the tone of the proceedings had markedly changed in the few moments that she had been conversing with Fox Head. A certain lewd shamelessness informed the actions and attitudes of her companions that was quite out of accord with the way in which they were permitted to behave with the clients under the commanding eye of Mrs. Miggs. Several of the younger girls were sitting on their partners' knees and permitting considerable liberties to be taken with lips and hands. Mrs. Galloway—that exemplar of prudence—had been constrained to give an *ad hoc* rendition of "The Birth of Venus," not upon a darkened stage at some considerable remove from her audience, but standing on a table top in full view of all who pressed about her, raising their glasses and urging her on to more extremes of voluptuousness, to which she responded with great willingness, shedding her gauzy raiment and simulating the rising of the goddess from out of the bosom of the sea, whole, vibrant, born in the full glory of womanly nakedness. It was a performance that, though diminished through lack of the harpsichord accompaniment and missing the verse-speaking that informed the plot, had an earthy immediacy which was quite absent in the original. Mrs. Galloway, having been lifted down from the table by two willing swains afterward, did not trouble to replace her garment, but merely twisted it about her slender waist like a sash. She winked at Emmie and wiped a streak of sweat from her glowing cheek. Wild-eyed, slack-lipped and abandoned, she seemed to Emmie to have become possessed.

Possessed . . . !

The champagne! Emmie's first glass remained almost full, she having taken only a slight sip to pledge the health of Fox Head. Raising it to her lips, she took

a questing sniff and then a tiny sip. There was no
doubt about it, she had smelled and tasted that elusive
flavor before, that touch of the Orient, like the distant,
handy scent of joss sticks and frangipani. Once more,
she was translated to that curtained theater box, with
the insidious drug poisoning her mind and blunting her
restraints, so that she was stripping herself nude before the gaze of the man who danced before her, and
was joining him in the orgy of abandonment, hand to
hand, breast to breast, thigh to thigh. . . .

"Eeow!"

Mrs. Galloway emitted a most unladylike squawk,
as, when passing by Emmie with a brimming glass of
champagne in her hand, the vessel was struck to the
floor in splintered shards.

"What did you do that for, Emmie?" she demanded. At close quarters, her eyes were glazed with
strange lights, as if she were looking out upon a distant
landscape of her own devising.

Emmie whispered, "Listen to me! Whatever you
do, don't . . ."

"The divine Venus has broken her glass!" It was
he with the dog's head, who had apportioned Mrs.
Galloway to himself. Insinuating an arm around her
bare shoulders, he pressed his own glass to her simpering lips. "Drink deeply of the wine of passion, O
goddess of love."

Mrs. Galloway obeyed Dog Head, her glazed eyes
staring up at him in lustful adoration. Emmie turned
away, defeated.

Too late . . . !

Already the other women and girls had drunk deeply
of the tainted wine; the signs were all about her. She,
alone, was forewarned and could avoid the trap. But
she must be careful. Raising the glass to her lips, she
threw back her head, and, lips still closed, allowed the
liquid to spill over her chin and over her shoulders and
breasts. She lowered the glass, to meet the glittering

gaze of Fox Head. He was carrying a large champagne bottle.

"How deliciously abandoned, Scheherazade! Not content with drinking the wine of passion, you are offering it as a libation to your ravishing body! More libation for the bewitching Scheherazade! Salute a thousand and one nights of unbridled fulfillment!"

Shouting his lustful tribute, Fox Head upturned the bottle and proceeded to pour its contents over Emmie's front, so that the chilled wine cascaded down the deep valley between her breasts and over their proud orbs; following which, and still with his hand raised to continue pouring, he stooped, open-mouthed, to take the foaming liquid as it flowed in twin cataracts from the ends of her jutting nipples. When the last of the champagne had gone, after he had licked dry every inch of her satin skin, he pressed his mouth to hers, lips and tongue reeking of the insidious drug, so that she, not daring to resist his importuning tongue, was unwillingly obliged to ingest a considerable quantity of the poisoned wine.

This inflammatory exhibition was watched, and loudly applauded, by the rest. It served, indeed, as a key to release yet another and more abandoned round of license.

That the proceedings of the Bizarre Club might be totally unbridled, the footmen were dismissed, the doors were locked and bolted (as Emmie observed with a sinking heart), and, with wild hoots of savage delight, the men in the animal masks declared a banishment of all restraint.

Games were devised, together with improvisations of the most shameless kind. There was a "wheelbarrow race," in which a trio of girls—the youngest, the most vulnerable to the drugged wine—raced upon their hands, with male partners supporting their legs by the ankles, and the better to perform the feat they allowed themselves to be stripped. There were guessing games,

games of pass the parcel, where the "parcel" began
as a fully clothed woman who was passed around a
seated circle of masked roisterers, each man attempting, in the brief moments she was in his clutches and
before she was dragged away by his neighbor, to rip
off as many rags of her clothing as possible, till she
ended—hysterical, shrieking, totally compliant and
nude—in the lap of the winner.

From all the abandonment, Emmie distanced herself
as much as possible, while still contriving to be part
of the gathering. She received casual kisses and embraces with seeming ardor, remembering always to
keep a brimming glass of champagne in her hand.

Forfeits were in the air. . . .

"Any wench who won't join in this game must pay
a forfeit!" This suggestion came from Owl Head.

"You shall devise the forfeits, Owlie, and collect
'em!"

"Right you are, Ratty!"

For being too bemused to play in a salacious guessing game, one young girl was compelled to lift her
skirts and be brutally slapped on her bare behind by
every man present. The tempo was increasing, the
needs ever more demanding, the forfeits crueler.

"Forfeits for any wench who hasn't taken part in
a game so far!"

And surely, thought Emmie, *that shaft must have
been aimed at me. . . .*

The end came soon after. There was a girl, a soft-
scented little thing held in much affection by everyone
at Miggs's Diversions. Though far advanced along the
licentious path down which the drug had enticed her,
her native modesty asserted itself and prevented her
from performing an act of shameful indelicacy upon
the person of he who had ordered it: the Master of
Forfeits, Owl Head. Her fastidiousness did not save
her, any more than did her extreme youth and gentle
loveliness. Two monsters took her by the arms and
another by the hair, and she was forced to perform

the abomination under duress, with the masked members baying. In her frantic threshings, she contrived to bite her principal tormentor, whereupon the shout went up: "Duck the bitch! Cool her off in the fountain!" And she was dragged by her hair to the fountain bowl in the middle of the chamber, carried into the water by four masked torturers, ducked, face-downward, and held there.

"One! Two! Three! Four! . . ."

The chant continued. The girl's struggles, frantic to begin with when her head was immersed, grew more feeble.

"Ten! Eleven! Twelve! . . ."

Somebody stop them! thought Emmie. *They're going to kill that sweet marmoset. But who will stop them . . . ?*

"Sixteen! Seventeen! . . ."

"Best to bring her up now, Owlie!"

"Damn you, she'll come up when I say, Piggy!"

"Twenty! Twenty-one! . . ."

"That's enough—up with the bitch!"

The girl was lifted out of the water, head lolling on her slender neck, thin white arms trailing, and put on the floor by the side of the fountain bowl, where she lay, eyes closed, with no sign of breathing.

"By God, I think the wench is drowned, Owlie!"

"By God, sir, I think she is. Damn her for a confounded spoilsport!"

Oh, don't let it be so, prayed Emmie. *Please . . .*

And then the girl emitted a feeble, plaintive cry, like a babe roused in sleep. Her unformed breasts rose and fell. Her eyelids flickered open, and terror possessed her to see the hideous masked heads looking down.

"The whore was fooling all the time!"

"Give the cunning strumpet another dose of the same medicine!"

The unbelievable was happening, the unrepeatable about to be repeated. Members of the Bizarre Club howled their approval, and the bemused creatures from Miggs's Diversions looked on with lackluster eyes, as the frightened girl—no longer struggling, but piteously pleading with her tormentors, offering herself in any way each and every one of them chose to take her, and all in vain—was again being dragged into the water. Once more, her head was thrust under and her voice silenced.

"Leave her be! Let her go, murderers!"

Emmie was among them, leaping into the fountain bowl and laying about her with small, clenched fists. The man, utterly taken aback by the unexpectedness of the attack, let go of their victim and turned to face the beautiful, furious creature who stood, bared breasts heaving with passion, arms akimbo, splendid eyes flashing hatred and contempt.

"Aye, murderers all!" she blazed. "I have met you before, some of you, maybe all of you. Some must have been present on the night when poor little Perry Manners was gelded like a farmyard ox, the night when I would have been ravished and maybe murdered. Some of you, perhaps all of you, must have laughed to see me lying in that theater box at Drury Lane, enticed—like these women here, drugged and debauched—as you have drugged and debauched this child, and half drowned her when she had the effrontery to protest against the indignities you heaped upon her body, her soul, her womanhood, ravished by your ringleader, your precious Snakey—as you planned to ravish all the women here tonight!

"Where is he?" she screamed into the masked faces circling her. "Bring me to him, and let's have an end to this mummery! Take me to your damned Snakey! I want to demand of him, to his accursed face, why he should have found it necessary to kill my poor, my sick, my old and lovely husband, the kindest man who ever lived!"

A long silence followed, in which a great deal of Emmie's wild assurance evaporated, leaving her with the feeling that she had allowed her hot Cradock blood—augmented, no doubt, by the small quantity of drugged champagne she had drunk—to guide her passions where her reason would not have taken her.

And then—a voice: "Lady Devizes has spoken—and her ladyship's demand will be obeyed. Seize the whore!" The speaker was Fox Head, who had first selected her for his companion of the evening, who had drunk the wine that poured from her incomparable breasts.

They took her, one to each arm, a dog's head to one side and a lizard's to the other, and marched her roughly out of the door, which was opened by Fox Head. As it closed behind her, she heard the thin, plaintive wail of Mrs. Galloway calling her name.

Beyond, there was a wide staircase leading to an upper floor, where a gallery ran around the entire vault of the hallway. Reaching the top of the stairs, Fox Head knocked upon an oaken door, entered and closed it behind him. Emmie stood, heart pounding, with the masked brutes who pinioned her.

Footsteps. The door reopened and Fox Head stood before her again. "Snakey will see you now," he whispered. "Such a pity that you have chosen—this way. I bid you goodbye, my lady."

He seized her to him, one arm held tightly around her waist, the other hand molding her breast, and mouthed her hungrily. The sickly scent of the drug was still upon his breath. "Such a waste of an exquisite experience," he murmured between her lips.

Next instant, she was thrust roughly through the door, which slammed behind her with a hollow finality.

It was dark within the chamber, dark as hell's gate. Emmie heard a scratching sound, as of a rat's claws scrabbling to get out of a cage trap. A tiny spurt of flame grew from out of a struck spark; the flame became a shielded candle. By its light, she saw the lower part of a dark-clad figure seated in a chair behind a table.

"Well, we meet again," came a familiar, drawling voice. "The little madonna of the railings. You really have quite grown, Emmie. But you were an incomparable virgin of nineteen. I wish I had had you then."

"I know you!" cried Emmie. "I know you well!"

"Do you, now—do you? Are you sure?"

She screamed. The candle was suddenly lifted up, so that the unshielded part shone upon the head of a seated figure. And the head was the head of a snake— a hooded cobra, whose scaled skin glittered greenly in the shifting light.

"Horrible—*horrible!*" she breathed.

"We all take the name and mask of an appropriate animal," said the apparition. "The chairman of the Bizarre Club, who is elected annually, assumes the mantle of *this* wise and greatly maligned reptile for his period of office. Whereas I—as founder and lifetime president—will retain the sobriquet 'Snakey' to the grave and beyond."

Whereupon, he raised his hands and took off the mask, revealing the face of Lord George Delavere, member of Parliament for Bath, bachelor and sardonic wit, beloved of smart Society hostesses throughout the kingdom, and—incidentally—rapist, torturer and murderer extraordinary.

He was speaking; she was listening, after the manner of a rabbit watching a snake: struck dumb with horror and fascination, unable to move, powerless, even, to think.

"That fool of a nephew of mine," he said, "the absurd Simon de Mazarin—it is he you have to blame for the plight you are now in. I killed him after he had made his confession. I will explain.

"It was at one of our meetings, after I had first met you as Lady Devizes and divined you to be the pretty creature we so very nearly enjoyed that night near Leicester Square. I regaled the company with a highly colored account of your physical excellencies, so that fool Simon—who was this year's chairman, God help the club!—contrived the adventure of possessing you in a theater box after he saw you alone there.

"Imagine my position! He gave you his name! A casual inquiry among Society, a word to your relations the Beechboroughs, would have elicited that he was my nephew. And to think that I walked for weeks on end in daily hazard of being publicly associated with the doings of that bungling fool! I, who by exercising my wits, have enjoyed the life of complete license for thirty years on the one hand, and that of a respectable public servant on the other.

"For, would you believe, he never told me about you till a fortnight later? Even when I drove you home from the Beechboroughs' party, I was not aware that you had taken fright at seeing him. And when I discovered—well!—you had to be found. And found you were, in very short order, at Miggs's Diversions. Prancing around in your nightshift—ha!"

The act of watching him—after all, without the hideous mask, he was a perfectly ordinary-looking man, past his prime and lame in the bargain—gradually broke the spell of silence that shock had imposed upon her.

"Why did you murder my husband?" she demanded. "What harm had that good man ever done you that you had him squashed like a beetle?"

He was not listening. His face, singularly unmarked by evil, a scholarly yet bucolic face, like that of a hunting parson from the shires, was set in a dreamy expression, and the eyes were not on her, but fixed upon scenes and events long gone.

"What days they were," he mused, half to himself. "The early days of the Bizarre Club! And what nights! I founded it in emulation of the Mohocks, you know—those fine, roistering bucks of the upper class who were sickened by the mealy-mouthed priggishness and hypocrisy of the damned parsons and judges, the Mohocks who held that a gentleman was entitled to take a wench by force if he felt so inclined, and slit the nose of common fellow if it offended him. What days—what nights we had!''

"You're mad!' cried Emmie. "*Mad!*"

The wild denunciation penetrated the carapace of his private world, but not so the meaning of her words.

He stared at her dully for a few moments, and then he said, "Your husband was a fool, also. Why did I kill him? (And, by the way, the task was carried out by one of your own servants, for every man has his price—particularly when he has not been paid for weeks. Indeed, such a circumstance hardens a man's heart most conveniently against his master.) I killed him for this reason: when Devizes lost almost every-thing following the panic of Napoleon's escape from Elba, he came to me for advice. I gave him that ad-vice, told him to go into the slave trade, and intro-duced him to secret connections in Guinea and in the East Indies. I took a great risk, to trust an honest man, but I demanded a half-share of the profits, so the risk was justifiable.

"For a while, all went well. Then—disaster! That hot-head Vanbrough, when challenged by a navy ship opened fire. (Did you know, by the way, that Van-brough was caught trying to flee the country with a pocketful of expensive bric-a-brac? He was tried in Dover for piracy on the high seas. They hanged him last week.)

"When warrants were issued, Devizes became a danger to me. Honest men, when forced by circum-stances into courses of action that lie contrary to their natural inclinations, are always a danger, for, if dis-covered, they will tend to forswear, to confess, to throw themselves and their associates at the mercy of the law. So I had him—as you say—squashed like a beetle.''

This bald account of her husband's murder having been delivered—and quite unemotionally—he turned his gaze upon the woman before him, in the splendor of her half-nudity, proud, disdainful, contemptuous, suffused with loathing for him.

"With commendable selflessness," he said, "you have inquired only of your late husband's fate. You have not asked about your own."

"What is—my fate?"

"With what you know about me, about the aims and objects of the Bizarre Club, about the circumstances of your husband's death"—he spread his hands— "need you ask?"

"And what about the others—the women and girls who were also lured here?"

"I do not know about them. They have—regrettably—learned too much. I shall have to give the matter some thought. Perhaps I will offer to buy their silence, for such canaille will sell their souls with the same eagerness that they sell their bodies. But you, my dear Emmie . . ." He rose unsteadily to his feet on the two sticks propped by his chair, then carefully placed the sticks on the table and stood upright, unaided.

"You'll not attempt to buy *me*?"

"I know it would be useless."

"So I, too, must be squashed like a beetle?"

"How wrong you are, my dear, how wrong." With some assistance from holding the table, he took a few paces around it and faced her. "You see, I am not half so decrepit as I would have the world believe. Nor is my infirmity caused by a fall, but by a blast of buckshot fired at close range by a Bow Street runner's blunderbuss. You will find me a good performer, still, at the ancient game of the handy dandy." He took a pace toward her.

Emmie drew breath sharply. "No!" she breathed.

"It has been a long time," he said. "That little virgin hung there upon the railings. I never did forget you. The sight of you. One grows older, and it's the thought of the women one never had, the chances that one lost, which haunt the mind. Come to me, child!''

Emmie took a step back, and met the unresisting wall. There was no further escape.

"Get away from me!" she whispered.

"I will pleasure you greatly," he said, and his eyes were slack and dead, "albeit I am far gone in the pox. But that is an elegance, merely, and scarcely matters to me, and—considering your position—not at all to you. Come! Come to me!"

"Don't touch me!" she cried. "You are evil! Foul! A sack of disgust! You should never have lived!"

His hand advanced. It trembled as it groped for the peaks of her splendid breasts.

"I would wish to die embracing you," he said. "For you are exquisite, Emmie! You are supreme! You are—*perfection of woman!*" His voice rose to a shout.

His hands were upon her, molding her. His lips were closing upon her, mouthing her. She felt the foul miasma of his diseased breath fanning her face, felt his spittle bedewing her cheek. He was strong, stronger than she would have believed. The arm that locked about her waist was not to be moved by any power of hers. With his other hand, he was ripping away the rest of her clothing, till all that remained was the turban and slight veiling secured by the pin.

The pin . . . !

"Feel free to resist me with all your might," he hissed in her face. "Scratch! Bite! Pummel! Kick! Punch! Scream! Writhe! For in the moment that we shall presently know together—the supreme emission—I would have no dearer wish than to perish on the instant, to be transported in the ecstasy of . . .

"Aaaaah!"

His hands dropped away from her, his pouched, red-rimmed eyes fell to his breast, where, from just below the breastbone, the glittering head of a cheap paste-and-pinchbeck hatpin protruded from the shirt-front already stained with a sudden seeping of bright carmine. He plucked at it. Screamed when his fingers touched.

Emmie, nude, pressed herself back against the wall and waited for the last grains of the sands of her life to run out. She had made her final gamble. Nothing else remained but to die at his hands.

Lord George Delavere had style if nothing else. The life already ebbing from him, he met her eyes again. Lips twisted in the mockery of a smile, he bowed, with something of a flourish, as at Court. When he fell, he fell against the door. Next, he wrenched it open and staggered out onto the gallery beyond.

There was a tremendous shouting and coming-and-going down in the hall below. A woman screamed. A whistle blew. In a great gathering of sound, Delavere took three paces forward and came up against the wooden balustrade of the gallery. His appearance—and his last declaration—commanded instant silence.

"To my aid, the Bizarre Club!" he cried. *"Or I'll stone all your damsons!"*

That delivered, he folded over slowly and with great dignity to fall from the gallery, and to end himself upon the elegant Italian tiles thirty feet below.

A woman was sobbing drunkenly. It sounded like Mrs. Galloway. Men's voices were raised in haughty protest, with talk of: "My friend the Lord Chief Justice," "I would have you know, my good man, that I am a member of the House of Lords and you will pay for this outrage with your career," "I demand that the Prince Regent be informed of my present predicament," and so forth.

Emmie, slumped on the top step, her head resting against the wall, naked still, her cheeks wet with unbidden tears, gave a start at the touch of a gentle hand upon her shoulder. It was Jock Ballantree, who ripped off his coat and placed it about her shoulders.

"Jock!" she whispered. "Again—*you!*"

"We all have a role in life, it seems, Emmie," he said. "Mine is predestined to be that of the fellow who clothes the naked. Are you all right, Emmie?"

The giant Jago stood a few steps behind and below his master. He raised his tall hat to Emmie. "Evenin', m' lady," he said. " 'Orrible weather for the time o' the year."

"I searched high and low for you, Emmie," said Ballantree, "till a fellow from the regiment swore that he had seen you at Miggs's, upon which Jago and I sought for you there, only to be told that you had been hired for a party at this place. Well, when we tried to gain admission, the lackeys showed fight. We made such a ruction that the Watch arrived in force. Those fellows down there—the ones in the masks—made the mistake of trying to bribe the Watch, and they'll all be cooling their heels at Bow Street tonight. But, Emmie, what of Lord George Delavere? What of *him*, Emmie? You know that he's—he's . . . ?"

"He was a devil," said Emmie. "But the devil is dead!"

Chapter Three

Return to Bristol, to Annabel and devoted Reilly—
that was her decision—to find work as a tavern wench,
at which she had thrived in the manner born under
Mr. Winkley, who had espied her talents on first sight.
The decision made, it only required her to fetch a few
traps that she had left behind at Miggs's Diversions—
though that was only an excuse to say goodbye to
Mrs. Miggs, Clarence Pritchard, Jack Pickersgill and
the ladies.

It was a clear, frost-girded morning when she went
to the steps. The tide was at the flood. A single wherry
bobbed in the oily shallows down below. The wherryman's head was bowed in sleep between his knees.

She called out to him: "How much to Miggs's?"

Without raising his head, he lifted a hand with four
fingers splayed.

"Too much!"

One finger fell, leaving three.

"That's better." She stepped into the boat, and
turned to look out across the water, which was flat

calm, drifting, glassy, with screeching seabirds swooping low; they were bunched in massed clouds about the stern of the black hulk, for that was where the French chef tossed the remains of the previous nights' suppers. No seagulls in London lived better than those that ate the unconsidered scraps of Miggs's Diversions.

A single, powerful sweep drove the wherry far out into the river. Emmie watched the hulk come nearer. Not a sign of life aboard, though surely at such an early hour the girls would still be breakfasting after the long night's work. It was still only five-thirty A.M.

The wherryman shaped course to point up-tide, abreast of the ship's gangway. The forest of masts and rigging loomed above her, the eyeless, black hulk casting the shadow of the early sun. Emmie, who had known warmth and friendship behind those stark and uncompromising walls, felt tears prickling her eyes.

And then—it happened . . . !

From every spar and boom, from bowsprit, main and mizzen masts and from the mizzen gaff, there ascended streams of brightly colored signal flags, rising to the morning sky, dazzling, flapping, proud. Within instants, the tired old hulk was a 64-gun ship-of-the-line again, fit to sail the seas for England as she had sailed them under Nelson, one of the far-off, storm-tossed few who had held the battle line.

Heads were appearing everywhere: on her upper deck, from opened gun ports. Figures clung to the rigging, waving, crying out for joy and love.

"Good luck, Emmie! We'll never forget you! We love you, Emmie!"

The wherry drifted past on the tide, made no move to go alongside the hulk. In a few moments, the current had carried them far past the beflagged old third-rater, and the joyous cries died on the wind.

Slowly, with intense care, Emmie looked upon her wherryman.

Nathan Grant rested on his oars and pointed a free hand at her.

"I thought you a whore!" he said.

"And I thought you a slaver!" she retorted.

"I was never a slaver," he said. "Sir Claude, who brought me to England because he knew about us, never allowed me even to know that part of his business."

"If I was a whore, I whored for you—and I'm glad."

"I know it. Will you marry me, Emmie? I would add that I am a widower. I was a widower, though I didn't know it, when we were together aboard the *Delaware*."

"Nathan—you never told me when you came to Bath!"

"You never told me that Annabel was my child. It was left to Reilly to tell me that only last week."

"Reilly? But—where . . . ?"

"She's in London. Here. With the babe. I brought them both here."

"Where, Nathan? Where, my darling—tell me *where?*"

He pointed downriver, to the smudge of buildings rising above the morning smoke of the great city: the Tower and the Monument, the spans of bridges one behind the other, spires and steeples uncountable and, soaring above all, the majestic dome of St. Paul's.

"Take me there, Nathan!"

He plied the oars, and, borne on the flood, they were swept toward the haven they together sought, Emmie and her beloved.

82